THE DAY TIME WAS HACKED

A Novel by

CAREL MACKENBACH

All the characters in this book are fictitious, and any resemblance to actual persons, living or dead, is purely coincidental.

Copyright © 2010 Carel Mackenbach.
All rights reserved. No part of this publication may be reproduced, stored in a retrieval system, or transmitted in any form or by any means, without the prior permission in writing of the author.
Maps by David Lindroth.
Front cover photograph by Dirk van der Eecken. Basilica St. Mary Magdalene in Vézelay, France.
Author photo by Laura Prins

ISBN-10 1439227853
EAN-13 9781439227855
LCCN 2009901138

For Charlotte, Caroline, Marc, and Josephine

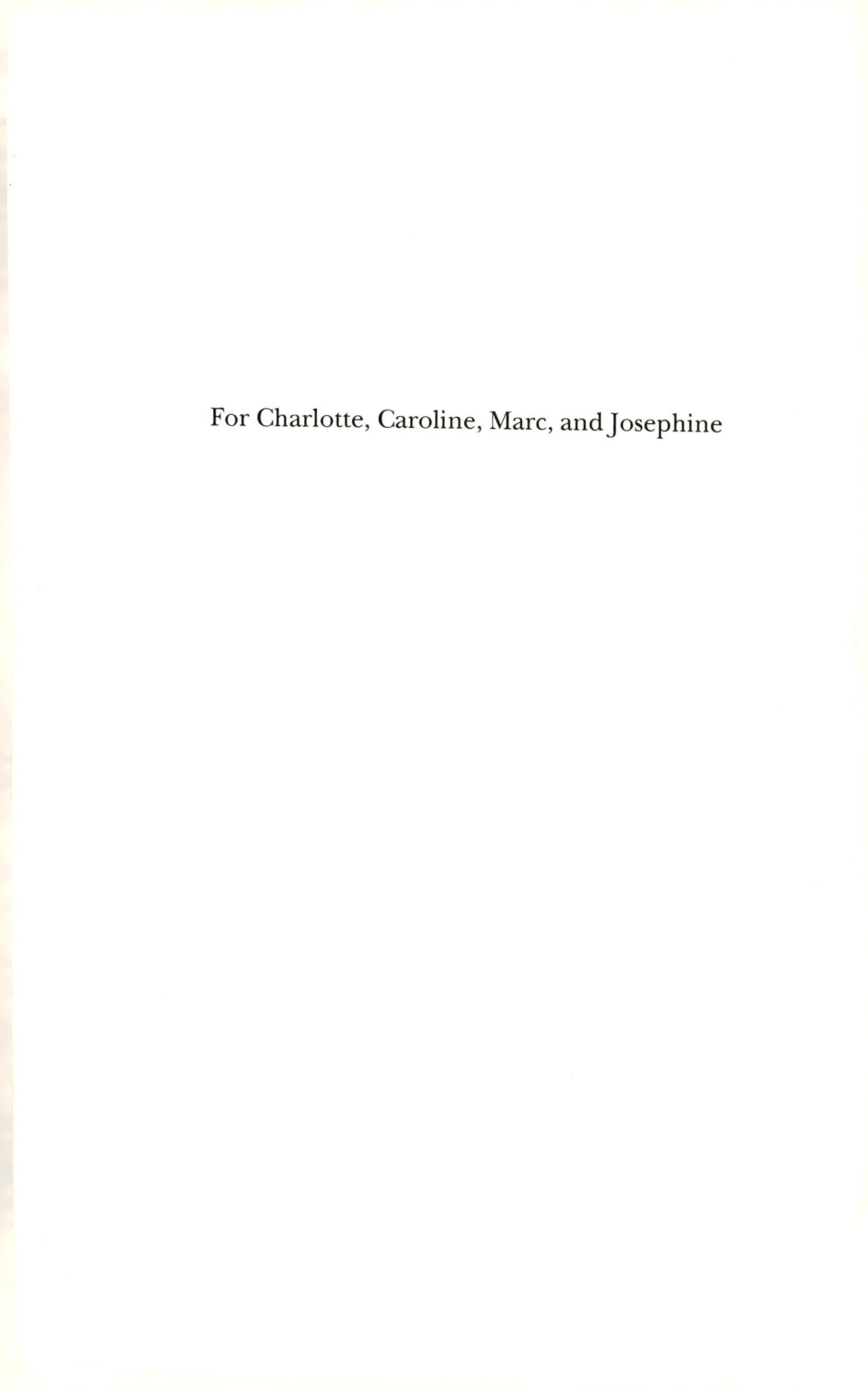

Acknowledgments

Special thanks to the Leadership of the U.S. Navy at the time of my visit. Rear Admiral "T" McGreary, the Navy Chief of Information at CHINFO, and Donna-Grace Schwenter, Special Assistant for Field Activities of the Navy Pentagon for allowing me to access the United States Naval Observatory (USNO) while 9/11 was still a painfully vivid memory. My sincere appreciation to the Leadership of USNO, especially Commander Susan N. Greer, Librarian Brenda G. Corbin, and Public Affairs Office Geoff Chester, who showed me around and whose email signature always brings a smile to my face: "Outside of a dog, a book is man's best friend. Inside of a dog, it's too dark to read"—Groucho Marx.

Special thanks to Sabino Maffeo S.J., the retired director of the Vatican Observatory in Castel Gandolfo, who showed me around and gave me his excellent book on the Observatory's past; and to Guy Consolmagno, who showed me the beautiful meteorite collection and inspired me with his book *Brother Astronomer*.

Special thanks to the Prefect of the *Archivio Segreto Vaticano* (ASV), Father Sergio Pagano, who authorized my visit to the archives, and most importantly, to the *Torre dei Venti*, which is normally closed to visitors.

Special thanks to Professor Dr. Ronald Mallett, who encouraged me to write of things that are not (yet) possible. His often quoted comment, "the first yards of the Wright Brothers' historical flight could not foretell the future of our aviation," is an inspiration to us all. Professor Mallett just so happened to be in the process of penning an autobiography, and his book *Time Traveler* (Thunder's Mouth Press, 2006) is an inspiring journey of a scientist who discovers the theoretical possibility for an electron to travel in time. I'll never forget his response when I told him to use his machine to send brainwaves back and forth in time. After a thoughtful pause, he said, "That may very well be possible in the future."

I would like to thank my first-, second-, third-, and even fourth-time readers, who offered invaluable comments and advice to further improve the manuscript.

Amongst the most precious sources of my research about the Vatican is *Power and Religion in Baroque Rome, Barberini Cultural Policies* (Brill, 2006) by Professor Dr. Peter Rietbergen. This book offers a rich account of the mysterious and fairly unknown other side of Maffeo Barberini, the later Pope Urban VIII. The saying "the devil is in the details" is more than applicable for the dark sides of Urban VIII. The theft of the reliquaries of Mary Magdalene, putting astrology on the list of forbidden sciences, and practicing it in secret all added to the magnificent background story.

The proof of a Brahmin relation to the poems of Urban was also discovered by Professor Rietbergen, who had luckily memorized the exact wording, as referred to in a footnote in his aforementioned book, since the *Biblioteca Apostolica Vaticana* (BAV) has been closed for five years.

A special word of deep gratitude for my friend Kuldeep Sharma, who has taught me the Vedic perspective on time.

A word of thanks for Professor Dr. Joost Kircz, who invented the as-yet-undiscovered phenomenon of 'thinkwaves'.

Finally, I want to thank my team of editors, especially Autumn Conley and Michael Carr, for their meticulous and thoughtful advice. But most of all, I want to thank my friend Peter van Gorsel, who has been with me from the start.

Abbreviations

ASV *Archivio Segreto Vaticano.* "The Secret Archives of the Vatican". This archive contains all religious documents related to the pontificate.

BAV *Biblioteca Apostolica Vaticana.* "The Apostolic Library of the Vatican". This archive contains all non-religion documents of the popes.

GWUMC George Washington University Medical Center.

NETWARCOM Naval Network Warfare Command.

M.E.T. Metropolitan Police Washington.

USNO United States Naval Observatory.

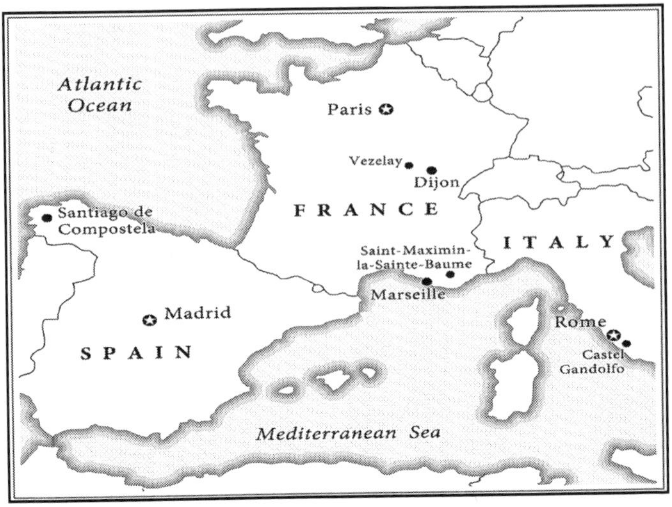

Atlantic Ocean
Paris
Vezelay
Dijon
FRANCE
Santiago de Compostela
Saint-Maximin-la-Sainte-Baume
ITALY
Marseille
Madrid
Rome
SPAIN
Castel Gandolfo
Mediterranean Sea

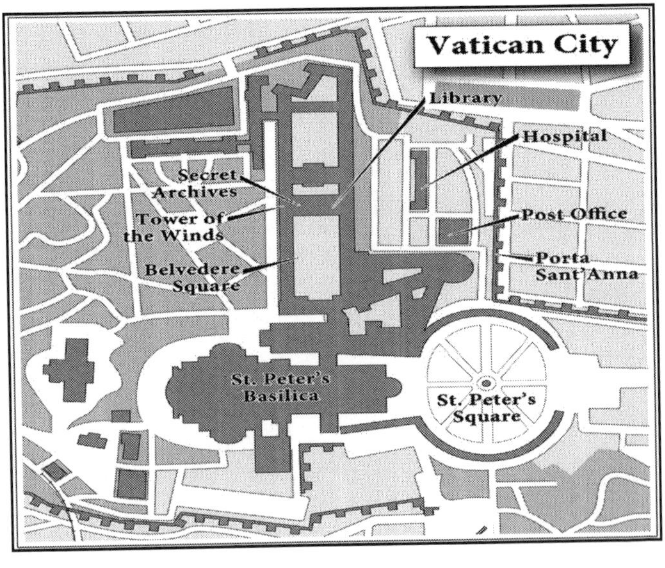

Vatican City
Library
Hospital
Secret Archives
Tower of the Winds
Post Office
Porta Sant'Anna
Belvedere Square
St. Peter's Basilica
St. Peter's Square

Prologue

2115: Beijing

Ten floors below the former Beijing Ancient Observatory, close to the Forbidden City, the immense hall was deserted. The lone, luminous platform stood out among its dark counterparts as if it were floating in a dark, void space. The only sound came from huge two-bladed fans hanging from the ceiling, flapping recycled air around, along with the frantic brushing of ten fingers over a built-in screen on a mahogany desk, an asynchronous piece of furniture in the center of the floor. These fingers were the only moving parts of Colonel Malik, a stout figure frozen in a gazing disbelief across the rising foggy hologram in front of him. "Why haven't I seen this before?" he moaned. If his jet-black face could have paled, it surely would have. "Why is it here in the first place?"

While his fingers rapidly merged freshly digitized sources of the Army Analogue Archive, the foglet morphed into a 3D landscape of France. Malik launched a text-to-speech synthesis, then closed his eyes and listened: "According to the legend, Mary Magdalene was active in Southern France, spreading her deep-felt beliefs in Jesus as the Son of God. She also worked on an extraordinary plan...a plan that required the services of an architect. Allegedly, while on her deathbed, she finally shared her secret with the priest of Sainte Baume, who gave her the last sacrament."

The sonorous voice calmed him down only a little. "...And Jesus said to me, '*noli me tangere.*' Do not hold me, because I have not yet ascended to my Father..." Malik's eyes were now suddenly wide open. "She had made a vow to commemorate this event and had him pledge to continue searching for an architect. The secret was passed on to the priest's successor, and during the next several centuries, it became the most important prerequisite for becoming a priest of the church of Sainte Baume—never to reveal the secret to anyone and to keep the quest for an architect alive." Meanwhile, the contours of a huge church became visible, rising rapidly on a small hill. Malik whistled softly, the effort eased by the adequate gap between his two front teeth, as a small sign popped up. It read: NO LONGER EXISTENT.

"In the early eleventh century, the relics of Mary Magdalene were transferred to Vézelay for reasons unknown. However, the priest fulfilled Magdalene's last wishes. Her secret was magnificently perpetuated in the architectural design of the Basilica of Sainte Madeleine in Vézelay. In spring, the sun's rays crept steadily farther across the floor until the summer solstice, when the beams of sunlight formed a pathway on the tiles, straight down the axis of the center aisle, almost like a code." At the word 'code', Malik suddenly looked around, as if he suspected he was being watched. Satisfied that he was indeed alone, he continued rifling through even more 3D material, his mind spinning all the while. *A source code?*

Ten floors up, two officers had been watching Malik all the time. "What is he thinking right now, Lieutenant Tong? How does this relate to the mission?" the general asked, standing next to Tong in the dimly lit control room packed with surveillance screens.

Tong looked down on the chisel-faced woman and carefully chose the words. "We need a few more seconds, General. We're processing the colonel's think waves. He believes the code is somehow linked to the scientist."

"Does he suspect we're monitoring him?"

"No, General. We're observing him now every night, when he feels nobody is watching him. He has no way of knowing that the paint on his office walls is capturing his brain activity from four angles." Tong pointed at the monitor, and a 3-D laser image of Malik's brain circled around. "Areas 21 through 28..." He stopped; something was happening.

Malik was hastily perusing the complete digitized Vatican Archives. He accessed the phone logs of the *Guardia Svizzera*. The Vatican police had confirmed a French student's last telephone call to the astronomy summer school teacher in Castel Gandolfo, asking for Brother Frank Bootsma and rambling about his astounding discovery of the code origin. When Bootsma couldn't take his call, it was routed to the Vatican switchboard. Malik's hands trembled as new chunks of data presented themselves. The student had been murdered, and his revelatory notebook was missing. This Bootsma had accused a U.S. Naval officer, one Captain John Pakula.

"Why is Colonel Malik so disturbed?" the general asked, jerking her head toward the lieutenant. Her neck cracked like an old tree. "He knows Pakula is Major Roto Ashlev's prime target. Do we have a full transcription of his thinking process?"

Tong looked stubbornly at the general and noticed her skin didn't cover completely her newly implanted synthetic atlas, but decided it best not to mention it. She was known for her extremely dangerous and unexpected outbursts, especially toward anyone advising her on spare-part implantations. "Since we informed the colonel he has to assist Major Ashlev on his mission, he has started to do some research on this priest, Frank Boohtsma. Right now, he is trying to figure out who killed this student. As you can read, he suspects the major, but he cannot explain this, because the major has not yet been sent away. And now he's not sure he should tell him about the student in the first place. He's worried about the time-travel paradoxes… and he's correct on that one, if I may say so."

"Are you absolutely sure he is *only* worried about time-travel paradoxes?" the general asked, her suspicions growing.

The monitor filled with a series of mathematical calculations. Tong said, "The probability that Colonel Malik can figure out our plan is zero, and—"

"I am not interested in your calculations, Lieutenant! And I think you are incorrect. He cannot and will not—"

The general did not have a chance to finish her rant because the surveillance screen suddenly started to show a series of rectangular boxes, each in a separate foglet and each divided into twelve numbered compartments, which were, one by one, filling with words. Malik was typing information into each of them and had switched on a printing facility. Carefully, he picked up the small swatch of cotton cloth that was rolling slowly out of the 3D printer. It had no trace of ink.

"Lieutenant," she barked, "do we have intel on that printing device?"

"No, General. Colonel Malik must have fabricated his printer out of range of our surveillance." Tong paused another second. "Our best estimate is that he knows we're watching him. He's using an extinct language to compose a message."

As the general turned her head toward Tong, her neck cracked open a bit farther, displaying even more synthetic parts. She took a deep, hissing breath. "This is not looking good. Get us a copy of that tissue, the solstice, the notebook, secret messages—all of it. But their *sources* are what this is all about—both the priest's and the scientist's. When the major has left, we'll deal with Colonel Malik."

Part 1

larger chunk released...but, strangely, it seemed to be in a perfect square, not at all like a piece of randomly torn, aged carpet. "What in the world!" he said. He tugged on the edge again, and a piece at least three feet square pulled free from the wall and thumped between the legs of the cabinet.

He struggled to sit up and bumped against this desk, toppling a framed photo. For a brief moment, he glanced at the cracked glass and the picture of his mother with him at his graduation. He looked at the carpet piece in his hands. It was full of dust, but the edges were rather perfect, as though they had been cut with a sharp object, albeit a very long time ago. Standing, he stared at the cabinet and then at those on each side of it. Only on close examination could the slight differences in color ever be discerned.

Tossing the carpet segment onto the table, he reached out to grasp the sides of the cabinet and slowly inched the entire unit away from the wall and toward the center of the room, closer to his working table. Peering behind it, he saw the bare area in the rug. Bending closer, he noticed that it was covered by another more faded layer of carpeting.

"What the hell?"

Frank inspected the carpet with the eyes of a scientist and discovered the imprint of what looked like a door pushing its frame through the carpet.

Okay, this was interesting, he thought. Needing answers, he hesitated only a few seconds, then dug his fingers into the older carpet and started ripping it off. Thankfully, no one would know he was disturbing a part of Vatican history. He could always replace the carpet piece and push the cabinet back into place, and no one would be the wiser.

A minute later, he gasped aloud. *A door!* There it was, created by some much smaller Italian, perhaps in a previous century, and carefully hidden from curious eyes.

Frank pulled on the carved-out section in the wood that neatly fit the curvature of his fingers. Tugging, he was surprised to see how easily the door opened. He peered into a dark, dank hole that was clearly the beginning of a secret passageway.

Chapter 2

Tuesday: DuPont, Washington DC

Sometimes Max didn't open his bedroom drapes for weeks. The light coming through the windows cast reflections on his two computer screens, one twenty-three-inch full-HD widescreen for gaming and a regular nineteen-inch one for coding. He preferred his room to be dark, especially when he was kicking ass in a war with other gaming soldiers from around the globe, and light interfered with his focus. The first release of *Call of Duty* was still his passion because he liked WWII so much. As was typical, his private sanctuary was littered with clothes (both clean and unwashed), school books, and stacks of papers, and he was just fine with it the way it was. It was the only place where he didn't feel the throbbing pain somewhere behind his eyes. He couldn't remember when the pain had started, but that was irrelevant for his father, Jacob Burkowski, a radiologist in the Neurology Department at George Washington University Medical Center (GWUMC), who was determined to find a cure—a cure for his pain, his depression, and his 'hallucinations', as his dad kept calling his visions. It made him feel even more depressed.

Max was the seventeen-year-old carbon copy of his father in appearance, but that was where the similarities stopped. The two of them didn't share much more than the same address. Since his parents were divorced, he pretty much had full authority over his life. Both of his parents were too busy with their own interests to bother with him. He still lived at home because his father insisted, partly blaming it on his 'mental situation', as he had typified it. And it could've been okay, weren't it for those pesky therapeutic sessions at his dad's clinic.

With one hand, Max operated the machine gun, rapidly tapping the spacebar and the cursor. His chin rested on his other hand, which he had planted on the table. Frequently, his eyes fluttered as he fought against his drowsiness. Other than an hour or two of sleep in his bed, he had played the game nonstop for the remainder of the night. He had been fighting a highly successful war until the worst of all possible things happened: his PC had crashed mid-game. He had beefed up his internal memory to the max, but the number crunching he needed for calculations on his other screen had taken its toll. For weeks, he had endured increasing episodes of unexpected endings in the midst of his game, and his frustration had finally evolved into anger. Although he had been able to rejoin the competition, it was always at a lower level—the harsh price he had to pay for accidentally 'quitting' in the middle of an attack. Now, he was just a soldier, and somebody else with a more reliable PC had claimed the title of platoon leader. To make matters worse, the new lieutenant kept on giving him directions that made no sense to him.

Max preferred to play *Call of Duty* at night because that was when all his friends were online and available to play. They were the blue dots on the screen; the red ones were the enemy. He didn't know them and didn't want to. Sometimes they had their mikes switched on, and from the sounds of their voices, he guessed they were Russian or something. He could understand their cursing though. They used the same cuss words he did, which was weird.

His dad hadn't been completely deaf to his requests. He had received a new audio set for his birthday, as well as some high-powered sound blasters, which added exponentially to the battlefield experience. For now, he used earphones so his dad wouldn't notice. The graphics were much more advanced in the version he had now, and he had downloaded a pretty expensive photo-editing program for changing the color and texture of the uniforms worn by his platoon. He'd even written some code to insert new uniforms into the game and shared it with his friends. "Pretty cool," they'd all agreed. What you could expect from a student in artificial intelligence, especially a talented one like me? he thought without smiling.

Of course, these changes were invisible for the enemy, since they rested with the client and not the server. If they could get in without being noticed, he knew his friends would love to do it, but he wasn't sure if they could mask their IP addresses permanently and stay invisible while they committed their first computer crime. So far, his friends had only downloaded games and movies and shared them with him. That wasn't illegal, because everybody did it, they said. And besides, they had been paid for once already. He didn't disagree, but it was so old school. What they were doing was so small fry, at least compared to what he'd managed to do, Max thought while he watched a black window on his other computer screen rapidly fill with white lines of code, word by word. Finally it read: COMPILED. The black window closed automatically, and an hourglass showed up, turning around and around almost endlessly until it stopped and disappeared, leaving his code screen empty. After a few seconds, his other screen beeped, and there it was; there HE was. It had launched itself autonomously again! He switched on his mounted webcam and established a connection.

"Hi, Max," the avatar said, nodding at him. Max nodded back at his duplicate, confirming their eye contact. "How are we feeling today?"

"Not so bad," Max replied. "Wait...I first must leave the battle."

"How's the pain?"

"No pain right now."

"Any more memory flashes?"

"Don't want to talk about it." Thinking about his father and his lab only depressed him again. "How are you doing over there?" he asked, switching subjects.

"Fine. I managed to gather some info about the target. We cannot break their firewall, but…" His avatar paused for a second. "… I discovered a COM port we hadn't thought about."

This was great news. Max was so glad his avatar didn't mention the name of their target. He never knew if anybody was snooping around in the game control center, where the online version of *Call of Duty* was hosted.

"How're the seeds progressing?" Max asked.

"Don't worry about my capacity. Our app is now installed on a mere 35,67 percent of game consoles, especially the PS3. The moment they're on, their processing power begins flowing toward me…but there's more."

"More? What is it?" Max knew what he had coded. He just could not believe his creation had been working overtime.

"Well," his avatar continued, "I managed to stay connected to the consoles even when they are on standby. I think we've just passed the 200-petaflop barrier, which means we've left behind the most powerful supercomputers of the world like the Jaguar Cray XT5 in Oak Ridge and the Nebulae in Shenzen, boasting less than 2 petaflop."

Max didn't know what to say. He had created his avatar a few months ago, when he had a sort of brain surge about how to compose a tiny package of software that could replicate and enhance its core functionality, feeding itself by thousands—and now apparently millions—of game consoles worldwide. Although his creation had started talking to him a week earlier, he now realized his avatar had a will of its own. It didn't just follow his instructions anymore.

"What's the next step?" he asked, almost afraid of the answer.

His avatar smiled at him and winked. "With this superpower, there is no password we can't crack. My first aim is our target. I located the subcontractor of their server park. It turns out they have outsourced the building of these kinds of facilities. It downloads updates at a regular interval. If we get into those updates…"

For some reason, instinctive or otherwise, Max's attention wandered to the clock on his computer. Shit. Almost time to go! He jumped from his chair and promptly promised his avatar he would log-on with his cell phone. Speaking of phones, where was it? He searched under the piles of junk on his desk, under the sheets on his bed, and finally located it in his jeans, which he had dumped on the floor in the middle of the night. He returned to the PC and mumbled "Be right back" to his avatar and quickly switched off.

After pulling on his jeans, he picked up a sweater from the floor and sniffed it. It smelled okay. He stuffed his arms in the sleeves and yanked it down over his body, all the while cursing the washing machine. The sweater needed to be baggy, and it had shrunk. It was way too short. One day, he would be muscled enough to wear tight sweaters, but for now, he preferred loose-fitting stuff.

Dashing to the bathroom, he took a good look at himself in the dirty mirror over the sink. *God, I look pale.* He splashed some water on his face, hoping he could wash away the hard evidence that he'd stayed up almost all night. He combed his short, dark hair and carefully pulled at it before putting a handful of gel in it. It was crucial that it stayed in shape all day.

He rushed down the stairs, three at the time, and landed in the kitchen. Pulling open the door of the fridge, he removed the orange juice box and shook it. Damn. *We're out of juice.* With the door still open, he suddenly froze. Something was wrong. It was awfully quiet—too quiet. Normally, he'd hear his dad upstairs going through the motions of getting dressed.

He glanced at the wall clock. It was already after eight o'clock! *I missed the bus!* He was in deep trouble. He'd been this late once before, and the dean had told him that if it ever happened again, he'd be suspended from university. *Why didn't Dad wake me up?* This was not something they agreed on, of course.

Max removed the receiver from the wall phone, punched in the number of the hospital, and reached the head nurse. "This is Max Burkowski, Mrs. Williams. I know my dad is probably busy, but I have to talk to him. It's urgent."

"Of course he's busy, Max. We all are. What is your so-called urgent business about this morning? I'll relay the message to him."

"I prefer to tell my father myself."

"Then you'll have to wait. The doctor is in the middle of a procedure."

Max switched the phone to his other ear and waited… and waited.

After several minutes, he heard Mrs. Williams's voice again. "Your father says he's too busy to come to the phone, Max. He wants you to know the dean called him this morning. You're evidently suspended for two days. Too many unpardoned absences. You're to report back on Thursday morning…on time. Is there anything else?"

"Nope. That's all I need to know. Thanks," he said as normally as possible and hung up.

Shit! Max threw the empty juice carton into the sink. Now what was he supposed to do? He fumed in silence while pacing the floor. His life sucked. He'd lost his appetite. Slowly mounting the stairs, he returned to his room. He stared for a full minute at the mess that littered the floor, his bed, his desk, and every other surface. He could clean his room, he supposed. At least some of it. No, later.

He slumped onto his chair and rebooted his computer. He wanted to finish his conversation with his avatar. He could've used his cell phone, but this interface was much better.

What the hell! He sat up straighter. His PC clock was out of sync, and the time zone had changed. He clicked on a map and discovered his clock was set for Beijing, Chongqing, Hong Kong, and Urumqi, thirteen hours later than his time should be. This was weird, he deliberated. Wait a second. Could this be a hack job? Had someone hacked into his computer?

Max suspiciously looked around and stared at the closed drapes as if expecting to find the answer behind them. If his PC had been relayed to another network—supposedly somewhere in Asia—that meant someone had somehow gained control over it. Everything he did could and would be monitored, and that would be a disaster. He logged into his wireless router but didn't find anything suspect. His PC firewall was operating and didn't show anything out of the ordinary either. What the hell was going on here?

The game.

Max quickly launched *Call of Duty* again. It needed a full five minutes for all the components to load. With his eyes glued to the screen, he watched as the series of install windows flashed by; none appeared to be anything other than the normal setup. Wait! What was this? He'd never seen that progress bar before.

Two seconds later, it was gone, and he was left wondering if he'd seen it at all.

Shrugging, Max started the game. There was only one other player on the server—his avatar, which stood there motionless. As soon as Max pointed the cursor at him, a short horizontal blue line lit up above his head, indicating he was on his team. Max clicked on him to send a message. "Hi."

The other player just stood there looking at him. He said something, but there was no sound. A week earlier, it would have immediately responded like a good little avatar slave, but now it had a life of its own.

He peered more closely at his avatar. He's wearing my fatigues, Max thought. That's my design! Still... Max hurriedly launched another program that allowed him to download the uniform and open the source code.

Wow. Who is screwing with my system? Homeland Security?

Max clutched his head with both hands. His eyes grew wider, and he stared with gaping mouth at the screen, holding his breath. The graphic code was written in Chinese or something! He had never seen anything like it. The only thing he understood was the number 2115. This was definitely an attack; his computer was seriously infected. "Fuck!" he swore aloud as he quickly launched his virus scanner. The process would take at least half an hour, but there was nothing more he could do but wait for the results.

Leaning back in his chair, he counted the minutes. He fought a yawn. His eyes blinked several times, and his head nodded. He may as well get some sleep, he decided. He pushed himself to his feet and flopped facedown onto his rumpled bed.

The last thing he thought of before falling asleep was what his father would say if he found out his online gaming had infected his PC...or even worse. He'd be in deep shit. Hopefully, the virus scanner would automatically delete the malware or whatever the intrusion was.

Chapter 3

Tuesday: Castel Gandolfo

Frank struggled to move through the narrow passageway behind the cabinet. He swallowed hard to push away his billowing claustrophobia, but it was getting worse. The further he went, the less oxygen there seemed to be. If all of these problems weren't bad enough, the poor light from the meteorite room wasn't powerful enough to illuminate anything other than the direct entrance. His eyes strained to see into the blackness beyond. Yet strangely for him, none of that seemed to matter, because his curiosity was growing with each step he took. He flipped open his cell phone, and the glowing screen offered just enough light for him to catch a shadowed glimpse of the walls and the makeup of the tunnel.

There appeared to be a myriad of passageways, but where did they lead, and what were they doing there? After squeezing through several hundred feet and running out of breath, he had to stop to get his bearings. He was sure he was moving in a circle. Suddenly, he saw a stairway, but it only had seven steps, and there was no doorway at the top. A stairway to nowhere?

Interested in this bizarre construction, Frank climbed the stairs to more closely inspect the landing. Maybe there was another hidden door. On the seventh step, he suddenly grew dizzy, and a wave of nausea stopped him in his tracks. Bracing himself against the wall and waiting for the feeling to pass, he decided he'd better return to the exhibition room before he fainted. He could return later, when he was better prepared.

He had just turned around when he painfully banged his shoulder against the wall and dislodged a chunk of the surface material, which fell at his feet and rolled down the other six steps. Gripping his shoulder and stifling a curse, he reflexively turned to the wall, and in doing so, he felt a sudden coolness on his cheek. Using his cell phone as a mini flashlight, he rubbed his finger against the rough area until he found the source: a forceful stream of cool air—not much, but certainly better than what he had. Was this the Lord's doing? Poking at the area, he discovered a perfectly round hole, slightly smaller than his eye. He pursed his lips around it to suck in the clean air and, after several inhalations, felt relatively revived.

Then, he placed his eye against the hole and gasped in realization. This was a peephole! Blinking to clear his vision, he stared through the peephole again, quietly whistling to himself in shock. He recognized the Papal Key on the Goblin tapestry near the four-poster bed. He was directly behind the bedroom wall of the pope! Anything discussed in the room could be overheard by anyone standing in the hidden passageway. Someone had spied on the pope! Who? When? Was it centuries ago? Why?

Frank sucked in another draught of the fresh air and forced himself to calm down. He gazed through the peephole with increasing interest. No one was in the room, but the windows and wooden shutters were wide open. The room was obviously being prepared for the arrival of the pope in the next couple of days.

What should he do? Report his findings? To whom? The Vatican authorities would want to know why he had been snooping in the exhibition room and why he hadn't immediately reported his discovery to someone before entering the tunnel himself. Maybe his curator privileges would be taken away from him. Maybe he'd even be dismissed from the brotherhood.

Frank forced himself to think rationally. This could be something big. He couldn't stop now.

He squatted and pointed his cell phone at the floor, hoping to find some sort of clue—anything to answer his questions...but he found nothing.

Impatient now, he moved a bit farther down the passageway, paying more attention to the floor than to the walls this time. Unexpectedly, his foot hit something hard, bruising his toe. *Damn!* He stooped to take a look and used his hand to sweep away any loose rock and compacted soil. His fingers detected something metallic. He got down on both knees and held his cell phone to the area. It was an iron ring, partially imbedded into a carved-out indentation! Setting the phone down close by, he used both hands to clean away the decades of debris clinging to its surface and the surroundings. Amazingly, the ring lifted as soon as he wrapped his fingers around it. He pulled tentatively at first and then harder. Initially, nothing budged. Then, after one more energetic tug, he heard a hissing sound as the hatch gave way. Once again, he was stunned when yet another secret door opened before his eyes. He rocked back on his heels as a wave of cold, moist air rolled toward him, and he felt his pulse accelerate.

Another flight of stairs? What in God's name? The stairs seemed to lead at least two floors beneath the ground level of the Castel. Frustrated at his inability to see beyond two feet in front of him, he stopped. *What's the sense in continuing?*

Suddenly, Frank's eyes caught the outline of what looked like burned-down torches. Maybe he could... Digging into his pocket, he withdrew a cigarette lighter. It shamed him to think he couldn't forgo his daily Petit Corona cigar, but for once, the habit was going to pay off. He reached for one of the torches and held the lighter to it. Immediately, it lit up several feet of the underground room. Holding the torch high, he descended another couple of steps and lit up another one, leaving it on the wall.

As his eyes adapted to the light, he gasped in wonder. The walls to his left were painted with light blue frescoes depicting biblical scenes, but it didn't make sense. If this excavated room were part of the escape route for those who spied on the pope, why would they have created these spectacular works of art? And *how*, without being discovered by others in the Castel?

Frank descended a couple more steps. Time had taken its toll, and parts of the frescoes were covered with green mold. But considering the passage of time, most of the paintings were amazingly well preserved.

He took a few more steps downward. At first, the wall to his right appeared to be without paintings, but looking more closely, he saw that this wasn't the case. Closer to ground level, he saw drawings of a totally different nature. The most prominent color had been a deep red at one time, and although it was difficult in the dim light to see details through patches of mold, he could identify signs of the Zodiac. Three remarkably bright yellow bees surrounded several of them. Making a quick count, he determined they numbered fifteen in all, and every part of their bodies, heads, wings, and legs were painted so realistically that it looked as if they could fly away with a snap of his fingers.

It was at that moment Frank realized he had it all wrong. Because the yellow bees had survived the devastating effect of time, he knew the true meaning of the stairway and passageways. The peephole was not intended for someone to peer *into* the papal bedroom. The pope and his assistants had used it to look *out*—as one uses the peephole of a modern-day hotel room—to see if anyone was present before making a secret exit. The room and passageway in which he stood were decorated to make the pope's comings and goings worthy of his stature.

Frank rubbed his face with his free hand, which was now trembling. He had never read about such things during any of his years of study and had never heard anyone utter a word about it in theological discussions. He had seen the yellow bees before; the famous bees depicted on the heraldic emblem representing the noble Barberini family—the family that produced a pope of their own blood, Pope Urban VIII.

A second thought entered his mind. He was convinced the entire tunnel system had been Pope Urban's secret passageway into and out of the Castel. It had been a covert part of the edifice during his 1623 to 1644 tenure.

BANG!

Frank turned with a start and felt his heart leap into his throat. What was that?

Nothing but silence filled his ears. The hatch door!

He panicked. Did he just lift the ring or was there a locking device? Would he be able to get out of here? He quickly ascended three steps and then stopped. If he left now, he might never have this opportunity again. Anyone entering his office would see the hole in the wall, and...

He held the torch higher and peered at the walls again and then at the stairway heading even further downward. Before he could change his mind, he moved down the stairway, this time more rapidly. He was not ready to leave yet, he firmly convinced himself.

The flight of at least a hundred stairs descended at a forty-five degree angle with no intermediate landings. At one point, Frank imagined hearing the muffled sounds of the Swiss Guards moving about but decided it was just the pounding of his heart. The air seemed less suffocating. There must be a ventilation shaft somewhere. That was good, because the mixture of guilt and excitement and his claustrophobia was making the simple process of breathing difficult.

Minutes later and floors beneath his exhibition room, he finally came to a stop in a vaulted, empty crypt. In the dank air, the flame from the torch flickered over the mildewed walls that seemed to cover remnants of additional frescoes. Sucking in a long, deep breath, he coughed and staggered against the stairway. It hadn't been a good idea to hurry. Although he was accustomed to working in clammy, windowless rooms, the lack of oxygen was ultimately causing a serious breathing problem. He realized if he stayed any longer, he knew he would pass out. He took one last glance around. Except for some frescoes, there was nothing but dust.

More slowly this time, he climbed the two flights of steps, hoping he would be able to make an exit without exposing his presence by shouting and banging on the hatch door. Panting and finding it increasingly difficult to haul his frame up the narrow stairway, he found relief when the door moved as soon as he applied pressure. Once more, in the passageway that led to the exhibition room, he paused to gaze at the top of the seven steps leading to the peephole. He thought he saw the faint outline of what could have been the framing of a door.

Five minutes later, he climbed through the hole into the meteorite room and fell forward, coughing and gasping for breath. Sweat poured down his face and dripped into his eyes.

What's that?

His heart was still in his ears, and he felt decidedly dizzy, but he had clearly heard movement close to the room. He glanced at his watch. It was seven thirty, dinner time. He had completely forgotten about dinner! He dragged himself to his feet and dropped his head into his hands. He had a dreadful headache. Moving like a zombie, he closed the secret door, covered it with the square of carpet, and moved the cabinet back into place.

Leaning over his study table to catch his breath, he battled with his conscience. The right thing to do was to immediately inform the former *Direttore di Specola Vaticana*

Father Gabriel Bonomelli, but as quickly as that thought entered his mind, he dismissed it. Although their relationship had been professional, he wasn't sure how Bonomelli would react to his confession because he was a converted Catholic. The rather crotchety old man was famous for snapping off Latin quotes from the Bible and questioning how a Protestant could possibly see the Light while staring into the wrong lamp.

Putting the broken frame upright, he suddenly shivered. In a flash, his father's stern warning resonated: "*Never become part of the Vatican!*" In a dark way, his father was like Father Bonomelli. Years earlier, during an argument, the old man had compared Frank to naïve, prewar, pro-Nazi politicians. He had left his parental home that same evening, never to set a foot there again. Looking back at it now, his skin crawled as he realized he had brought along a whisper of doubt that had never left but only waited quietly for the moment to strike. His breathing accelerated. *Mustn't panic,* he told himself. *Focus...focus.*

He slapped his face lightly and glanced at his watch. He would have to hurry.

First, he should show up for dinner—try to act normal, whatever that was.

Forget about dinner, he then told himself. He strode to the door of the exhibition room and cautiously opened it to scan the hallway. Good. This part of the Castel was usually deserted, and those likely to show up would be eating.

Frank hurried to reach the room next to his. It was a private archive, off limits to him. However, because the Castel itself was guarded night and day, no door in this section was ever locked. Once inside, he turned on the overhead lights and rushed to skim the shelves for anything that might contain the information he needed. Nothing caught his eye. He scanned the entire room and noticed a steel filing cabinet on the back wall. On the left door of the cabinet, a plastic plaque read: ARCHIVIO. He suspected that anything of real importance would have been moved to the one and only *Archivio* in Rome—the *Archivio Segreto Vaticano*. Besides, it was probably locked.

At that moment, his eyes fell on the writing desk of the librarian who worked only certain days of the week and always left by three in the afternoon. For some reason, he felt compelled to go through it. In the second drawer on the right, he found a set of keys. He shook his head at the ridiculousness of his current situation. The Castel was only protected at the gate. Once admission was granted, free access to any room was permitted, except for the papal suites. Of course, those in charge trusted people like him to obey the rules.

Frank used one of the keys to open the steel doors of the cabinet. Inside, he found shelves lined with a collection of rare astrophysical books. He was just about to relock the doors when his eyes fell on what appeared to be a drawing peeking out from two of the largest tomes. Curious, he pulled it out and held it closer to his eyes. A label said: CASA BARBERINI. Below this was a signature: PIRANESI F. On the backside of the drawing, he read:

> VOL. 11. PARTE III.—DI DUE SPELON-
> CHE ORNATE DAGLI ANTICHI ALLA
> RIVA DEL LAGO DI ALBANO. GIOVANNI
> BATTISTA PIRANESI.

Frank lifted his eyes to the ceiling. "Thank you, God!" he muttered aloud, wishing he had time to dance a jig around the room. The '*due spelonche*' was a reference to caves beneath the castle, one of which he had just discovered. The etching in his hands was made by the famous eighteenth-century artist Giovanni Piranesi, and it clearly depicted the period *before* the Papal Palace had been built. As he studied it, he was positive the site depicted the ancient tunnels or caves that existed under the *Casa*

Barberini, the family home of Pope Urban VIII, which had been expanded later into the Castel in the 1620s.

Frank was ecstatic. Within ten minutes, he had found the answer to his newly discovered secret. *Now what?* He replaced the etching and relocked the cabinet.

The Barberinis had built Castel Gandolfo atop a series of caves. But why? And why did they connect them with a maze of apparently secret corridors and then hire painters to decorate the walls with beautiful frescoes...of Zodiac signs? It was reasonable to assume it was for no other reason than to make use of the caves, perhaps as a cool place to congregate when the weather turned hot during the summer months, or even as a cellar for food storage.

But still, that didn't explain why the arrangement ended in a vaulted crypt with no doors. It couldn't have been a secret exit unless the door was hidden from him. Frank shrugged. It was time to get back to his room and put away the meteorites he had earlier removed. He could ponder the imponderables all night in his bed.

On the way to the door, a mix of guilt and doubt assailed him. He should never have come here. He should never have opened the steel filing cabinet. He should never have been poking around at all. He was going to have to tell the former director right now. But once again, he argued with himself, deciding instead to slow down and think this through first. The cave definitely had something suspicious about it. What *was going on* down there?

"Brother Frank? Exactly what you are doing in this room? I believe it is off limits to you," the unusually soft voice of Bonomelli sounded directly behind him.

Frank whirled and swallowed; he was caught red-handed.

"Well?" Bonomelli provoked, raising his bushy white eyebrows over the rims of his wire-rimmed glasses. His hand was still on the doorknob, and he didn't step into the room.

"H-hello, Father. I, uh, forgive me for looking like a raccoon caught in the garbage. I-I didn't hear you enter. Have you had your dinner already?"

"Follow me." Bonomelli snapped his fingers and turned to shuffle down the hall and into a small pantry. Without turning to see if Frank had followed him, he seated himself at the square table and wagged his finger at the industrial-strength espresso machine, an investment condoned when President Bush and his wife visited Pope John Paul II in 2001. Thus, it became the most advanced machine of the *Specola Vaticana* in Italy, a sharp contrast with the spectacular astronomical array of its headquarters in Tucson—not that the director would appreciate the joke.

"*Padre*, would you like me to make you an espresso?" Frank needed time to think about what he'd say when asked the questions he knew was coming. Although Bonomelli was forced to step down at the age of seventy-five, he behaved quite like he were still director of the Vatican Observatory.

When Bonomelli nodded, Frank switched on the machine, noting that his hands were trembling. Keeping his back to Bonomelli, he prayed the man wouldn't notice his uneasiness. With two cups of steaming hot espresso in his hand, Frank finally joined the elderly man at the table. "Here you are, *Padre*."

Bonomelli brought his cup to his mouth and blew on the coffee. He then squinted at Frank though the thick lenses of his glasses. "I went to the meteorite room and didn't find you there. What were you doing in the library? I hope you didn't disturb anything."

Frank felt uncomfortable and hoped his anxiety wasn't noticeable. He kept his eyes on the dark brew in his cup. "Actually, Father, I, uh, I needed some answers to questions that have popped up in my newest research. I thought the library might provide them for me. I noticed the metal cabinet with ARCHIVIO on it, and—"

Unexpectedly, Bonomelli spewed the espresso from his mouth across the table. At the same time he dropped his cup on the floor, spilling the rest. A paroxysm of coughing choked off his immediate response. Frank leaped from his chair, but before he could step forward to help him, Bonomelli had regained his composure. "The *Archivio* is reserved for the *Direttore di Specola Vaticana*, and...and *nobody else*, Brother Bootsma!" His voice trembled, but it was stern.

Before Frank could offer an explanation, Bonomelli slowly pushed himself to his feet and hobbled toward the door of the pantry. Before leaving, he turned to glare at Frank. His anger had needed some time to grow. "The *Archivio Segreto Vaticano* is taking care of our archives, and if you have any questions about *anything*, I am the first person to handle them. Is there anything you need to know right now, Brother Bootsma?"

Frank shook his head. "No, Father, not right now."

Bonomelli raised a bony index finger and shook it at him. "Well, let me tell you something. I had a dream last night—quite an extraordinary dream. Do you know what I dreamed?"

Again, Frank shook his head.

"It was a dream about you! A rather unpleasant dream. I saw you in the Secret Archives in Rome, within the Vatican walls." Bonomelli narrowed his eyes and seemed to get lost in his thoughts. "There was something strange about the situation. You knew you would never leave those walls alive. You were about to be unified with our Father, deep, deep down in the catacombs of the Archives."

Frank watched him closely. How should he respond? Was the man demented?

Again, the elderly *padre* shook his finger at him. "Stick to your job and take care of our meteorite collection, Brother Bootsma. Stop searching for 'grand schemes'. You won't find them. Don't let your quest for greatness distract you and make you smaller than you are."

Frank was stupefied by the unexpected revelation. Bonomelli's words showed an uncanny perception about who he was and what he was up to. But how could he? How could he know about his work on the GOD project? He had never shared it with him and had always used a secure space on the Vatican servers; everything was encoded and encrypted quite meticulously.

Bonomelli stepped out of the pantry, but a couple of seconds later was back in again. "I have to leave for a few days, Brother. I have urgent matters to attend to that won't allow me to fulfill my duties in the coming days. You will replace me at the morning sermon and finish preparations for summer school for the rest of the week. This is not a request." With that, he turned his back on Frank and hobbled from the room.

Frank stared after him and finally dared to breathe again. He moved to clean up the floor and the tabletop. He opened all the closets in the pantry. He had to find something to eat, and he had to think. There was nothing there except some sugar cubes. He took a handful of them and stuffed them into his mouth while making another espresso for himself, and then another one, all the while pacing the room and thinking about what he had just learned. The caffeine and sugar were working. Something strange was going on in the Castel. Bonomelli knew about it and was trying to conceal it from him. His advice to stop doing research right now was just way too coincidental. Again, Frank felt pain; his mom had begged him to listen to his father, himself a scientist, only too late. She had made the plea for the last time on his graduation, when she came over to Tucson. When his father died soon afterward, Frank's feelings blurred into one big soup of sorrow, self-pity, and mistrust.

He took a deep breath. How long had he been sitting here? With only a couple of days left, he would have to move quickly if he wanted to investigate further. *Yes, I have to.*

Back in the exhibition room, Frank searched the Internet for the next two hours and learned a few astounding facts about Pope Urban—facts that now clouded his thoughts. He took some printouts and headed back into town for a late-night dinner to reward himself for his shocking discoveries. Over a nice meal, where he made most of his decisions, he decided to go back to the cave the next day... just one more time.

Chapter 4

Thursday: USNO, Washington DC

Roto Ashlev pushed open the door to his office at the United States Naval Observatory in Washington and stopped for a moment to scan it. Good, he thought. Everything was in order. As he strode toward the massive desk near the window, he tossed his coat over a chair and dropped his suitcase onto the floor next to it. He was exhausted, and his back ached. The early morning flight from Rome had been crowded, even in business class. The sleep he desperately needed had managed to elude him.

Scrubbing the hint of whiskers on his face with his hands, he tried to push away the thoughts that had persisted throughout the flight. All had not gone well on his trip, and he had regrets—regrets that would be best forgotten. He regretted he had not been able to visit Castel Gandolfo, for instance, but the Time Committee meeting scheduled for that very morning was crucial for getting the infrastructure of his project up and running. He rubbed his eyes and yawned. It would never do to be less than alert during the next few hours. Dropping onto the leather chair behind his desk, he patted his cheeks several times to free up his mind.

Unfortunately, his efforts didn't work, and once again, his thoughts drifted back to his stay in Rome. Try as he might, he could not block out the unanticipated fight that had ensued in the Vatican. He had checked and rechecked himself many times in the airport and on the plane, and fortunately, there was no trace of the fight on his face or body. It had been his first mistake. How could he have been so careless? Killing the man had been in self-defense, but it could have ruined everything.

Ashlev inspected the office again. With John Pakula, it had been different. There was no body, no evidence. After that fight, however, the room had been a mess. Desk papers had littered the floor, and a chair had been overturned. Now, the room was restored to its original state, and he appreciated its appearance. The late nineteenth-century mahogany wall panels, ceiling, and floors gave it character, warmth, and elegance. The dark cherry furniture blended and contrasted well against the room-sized Persian carpet and maroon leather couch. It was a suitable office for someone with clout.

Ashlev took a close look at himself in an old, glass-framed Navy map that reflected his face and upper body. Pakula had a slim, athletic frame; short, but not ultra-short jet-black hair; and an aquiline nose—all physical attributes that made him present well in his C.O. position with the U.S. Navy. He liked his deeply sunburned skin, most likely the result of his years at sea. He stared into his dark eyes; they looked troubled.

He had killed a man.

Well, it was a necessary part of the mission.

Pakula had resisted, but he hadn't fought like a man. He had surrendered almost immediately, probably because he'd been taken by surprise. The fact that he hadn't seen his victim made it all feel dreamlike. Who was he trying to fool? Ashlev thought. He knew better. He'd prepared several missions—been there, seen it all. But the wonder of the missing body still amazed him.

Ashlev stared at the center of the carpet and tried to relive the scenario. He felt no remorse. No officer was immune from dying in combat, and—unexpected or not—

killing and dying in the line of duty wasn't the issue. A soldier's job was to fight. Dying was just part of the equation. That he had taken out a civilian was different, though only slightly. His instructions were clear. The completion of his mission allowed him to kill as needed. He was instructed to leave no witnesses and, more importantly, to have minimum contact with the target. Hostages were out of the question. He could take nobody with him.

Nobody, that is, except for the scientist and the priest. Their abductions had been carefully planned and would surely pose no problems.

Ashlev stretched his arms above his head and arched his back, still hurting. He couldn't remember the details of the fight with Pakula, but he must have been smashed to the ground or against a wall. It had hampered him in his fight with the old man in Rome. With each aching pain in his back, Rome came rushing back to his memory.

Everything about Rome had been a big surprise. Nothing in his preparations could have equipped him for the almost suffocating noise and crowds of humanity. The smells of gasoline, food, and perfume, and the scantily dressed women… He had been overwhelmed by it all. Even for a warrior on a mission, the sensory overload had been almost too much to handle.

Not everything had been a failure. Gaining access to one of the most secured Archives of the world at that time had been remarkably easy. His uniform, fake ID, and a forged letter had done the job. As a founding member of the Society of Observatories, he was allowed to study the origin of the Italian birthplace of the Vatican Observatory the *Specola Vaticana*. He had been shocked about the absence of modern security technology for such an important place. DNA and iris scanning had been available since the early 2000s, but he wasn't about to complain about that.

Unfortunately, nothing had gone smoothly. In fact, his plan had dissolved into a catastrophe. Thankfully, he had confiscated the original document on his list, but the price had been too high. He still couldn't understand how it came to be that the old man had been searching for the same document, in the same place, and at the same time as he. Moreover, it seemed as if he had been waiting for him. It was not only absurd, but impossible. Logic prevented it, yet it had happened. So, what could he do? He had no choice. He had to kill him.

Unfortunately—and this is what bothered him most—he'd killed an innocent student as well, though accidently, of course. The boy hadn't wanted to hand over his notebook...and he needed it. He needed to put the notebook away. He began a systematic search throughout the office to find a safe. Finally, he focused on an office cabinet that was not of the same cherry-wood as the others in the room. He opened the door, which wasn't locked, and there, in plain sight, he saw the metal safe. It was locked. It would have to wait.

Ashlev straightened his tie and smoothed back his hair. It was almost time for his meeting. He sighed deeply and peered out the window. It was always quiet at this time of morning. To the right, he could see the main entrance to his building. Wherever he looked, he noticed familiar things. Straight ahead, several yards further down the hill, he saw the top of the building housing the Atomic Clock, barely visible through the sprouting branches of several trees. It looked as if time had come to a standstill. Just then, his eyes fell upon a digital ticker tape attached to the top of the door of the building. It showed the time in oversized numbers, ten digits behind the colon. One of the digits was out of order; it flickered.

Ashlev couldn't help smiling to himself. He had been in Washington for fourteen days, six minutes, forty-five and almost three-tenths seconds. According to plan, he had arrived exactly on time. His victim had been seated behind his desk, and he had taken him out in exactly one minute and ten seconds, thirty-five seconds quicker than planned because he was easier to overcome than expected. The task could have taken place a couple of seconds faster if he had ignored Pakula's question. The officer seemed compliant for the most part, but he had asked, "Why?" It had sounded like a prayer.

Ashlev frowned. He hadn't answered Pakula, but he had hesitated because of the nature of the question. It implied that Pakula understood what was happening and only wanted to know why he had to be taken out.

What did it matter now? Ashlev shrugged. He was tired of dwelling on the issue. He and his men had a mission and couldn't afford delays of any sort. The longer they stayed, the more they could contaminate the plan and its future. He hoped his two aides had been more successful in taking their target into custody.

Time to move on. Ashlev turned and walked briskly to the door. He opened it quietly, quickly scanning from left to right into the corridor; it was deserted. He heard no sounds of activity. He was alone in the building for at least another hour. Pakula had always arrived early to his office in order to monitor the arrival times of his men, so he had plenty of time to work undisturbed. Good habit, Ashlev thought. Pakula also had other worthwhile habits. He had maintained a daily diary, which he stored on the Navy's mainframe network. Since the beginning of Arpanet, the Navy had archived all information entering its network, and now he needed to gain access to it and delete certain data.

Ashlev returned to his desk and adjusted the PC screen. He had ignored this particular task since his arrival, but he couldn't put it off any longer. He was an expert at wiping away every trace of data history from computer files, including those on the Net, and he didn't anticipate encountering problems. He was still surprised to see that a keyboard and mouse were required for data input however. That would slow him down a few seconds.

He lifted the keyboard. There had to be a wire connected to the system to prohibit wireless sniffing. He was right. The system was hardwired to the desk. He followed the wire and saw where it disappeared into the inner workings of the desk and then exited on the left side of the desktop to connect to a box on the floor next to a filing cabinet. He leaned closer to the cabinet and heard a soft humming. Once he understood the setup and thought about how to bypass it, he returned to the keyboard.

When Ashlev moved the mouse, the screensaver flicked off, and a window popped up, asking for a username and password. What do I do now? he thought. He lacked the tools and the processing power he had at work to crack any username-password combination, regardless of the length of the codes. He pulled open the drawer on the right side of the desk to see if Pakula was as sloppy as most people. After pushing aside containers of paperclips, pens, Post-it pads, and boxes of Scotch tape, he closed the drawer and opened the center one, pulling it out of its frame and tilting it to the side so he could see under it. He stifled a laugh and shook his head in amazement, once again bemused by the naïveté of people in positions of power. At the bottom of the drawer was a sticker showing a range of numbers in clearly visible black ink, along with a password. Next to it, Pakula had taped a double-edged key. He tore it loose and placed it on the table. Good.

First, Ashlev typed in the numbers and the word on the sticker to see if he could access the computer. If he wanted to be Pakula, he'd better start acting like him, and asking for computer help was out of the question. Miraculously, the screen opened, and he gained immediate access to the system. The homepage revealed all the access points he needed for his task. He quickly searched through Pakula's documents folders but found nothing on the hard drive as he expected. There were five network drives. He started with the one carrying the name of JOHN PAKULA.

The folder on Pakula's private drive contained several personal letters and a few downloaded documents that seemed to relate to holiday destinations. His official folder, marked SUPERINTENDENT, contained a list of subfolders, one for each of the officers reporting to him, including that of Deputy Superintendent Ellen Meyer. Ashlev opened it and found a résumé, a photo ID that contained her signature, and numerous evaluation reports. He clicked on her signature and saved it as a picture; he would use it later on. He found himself staring at the photo ID and wondering what she would look like as a real person. IDs were too formal to reveal personal traits. He would deal with her later, as he had other priorities right now.

After working on the files for several more minutes, he turned to the key. Why had Pakula hidden it under the drawer? Rising from the desk chair, he took the booklet and walked over to the safe. After he inserted the key, he wasn't surprised when it opened with one simple twist. The safe was empty. He leaned over to have a closer look and ran his hand inside to make sure he wasn't missing something. The inside seemed to be lined with a soft, velvet-type material. He carefully touched every surface of the enclosure and felt nothing. He placed the notebook inside the safe and closed the door. With no need to lock it again, he left the key in the lock.

Returning to his desk, Ashlev reviewed his plans. His men would go after Burkowski; he would concentrate on the priest. He took the phone receiver off the cradle and pushed several numbers he had committed to memory. The Vatican Embassy was located directly opposite the main entrance of USNO.

"Vatican Embassy speaking. How may I help you?"

"Good morning. This is Superintendent John Pakula of the United States Naval Observatory. I have a special request. We need to meet with Brother Frank Bootsma as soon as possible. In fact, it is fairly critical that we meet with him personally. I understand he is based in Tucson, Arizona, but he may be in your facility today. Is that right?"

"One moment please." After too many seconds of static, she returned. "Are you still with me? I'm so sorry, but Brother Bootsma is in the other office right now."

"The *other* office?"

"May I know the nature of your call, sir?"

"Unfortunately, I'm not at liberty to discuss the matter with anyone other than Brother Bootsma. It's an official matter."

"I'm so sorry, sir, but Brother Bootsma has been interviewed a lot lately. He has had some very unsettling experiences. The press—well, you know, always turning things around, calling him under false pretenses."

"I fully understand, ma'am, but I'm sure if you tell him this is an official call from the USNO, he'll take my call. Where is this 'other' office? Would I be able to visit him there?"

"Not sure I may share this with you, sir. Brother Bootsma is still in Italy, sir. I believe Brother Bootsma will be returning today. He sometimes takes a connecting flight through Washington."

"He's still in Italy?" Ashlev quickly evaluated his situation. If he'd taken the extra time to drive to Castel Gandolfo, he'd have the priest in custody. "Do you know the number and time of his flight? We can pick him up."

"Oh, no, sir, we'll pick him up. We have standard arrangements. I'll make a note and tell him immediately that you want to meet him here."

As soon as he hung up, a light started to blink on his phone, indicating a voice message. Ashlev pushed the button. The message was short: "The Atomic Clock is now fifteen seconds behind Earth's rotation speed."

Ashlev felt a moment of anxiety. He had even less time than he thought. *Bootsma is arriving today?* He had to call NETWARCOM immediately. In only a few hours, he'd have to preside over the Time Committee meeting, and he anticipated serious problems with Meyer.

His phone rang. Bucket wanted him at the gate... immediately.

Chapter 5

Thursday: DuPont Circle, Washington DC

Max awoke with a start to the buzzing of his alarm clock. He thrashed through the bedding to locate it and finally found it under a pillow. He was better prepared this time and leaped off the bed and into his jeans he'd purposely dropped in that exact spot the night before. He reached for a sweater from the floor and sniffed at it. *Not too bad.* After slipping into his sneakers, he fled to the bathroom and carefully fixed his hair before putting a handful of gel in it.

His two screens were asleep. He awoke them by pushing his mouse and waited for his avatar to launch itself, but there was no such luck. He tried to launch it manually, but it still didn't respond, so he didn't manage to find the sources of the Chinese code. He had to go, so he switched off his machine, hoping for some luck when he logged in with his cell phone. Max was no fool, and he knew he couldn't risk being late again.

In exactly five minutes, he was sprinting down the stairs, three at a time, and bursting into the kitchen. Next to the sink sat the paper bags his dad hadn't bothered to unpack the evening before. He rummaged through them several times, finally dumping everything onto the counter. *Where the hell is it? Shit!* Once again, his dad had failed to remember his promise. He hadn't bought his one urgent request...unless it was somewhere else. "Dad!" he shouted at the top of his lungs. "Did you buy that tiny memory card for my cell phone?" Damn, he should've just bought it himself. Why still living at home?

During the divorce proceedings, the judge had asked him whom he wanted to live with. "My dad," he had said. He still remembered the expression on his mother's face. Clearly, she had felt the sting of rejection. Well, she had told him when he was little that babies choose their parents, and it was something he never forgot.

But that was years ago, before his dad discovered he had chronic headaches and felt down most of the time, as he did right now. He still wished he'd never mentioned it. The moment he had told his father about the throbbing pain behind his eyes, he was whisked to his dad's lab and put inside his fMRI. He never forgot the smile on his father's face when he had told him his great discovery. He had what his dad called an "Area 25 problem," which he explained, showing a map of the brain, as "a tiny part deep inside your brain that causes depression and pain." Maybe his dad smiled when he said it because he had thought he could cure him. He didn't know and wasn't interested either. All he knew was that his father had written an article about it and had used him as a guinea pig. When he had turned seventeen, he had refused to be tested ever again, and they had a big fight over it—a fight Max had won. It had been a turning point in their relationship. Running upstairs, he reminded himself not to mention his pain, knowing full well it was only a means to getting himself in trouble.

His father had forgotten—again—to buy the memory card for his cell phone: no memory card, no app, no more talking to his avatar. He found his dad walking between the master bedroom and the bathroom, trying to dress for work while shaving. "What time did you get up?" he asked. "Didn't hear you." Jacob lifted his chin to swipe the razor over his neck. Then, wiping his face with a towel, he turned to examine Max and wait for his reply. He reached out and tried to smooth down the fancy forelock Max had so carefully arranged, but the he'd ducked just in time.

"Don't know," Max said, lying. "Think it was about seven." He wanted to say that at about that time, he'd died a horrible death…just around the corner of the bell tower of *Sainte-Mère-Église* after that fateful night of June 6, 1944, when his parachute regiment was slaughtered by the Nazis. It would have been partly true while still carefully hiding the fact that, in parallel, he had his own secret project with the avatar. He decided not to mention it. He was in no mood for an interrogation. Instead, he shuffled his feet and stuffed his hands into his jeans. "Did you buy me the memory card last night, Dad, yes or no? The shop is next to the supermarket. Remember? You said you'd buy it, but I can't find the damn thing. Simple question, simple answer please."

Jacob shrugged and turned back to the sink to comb his hair.

"Hey, does that mean you didn't buy it or you don't remember if you did?" Max couldn't keep his annoyance from creeping into the question. The pain was back, right there behind his eyes.

Jacob looked directly at him again and peered at him. They were at eye level. "No, I didn't buy it. Yes, I remembered, but I was already in the car and didn't want to get out again. Next time, okay?"

"No, it's *not* okay, Dad. As I told you before, I can't play the game without a card. Why don't you understand this? I've begged and pleaded…and you promised."

"When did you get to sleep last night? Is your headache back?"

"Don't change the subject. Why didn't you buy the card? This is the second time you've forgotten. And my headache is none of your business. We've been there, remember?"

"First of all, tell me, is the pain back, yes or no?"

Max threw his hands into the air. "What does it matter to you? I want to know why you didn't buy me the damn card. I need it!"

"You *need* it? Don't we live here together? *I need* a little respect." Jacob returned to the bedroom with Max close on his heels.

"You're not taking me seriously, Dad. You think I'm still a kid—someone you can either boss around or put into one of your machines!" Max instantly he realized he'd made a mistake as Jacob briskly turned around

"What did you say?"

"Sorry, Dad. I didn't mean it."

His dad contemplated his apology for a moment and then nodded. "Okay. Take it easy, son. It's okay. Nothing to get all riled up about."

"It's not okay, Dad. If I treated you and your 'time-travel' tech the same way you treat me, you'd never even talk to me." Max made quote-unquote gestures in the air.

His dad squinted and tilted his head. "Did you sneak into my study, Max? I thought we had an arrangement."

Max shook his head. "I'm not stupid. Sometimes you're so clueless. You leave stuff on the freaking kitchen table, Dad—*our* kitchen table. Okay? I see things, whether I want to or not. Anyway, I need that memory card...TODAY!" Hating to show the depth of his disappointment, he fled the room and ran down the stairs again. In the kitchen, he snatched up his backpack from the kitchen table and wrenched open the fridge door to find something for his lunch. He saw nothing he liked and slammed it shut. "Why do I live here?" he groaned.

He dashed through the living room and out the front door, slamming it shut with a loud *bang*, and then ran across the lawn toward the bus that was already waiting for him at the corner. The driver was honking to speed him up. On the way, he almost bumped into the newspaper boy. "Sorry," he said. It was at that moment he noticed a van pulling to the curb directly in front of his house. A movement behind the windshield caught his attention, and he stopped to stare. Two unsmiling men were eyeing him, and one of them pointed in his direction. The other one shook his head and pointed at the newspaper boy.

The bus driver honked again and opened the door. Max hesitated. *Who were those dudes?* he wondered. The bus driver honked again. Max sprinted the last yards toward the bus and jumped aboard. The sliding doors closed with a loud *hiss*. He took a seat and pushed his nose against a window. The two men were still watching him from their van. It looked as if they'd been waiting for him. Max groaned to himself. Life wasn't a computer game. His imagination was running wild.

"Hey, Max," a girl's voice sounded close to him—way too close. He looked up to find a petite brunette with too much makeup, about to sit next to him. She was smiling. Max ignored her, as he didn't like her very much. Except for maybe one or two of his female classmates, he didn't like girls at all. As far as he was concerned, they were just too dumb and annoying. He took at his Smartphone and tried to launch his app. He stared at the hourglass that was turning somersaults. He felt the girl take the seat next to him. When he finally cast a quick sideways glance, she was still smiling at him. He held the phone closer to his face and focused on the screen, not sure the hourglass would stop turning around.

Chapter 6

Thursday: DuPont Circle, Washington DC

Dr. Jacob Burkowski hated that he'd disappointed his son again. He still felt incompetent in dealing with the boy. Modern kids were exposed to megadoses of television and online chat. Nevertheless, he had to admire Max's independence and intelligence. He might spend too much time gaming, but he managed to get his studying done. Thankfully, he was one smart kid. However, his brain problems troubled him, especially because Max didn't want to talk about it anymore.

He should have bought him the damn memory card, but he was anxious to get home and back into his studies. Max should understand by now that his work had to come first. A staff position in a medical school meant he worked 24/7 if need be. There were no eight-hour days for academic physicians, especially for those involved in research. He was about to head after him when he dashed out of the room but changed his mind. Instead, he struggled to put on his slacks. The top button was causing problems. He was gaining weight for some reason, even though he jogged and paid attention to his diet. There had been a time when people thought he was considerably younger than his real age. He was of average build and still well proportioned for his height, but it was his youthful face that caused all the comments. He cursed under his breath.

Once more, his thoughts turned to his son. It certainly didn't help their relationship when he avoided answering Max's questions. The boy had been primed to start a fight. The fMRI clinical trials had popped up again. He was about to lose his own temper because, like his son, he wasn't a morning person, but he'd managed to get his under control. The two had devised a workable shopping system. Max would email or text him his grocery list, and he'd pick up the items on his way back from the hospital, but sometimes, their system failed. Memory cards weren't groceries, and he'd been focused on providing food for his son and getting home. His special project was nearing completion; it was not the time for interruptions and extra errands.

He realized he was looking for an excuse to defend himself, but he'd come to learn that kid only look at the bottom line. Max had most likely sent his request from his new phone while multitasking, probably gaming with his friends. Anyway, he had wanted to tell his son memory cards were not the end of the world when he had run off. Stubborn kid.

He heard the fridge door close with a *whoosh* and then the front door slam. Max was off to class for the day. Their little collision wasn't the first and wouldn't be the last. He needed to be more sensitive to Max's needs. The boy was growing up so fast, and Jacob hadn't been an easy piece of work himself.

Jacob heard the bus honking and strode to the bedroom window to peer out. Was Max dawdling again? He'd better not miss the damn bus. He lifted one of the venetian blind slats and saw his son running toward the bus. Then, he stopped and turned to gaze at a van.

Jacob froze and felt his heart kick in his chest. Two men had stepped out of the vehicle. They took a couple of steps toward Max. The impatient driver honked again, and Max jumped onto the bus. The men watched it disappear around the corner at the end of the street. They said something to each other and then turned to stare at the house. One of them looked up.

Instinctively, Jacob stepped back from the window. This wasn't in the plan. He recognized the men from their uniforms. They were supposed to meet him at work and not bother him at home. "What are they doing here?" Jacob cursed aloud. He had been too trusting, too eager to cooperate—though actually, he'd felt he hadn't have a choice. They were government officials and knew details they couldn't or shouldn't. They insisted their mission was critical. But . . . what if they weren't who they said they were? Why didn't he go to the department head? Now it was too late. This was all way over his head. What should he do now?

As Jacob inched toward the window to peek out again, his heart jumped with the sound of a knock on the front door, followed by a persistent ringing of the doorbell. "Oh God! They're here!" he whispered aloud, panic-stricken. Cold sweat dripped down his back. He wished he could turn back the clock, but he thanked God Max wasn't there.

Slowly, Jacob descended the stairs. With every step, he felt the ominous weight of an impending catastrophe. For some inexplicable reason, he felt his life would never be the same. He pictured himself dragged away by the police in handcuffs, convicted for the illegal and unauthorized use of medical equipment. These guys were indemnified because of national security, but he was just a first-class loser—somebody who could be tossed away and forgotten. He was just one more guy in the wrong place at the wrong time.

He was going to lose Max. Hannah would never let him have Max again. She would put him in an expensive boarding school, most likely in England. What difference would it make anyway? Max would never be able to visit him in prison.

By the time Jacob reached the bottom step, he had gone over every worst-case scenario in his mind. He could already see the familiar silhouettes through the glass panes in the door. One of them couldn't stand still; he was in constant motion. The other one was trying to peer through the frosted glass. Beads of sweat dripped from Jacob's forehead onto his shirt, and he felt nauseous. There was no way he could back out now. They had told him they would bring their test subject in at nine a.m. to be sent back in time, but they were supposed to meet him at the Medical Center, not at his house. He reached for the doorknob and hesitated one more time.

At that very moment, he heard a cell phone ring and the voice of one of the men speaking into it.

Two seconds later, both men turned and hurried back to their van.

Jacob dropped his head into his hands. Feeling a rush of relief, he remained rooted behind the door. What should he do? Go to work and meet them there or call his chief and ask for advice?

❖ ❖ ❖

The call had come on his cell phone shortly after he'd arrived at home. He was still in the kitchen, about to start dinner. Max was upstairs in his room. The speaker identified himself as "Superintendent John Pakula of the United States Naval Observatory." Jacob wasn't fully cognizant of the USNO activities, but he remembered reading something about them in the *Washington Post* right after 9/11. Rumors said they were building underground housing for the vice president, who happened to have lived in the former superintendent's house. He remembered every word of that initial conversation with Pakula.

"Sorry to bother you at home, Professor Burkowski, but I need answers to a few questions that are vital to our national security."

He'd felt flattered to receive a call from such an important person, especially when the man addressed him as "Professor," a title he rarely heard at med school since he hadn't yet earned a full professorship. He had no idea what the man's position implied, but it sounded important. He had listened politely.

"We understand you're working on a project involving the transmission of brainwaves. Is that right?"

Jacob had found himself speechless. *How did this Pakula find out about my special project?* Why would anyone at the USNO care about his research, and how did they learn of it?

"Professor Burkowski?"

"Well...yes, I guess you could say so."

"It's important that we interview you as soon as possible and would appreciate your cooperation. We'll send two officers to interview you sometime in the next couple days. Will you be available?"

Jacob was puzzled. Did he have a choice? Probably not. "Sure, no problem. That's fine."

"We're particularly interested in the side effects you've identified in your brainwave experiments. We understand you have an important paper about to be published on this issue, pending approval."

He had dropped onto a stool next to the kitchen table. "Yes, I do, but how did—"

"You're probably wondering how we learned about it. We have contact with certain members of the editorial board of *The Lancet Neurology*."

"*The Lancet Neurology?*" They knew about his article? Jacob had been impressed. It was gratifying when someone seemed to understand and appreciate the relevance of his work. He was convinced it could change the future of medicine.

"We know you've endured personal sacrifices to achieve your scientific breakthrough, Professor," this Pakula had said. "The U.S. government would like to pay tribute to you."

Did the guy know he had accidentally discovered that his son suffered from neurological depression related to a prefrontal cortex region known as 'the factory of depressions'? He had felt it his duty, both as a scientist and as a father, to do some testing on his son. Had he committed a criminal offence? Was this a legal trap?

"Don't worry about your private tests, Professor," Pakula had said, interrupting his dread. "From your article, we concluded you've built on the brain mapping of the famous German researcher, Dr. Brodmann—especially with Areas 25 and 27, working as a reset button for the human brain to cure post-traumatic stress. We're pretty impressed. Your search for this mental 'system restore point' is vital for the U.S. armed forces, as I'm sure you can understand."

Jacob had just mumbled "Yes." A *click*, and Captain Pakula had disconnected.

How did he know all this?

The next morning, two men from the USNO had paid him a visit, after Pakula's strange call at his home. They had introduced themselves as Simon Calder and Thomas Bucket, both typical Navy types, with military haircuts, arms bigger than his own legs, and necks that formed a bulging line from the tips of their shoulders to their ears. Calder was a head taller than his colleague. Their IDs showed no rank—only that they were based at the USNO in Washington DC.

Jacob wanted to explain his motives, but the bigger of the two was not really interested. "It is our understanding, Professor Burkowski, that one can use your procedure not only for this 'brain reset' business, but also actual time travel back in time. Am I stating that correctly?" he'd asked.

Jacob had instantly forgotten his name. He often suffered from brain fog, especially when it came to names. For a moment, he had been puzzled, because the mention of time travel had only been a footnote in his article, nothing to be taken too seriously. But they seemed interested, so he decided to start his lecture on the subject.

"Einstein was the first to confirm the concept of time travel. Perhaps you already know of his well-known example. If an astronaut were to travel at the speed of light to a planet, he would theoretically return to Earth younger than the people he left behind. The reason behind this is that the personal body clock of the astronaut would have slowed down when his body reached a speed where time and space become disconnected. So, time travel in the days of Einstein hadn't been *real* time travel, but a sort of 'slowing-down-time travel'." He smiled boyishly. "This is called the 'Special Relativity Theory', invented by Einstein in 1905. The problem is, of course, that attaining such a speed would be impossible for any human being, and even more importantly, physically impossible to endure because of pressure and heat. The same equation could be used to take a few atoms apart, and as a result, an immense source of energy would come of it. So, the $E=MC^2$ was really helpful for building atomic bombs, as you are surely aware of, but not necessarily for traveling in time."

He had laughed forcedly, then realized his visitors weren't amused. The shorter one, who was far more muscled than Jacob himself, had laid a strong hand on his arm. "I'd prefer you not comment on any military issues here, Professor Burkowski."

"Sorry." The man's grip was bruising, alerting him this was not a social call.

"Continue, please."

"Okay. Well, ten years later, Einstein discovered that gravity—the same as speed—has the capacity to change the link between space and time."

He had paused to scribble a formula on a piece of scratch paper: $G(\mu v)=8\varpi T(\mu v)$. "This is the formula of the so-called 'Einstein Field Equation', or EFE, which is a little more complex than the $E=MC^2$ formula, as you can see.

For that reason, it never reached the Hall of Fame. In essence, it predicts how much gravity is needed to bend time."

From the glazed look in the men's eyes, Jacob realized his explanation was far too complex.

The small man pocketed the piece of scratch paper containing the formula. "Keep it simple please. We're not scientists."

"Well, just remember that this formula gives way more possibilities to travel in time. Even better, it allows one to travel *back* in time, so no more slow-motion travel into the future."

The smaller man had nudged the other one. "Now we're talking," he'd said. "That's what we needed to know."

Jacob had gestured toward a couple of stools and taken one himself. More comfortable, he'd continued with his explanations. "There's just one problem, gentlemen. Time travel would only be possible for an electron, not for an object like a human being. But I believe I've solved the problem. I discovered something I call 'thinkwaves'."

Officer Bucket had grinned. "We know, sir. That's why we're here. We—"

Officer Calder had raised one hand, neatly silencing him.

Jacob had watched the exchange and squelched the questions that came rushing in. "This is still in a very early stage and highly speculative. We know a tiny part of the brain—Area 27, or the CA1 region of the hippocampus—stores memory in some sort of code that is traceable by the formation of proteins. You can see this with the latest brain scanners like the new fMRI, or functional MRI. We have one at the lab now. However, nobody has yet figured out how to capture these tiny proteins. The problem is they vanish the moment we want to measure them. It's more or less like the phenomenon of measuring photons. Do you know what I mean?"

The two men shrugged.

"Anyway, I've solved that problem too," he'd said, giving in to his sense of accomplishment. "This CA1 part of the brain is capable of transmitting these thinkwaves. They weren't discovered before this because we didn't know where to look for them. It turned out they're small bits of memory code followed immediately by the brainwaves... like a shadow, as it were. Basically, by tuning the fMRI into the flow of these memory bits, I have been able to capture them digitally."

"We're not at all surprised," Bucket had said. "You're a genius. We read about—"

Once more, he was hushed by a gesture from Calder.

Reading something ominously greedy on their faces, Jacob had found himself wondering again if he was disclosing too much. He discarded the thought of explaining the interplay with Area 25.

"I, uh, I almost lost my job at the GWUMC," he'd confessed. "My chief learned I wanted to publish my rather sensational theory that time could be turned back for the sake of a malfunctioning brain. I only referred to time travel in a footnote, but I was asked to withdraw any mention of my theory in the paper. That's why I'm curious about how those at the USNO learned of it from the *Lancet*. Perhaps you can enlighten me? I don't want to put my position here at risk."

Calder had smiled. "Not to worry, sir. The Navy is considering offering you the position of Chief Neuroscientist at the USNO in order to facilitate your groundbreaking work on time travel. Think Oppenheimer in a Manhattan Project II," he added. "Before such an appointment can be made, however, we need to see some proof of your concept. Only then can we go to the Joint Chiefs of Staff with our recommendation."

Bucket had nodded. "We also need to know who else is working with you on this project. You didn't figure this stuff out all by yourself, did you?"

Baffled, Jacob had stammered, "As a matter of fact, I—"

Calder had interrupted again. "Actually, that's not a problem, sir, but we will need to try your theory on a test subject first. This week...tomorrow, in fact."

"But that's impossible. It would be a clinical trial, and there's a lot of red tape—a lot of time. It might take weeks, even months to find someone who—"

"Don't worry about the test subject. The government already has one arranged. The individual has been handsomely paid. He's signed all the required documents and is eager to participate."

Jacob had squirmed on his stool. He was both nervous and excited. Surely, if the government were already involved, the procedure could take place without delay. Calder's blue eyes hadn't shown any emotion, but military types were usually cold. He supposed they were used to making snap decisions and not spending excess time rehashing things.

Still, he had hesitated. "Please understand. I've never conducted specific experiments with my theory. To be honest, gentlemen, I'm not entirely certain about how to send the thinkwaves away. The only component I've designed is the double-helix glasses. In theory, we could connect these glasses to the fMRI, yes, but what should we do with it then? How would we be able to send these waves to a specific location?"

Both men had smiled thinly. Bucket had reached into his briefcase and pulled out a memory stick. "Just insert this into your fMRI machine and follow the instructions, Professor Burkowski. There's a read-me file that explains how it works and why you *are* going to work with us."

Calder had winked at him. "Nothing to it," he'd said. "Trust me."

"Yeah," Bucket had added. "That's the basis of the whole mission. Trust."

Now, as Jacob watched them drive away from his house in their van, he thought of the remainder of their conversation. He had iterated the importance of limiting all discussions of their project to the hospital. There were to be no more calls to him at home, yet now, they had showed up at his door, thereby breaking their promise. He wondered what would be next. *Trust?* he thought. *Yeah, right.*

Chapter 7

Thursday: George Washington University (GWU), Washington DC

Max hunched over his desk in the back row of his C Sci 270 class, one of his favorites. Computer science had not yet fulfilled its promise, but machine intelligence and cognition was the field he definitely wanted to specialize in. Most of the other classes—especially mathematics—seemed utterly pointless to him. He couldn't see why he'd ever need it, although his dad had lectured him about the importance of knowing how to crunch numbers if he wanted to become an engineer. "Being highly skilled in math is essential to your success in any engineering field," he'd preached more than a few dozen times. Max rolled his eyes just thinking about it. He still couldn't see the rationale behind the statement. If he needed to know something about anything, including complex calculations, there was always Google. Education these days meant knowing where to find the answers, not having them already catalogued in your brain. Fortunately, he was good at the subject without having to pour over the books. Besides, Professor Robinson was a real pain in the ass. He especially disliked the man, who Max surmised couldn't teach his way out of a hole. He had just announced an unexpected verbal exam and demanded all textbooks to be stored away and to switch off all cell phones and PDAs, while he handed out the test forms.

Before Max had a chance to switch his cell phone to vibrate only (he wasn't an idiot), it beeped to announce an incoming message. He glanced around the room to see if anyone had noticed, but his friends already had their noses buried in their test papers. He cast a quick peek at Professor Robinson; he hadn't seemed to hear the beep either. He hoped it was his avatar coming online. Last night, they had moved so close to the final target. He was almost too afraid to think about the name of their objective: Prometheus, the supercomputer of the Navy Cyber Defense Operations Command, NCDOC, located deep inside NETWARCOM. As his avatar had discovered, this machine was so big that it encompassed one-third of the 4,000-square-foot data center. The most surprising thing, however, was that his avatar had come up with this Prometheus in the first place.

His thoughts were interrupted as Professor Robinson pointed at him. "Mr. Burkowski, go to the first question on your form and please tell us, what is the ultimate fear most scientists share regarding self-replicating machines?"

He didn't have to think about it for a second. "Self-awareness, sir...the likelihood these machines will ultimately evolve beyond human ability to control or even understand them."

"Excellent answer, Mr. Burkowski. Where did you find this nice summary?" Professor Robinson continued sarcastically.

"Just following your class, Professor... and reading *Scientific American*," Max added, a bit too fast. Thought *Sci Am* sounded better than his Wiki source, it was a lie, of course. Most of what he knew came from his clone on the Net.

Robinson's eyes narrowed, but apparently he decided not to correct him as everyone smiled. "And what would be the problem with that, Mr. Burkowski, *evolving beyond mankind?*"

Max couldn't think of any reason, but he had to come up with something now. "Legal implications?" he suggested, not so convincingly.

His hesitation satisfied Professor Robinson. "You're not sure, Mr. Burkowski, but that's okay. It show's you're still learning. The correct answer is that it is something difficult to predict."

While the professor turned away to another student, Max felt the throbbing pain again. This was his moment, and he wanted to teach *him* a lesson. Now he could show what he had learned from his dupe. "I think you missed the point here, Professor. May I tell you why?"

As Professor Robinson turned back to him, he flushed, clearly annoyed by the upcoming attack. *Good*, thought Max as his adversary stared at him. "Well, are we going to hear your bright idea?"

Well, thank you, I accept your challenge, Professor. "Sir, the biggest promise for machine intelligence is in the field of supercomputing as a supporting science. If we could build a 200-petaflop computer with unlimited data intake, we could then bring synthetic biology to the next level. In other words, we could start creating life."

"Synthetic biology? This is the C Sci 270 class, Mr. Burkowski, in case you've forgotten where you are right now."

Some students snickered.

"With all due respect, it is projected that in the next ten or twenty years, way after your retirement, sir," he added, while he could've bitten his tongue off for those last words, "synthetic biology will be a booming business, and not just on the level of a bacteria with a full synthetic genome. No, we're talking here about the first synthetically created human brain."

Now the professor burst out in laughter, and the class followed suit. "A synthetic human brain? Are you out of your mind? It is obvious you have no understanding at all of the complexity of life, young man. Are you sure you haven't been reading *Science Fiction Quarterly* instead of *Sci Am*? No, your ideas are an insult to the scientific community."

He took a few steps closer as he zoomed in on Max's cell phone. "Did you take this exam with your cell phone on?"

Max looked down in a panic as he realized he had completely forgotten to hide his phone. He quickly scrolled through his message folders. First, he didn't find it. Then he browsed his text messages. Almost nobody used it these days, except for his mother. *What's this?* he thought, scowling. The rather cryptic message was from her! It read: GETYOUR. He checked the time. Her message had been sent a little over two hours earlier. That's a little weird, he thought. She was an expert at texting by now, though she seldom texted him, yet she'd used some sort of shorthand he'd never seen before. A flash of guilt swept over him. He hadn't even talked to his mom for about three weeks.

Max felt a grip on his shoulder. He froze and then tried to put the cell phone away, but he was too late. Mr. Robinson snatched it from his hands, grinning, and mumbled something like, "You won't see that one again."

"It was from my mom, sir. She never sends messages. I think it's urgent."

"Yeah, sure," Mr. Robinson said, stalking back to his desk, where he stashed the phone in a drawer with other confiscated belongings of other unfortunate students.

Max silently fumed. He had no other option than to sit tight. Maybe if he did a good job, Mr. Robinson would reward him with the return of his cell at the end of the class, but he couldn't focus. Over and over again, he mulled over the strange text message. His mom rarely texted him. He hated that he wasn't able to reply. What if Robinson stuck to the rules and quarantines his phone for at least a week? He had to stay in contact with his avatar, especially because they were so close to the target. He needed his phone back—pronto.

Chapter 8

Thursday: USNO, Washington DC

When Commander Ellen Meyer exited onto Massachusetts Avenue and turned right into the narrow Observatory Circle, she noticed a police car parked on the shoulder of the road with one officer behind the wheel reading a newspaper. He looked up and waved as she drove past him. She decided not to respond once she recognized him. For some time now, she had determined he was more interested in her looks than her ID.

She entered the South Gate of the USNO and thought about the lax security measures employed by those charged with the responsibility to be more vigilant. The guards at the gate waved her through without asking for an ID either. Sure, they knew her car and recognized her face, but for the life of her, she couldn't understand why getting on the USNO premises should be so easy. It was protected with a double fence, surveillance cameras, and armed personnel, but that didn't excuse security personnel from executing their duty. The guards hadn't saluted her and could have been watching over a museum full of mummies, for all they seemed to care. The presence of the Atomic Clock was reason enough to tighten security, at least in her opinion.

Shrugging off the issue, Ellen left her red Chevy Camaro in the parking lot and walked briskly uphill to the main USNO building, which was positioned in the center of a circular compound. On the way, she took in the grounds and appreciated the beauty all over again. She turned around and glanced at the modest white building that housed the Atomic Clock. She was surprised that most people didn't know that their cars' GPS originated at the USNO. Its precision not only directed cars and the time on cell phones and video recorders, but also space odysseys like the mission to Mars. A slight deviation in the coordinates, and the space mission would have landed on Pluto. It was her regular party talk, but most people couldn't care less. Most of her friends had no idea that a service period at the USNO was considered a step up career-wise, and turning down the post would reflect badly in any officer's files. Not that she had that many friends. She was a loner and liked it that way.

Entering the foyer of the building, she turned right and sneaked toward her office, which was next door to Pakula's. His door was ajar, and she could see he was already at his desk, working on a huge pile of folders. She had to shake her head. The man was all caught up in creating the image of an officer who took his post seriously. He arrived long before anyone else, probably hoping his industriousness would rub off on his underlings. Once again, she stewed over the fact that it could have been her in his chair. She was usually early to work too. She was already closing her door when Pakula's voice sounded behind her. *Damn.*

"Have a minute, Commander?"

"Yes, sir." Ellen stepped outside and snapped a salute.

Pakula answered in kind. "We have a meeting with the Time Committee in about ten minutes," he said. "I intend to bring forward an important request and would appreciate your cooperation." He motioned for her to step into her office.

Ellen watched him move toward her desk, revealing through his carriage his many years of military training. All his motions seemed in concert. It struck her that he looked taller than she remembered, and his skin seemed a little darker. "What is the nature of your request, sir?"

"I want to bring the Atomic Clock to the web."

She worked at controlling her shock. "What part of the Atomic Clock, sir?"

"The whole damn thing, Commander—all twenty digits."

Ellen's eyes widened. "You want *civilians* to have access to the highest level of GPS?" she asked. "No…restrictions?"

"Yes, that's exactly what I want."

"Sir, I don't know if we can get permission for—"

"Have I mentioned who would have authorization to visit this website, Commander?"

"No, sir, but you weren't explicit about—"

"You're here to execute my orders, Commander, not to question them. I will expect you to support me in the meeting."

With her jaw hanging, Ellen watched as Pakula turned on his heels and marched from the room in a manner not unlike the changing-of-the-guard ceremony. If his antics weren't so preposterous, she would have laughed out loud. Instead, she dropped back into her chair.

Supposedly, Pakula would be working with other units in the Navy, communicating up through the chain of command; Ellen was more internally oriented and worked with staff members to ensure things went smoothly within the operation. She was his lieutenant, and it was this that required mutual respect.

Nevertheless, her military instinct told her there was something going on with him. She had been in combat in Afghanistan and Iraq and had seen what war could do to a man's mind. She had to check him out. The longer she thought about it, the more she became convinced Pakula could have a problem, involving a possible breach of USNO security.

✤ ✤ ✤

Ashlev had mere hours to sequester the Jesuit priest. Fortunately, the Vatican Embassy was just across the street, convenient, to say the least. But first things first. Thanks to their commander's cooperation, he gladly had the uplink to the Naval Network Warfare Command (NETWARCOM) almost organized, and he was well on his way to accomplishing that goal.

He was determined to connect the USNO directly to NETWARCOM. Besides high-resolution imaging, the space satellites of NETWARCOM were outfitted with high-precision lasers, capable of hitting a target within a five-inch range. Their primary goal was to avert a missile attack. And, as an added bonus, these lasers could also easily reach the surface of Earth.

This was exactly what Ashlev had in mind for his mission. They were going to attack specific humans with these lasers by sending electromagnetic waves. However, in order to hit the targets exactly in the left temple, the ultra-precision of the Atomic Clock was essential.

With only a few minutes to go before the Time Committee meeting, he had browsed the Navy Net and located the website of the leadership of NETWARCOM. The commander of NETWARCOM, Vice Admiral Terry Shields II, smiled at him from his official photograph. Ashlev had him on the phone in the next two minutes.

"Commander Shields, this is Superintendent Pakula at USNO speaking. I'm afraid we have an emergency situation that requires immediate action. Our data indicate that the accuracy of the Atomic Clock has altered considerably, and the discrepancy between it and the rotation of Earth is now out of sync."

"Is that so? How bad is it this time?"

Ashlev had smiled to himself. It was a known effect of the gradual slowing down of the Earth that, once in a while, a so-called 'leap second' had to be added to the clock to avoid miscalculations. The normal procedure was for USNO to contact NETWARCOM if the adjustment was out of range, which was routinely three seconds in a two-year period. His two men had already eliminated the two Navy guards that watched over the Atomic Clock and had manually changed the calibration of the helium-operating clock. He expected some flak from the Time Committee in a few minutes, but at that moment, he needed Shields's cooperation.

"Sir, the situation is serious and deteriorating," he'd said. "We anticipate a further slowing down of at least fifteen seconds in the next five days. Right now, we have no understanding of why this is occurring. It could be the Chinese. We do have some intel on their nuclear tests running several miles under the Mongolian heights, but that's only speculation. Commander, for the moment, we request permission to have direct access to the satellite operation of NETWARCOM to recalibrate the Atomic Clock. We need to measure the rotation of the Earth from the outside, using your satellites as external points of reference."

"How long will you need this direct access, Captain?"

Ashlev had tightened his lips. Commander Shields was well aware of his rank. "No longer than forty-eight hours, sir."

"Hang on the line, Captain."

Ashlev had heard a faint *click* that indicated the commander sought counsel. In less than a minute, he was back. "Permission granted, Captain. The uplink will be effective in ten minutes."

"Thank you, sir." Ashlev had pumped the air with his fist. Everything was going according to plan again. His trip to Europe had been a disaster, but maybe the stars were on his side now.

He glanced at the clock. *Just in time.* He stepped into the corridor to see Commander Meyer walk toward him. He had to admit she was attractive. Even though she appeared well muscled, she was every bit a woman, even in her uniform. He had only seen her smile once, but when it broke across her youthful face, her entire appearance had changed. But it would never do to become more than businesslike with Commander Meyer. It was just too risky.

At the moment, however, he needed her cooperation. He had learned she was a stickler for military protocol. She would comply with his command and be an effective partner in his further deception, like it or not.

He cast a sideways glance at her as they entered the Time Committee meeting. Yes, duty, honor and country were firmly imprinted on her lovely face.

Chapter 9

Thursday: Rome

During every part of the morning prayer, Frank Bootsma's thoughts wandered to the very purpose of it. Out loud he prayed to God, but silently he begged for guidance, clarity, and faith. He had been awake for most of the prior night, arguing with the growing voice inside him, battling the horrifying thought that he had made the wrong choice. Had his father, the historian, been right? Ever since his discovery deep under the castle, he had trouble getting warm. Indeed, he shivered all the time, as if he had a fever.

As he hurried toward the gate, the guard was on the phone. "Brother Bootsma," he said, "I have a long-distance call for you."

"I'm so sorry," Frank said. "I'm in a terrible hurry. I've got to catch a train, and I'm already late." Without waiting for a reply, he scuttled down the winding path to the railway station. He couldn't afford to miss the first train from Castel Gandolfo, which would arrive around seven-thirty at *Roma Termini*. Unfortunately, it was a local train and would stop at every station, taking more than an hour to cover such a short distance, but he had no other option.

From *Termini*, Frank took the subway to the *Piazza del San Pietro*. First, he ordered a piping hot espresso and a divine-smelling crispy croissant because his breakfast had been ages ago. In his hurrying, he almost forgot to stamp the ticket he had purchased from one of the vending machines.

It was only a short five-minute walk to the *Porta Sant' Anna*, the gate all staff used to enter the Vatican State. The Swiss Guard noted his clerical collar and waved him in. He headed directly to the office of the Vatican to get a pass. The admissions office was situated in a modest building that looked more like a refurbished trailer. Again, his clerical collar spared him the questions; the purpose of his visit was sufficient. Within a couple of minutes, he walked away with the precious *Permesso di accesso alla Città del Vaticano* stamp on his ticket. In large capital letters, it read: BIBLIOTECA-ARCHIVIO.

Outside the admissions office, Frank turned right and immediately ran into two Vatican policemen in impressive buttressed capes, blocking his passage. He showed them his *permesso*. One of them glanced only briefly at it and waved him on. Again, he was surprised his access was so trouble-free. The scratch-pad permit could be easily forged with any copy machine.

Frank passed the rather non-descript Vatican post office and only a couple of yards further reached another gate that blocked access to the *Cortile del Belvedere*. Again, he showed his *permesso* and was waved on. He turned right and strode across the square, peering up at the impressive Vatican Museum. The *Torre dei Venti* had been constructed atop the second floor and was closed to the public and to scholars. No one could enter without authorized admission by the Prefect of the Archive.

Frank knew he shouldn't slow down while crossing the square or reveal any hesitation in his progress, or the police could become distrustful of his intentions. As in any other city, they could question him, and if he were unable to answer satisfactorily, they could detain him for further interrogation. The left entrance led to the *Archivio Segreto*

Vaticano (ASV), where he had to acquire a *tessera temporane*—the all-important pass to gain admittance.

When Frank stepped into the hall, he was struck again by the facility's modest proportions. This was the ASV, a place so many people wanted to visit, yet so few were allowed to enter. Frank had learned that the two requirements for gaining access to the ASV were to be either a priest or historian and to have a document from a professor assuring that the holder was about to carry out important historical research. Strictly speaking, he was a priest, but he lacked the letter of reference.

The concierge in the gray cloak stared at him. "Well?" he asked.

Frank worked at controlling his nervousness. He hadn't had time to ask his director in Tucson to fax him a letter stating he needed to continue his research, not that the director would have written it anyway. His job description didn't mention doing historical research in Rome. Besides, the Vatican Observatory budget was limited, so his request would likely be denied.

Knowing this, Frank had devised a better plan. The night before, he had reopened the filing cabinet in the library next to his meteorite exhibition room. Just as he had hoped, the historical etching was exactly where he had replaced it.

"I have something of great interest for the *Prefetto di Archivio Segreto Vaticano,*" he said. "Would you please be so kind as to ask permission for me to meet with him?"

The concierge didn't blink. "Well?" He held out his hand.

Frank opened his briefcase and removed the folder containing the document. "This is a rare print that should be stored in the *Archivio Segreto Vaticano*. I am certain the *Prefetto* will want to include it with all the other documents transferred from the Castel Gandolfo centuries ago," he said.

The concierge examined the etching without comment.

"The print shows the origin of the Castel Gandolfo building long before it became the summer residence of our Holy Father," Frank added. "The ASV will be interested in seeing it...or do you want me to go next door?"

How about that one? Frank thought. The Vatican Library—the *Biblioteca Apostolica Vaticana* (BAV) —which was directly next door, contained a significant collection of non-religious manuscripts related to the Pontificate. Frank knew that many of Cardinal Maffeo Barberini's manuscripts were located there—manuscripts he had written before being appointed as Pope Urban VIII. He also knew the ASV and the BAV had separate entrances and separate staff and were governed by two different *Prefettos*. The staff rarely talked to each other, and even more importantly, their facilities contained no cross-reference system for their collections, neither physically through an index card system nor digitally.

Frank realized the etching belonged to the BAV. Most of the historical documents of the Vatican Observatory were archived there. But then, that wasn't his strategy. If the Vatican had any information on the Barberinis, it would be in the ASV. Anything secret—*really* secret—had to be buried deep inside the ASV, and to clear his conscience, he needed to find it.

Frank's eyes never wavered from those of the curious concierge's. He played his final card. "I would strongly suggest you pick up that phone behind you and make my request, or I'll ask the Father General to inform the *Prefetto* that we handed over this precious document to the BAV." He knew the concierge was well aware that the Jesuit superior outranked the Prefect but would never intercede between the two rivaling institutes. When he flipped open his cell phone and started to punch in a few random numbers, the man grew visibly uneasy. Frank could tell he was making a quick risk analysis.

"Okay," the concierge said, holding out his hand to stop Frank's activity. "Hang on." Clearly annoyed at having to suffer loss of face, he turned and picked up the receiver of a red phone mounted on the wall behind him. With his back to Frank, he spoke softly for a full minute. When he finally turned to face Frank again, his attitude had dramatically changed. "The secretary will be with you in a few minutes, Brother Bootsma. We kindly ask you to wait here."

"Thank you." Frank maintained his posture, although he wanted to sag in utter relief. He reached for the folder containing the etching. "I'll take that now," he said.

Within three minutes, he saw the elevator door open at the far end of the corridor. A black-suited man who appeared to be in his forties stepped out and strode toward him, smiling with both arms outstretched in a welcoming stance. "I am so very sorry for the misunderstanding, *Dottore* Bootsma." He took Frank's right hand in both of his and shook it a little too heartily. "Please follow me."

The secretary unlocked the door next to the check-in counter and motioned him inside, but not without first shooting the concierge a harsh look. He hurried across the room and gestured toward two chairs next to a table. "Please sit down, *Dottore*. We'll be more comfortable. Again, our sincere apologies for this misunderstanding. It is difficult to find qualified personnel these days."

Frank didn't know what to say, so he only flashed the man one of his disarming smiles and opened his briefcase for the second time. Carefully touching only the very edges of the etching, so as to elevate the importance he placed on the document, he removed it from the folder and placed it on the table before them.

The secretary removed his spectacles from the breast pocket of his jacket, stretched the wire rims over his eyes, and hooked them behind his ears. Then, he leaned forward to study the print without touching it.

Frank watched him. "As I said to the concierge, this obviously rare print probably belongs in the BAV, but I just wasn't sure."

The secretary didn't respond.

Like all senior Vatican staff members, he had probably been appointed to his position because he had the right connections, Frank decided.

Finally, the secretary removed his spectacles and peered directly at Frank. "Is it your intention to turn over this print to us for safekeeping?" He pressed his thin lips tightly together while stuffing the eyeglasses into his pocket again.

"I am most interested in assuring that it finds its rightful home," Frank said. He paused and narrowed his eyes, gazing for a moment at the ceiling. "It wasn't my original intention to bring this with me today, but I was stopping by the ASV anyway on another matter. I know I would ordinarily need a letter of recommendation from a professor, but since I leave for the United States today after studying these past few weeks at Castel Gandolfo, I would appreciate it so much if I could be allowed—as an exception, of course—to investigate a few documents." Frank paused again and took on the humble look of a low-level servant. "Of course, before I leave, I intend to leave the print here. I don't believe we need any formalities right now, do we?" He was certain the secretary was fully mandated by the *Prefetto* to make a decision on the spot, and he was right about that.

The secretary rose from his chair. "You may leave the print with me. I will now ask the *Officio di Permessa* to bring you a pass. If you will excuse me, I must return to my duties."

The secretary shook his hand and left the room with the print ensconced in the folder and hidden from sight. Another black-suited man stood directly outside the door. They exchanged a few words, and the second man entered and seated himself behind a desk near the window and turned on a PC without saying a word to Frank. After a few minutes, he pointed toward the corner of the room.

Frank turned and saw a camera mounted on a tripod. Somehow, he had missed it when he had followed the secretary into the room. "You want me to look into that camera?" he asked.

The man smiled and turned his hand palms up. "*Non parla Inglese,*" he said.

That explained a lot, Frank thought. This was even better. No English, no questions. Now that he was so close to getting his pass, he felt the tension grow. The shivering was gone. In a few moments, he would be inside. *There will be no turning back.*

A minute later, the man handed him an ID document that had squirted out from the printing machine next to the computer. His photo appeared next to a number and the date of validation, which was today. He looked tense.

"Thanks," Frank said, rising from the table after examining the pass. He glanced at his watch. The ASV would close in four hours; it was only open until noon.

While he headed for the locker room on the mezzanine next to the front desk, it dawned on him that stealing a print and using his Jesuit order to get into the ASV would make this visit his last. As he put the key in the locker, he suddenly understood that Bonomelli's ominous dream prophecy was coming true. The old Frank was about to die.

Chapter 10

Thursday: GWUMC, Washington DC

Jacob waited with his hand on the doorknob of the front door until he heard the black SUV drive off. Carefully, he opened the door just enough to search the street. Breathing another sigh of relief to find the two government men gone, he stepped out and darted down the sidewalk to fetch the morning newspaper that was delivered with the precision of a Major League pitcher every morning.

Jacob tucked the paper under his arm and took one more look down the street to ensure the SUV hadn't returned. Located on Waterside Drive, their property had so many full-grown trees that their house almost appeared like the center of a forest. He knew the neighbors, but they minded their own business. He was hoping none of them had noticed the arrival of the black SUV or the quick departure of the two men driving it.

He hurried back into the house. Upon entering the kitchen, he glanced at the wall clock, stashed his papers into his briefcase, and headed out the back door, skipping breakfast. He was already running behind schedule. As he climbed behind the wheel of his silver 1990 Volvo 240 sedan, he felt more relaxed. He enjoyed the powerful sound it produced. No sooner had the engine roared when he heard his cell phone ring. Out of habit, he didn't answer the call. He checked the display. He'd arrive for the scheduled meeting at the MC in plenty of time.

Work or not, Nurse Jenny Williams would have to be patient. He wasn't her whipping boy.

Perturbed by the call from the hospital, Jacob followed the quickest route to Connecticut Avenue, which took him straight to DuPont Circle and New Hampshire Avenue. It was only a six-minute drive if he didn't encounter traffic congestion, and he didn't. He used up another five minutes to park in his assigned space and trek into the hospital and another couple of minutes to take the elevator to his floor.

As he entered the floor and walked past the reception desk, the head nurse on duty gestured toward a man strapped onto a gurney near the entrance of his lab. "He was rolled in by two military officers. Navy, I think. I tried to reach you, Doctor Burkowski," she said. "They insisted you agreed to be ready by eight o'clock sharp."

Jacob glanced at the man and saw that his eyes were closed. "Did they give you a name and reason for his admittance?" he asked.

"Motor vehicle accident." The unsmiling nurse, whose badge read JENNY WILLIAMS, held out a plastic card.

Jacob studied it without comment. The card showed the name of a construction firm, a photo, a personnel number, and the name BASIL BUDDHADEB. He glanced over his shoulder at the man on the gurney again. "They told you he had an accident?"

"That's all they said. Well, also that you'd been briefed in advance and expected his arrival, Doctor."

Jacob grimaced. *Can't these government people stick to their own plans?* "Looks like someone from the Middle East, and his name reflects that. Does the patient speak English?"

Nurse Williams shrugged. "Don't know, sir. He was unconscious when they rolled him in. He's only been here a couple of minutes. The officers said he had an injury at their base. They wanted an fMRI, but I haven't found the paperwork for it yet. What do you want me to do? It doesn't seem like normal procedures have been followed."

Jacob fought to control himself, steaming and ready to vent at Nurse Williams, but he knew he had to calm her down to make sure she wouldn't call anyone. He'd lose his job in a heartbeat. Heck, maybe he would anyway. This was not what he had anticipated. "I'll take care of it," he said through tight lips. He pushed open the door into his lab and pulled the gurney into the room himself. Closing the doors, he placed his fingers on the man's carotid artery on the left side of his neck and felt a strong pulse. Assured by the steady breathing, he went directly to the instrument panel. It showed the fMRI unit had already reached maximum power. Nurse Williams had performed her routine and switched it on when she arrived for duty, a standard procedure for the daytime shift.

Jacob left the examining area and entered a glass-fronted adjacent room built with magnetic shielding to prevent exposure when the fMRI unit was in use. The unit itself had to be shielded from the computer equipment because radio frequency signals could disturb the magnetic measurements. As soon as he booted his computer, it beeped to indicate it was ready to manually bypass the control system of the fMRI mechanism by asking for the access code. Jacob inserted the memory stick he kept on his key ring. The program recognized the code and opened up within seconds. He typed in his username and password and waited only another few seconds before the system was ready. He had completed the first part of the procedure.

He opened a cabinet behind him and removed a glass setup the size of a twelve-cup Mr. Coffee machine. The structure contained two helix-formed glass tubes that he'd connect to his computer and the fMRI unit. The patient's captured brainwaves would be sent through the two tubes and would connect, in real time, to a U.S. Navy satellite—at least that's what he understood after studying the read-me file he'd been given by Calder and Bucket, that, and the other program instructing him how to set up communication with the USNO. He'd learned that the fMRI would be connected to the USNO and then rerouted to their Navy satellite operation—the defense satellites of NETWARCOM. This unit would use lasers to fire the brainwaves with ultra-precision to their target somewhere on the globe.

Next, Jacob opened the autoexec file. No user name or password was required. He watched and waited while the program set up connections to the satellite. A pop-up box asked for the destination. In parallel, a window opened showing a large section of the Northern Hemisphere.

Damn. What was the destination…and where were Calder and Bucket?

At the very moment he thought it, the door to the examination room swung open. As if summoned by his mental questions, both of the officers entered and saw him behind the thick glass barrier. "Good morning, Professor," Calder said. "Everything under control?"

Jacob rose from his stool and returned to the examination room, glaring at both men. "Everything under control? You tell me! Seems like neither of you is sticking to the program." He had to control himself, but it was difficult. "We have hospital procedures, and they have to be followed. I could lose my job because of this."

Calder touched his arm. "Don't get upset, Professor. In the war on terror, we all have to make sacrifices."

Jacob stared at him. *He can't be serious.* But while Jacob stood speechless, Bucket maneuvered the gurney toward the examination table appending the fMRI unit and unstrapped Mr. Buddhadeb, who was still lying there, inert. Calder joined him, and they lifted the man onto the table. Bucket stripped off his shirt and strapped him down again, including a strap to hold his head still. Calder motioned Jacob over to examine him.

Jacob moved closer and lifted an eyelid. The pupil reacted to the overhead light; he wasn't in a coma. It was then he noticed the red bruises on his temples. "What are—"

"Okay, Professor," Calder said, "let's see where we are." He headed for the glass-enclosed room, seated himself at the computer table, and scanned the data on the screen, throwing a fleeting look over his shoulder to ensure Jacob had followed him. "The fMRI is active, the time machine is active, and the connection to the satellite is active. We're almost ready." He removed a piece of paper from his pocket and typed in a few coordinates. Then, he threw another glance at Jacob. "What's wrong, Professor? Haven't you got things to do here?"

Jacob felt paralyzed. He cast another look at the man called Basil Buddhadeb. "Exactly who is this man? I haven't examined him, and I don't know his physical condition." He shook his head. "This is no way to conduct a test. I can't allow this."

"It is too late to back out now. Start the machine, Professor!"

"No, sir. I can't...won't do it," Jacob said. "I need more time—more information." He looked at Bucket, who had joined them after leaving his post by the gurney. He had a rather insipid look on his face.

Calder's face had grown red, and his eyes narrowed. He motioned to Bucket, who left the room without comment. He returned a minute later with Nurse Williams, pushing her roughly into the examination room and then into the adjacent room behind the magnetic shield. He pushed her one more time, and she fell heavily to the floor with a groan. She peered up at Jacob with terror in her eyes.

"Don't make a sound, bitch!" Bucket said, towering over her.

"As you can tell, Professor, this is not a game." Calder motioned to him. "Turn on the machine! This is your last warning."

Jacob glanced at the nurse but couldn't meet her eyes. "Why won't you listen to me? This machine has never been tested for the experiment you are instructing me to—"

"He's not getting it," Bucket said. "Shall I proceed?"

Calder shook his head. He rose from the computer stool, grabbed hold of Nurse Williams's arm, and dragged her into the far corner of the room. He pulled a gun from under his jacket, cocked it, and placed the barrel against the back of her head. He stared at Jacob and ordered, "Do it now! We don't have time for this."

Jacob trembled. Bile rose in his throat and almost choked him. Did he have a choice? Calder had every intention of killing an innocent woman, and it was his fault. A million thoughts raced through his head. He shouldn't have instigated research on the fMRI machine in the first place. He shouldn't have submitted his research for publication, and then no one would know about him. If he threw the switch, he could kill an innocent man; if he didn't, Nurse Williams could lose her life. While he deliberated, the sound of a gunshot exploded in his ears. He inadvertently blinked. When he reopened his eyes, he saw the nurse fall over onto her side, lacking part of her skull. Brain tissue and blood sprayed all over the floor and on the wall. He gagged.

Calder stepped back and stashed the weapon in the holster under his jacket. "I assume you're ready now, Professor?" he said.

Jacob couldn't take his eyes off the nurse he'd known for several years. Calder had executed her in cold blood. He felt sick. He had to throw up. He held a hand over his mouth and gaped at Calder as tears clouded his vision. He felt his body tremble.

Suddenly, someone kicked him in the shins. It was Bucket. "Professor? Hello there. Wake up. We've got things to do." He danced and waved his hands in front of his eyes.

Jacob recoiled. He was kicked again.

"Turn on the damn machine!" Calder ordered.

With shaking hands, Jacob flipped the switch that initiated the movement of the fMRI bed. The test subject rolled slowly into the cylinder-shaped tube unit until his head and the upper half of his chest were inside the chamber. Then, the examination table stopped.

At first, nothing happened. Suddenly, a blinding white light whirled inside the neon tube, creating a crackling sound. On the computer screen, the brainwaves of the test subject showed steady green sine waves. As the light increased its speed, the sine waves became longer. The test subject became visibly restless and started to moan and writhe. Only the strength of the straps held him in place.

Jacob watched the wires inside the neon tube and globe of the world on two split screens. The tube and the globe were connected by a stream of brainwave signals shown as zeros and ones. At first, these signals were pointed at the United States, zooming in on Washington. Then, the globe turned, and the screen zoomed in on Burgundy, France. The flow of brainwave signals increased in speed. In the upper right corner of the screen, he saw the GPS location change from a parallel of 42n22 71w04 to 47n28 3e44, stopping in Vézelay. Suddenly, the camera lens zoomed in on an area outside a huge cathedral.

"We have a connection with the satellite, Professor," Calder said. "Increase the speed. Wait for my signal."

Jacob increased the velocity of the circling light inside the tube. On screen, a meter showed it was traveling toward the maximum rate of 670,616,629.2 miles per hour.

The test subject cried out. His chest and face were a bright red, and he was covered with beads of sweat. His muscles contracted as if he were being electrocuted. The contractions caused uncontrolled spasms as he tried to free himself from the straps.

"We've got to stop this!" Jacob shouted. "This is insane. This man's going to die!"

Bucket blocked him from reaching the switch that would turn off the fMRI unit. He wrapped an arm around his neck, almost suffocating him. "We give the orders here, Professor!"

Calder pointed at the satellite image. The movement of a figure leaving the church appeared on screen. They watched it move steadily away from the structure. "Start the double-helix," he ordered. "Now, hit that target figure at minus three seconds."

Jacob switched on the double-helix tubes and watched a vivid light circle inside them moving faster and faster between the computer and the fMRI machine, but he hesitated to press the key that would zap the unknowing target.

"Hit the key, Professor!" Calder repeated.

Jacob held a trembling finger above the ENTER key that would gave the input minus three, hating himself and regretting the time he had spent on his secret project.

Calder slammed his hand down, and the electronic package left the fMRI and flew through the double-helix up to the satellite. An appalling steam emerged from the opening of the chamber, and a second later, Buddhadeb's entire body had literally evaporated.

Bucket released his grip on Jacob's neck. "Now that wasn't so bad, was it, Professor? Behave yourself, and I won't have to hold you down."

Jacob stared at the machine. They had just killed a man named Basil Buddhadeb, and Nurse Williams lay dead only feet away. This would be the end of his career, the end of his life.

Calder focused on the screen and zoomed into the area outside Vézelay. "There is always some time delay," he said. "That's why we had to travel back in time three seconds." He paid no attention to the fMRI unit or to what had happened to his test victim.

At that very moment, Jacob saw the small figure on the screen collapse. Other figures seemed to gather around it.

Calder threw his arms into the air. "It worked! Good job, Professor. Congratulations on your first time-travel experiment." He peered at Jacob with widened eyes. "We were convinced you could do the job. Now, tell us who gave you the code."

Jacob's mouth was almost too dry to talk. His lips seemed stuck together. *Why do they keep asking me about a code?* "As I...as I've said before, sir, no one has given me any codes. This is my project and mine alone. No one else knows about it—except you, I guess."

"This isn't going to work, Simon. I told you so. We've got to switch to Plan B," Bucket said.

Calder nodded, and once again Bucket headed out the door of the lab.

"Where's he going? What's he going to do?" Jacob asked, alarmed and afraid they would bring in another innocent hostage to bribe him with.

Calder locked the door behind Bucket. "You'll know in good time. We'll just wait here."

"Wait for what?"

Calder grinned. "You need to know now? Hmm. Maybe having time to think about it will do you good. Bucket is going for your son, Professor. I believe his name is Max? We'll do a little experimenting on him—you know, just to ensure you're properly motivated to tell us all about the technology sources you use to safely travel back in time."

"Leave my son out of this! I don't know what you're talking about! I can't tell you something I don't know!" Jacob lunged at Calder, but he was no match for the well-muscled officer. Calder gave him an uppercut under the chin, and with that one blow, he went crashing to the floor.

Chapter 11

Thursday: GWU, Washington DC

If Robinson thought he could take his cell phone away and keep it, he'd made a serious mistake, Max thought. The exam was finished, and he was just about to rise to stride to his desk when he noticed one of his friends motioning to stay low. He pointed at the glass-windowed door of the classroom; the dean's head was clearly visible.

At that very moment, the dean entered the classroom, closely followed by two men in military uniform. The whole class fell silent, including Robinson, who rose from his desk to wait for an explanation. The dean's eyes scanned the room and finally rested on Max.

Max swallowed and felt his heartbeat accelerate. He knew instinctively that something was wrong—terribly wrong. The dean motioned for him to come to the door. As Max stared questioningly into his eyes, he saw something that resembled pity.

The dean put a hand on his shoulder and whispered in his ear. "These Navy officers are here to escort you to the USNO, Max. Your mother has been in a serious car accident near the entrance gate. Your father will meet you there."

Max went numb. The words "serious accident" echoed in his head. He nodded, unable to find his voice, and cast a nervous glance at his classmates, who were staring at him to watch his reaction to the news. His vision blurred, and he felt confused, sort of like a zombie looking at himself from a distance. He hated his mother, so why was he crying? *Is she dead?*

Feeling somewhat bodiless, he started to follow the dean and the two Navy men to the door of the classroom and then felt something pushed into his hand: his cell phone. Professor Robinson mumbled, "I'm so sorry," and his face showed he really was. Max clutched the phone tightly and nodded at him. He certainly didn't like the sucker, but somehow, under the circumstances, he felt differently about him.

Once he was outside the school building and walking down the sidewalk between the two officers, he glanced up and saw a black SUV waiting at the curb. It looked vaguely familiar to him, but he shrugged it off. One of the officers opened the door and motioned for him to sit in the back seat. Neither of the men said a word to him as they climbed into the front. When they pulled away from the curb of the campus parking lot, he heard a loud metallic *clunk* as the doors locked. Instantly, he remembered the car. It was the same one he'd seen pull up to the curb as he had dashed to the school bus that very morning. A sudden coldness had him shivering.

The guy next to the driver turned and looked at him. He didn't say a word for several seconds and just stared, leaving Max feeling even colder.

Max stared back. "Are we going to see my mom?" he asked. "Did she really have an accident?"

The driver adjusted his rearview mirror and eyed him. Then, he nodded at his friend and mumbled, "Tell him."

"Yes, she did. We'll show you soon enough. Just sit tight and don't do anything stupid. We don't want you to get hurt. If you cooperate, everything will turn out fine."

The response wasn't what he'd expected. It wasn't a simple answer about his mother's accident, but some kind of disguised threat. *But why? What is going on here?* Max wanted to ask more questions.

Moments later, the driver stopped the SUV at the curb on a quiet street. Max watched both men get out and start up what looked like a serious discussion. It was clear they disagreed about something. He examined them more closely. The driver had one stripe on his sleeve. The other one had to be a more senior officer, because he had four stripes and a star. He remembered this from his games. This man shook his head and stepped into the car without looking back at Max.

Suddenly, the door next to him opened, and the driver reached in to grab hold of his arm. "Come on, get out," he said, literally dragging Max onto the street. He grabbed hold of the nape of his neck and herded him toward the back of the SUV, pushing the button on his handheld key holder to snap open the trunk. "Take a good look," he said.

Max took one look and collapsed. The driver caught him before he hit the ground and hauled him around the car and into the back seat again.

While he fell on the back seat, the throbbing pain behind his eyes came harder than he'd ever experienced, as if the inside of his forehead had exploded. He grabbed his head. A series of flashbacks played out so rapidly that it hurt when he tried to look at them. He couldn't make sense of it.

At some blurred distance, he heard the driver slamming the door shut, stalking behind the vehicle to close the trunk, and then returning to his position behind the wheel. The man cast a glance at his companion. "This part of our mission is almost accomplished. It has gone more smoothly than I expected. You still don't know why we picked up the kid, do you?"

"Can't say that I do," his colleague said, his words echoing in Max's head. But then, Max realized they weren't echoes at all; he'd heard those words before. He'd been here before!

Somehow, in spite of his tremendous pain, he was alert enough to listen. *Do we know each other?* he wondered.

What is this? He suddenly realized the door hadn't locked. He tried, and it opened a crack. The Navy men were too busy arguing to notice.

Once more driving and watching the traffic, the driver suddenly chuckled. "You should have seen the woman. In her final minutes, she actually tried to negotiate her way out of it. What an idiot."

"I don't remember the boy's mother being part of the plan," the other officer said.

Max had to wait until they stopped at a traffic light, and they hadn't progressed that far yet.

"She wasn't, but she turned out to be instrumental in getting the beacon." The driver accelerated and turned onto an access road, heading in another direction.

"The beacon?"

"I don't get it. You're the officer. You're supposed to know everything. The boy's the beacon."

At that moment, the officer turned to peer over his shoulder at Max.

Max glared back at him only for a second. The officer seemed disturbed, like he had heard something he either didn't know or didn't want to know. *I'm going to be killed,* Max thought, though he didn't know what the stupid reasoning was behind it. There was not a second to lose. He jerked at the handle and let himself fall out of the car. A second later, he was on his feet, running back to the entrance of his computer science building. He didn't look back but kept on running.

Chapter 12

Thursday: Vézelay

Marguerite Favre had just finished giving her tour around the *Romanesque Basilica of Sainte-Madeleine de Vézelay*. She doubted the Chinese tourists had grasped the true meaning of the architectural design, except maybe for her comment that the mysterious feature marking the solstice could be paralleled with that of Stonehenge.

She had watched the last tourist in her group leave the Basilica and barely started her march across the *Place de la Madeleine* to her favorite café when she abruptly fell to the ground, crying out in alarm after receiving what seemed like a heavy blow to the head. Her body began to convulse as if she were having a seizure. Some of the Chinese tourists rushed back to help her but were unable to get close because of her flailing. Then, just as suddenly as the seizure had begun, she quieted and lay motionless. Soon, her eyes blinked rapidly several times, her head rolled slowly from side to side, and she pushed herself to a sitting position. Seeing the audience of gaping tourists, she rose to her feet and shook herself, much like a dog shaking itself dry after a plunge into the water.

"You okay, madam?" one of the Chinese asked.

"What the fuck are you talking about?" Marguerite gasped in unison with her onlookers. Her voice sounded deep and masculine, and she never, ever cussed!

Alarmed, she stumbled forward a few steps and then noticed her body and the way she was dressed. "What the hell is going on?"

He was no longer himself! He was someone else—a woman, to be exact. *A woman? What the hell happened to me?*

Basil Buddhadeb rubbed his arms with frantic motions, as though he could brush away the sleeves of his blouse. He gawked back at the bunch of foreigners, who seemed as much in shock as he was. *Think!* he demanded of himself. He had left home for work at six thirty that morning. Out of nowhere, a car had raced up next to him. In a matter of seconds, he had been dragged onto the back seat next to a hefty, well-muscled man in uniform—a military uniform, to be exact.

Basil scratched his head. The man hadn't said a word. He had raised his right hand and...and clubbed him over the head.

Now, he was...he was seemingly a *woman* with his same voice, in some weird place he didn't recognize. He gazed about, increasingly perplexed, shaking and struggling to make sense of what seemed like the weirdest dream he'd ever had. He ignored the bewildered faces and the muttering of the Asian strangers and staggered toward the steps of what looked like a Middle Age cathedral.

Maybe I wasn't kidnapped. Maybe he was hit by the car and killed and then somehow sent back to Earth for some reason. Yeah, maybe that's it. He saw that once in a movie.

Chapter 13

Thursday: GWU, Washington DC

Inside the building, Max dared to look back. He didn't spot them at first through the sliding glass doors, but then he saw the SUV make a U-turn and approach the small parking lot that was reserved for the dean and senior staff members. Several spaces were vacant, and in no time, the doors sprang open. The two Navy men didn't waste a second and ran straight toward him. He had no choice but to run. He dissolved into herds of students moving in and out of the building. He knew he had bought himself a few minutes because they would have to pass the metal detector first and show some ID.

He had to come up with an escape plan now. His first instinct was to seek refuge at the dean's office, but he dismissed the thought immediately. The dean had handed him over to these guys and believed everything they had said. He stood on his toes and peered over the shoulders of his fellow students to catch a glimpse of his two pursuers. They had passed security and were pocketing their stuff. The nasty one already eyed him and said something to his superior. Max ducked and zigzagged away, desperately searching for a place to hide. The closest place he could see was the men's room, but he reasoned it would be better to go in the ladies' room because they wouldn't expect it. While he sneaked into the ladies' room, he prayed no girl would be in there. He closed the door behind him as quietly as possible and had a glance around. Luckily, there was no one in there washing her hands—or worse. He inspected the stall doors frantically, and none of them were locked, so he chose a stall and locked himself inside it.

He sat down on the toilet, pulled his headset from his neck and put in on, connected it to his Smartphone, and switched it on. As he hoped, a green light was blinking, indicating his avatar was waiting for him. He muted the sound and launched the app. The familiar face of his duplicate calmed him down a bit. Reading his lips, he understood his question. He had to switch on his cam to make eye contact. It had been his dupe's idea to use iris scanning for authentication. A soft *beep* indicated they were in sync.

"What's up, Max? Where are you?"

"You don't wanna know, dude."

"You're in trouble right? I hear you breathing heavily and talking very softly."

"Yeah, sort of."

"Please, Max, I don't think this is a time for playing games. My GPS information tells me you're in the ladies' room. Am I right?"

Max just nodded.

"And, based on the cam position, you are sitting on the toilet…with your pants on."

Max almost had to laugh at the cute little bastard.

"The bad news is that every girl can see your big feet below the door now, so I suggest you lower your pants to hide your shoes immediately."

Fuck. He hadn't thought about it, of course. Max instantly unzipped his jeans and draped the legs over his shoes.

"But it's not really the ladies I am worried about, Max. Who's after you?"

Max quickly explained about the two Navy men. When he arrived at what he had seen in the trunk, he suddenly felt a knot in his throat. Unbidden tears welled up in his eyes, and he started to sniffle.

His dupe seemed to understand. "It's okay, Max. We'll find a way out. Please try to focus on your escape first. I think I know a way out. Look at the screen." On the screen, a tiny map emerged showing the street-level layout of the campus. It made way for a map of all basements and connecting tunnels. "I checked out the immediate surroundings, and it turns out that all university buildings are connected in a maze of tunnels. If we can get into the tunnel system, I am you're your assailants will not be able to find you."

Max felt relieved, but he looked up quickly when he thought he had heard something. There was nothing there, and the noise was coming from outdoors, much to his relief. "What are we waiting for, dude?"

"The problem is, I am not so sure we have coverage in those basements. I think you'll lose the signal and the guided assistance I planned for."

Instantly, the pain behind his eyes popped up again. He rubbed his temples.

"Try to shut out the pain, Max. We need to stay focused."

Max nodded slowly, trying to memorize the nearest subterranean exit. "I want to get to my father. He's only a few blocks away," Max suddenly blurted out. He was so scared and wanted to get to his dad.

"I'm not sure that is good idea," his dupe objected.

"Why? My father is the only one who can help me," Max snapped at him, "and he's for real, not like you." Immediately, Max regretted the harsh words he had spat at his new friend.

It took his avatar a few seconds to come up with an answer. "Okay. Let's move toward him, but there are no guarantees. Before we're there, I have to talk to you." Max was staring at the screen, still surprised about the omniscience of his virtual buddy. His friend was so determined to get access to NETWARCOM. *Is this somehow connected to those Navy guys? Do they somehow know?*

"Hey, pull up your pants and get moving," his dupe said, interrupting his thoughts.

At the very moment when he had zipped his fly, the door swung open, and a group of girls swiveled in, giggling and making camp in front of the mirrors.

"Oh my God, he's soooo cute," one said. "Ooh, what color is that?"

"It's called Naked Ambition," the other one answered with a ridiculously stupid and annoying giggle. "I sort of stole it from Mom's purse."

Damn it, Max thought. *I'm stuck.*

Chapter 14

Thursday: Rome

After hanging his coat in his locker, Frank took the elevator to the fourth floor of the ASV. There was no reception desk and no one was waiting for him, so he wandered around a bit before entering the first room, where several scientists were studying massive tomes and manuscripts. Nobody paid attention to him.

At the back end of the room, he noticed two male archivists in similar gray suits, sitting at a desk. They seemed to be handling requests. As he approached, one of them looked up and smiled. "Do you have the number for me?"

"I would like to see these," he said, showing him the number MISC. ARM. X, 204.

"Very well," the archivist replied. "Please have a seat." He gestured toward the row of tables where others were mesmerized in ancient books, some so large they almost filled the entire surface of the reading table.

Frank took a seat and heaved a deep sigh. He was inside. If they really did hand over the Galileo trial papers to him, he knew where to look. It had to have some clues about Galileo's best friend, Pope Urban VIII, the one who sentenced him to lifelong house arrest—the one accountable for creating the Vatican Observatory, as a weak effort by the Catholic Church to atone for its mistakes. A painful knot formed in his chest.

The archivist was finally nodding at him. As he approached the desk, he saw that like a sales clerk in a music shop, the man simply reached behind him to remove a DVD from a boxful of them. Had he been keeping him waiting for nothing? Frank resisted the urge to say something about it.

Along with the DVD, the archivist handed him a short memo written in block letters stating that since the Galileo trial files were considered vulnerable, the ASV had digitally mastered them onto a disk. Frank reexamined the room and observed that the ASV had changed dramatically since his last visit as a student. It had moved into the twenty-first century and would likely be considered one of the most advanced document laboratories in the world. "I have no laptop with me," he said.

The archivist nodded as if he anticipated such a response. He motioned for Frank to follow him to the next study room.

This room surpassed Frank's expectations. Every table was equipped with a Mac flat-screen of at least twenty-four inches. A dozen analysts in white laboratory coats were assisting scientists with the digital archives. Frank was assigned to a chair halfway down a long table. The archivist clicked on the computer, inserted the DVD, and waited for the image of the Galileo trial files to pop up on the screen. "Do you have any questions?" he asked. When Frank shook his head, the man left the room.

What followed came as an unexpected surprise. He had been taught at the Jesuit college that Galileo had been on trial as an astronomer for claiming that the Earth turns around the sun and not the other way around. The title page on the screen showed differently. It read: " *7. Con Galileum Galilei Mathematicum. Processo di G. Galileo.*" Frank read it again and again. This was something he hadn't known. Galileo had been on trial as a *mathematician,* not as an *astronomer.* If this was the case, who was his opponent?

The file contained 464 photos. The analysts of the Vatican *Laboratorio di conservazione et restauro* had taken their job seriously and photographed both sides of every page. Almost 232 pages were blank, except for a few stamps here and there. Frank squinted at the screen and moved closer. He especially scrutinized the blank pages for unexpected clues. Immersed in his study, he didn't see or hear anyone approach and jumped in his chair when he felt a strong hand on his shoulder.

"Hey, partner!" a muffled voice hissed in his ear.

Frank peered into the freckled face of Patrick McCormick, a red-haired Irish brother who had shared a room in his dormitory during their seminary years. Without thinking, he rose to hug his friend, but McCormick pushed him gently back while glancing around to see if they had disturbed anyone.

He sat next to Frank and leaned closer to him. "What are you doing here?" he whispered.

Frank found himself at a loss for words. He had just opened his mouth, when McCormick turned the screen far enough to read the text on the dark yellow photo.

"What on Earth is—?"

Frank put a finger to his lips. "I can explain it all, but not here. Is there somewhere we can talk in private?"

McCormick frowned. "Well, our offices are closed for non-ASV people," he said, "but I know a place. Wait here a second." He left the study room for the one next door and returned within a couple of minutes. He gestured for Frank to follow him.

"Did you speak with the two archivists who sent me here? What did you tell them?" Frank asked once they were out in the corridor.

McCormick laughed. "I told them I want to show you the bunker because you don't believe it exists."

"You have a *bunker*?"

"See?" McCormick laughed again.

Frank joined in. This was how he remembered Pat—always joking and laughing about his own jokes.

They took the elevator several stories down and walked through a series of corridors to end up in front of a massive sliding steel door, which McCormick easily pushed aside. As soon as the door opened, Frank saw how the bunker got its name. The concrete walls were at least a foot-and-a-half thick, and the space was so immense that he was certain it rivaled that of the complete Belvedere building that housed both the ASV and the BAV. He observed long steel racks stacked end to end with tomes and thousands of cartons.

McCormick smacked him on his back. "This, my friend, is the largest collection of ancient manuscripts stored in one place. Follow me." He strode randomly through several aisles until he stopped in a narrow one completely out of sight of the entrance door. "This is the only place I know of that doesn't contain a bugging device, because it's quite impossible to cover the whole area. I've done my part, space cowboy. Now it's your turn. What's going on? The last time I heard from you, you had just gotten a fancy job traveling between the United States and Castel Gandolfo to prepare for the first pope on the moon. Since when do you have any interest in the past?"

Frank grinned. "Where shall I start?" He took a deep breath. Could he trust his old friend? He had already taken an irreversible step to ask for a private conversation. On the other hand, they had experienced many personal 'chances', as they had coined it, when they shared more than a dormitory. These chances, which always pivoted around money and females, had marked dangerous turning points in their religious careers. Both had crossed paths several times since those days, but this meeting was totally unexpected and a little unnerving. But Frank was already too deep into revealing his reason for being in the ASV. He had to come up with something.

Starting with the secret door in the meteorite room, he guided his friend through his first visit in the hidden chamber under Castel Gandolfo and the print he had handed over to the secretary of the ASV. Frank decided not to tell his friend about Bonomelli's dream and all the rest—not yet.

McCormick listened without comment for some time. "So, you're telling me you stole a print from the Vatican Observatory, got access into the ASV under false pretenses, and now I have brought you into a place you would certainly never be allowed if my superiors knew anything about it?" He folded his arms across his chest and shook his head. "Oh boy. Pardon my saying so, but I do believe we're in deep shit, buddy. Give me one good reason why I shouldn't escort you to the exit door of the ASV right this minute."

McCormick wasn't laughing this time, and not even the hint of a smile creased his face. Frank knew he had to tell him more. "Promise me you'll never repeat to anyone what I tell you, Pat?"

McCormick smiled thinly now. "Have I ever let you down, Frank?"

It was true. He didn't want to be reminded about their wild dormitory years and Pat's finally abandoning the priesthood. He had noticed the wedding ring on Pat's left hand but dared not ask. "Okay," he said, "I wasn't much interested in the past in those days, but thanks to my position at the Observatory, I have access to one of the fastest backbones of the Arpa Internet. I didn't sleep last night, Pat. I did a little investigating...did my homework. I discovered considerable research has taken place on only one pope. Any idea who that might be?"

"Is this a damn quiz? Come on, Frank. Just get on with it."

Again, Frank hesitated. He hadn't seen Pat for a long time and thought maybe he'd changed. "We both know the history of the Vatican has had its black periods, and not all our popes have been the most respectable people on Earth, right? Well, when I Googled Urban VIII, I got a long list of entries—incriminating stuff they didn't teach us about at our little Jesuit college. The trial of Galileo was one big cover-up, Pat."

"That's it? Frank, we all know Galileo was f— ...uh, victimized. He was the wrong man in the wrong place. He had the wrong friends too. Not the most successful combination, in my estimation. But this is all public knowledge. It's nothing to get upset about." He examined Frank's face with a question in his eyes. "Your story has to be much better than what you've told me, my friend. Fess up!"

Frank grimaced. Pat was right, of course. He *was* holding back. "Okay," he said. "I went back into the cave, this time with some proper lighting." He hesitated again and peered over both shoulders to ensure no one was within hearing distance, then lowered his voice. "I went down a second time, Pat. You won't believe this. The first time, I didn't see anything too unusual—only a dank cave with some vague frescoes."

McCormick's eyes narrowed as he became fully engrossed in his account.

"This second time, as I strolled across the floor, the most spectacular thing happened. A strange wind whirled up all around me and whistled through the cave. It literally blew away the sand from the floor beneath my feet, revealing what I had missed before—a huge marble disk containing dark lines in a definitive pattern." He removed his cell phone from a pocket and flipped it open. "One sec...I took a photo of it." With a few clicks, he pulled the JPEG up on the screen and held it up to his friend. "Can you believe this, Pat?" The picture revealed an off-white disk with a pattern of concentric lines ending in eight points.

McCormick inspected the picture while biting the inside of his cheek.

"What are you thinking, Pat?"

McCormick cleared his throat. "I know of only one such disk, Frank. It's up here in the Tower of the Winds, in the so-called Meridian Room." He pointed to the ceiling over their heads.

Frank's eyes widened, and he swallowed. "How do you know that?"

"Except for the *Prefetto* and his secretary, there is only one person allowed to visit that room."

"*You?*"

"Yes, me. You question that? You, who tells me about a whirlwind in a cave and more? Come on, Frank."

"It's been a while, friend. Do you think it's another copy of the disk I found?"

"I don't think it, I know it. The disk in that picture is an exact copy of the one upstairs."

Frank stared into his friend's face, wondering if he was telling the truth. "May I have a look?"

"Nope. Impossible. It's just across the corridor where all the staff members of the ASV have their offices. We'd never make it there unseen. But I can tell you about it."

"Anything is better than nothing. Tell me more about this Meridian Room."

"Follow me." McCormick turned and zigzagged between the rows of racks. While they walked, he brought Frank up to speed. "You probably know only the highlights about the Tower of the Winds. In a way, it's the predecessor of the Vatican Observatory. Pope Gregory XIII appointed a committee to advise him on a fundamental reform of the calendar to better assign the Holy Days. It was all about showing its superiority over Protestantism, and it was no surprise that the Protestant countries were reluctant to adopt the far more accurate Gregorian calendar."

While he talked, McCormick eyed the labels on cartons as they passed by them, unaware of the impact of his words.

"They drilled a tiny hole in the south wall," McCormick continued, "which was covered with sixteenth-century frescos, positioned exactly in the mouth of Abraham. It allowed a sunbeam to pass through and indicate time on a clock the size of a manhole cover engraved on the marble floor."

McCormick finally paused and reached for a carton, pulling it off the rack. He showed Frank its label: MISC. ANEMOGRAPHIA, F. EGNATII DANTIS.

"What does it mean?" Frank asked, trying to appear nonchalant.

"This box contains the original architectural design of the *Torre dei Venti*. The *Torre* was famous for a major scientific breakthrough. Ignatius Danti was a genius. Did you know that?"

Frank shook his head. "Never heard of him. Didn't Pope Gregorian XIII have the evidence he needed to adjust the calendar?"

"That's what's in the official history books. First, unknown to the public, the calendar had been adjusted long before the Tower was finished. Second, there was something else in the Tower. Guess what it was."

Frank shrugged. "Come on, Pat, just get on with it! I've only got a limited amount of time here." Where was this leading?

McCormick grinned. "Sometimes you surprise me. You know so much about faraway galaxies, yet you have no idea what's happening right here under your nose."

"Tell me, Pat!" Frank almost yelled.

"Look at the title on the box, dumbo. An *anemograph*! An instrument to measure the direction and velocity of the winds, plus a solar clock to measure time. It was used in the days of the Gregorian calendar. This guy, this Danti, invented it!"

"How was I supposed to know that? I'm not an expert in art history. It doesn't really interest me." He still had no clue where Pat was going.

"Listen carefully, Frank. Here it comes. The anemograph is attached to the ceiling in the middle of a painted disk that has the same engraved lines as those on the marble floor disk. They are positioned exactly opposite each other. In other words, they were interconnected by design. In Gregorian time keeping, that had a meaning that few have clearly understood since. And now, you come up with another disk that seems identical to those in the Tower of the Winds."

McCormick turned the carton upside down to reveal the seal at the bottom.

Frank whistled. "The *Biblioteca Apostolica Vaticana*? I'm stunned."

"You're not listening to me. Don't switch subjects."

"What's this box doing here?"

McCormick chuckled. "You collect meteorites, right? Well, I collect original documents about the *Torre dei Venti*. Satisfied?"

"You *stole* this box from the BAV?"

McCormick sucked in a deep breath. "Well, *stealing* is a rather harsh way to put it. I wanted to study it, so I, uh, *borrowed* it when I was on a tour around their bunker. Nobody ever found out. By the way, you ask *me* about *stealing*?" He was about to laugh again when they both heard footsteps on the linoleum corridor outside the entrance door. Both froze and eyed each other in horror.

McCormick shoved the carton into Frank's hands. "Have a look inside. I'll see who's there and try to get rid of him."

Frank watched his friend until he disappeared at the end of the aisle. Then he dropped to his knees on the floor and opened the carton. Inside, he found the first print of Danti's manuscript. On the front page, he saw a diagram of the disk, just as McCormick had said. On each section surrounding the circle's center, the architect had painted the image of a cloud with a face inscribed with an open mouth: the personifications of the four winds.

Frank was so immersed in reading that he forgot where he was and with whom. It hit him as an afterthought that McCormick had not yet returned. He rose from the floor and turned in both directions. Utter silence. He was alone in the massive storage bunker of the ASV with a box of material stolen from the BAV.

He was instantly overcome by a sense of panic. He had to get out of there!

Chapter 15

Thursday: USNO, Washington DC

At the stroke of eleven a.m., Ellen seated herself around the conference table with the three men and one other woman of the Naval Time Committee (NTC).

Pakula peered directly at her. "Commander Meyer, since I'm still new to this, I'll have you begin with your report."

Although somewhat surprised at how quickly he deferred to her, Ellen rose from the table to move toward the laptop, which was connected to a beamer. "First of all, Captain, welcome aboard. As you already know, the rotation of the Earth is in a continual but gradual slowing-down process. This means we must routinely add a couple leap seconds to the Atomic Clock to ensure a more precise measurement of time. But recently, something has changed. The Earth's rate of slowing seems to have increased." She switched on the beamer and launched her presentation. "Notice that in this first sequence, the rotation of the Earth is visibly slowing while the digital clock simultaneously adds leap seconds." She used a baton to point to the screen. "The ticker shows the date running up from 01.01.01 to 06.20.09. Now, notice that the date slowed down on 06.19.09, and we had to add five seconds." She looked directly at Pakula. "What is most troublesome is that we have no indication that this slowing-down process will end."

He frowned. "Have other Navy units reported it?"

"No, sir. We've received no reports. We've only just recently discovered this phenomenon ourselves, but it won't be long before our friends at NETWARCOM find out and—"

"NETWARCOM?"

Ellen nodded. "The Naval Network Warfare Command in Norfolk, Virginia, sir. It was founded a couple of years ago to monitor all operational information systems, from ballistics to—"

"I'm aware of their existence, Commander. What's the relevance of this?"

Ellen read out the simple equation projected on the screen. "All guided weapon systems use our atomic time. A one-second error is equal to a difference of ten yards."

Captain Pakula propped his elbows on the table and folded his hands. "This slowing-down process...what are the consequences, apart from disrupting the accuracy of our Atomic Clock?"

"The problem, sir, is the questions that will arise from other entities. Our insertion of leap seconds has been a controversial issue for many years. It affects the 'purity of time', according to some of our opponents."

"Purity of time?" Pakula laughed. "That's absurd."

Ellen felt her face flushing as her irritation grew. "Sir, with all due respect, perhaps those who oppose the altering of the Clock have a point. They are mostly civilian scientists. If we continually adjust time, what is the value of it?"

"We won't continue with that discussion. Carry on, Lieutenant."

Ellen was taken aback. Why did he suddenly address her as 'Lieutenant' when he knew she's a commander? She glanced at the others around the table. Lieutenant Commander Hamilton had raised an eyebrow, and Lieutenant Lambert's eyes had widened. Even Abigail seemed surprised, although her eyes were focused on her note taking.

She decided to ignore Pakula's faux pas and go on with her presentation. "The rotation of the Earth may be slowing due to some yet-to-be-discovered gravitational fields active in outer space. Records show this has occurred before, only well before our time. I did a little investigation in our library, which contains several accounts by icons like Newton and Kepler and—"

"More fairytales concocted by our adversaries," Pakula snapped at her.

Once again, the other members of the NTC eyed Pakula in disbelief of his outburst.

"Excuse me, sir?" Lieutenant Hamilton raised his hand.

"Not now." Pakula pointed at Ellen. "Finish your presentation. I have other issues to discuss."

Ellen swallowed a retort. Never in her career had she been treated with such disrespect by a fellow officer, and she could see that Hamilton was more than a little chagrined. "I'm finished, Captain. You may take the floor."

Pakula rose from his chair and scanned the faces turned toward him. "First of all, I believe it is time to initiate a few changes. I don't agree with the Commander that we have a problem concerning how we handle the adding of seconds to the Atomic Clock. Our fine institution has a lot to gain through improved interaction with the public. To that end, I will issue an order later today for the publication of our Atomic Clock time records on the web. This will be on a full scale—all twenty digits behind the colon."

Ellen couldn't help it. Her mouth dropped open as if by reflex. It was obvious the other members of the Committee were just as shocked as she. *Is Pakula out of his mind?* She felt everyone's eyes on her, for she was next in command. They were waiting for her reaction before they spoke themselves. *Is this statement cause for dismissal from command? Can Pakula be relieved of duty after only a couple weeks at the USNO?* She pinched her lips. For now, it was best to watch, listen, and wait.

Hamilton raised his hand again. "Permission to speak now, sir?"

"Denied," Pakula said. "This matter will be handled in my office."

"Sir, with all due respect, the purpose of this Time Committee is to thoroughly discuss issues and come to a consensus. I would like to hear Commander Meyer's opinion on this matter."

"You're out of line, Lieutenant Commander. You're relieved of duty. Please leave the room." Pakula gestured toward the door and then crossed his arms over his chest.

When Hamilton remained seated, Pakula immediately reached for the telephone receiver on the table and called for security. A moment later, two men dressed in civilian clothes entered the room. Ellen gasped aloud. She didn't recognize the men, and they appeared so quickly that it was as if they had been waiting outside. They escorted the stunned Hamilton away; he was clearly too surprised to resist.

"Where were we?" Pakula asked, casting a quick glance at his watch. "Oh, yes, we will announce the publication of our Atomic Clock exactly thirty minutes from now. Lieutenant Lambert, you are responsible for getting the Clock online. Instruct the USNO webmasters to build it into our homepage."

Lieutenant Lambert visibly paled at witnessing his superior's arrest, and he quickly complied with Pakula to avoid the same fate. "Yes, sir. Right away," he said. "What clearance levels are applicable to this part of our website?"

"Good question. For the moment, only the superintendent of this base will have access. That would be me."

Ellen felt increasingly bewildered. Captain Pakula didn't seem himself. He was acting out of character, but who was she to object? If he only wanted the Atomic Clock accessible for himself, what was the big deal?

As Lambert left the room, he stopped in front of Pakula and saluted him again. It struck Ellen that some officers overdid the saluting, especially within the USNO, where saluting protocols were pretty loose. She'd never liked Lambert, the penultimate ass-kisser. He had yet to offer a personal opinion on anything.

"Okay, Commander, what else is on the agenda?" Pakula snapped his fingers and awakened Ellen from her thoughts.

"Nothing, sir. I believe we're finished." She closed the folder in front of her and started to rise.

"Not so fast, Commander," Pakula said. "The meeting is over when I say it's over!"

Ellen knew her face had become instantly inflamed. She was both furious and humiliated. Judging by the expression on Ms. Linden's face, her feelings were shared. Pakula's attitude was one of outrageous insolence. He had infuriated her to the point of no return, and now she literally hated the bastard. Not only had he disgraced her in front of others, but he had also personally organized a probable breach of national security, and she had felt helpless to respond appropriately.

Pakula waved at Ensign Linden. "You're dismissed. You stay, Commander Meyer."

As Ensign Linden headed for the door, she cast an anxious look at Ellen. The second she entered the hall, Pakula shut the door and locked it. Ellen was instantly on guard. What was the purpose of such precaution?

Pakula strode directly to her and, without warning, grasped hold of the lapels of her uniform. He lifted her from her chair and shoved her against the wall. At first, Ellen thought he was going to rape her when he pushed his body up against hers, but when he knew he had her pinned, he raised his right fist to strike her. Just as the blow was about to meet her face, she lunged sideways and jerked herself free. Pakula's fist hit the wall full force, and he cried out in pain, clutching his fingers in his other hand to massage them. His face was contorted with rage.

Ellen dashed to the other side of the table. "Captain! Get a grip on yourself! This is unbecoming behavior for an officer. We can sort out any differences of opinion in a rational discussion. If you stop this right now, I will not report you."

She regretted the words as soon as they left her lips. The bastard had touched her. He had violated the strict code of conduct for military personnel, and he could never justify his actions. And, the other members of the NTC meeting had witnessed his irrational behavior.

Even as these thoughts raced across her mind, she knew the odds were against her. It was better to talk him into letting her go and then try to forget the whole thing, as she had done many times in her career. Bracing herself with a hand on the table, she addressed her commanding officer again. "Let me leave, Captain. If you need someone to see to your injury, I will contact a medic."

Pakula glared at her with glassy eyes. "We'll talk about your behavior in the meeting later, Commander. You're dismissed."

Ellen hurried across the room, unlocked the door, and slipped out. Choking on both fear and anger, she headed immediately for the women's restroom. Ensign Linden stood by one of the wash basins. "Ms. Linden," Ellen said, hearing the stress in her voice, "would you remain here until I am ready to leave?" She turned on the faucet and scrubbed both hands vigorously with soap under the running water until she felt clean again. She wanted to rid herself of the feel of Pakula's hands on her body.

Ensign Linden stepped closer. "What's wrong, Commander? You look upset. Your face is all red and...and your blouse has become untucked. What happened in there?"

Ellen stared at her. "Please don't mention this to anyone, Ms. Linden. The captain was having a bad day, that's all." She noticed the notepad poking out from the folder the ensign had gathered up from the counter. "May I see that, please?" she asked. She flipped through the minutes of the meeting. "Why didn't you document the arrest of Lieutenant Commander Hamilton, Ms. Linden?"

The ensign's face reddened. "I'm sorry, Commander. Captain Pakula came into my office this morning and said he was going to have Lieutenant Commander Hamilton arrested for insubordination and ordered me not to make notes of it."

Ellen was about to express her disapproval when she remembered Pakula's instructions to her as well. He had literally ordered her not to voice an objection to his meeting input. *What the hell is going on?* Did Pakula plan that whole thing? She shook her head in disgust but didn't voice her concerns. Returning the notepad, she left the restroom, knowing Linden was gaping at her through the mirror.

❖ ❖ ❖

When the door closed behind Commander Meyer, Ashley dropped onto one of the desk chairs and buried his face in his hands. *What is wrong with me?* How did I manage to lose my temper in such a vile way? Attacking a female officer was a dreadful mistake. He had noticed symptoms of his uncontrollable temper before—like in Rome when the old man had tried to stop him—but he'd dismissed his actions then as necessary for self-defense. But this? What he'd done to Commander Meyer was something completely different.

He began to wonder if it was possible that Captain Pakula had a personal problem that had survived him or if taking possession of his body had caused some unexpected side effect. Maybe his transfer hadn't gone as smoothly as it appeared. Maybe time travel wasn't as uncomplicated as they'd originally surmised. And now? Now he was trapped in a body with the potential to become a significant threat to his own mission.

Chapter 16

Thursday: GWU, Washington DC

There was no way out for him. The talkative, gossiping, giggling girls showed no intention of leaving anytime soon, and he couldn't risk them tattling on him if they found him in there. It seemed like in the last few minutes, a whole new group of them had come in. What was this, some beauty contest? Why didn't they get out of here and go to class? Max thought, frustrated. Suddenly, it dawned on him they might have a free hour in between classes and could be there as long as they wanted. Sooner or later, one of the girls would want to use his toilet and would spot his feet. If they saw him, they would start shrieking. *What am I gonna do?* He started to freak out, and the migraine hit him hard. Bile rose up in his throat, and he had to puke. Fortunately, he was close enough to bend over the bowl.

In his hand, his cell phone buzzed. At some distance, he heard his dupe talk to him through his headphone. "Max, I hear those girls. You're no longer focused. We have no time to lose"

"I can't leave now," he whispered in his mike.

"You have to, Max. They will start searching your building—every room. In the end, they will look in the basement as well, but by then you'll be long gone."

He swallowed hard and tried not to feel the pounding inside his head. "When I get out, which direction do I have to go?" he mumbled softly.

"It's all about speed and surprise, Max. The second you open your door, just get the hell out of there. Go left. At the end of the corridor, you'll see a door, possibly with a sign indicating the basement. If there is a choice, take the right one. Don't look back and don't make contact. Go, go, GO!"

Max took a deep breath and took the bolt in his hand. He counted to three and then opened it as quietly as possible. There was no change in chitchat on the other side. In one fluid movement, he jerked open the door and tore off. One girl between him and the exit hesitated a second too long, and he roughly shoved her aside. She banged her head against the wall. As he entered the corridor, he heard her burst out crying. Some students looked at the ladies' room door and then at him. He adjusted his headset and quickly scanned around and checked the flight of stairs to the first floor; there was no trace of the two Navy men. He took a left turn and ran into the corridor, which made a sharp turn left. There were too many doors to choose from.

"Dude, I see three doors, all next to each other!" he yelled in his mike. "No signs. Which one do I take?"

"They must have rebuilt this part of the building. The floor plan is two years old."

"The right one has a small ventilation grid at eye level. Which one?" Max shouted.

"Max, are you alone there? I can hear footsteps closing in on you."

Just as he turned around, a dark voice bellowed behind him. A university policeman came 'round the corner, closing in on him fast. "Don't move! Put your hands where I can see them."

"Max, take the middle one! It has to be the middle one," sounded in his headset.

He hesitated because of the grid and tried the middle door first. "Locked! Damn it!" He tried the right one, and it opened just as he glanced over his shoulder.

"Hey, you there, this is a last warning!" the policeman yelled at him, while his hand moved toward his holster. He slowly and cautiously approached him.

Max tried to yank the door further open, but it was a heavy metal one. When he was almost through the door opening, a strong hand grabbed his shoulder. The policeman tried to drag him outside. He needed two hands and dropped his cell phone, now dangling free at the wire of his headset, banging against the door. With all his weight, Max tried to push the door back into its lock, crashing into the man's wrist, but he was no match for him. The door opened inch by inch again. His arm was already through the opening and waved around to grope him. The man's flailing movement tapped his headset off his head, sending it crashing to the floor. Maybe it was the instant thought of possible damage of his gear that unleashed Max's reflex, but a few seconds later, he had bolted the door as he sank to the floor, wiping blood and tissue out of his mouth. He looked at his sleeve. The emergency light made it almost impossible to see, but the sticky blood clots were undeniable. He could hardly believe he had just put his teeth into a man's forearm and torn away a mouthful of skin.

Chapter 17

Thursday: Rome

Feeling the rise of his pesky claustrophobia, Frank found his feet melded to the floor of the ASV bunker. He knew he had to take his leave, but how could he make an exit without rousing all sorts of questions. Where was McCormick? Why hadn't he returned for me? What should he do about the box of stolen documents? Taking a quick peek at his watch, he realized his pass would only be valid for another hour.

Wait...what was that? Frank cocked his head to listen and heard a distinctive grinding noise. *They're closing the damn door.* He would be locked in.

Quickly tucking Danti's original design of the *Torre dei Venti* into his jacket pocket, he left the open carton of BAV documents on the floor and ran through the maze of racks toward the steel door. "Hey, don't close it," he yelled. "Wait for me!"

Either his voice couldn't be heard, or someone was purposely ignoring him. No one answered. He knew without seeing it that the steel door was tightly closed by now, making his exit impossible. He dashed down several more aisles of storage racks, perspiring freely and coughing from the exertion. It took him another two minutes to reach the entrance to the bunker, where his fears were verified.

Frank banged his fists on the thick steel door, but no significant sound transpired. He peered over both shoulders and then dashed about in a circle, trying to find a nearby object that would make more noise. Then, he saw the fire extinguisher mounted to the wall directly next to the door. A brass plate signified it belonged to the Vatican Fire Department.

Without hesitating, he yanked the extinguisher off the wall and bashed it several times against the steel door. Each time, the metal ring on the bottom prevented a solid hit. Suddenly, the container fell from his hands onto the floor at his feet. The lead seal broke off. Instantly, he heard an explosion as white foam erupted and swathed everything around him with a thick blanket of the fire-quenching spume. Startled, he stumbled backwards and slipped on the wet floor. Recovering his balance, he scampered several feet away and watched in horror as the foam covered every square inch of the entrance area. It would impossible for him to get anywhere near the door for at least a couple of hours.

Frank gazed in dismay at his new dilemma, growing increasingly angry at his friend for deserting him. If McCormick didn't return for him that night, he could be stuck in the bunker for the entire weekend without water or anything to eat. He had to find a way to exit, but what good would it do to wander about the bunker without a plan? He concentrated on his breathing, taking several deep breaths and exhaling slowly through pursed lips. All the while, he assured himself he would be all right. He was a resourceful person; he would find a solution to his new crisis.

For the next hour, he walked the entire perimeter of the bunker, searching for a second door, but he found none. No emergency telephone was mounted onto any wall either. Despite his intentions, he found himself growing increasingly depressed. At that very moment, the overhead lights blinked off, and he was plunged into darkness.

Frank dug hastily into his pocket for his cell phone and flipped it open. It was useless for messaging, but it provided a faint bit of light. The energy indicator showed it was at half capacity. Somehow, he had to make it last through the night until the lights would hopefully be turned on again. Thankfully, it would be Friday in a few hours and not yet Saturday. And maybe—surely—Pat McCormick would find a way to reenter the building and come for him.

Unless Pat had been taken into custody.

Unless he had purposely locked him into the bunker for reasons unknown.

That new thought arrived at the same time Frank noticed the air supply had stopped with the dimming of the lights. He couldn't hear the familiar humming sound. The atmosphere in the bunker now seemed warm and oppressive. Why had he allowed his curiosity to overpower reason? Why had he been so trusting? He had told Pat everything. What would he do with the information?

He sank onto the floor and turned off his cell phone. He was both mentally and physically exhausted. His long night of research and the emotional rollercoaster he'd ridden over the past twenty-four hours was finally taking its toll. He might as well sleep; he could no nothing for the next few hours anyway.

❖ ❖ ❖

Frank jerked awake and found himself lying on a hard floor bathed in a cold sweat. At first, the pitch darkness didn't faze him, but then he remembered where he was: the ASV bunker! He pulled out his cell phone and flipped it open to read the clock. He had slept for three hours. He had to do something and not waste anymore time. He coughed several times and gasped for fresh air. The energy meter on his cell phone showed two bars. In a couple of hours, his phone would be dead. Maybe the foam from fire extinguisher had dissipated. Maybe . . .

Fire extinguisher! Why didn't he think of that before!

Frank bolted to his feet and pointed the screen of his cell phone toward the ceiling. Peering into the semi-darkness, he found what he was looking for: a sprinkler installation.

The trick was to trigger an alarm in a remote corner of the bunker, though he could only hope he would be able to run fast enough to reach the area of the entrance door before it opened. Despite his girth, he was still fairly nimble. He would do it or die trying!

Groping his way to the far end of the bunker, he stopped by one of the racks and searched for the closest smoke detector. Then, quickly emptying the shelves of cartons, he climbed until he was able to stretch out on the top shelf. He reached for his cell phone again and placed it strategically on his chest to get the most light from it. Then, he removed the plastic cover from the back of the fire detector. He inspected the workings and saw that two wires were soldered to a miniscule motherboard. As delicately as was possible with his chubby fingers, he broke them off. If he remembered his physics correctly, he merely had to reconnect the two wires and then run for the entrance door.

He peered over the edge of the metal rack to count the shelves he'd use as steps. This wasn't the time to fall and break a leg. He mentally reviewed his exit plan. "Okay, let's do it," he said aloud. He checked the time on his watch again; he'd have less than five minutes.

Holding his breath in case any extra movement might jar the wires, Frank twisted the two wires together. Instantly, the device started shrieking, and a little red LED flashed at regular intervals. As fast as he could, he slithered down the rack and fled toward the entrance door, holding his cell phone toward the floor so he wouldn't trip over his own two feet. Out of breath, he stopped just short of the door near the outer perimeter of the sodden clumps of white foam to wait for the fire crew.

Frank glanced at the digital time on his cell phone; three and a half minutes had passed since he'd triggered the alarm.

Without warning, the overhead lights flashed on, and at the same time, the sliding door slowly grinded open. Four firemen with masks and flashlights stepped into the bunker and waded across the excretion of the fire extinguisher. Except for some static from their walkie-talkies, they made no other sound. One of them pointed toward the far end of the cavernous space where the fire detector was blinking, and they headed for it. Not a single man looked in Frank's direction.

As soon as the fire crew had passed him, Frank inched his way forward through the foam. He didn't want to slip and fall. Once he reached the opening of the door, he bolted through it and down the corridor, not taking time to peer over his shoulder. The men would be busy. His greatest concern was where he could hide inside the ASV until it reopened again. He'd be seen if he tried to leave the institute now, but he could easily disappear amongst the tumult of morning visitors when the ASV opened at eight fifteen.

As he slipped past the doorways to other rooms, he inspected the walls and ceilings around them. As was the case in Castel Gandolfo, it appeared the ASV had not installed an alarm system. Other than the Vatican Museum, with its many treasures publicly displayed, the assets of the ASV were in the bunker and impossible to locate without knowledge of the archiving structure.

Confident his progress was unmonitored, Frank tried to censor his unbridled thoughts. If he intended to stay within the ASV for the remainder of the night, maybe he could use this one and only opportunity to visit the Tower of the Winds. If he were caught, so be it. One thing he knew for sure: McCormick would be the last person to help him.

Frank hugged the walls and scooted past the two study rooms to reach the central staircase. It wouldn't be prudent to take the elevator. He kept an eye out for alarm devices, but to his relief, he saw none. He took the stairs two at a time until he reached the third floor. Fortunately, the ASV kept enough nightlights burning along the corridors that he encountered no trouble finding his way. He felt in his pocket for the Danti document he had 'borrowed' from the carton. He would return it to the BAV by mail anonymously once he reached the States.

He sneaked into the room that housed material on the Old Testament patriarchs. According to Danti's plan, there were two doors opening into other extensions—the Apostle Room and the Meridian Room. He scanned the space, and a particular door caught his attention. Its surface was painted with a scene depicting the sacrifice of Isaac. A bearded Abraham raised a sword over the body of his son, while an angel gently blocked the blade. Next to it, Frank saw a faded fresco portraying Esau, who just had given up his birthright to Jacob. Frank felt his heartbeat accelerate until he could almost feel it in his throat. Surely, this unique door admitted visitors to the Meridian Room. If Pat hadn't lied about it, he would have the opportunity to witness something that verified his discovery in Castel Gandolfo.

Placing his tremulous hand on the iron handle, he gently pushed it downward. Instantly, the door latch clicked and the door swung open, inviting him to step inside. The room was dark. He felt along the wall just inside the entrance and found a light switch. As the space was fully illuminated, he gasped in disbelief. There, on the off-white marble floor, was the familiar depiction of the disk. Moving slowly and reverently, he walked until he stood exactly over it.

Suddenly, something else caught and held his attention—an egg-shaped oval near the perimeter of the disk containing two Zodiac signs: Aries and Libra.

He removed the Danti document from his pocket and studied it in detail. Nowhere on the original plan did he see the marking. It could only be the signature of one person: Pope Urban VIII.

Chapter 18

Thursday: USNO, Washington DC

After leaving the women's restroom, Ellen hurried back to her office. The first thing that came to her mind was to pick up the phone and make a full report to Admiral Ben Francisco. Although, as a rule, he usually remained in the background and didn't have direct contact with non-commanding officers, it was different with Ellen. He had personally appointed her to her current position.

Once she was seated at her desk, she thought again about her predicament. The admiral still maintained a few outdated viewpoints of the military, and when combined with his rather fatherly treatment of her, she knew he may not be the best one to consult.

Ellen set aside any more thoughts of seeking support from the admiral and focused instead on what she could do on her own. From experience, she knew her independence would serve her well in handling the situation. She was at her best on her own, without interference from anyone. She opened the bottom right drawer of her desk, knowing her gun would be there. She was not supposed to have one but had decided to keep it with. She shuddered to think of entering her home unarmed—or even worse, knowing the gun was inside her apartment if someone was waiting there for her.

She placed the weapon on her desk and removed the unopened box of bullets from the drawer. Her fingers trembled as she methodically opened the box and carefully loaded the magazine. The weapon was no ladies' gun, like a J-Frame Smith & Wesson; it was a nineteen-millimeter Glock 17. Even though she had never liked using the gun, she knew it would get the job done if it ever became necessary. Her mother had given it to her after her father's death.

Her plan was simple. Trained at most DEFCON levels, she was ready to act. It wasn't by coincidence that she had become Deputy Superintendent at age twenty-nine. She pressed a button on her phone to contact the head of gate control. The phone rang several times.

"A very good morning. This is Gate Control," a man's voice said. "What can I do for you today, Commander Meyer?"

"We have an emergency situation," she said crisply. "Shut down all gates without delay. No one gets in or out without my permission. Do you copy?"

"Yes, Commander. I'll issue orders immediately."

Ellen knew the man must be asking himself a dozen questions. Before gate control could change their minds, she left her office and headed directly toward Pakula's office, holding her gun with both hands, her index finger outstretched, fully prepared to open the door by force if necessary. She found his door ajar. Pushing it wider with her foot, she peered into the room. It was empty.

She rushed to his desk phone and contacted the South Gate. "Commander Meyer here. Has anyone left the base in the last fifteen minutes?"

"Good morning, Commander. Yes, madam. Captain Pakula left a short while ago."

"Exactly what time did the captain depart?"

"I can't provide you with that information, ma'am. We are not obliged to record the arrival and departure times of Navy personnel, ma'am."

Infuriated at the upsetting of her plans, Ellen sank onto the captain's chair and placed the Glock on the desk in front of her. Of course the arrival and departure times weren't required. This was the Navy's museum, not a restricted base. What should she do now? She felt her rush of adrenaline crash to zero and mused over why she felt so defeated. One setback didn't change a thing! Pakula had still behaved erratically and unprofessionally, not to mention that he had violated her person. *Just go get the bastard!* she thought.

She was about to leave Pakula's office when her eyes fell on the two stacks of files on his desk. Against all regulations, one file lay open. A memo from NETWARCOM addressed to Pakula stated that the accuracy of the Atomic Clock had to be recalibrated. The memo carried Wednesday's date. From the wording, Ellen found it unclear whether or not NETWARCOM was aware of the increased rate of the slowing of the Earth's rotation.

Ellen suspected NETWARCOM had already developed its own Atomic Clock, using the USNO Clock only as a cross reference. That would explain the lax security at the USNO entrance gates.

Standing beside the desk now, Ellen sorted through the shorter pile of files, skimming the titles. *Focus, Ellen,* she admonished herself. She knew she had to only focus on things she understood and then take action. Her training had taught her that the mind would filter out what it needed to survive.

Two minutes later, she rushed from the office to return to her own. She met no one on her floor. When she was within five feet of her office, she heard the phone on her desk ringing. Dashing to catch it, she barely had time to hold the receiver to her ear before she heard a familiar voice.

"Commander Meyer? This is Helen Bradshaw at the switchboard. I have a call for you from the Metropolitan Police, Third District."

Not now, Ellen thought.

"Do you want to accept the call, Commander?" Helen asked. "I have other calls waiting."

"Yes please. Thank you," Ellen replied.

"Commander Meyer?"

"Commander Meyer speaking," she said.

"This is Police Commander Diana Gomez speaking. Do you have a moment?"

"Is this about Navy personnel?"

"No, Commander. It's about a kidnapping. A teenage boy was abducted from his school, drugged, and transported to some other part of the country. We've tried to get hold of his father, but we haven't managed to contact him yet. A team of officers is on its way to the GWUMC right now. The father is a radiologist there."

Ellen placed the gun on her desktop. Why was she calling her? she wondered. "I don't want to be rude, Commander Gomez, but I have some serious obligations to attend to right now, possibly involving national security. I'm not at all sure I'm the one to assist you with this issue."

"Witnesses claim the kidnappers are Navy officers, ma'am. The nearest Navy base to the victim's school is the U.S. Naval Observatory."

Ellen sank onto her chair. *The USNO involved in a kidnapping?* She felt strangely disoriented. First, Captain Pakula's peculiar behavior, and now a kidnapping in downtown Washington by Navy personnel? What was going on?

"Hello? Commander, are you still there?"

"Yes, I am. If there are Navy officers involved, this is a matter for the Navy police. I'll see to it they are notified and sent over to you right away."

"I'm sorry, Commander. That's not why I'm calling. Superintendent Pakula is sitting in my office. He has informed me these two officers were under your command. He came in to report some irregularities. Will you come to my office downtown on your own, or should I send someone to escort you? We will need to have a firsthand report from you on this matter."

Ellen almost dropped the receiver. *Pakula is there, with the police?* He had left the USNO to set her up. She knew of no one who would kidnap and drug a young boy. Why was this happening? Should she call the admiral? Ellen heard herself say, "No, that won't be necessary. I'm on my way."

In a daze and feeling increasingly nauseous, she picked up the gun from her desktop and placed it back into the drawer. No, she should take it with her. Leave it in the car. She stuffed it into her purse, scanned her office, and realized her entire military career was about to take a serious turn. What had she done wrong to raise the ire of Captain Pakula? The last time they met, they had been on good terms. Today, everything had changed.

Chapter 19

Thursday: GWU, Washington DC

There was no sound behind the door. The policeman had groaned like a wounded dog when Max had bitten into his forearm. There was no way back anymore. He peered around, searching for his phone and headset. He got onto his knees and crawled toward them. He inspected them. With trembling hands, he put his set on his head and touched the screen. Unbelievably, it came to life, and it still worked. He checked the network signal indicator, and there was only one bar. "Dude, still there?"

"Yes, Max. I saw part of the action until your device was dropped on the floor. Good job, my friend! While you fought him, I accessed the university police network and called him back into the station."

"You did what?" Max was so surprised. Although he felt miserable, he was relieved he still had a friend on his side.

"Why did you think he left in the first place?"

"Because I ate part of his arm like a cannibal! I figured he needed a bandage or something."

"No, the man was distracted because of the message blaring in his ear. I had him on the phone for a few seconds before he backed off and left you alone."

"What did you say to him?"

"I told him we'd received an emergency call from the local police and he was needed badly at home."

"Was he?" Max got the feeling this was becoming bigger and bigger, in a nasty way.

"Max, there is no time to falter now. I'll do anything necessary to protect you."

"Did you hurt his wife?"

"*Hurt* is not the right expression, Max. The man called for backup and identified himself. I looked up the man's record in the university personnel department. It turns out he has a history of domestic violence. I only notified the Child Protective Services office in his hometown and tipped them anonymously about problems ahead. I guess they immediately notified the police, and consequently, they paid his wife a visit. These things can happen fairly quickly, you know."

"How did you do that so fast? Our fight lasted only a few minutes."

"Max, I did this while I was explaining it to you. I can do several things at the same time, in parallel. It takes approximately ten minutes for him to reach his base station. That left sufficient time for me to set it all in motion."

Max began to wonder how his dupe was so super smart, considering he certainly didn't program him that way.

"When you go down the stairs, follow the dotted red line. In case you lose connection, the map should still show you the way. I programmed it that way." A map opened up on his cell phone screen, and a red dotted line was pointing the way.

Again, Max was impressed and so glad he had a friend. He started to head toward the stairs to the basement.

"Hey, Max, wait a second! Not so fast."

"What's up? I thought you said we have no time to lose."

"Yes, but when you're down there, we will probably lose contact. I am not sure we'll be able to catch up."

On his feet again, he realized his headache was back at full force. Suddenly, he felt depressed, like he did most of the time with his parents. "Why do you say that, dude? Sounds like I'll never see you again."

His avatar just looked at him, and he didn't look any happier than Max did.

"Dude?"

His dupe took a deep breath. "The point is, we've tried so hard to get to our target, and we're so close. I only need a bit more time...and some more information."

"You think that's why these Navy guys are after me? Us getting to our target and all?"

"No. I can't calculate they know what we know."

"Calculate?"

"Sorry. My estimate is they don't know.'

"Then why are they after me? And did they really kill my mother?" The thought made him feel sick again.

"Max, that's why we have to talk, but there's little time now. I don't think they want you or your mother. I think they want your father."

"My dad? That's fucking weird! He's just a low-level scientist."

"Low-level? Are you sure?"

"Yes, I'm damn sure. My mother left him for that. His colleagues mock him because he's obsessed with some 'brain reset'. He even tried his theories on me," Max burst out.

His twin friend looked at him, expressionless.

"What? Your calculations came up with something?" He sank down on his knees, put his phone on the floor, and held his head in both hands. He could feel his skull pounding against his palms.

"Max, is there any chance your father has discovered something the Navy would want so badly they would kidnap you as a ransom, even kill your mother?"

He couldn't think of anything. "Sorry, dude."

"Not even this 'brain reset' you mentioned?"

"That's absurd," Max said, shaking his head 'no'.

"What are you thinking, Max?"

"Well," he hesitated, "my dad claims he has discovered a way to use an fMRI to restore the 'factory settings' of the brain, based on his research of a tiny part of the brain called Area 25. He told me the same technique could be used to send what he calls 'thinkwaves' back in time." Max smiled wryly at his friend. "Sounds weird right?"

"Max, listen carefully. Do you have any idea if this is solely *his* invention, or did he collaborate with other scientists?"

"Why?"

"Well, if other scientists are involved, maybe other families are in danger as well."

Max shrugged. "I'm pretty sure it's just my dad's thing."

"Okay, so no collaboration? Not with someone outside the hospital?"

"Nope. My father is a loner…like me."

"Have you ever heard of a man named Frank Bootsma?"

The moment his dupe said the name, a memory flash hit Max like a lightning bolt. *Bootsma? I know that name, but how?*

Chapter 20

Thursday: Rome

While trying to still his shaking hands, Frank studied the Danti document with the mysterious pattern on the Meridian Room floor. No matter how carefully he scanned every square inch of the drawing, nowhere on the document could he find the additional marking visible on the marble at his feet. Again, the thought persisted that it could only be the signature of one person: Pope Urban VIII.

Rising and walking the perimeter of the room, he marveled at the resemblance of the disk to the one in the underground cellar of Castel Gandolfo. Why had Urban VIII made a copy of the disk for his summer residence, and why was it hidden from public view in a dimly lit cave? He was assuming the disk in the Meridian Room was the original, but maybe it wasn't. When the wind in the cave whirled the dust into a mini-tornado that revealed the first disk to him, he hadn't seen it in its entirety. He had no way of knowing whether or not the same inscription existed there.

Frank fought against his fatigue and his concern that the fire crew would send an alarm to the Vatican police to search the building for a potential intruder. Every second of his time had to be devoted to finding answers to his questions—questions that involved a secret not revealed in any of his former studies.

The vaulted room in the summer palace was more simply constructed than the richly ornate Meridian Room. If the pope were curious about the relationship between the wind and the sun, he would want the best possible facility and equipment for his personal research. Accuracy would be essential to his findings. Frank examined the anemograph mounted on the ceiling, looking for confirmation of his theory.

He heard a noise outside the Meridian Room. His first thought was that they had come after him, that he must have left a wet trail from the bunker. He must hide, but where? There was only one other door. By some miracle, it was open! An iron spiral staircase led up to an attic over the Meridian Room. This was a dead end, yes, but it was the only way. He rushed up the stairs and found himself at the engine room of the wind vane.

For a moment, Frank forgot he was on the run. He was struck by the silence of the engine, which seemed more like an artifact of the Industrial Revolution than something invented in Baroque Rome. In all likelihood, the mechanism was unlike anything else in its time, and no one would have been allowed to see or work with it except Urban VIII and Danti.

Following the workings, he realized a wind vane must be mounted atop the Tower of the Winds. The room barely contained the machine. He tried to squeeze in around it to see if there was another exit and inadvertently bumped a small lever in the process. Nothing happened. *Thank God.*

He was only halfway up the stairs when he noticed a soft grinding noise. Running back up, three steps at a time, he followed the cogwheels. The wind vane at the ceiling of the Meridian Room was turning. *Oh God...*

Frank sneaked down the staircase and listened at the door. Except for the movement of the anemograph, it was as quiet as a tomb. It had to be a trap. The Vatican police would be waiting for him. He made the sign of the cross and slowly opened the door and looked around it. *Nobody?* He was alone. He found it difficult to comprehend that no police were waiting for him.

Back in the Meridian Room, exhausted, Frank sank to the floor, facing the wall where the committee of Clavius had drilled a minuscule hole into the mouth of Abraham. He looked up. The anemograph had stopped turning. He allowed his imagination to 'see' those whose curiosity compelled them to construct the room and the anemograph. About to nod off, he was startled awake when the mouth of Abraham lit up and sent a dazzling ray of light into the room and touched part of the intersecting lines of the disk. Gasping, Frank could do nothing but sit and watch in admiration.

Finally, he held Danti's plan in front of him and scanned the Latin text, hoping to find some statement of shared awe. Unexpectedly, his arms were covered with goose bumps, and he shivered. "Thank you, Lord, for my Jesuit teachings," he murmured. Then, sucking in a deep and tremulous breath, he translated the words aloud. "Wind, therefore, is the arousal of dry and hot vapor carried up into the air by virtue of the rays of the sun and movement of the stars."

He repeated the words several times before rising to his feet. His eyes followed the meridian line on the marble floor, dissecting it diagonally. That's when he noticed there were more signs of the Zodiac, hardly visible and most likely worn thin by centuries of footsteps.

"...by virtue of the rays of the sun and the movement of the stars."

At that moment, Frank remembered the words of Pat McCormick: "Moreover, these disks are positioned exactly opposite each other. In other words, these disks were connected by design. In the time of His Holiness Gregory XIII, this had a meaning." He remembered, too, that Pat had paused before adding, "...which no one has ever understood."

Frank envisioned the solar winds somehow connected to the winds on Earth. He had seen the anemograph moving! As he walked, he pondered what he had learned while doing his homework before coming to the ASV. Urban VIII was known for fearing astrological charts. That was why he had put astrology on the forbidden list. But there was the unproven allegation that, meanwhile, he had built a secret room where he held quiet séances to avert the negative influences of the stars—unproven, that was, until Frank discovered the secret room buried deep under Castel Gandolfo!

With that startling realization, Frank hit his forehead with the flat of his hand. Then he grinned and shook his hands in the air. He had been utterly clueless.

Father Bonomelli must have known all about the dark past of Urban VIII, and now his reactions to finding Frank in the library made sense. Quickly, other pieces of the puzzle came together. He remembered an incident that had almost made him quit his job. Two years prior, he had arrived at Castel Gandolfo a week earlier than planned for no other reason than that he liked Italy and was eager to begin his work. He had not informed Bonomelli of his early arrival.

"The Holy Father has been informed about the progression of our research, Brother Frank. It is a sunny day, and His Holiness is making a few personal observations with our solar telescope. That's all I can tell you," Father Bonomelli had snapped at him.

Now, Frank understood. That one sentence spoken by Bonomelli revealed a great deal about his recent discoveries. The donated golden telescope was used for watching the sun, especially sunspots. It was known to many in the Vatican that the late Pope John Paul II held a keen interest in astronomy. The fact that his successor had visited the dome to make "a few personal observations" was, on the face of it, not surprising.

Once again, Frank kneeled by the egg-shaped inscription on the floor and traced its shape with his fingers. The Vatican was officially involved in a covert project that necessitated Frank's absence. When he put all the elements into the right perspective—the Tower of the Winds, Urban VIII, Galileo Galilei, and the Vatican Observatory—he knew they were interconnected. The Holy Church had made the world believe she was sorry about the condemnation of Galileo and then built the Vatican Observatory in homage to the famous Italian astronomer. This rationale was passed on to those who studied at the Castel Gandolfo, but this justification was a cover-up.

In the centuries following Urban VIII, the Vatican had been planning something else—something important, something that involved counterattacking Protestantism. Pat had said it!

Frank returned to his pacing. What should he do about what he had learned? Would anyone believe him anyway? He had stolen an etching from the library of Castel Gandolfo, intruded into *the* ASV bunker where he had stolen yet another original document, illegally entered the Tower of the Winds, and probably broken a dozen other rules and regulations. But how could he sit idly by and see his Roman Catholic Church take yet another wrong turn? He started shivering again. *Is it still even my Church?* He had worked all his life to bring science and religion together, not to set them apart or to have one conquer the other. But now the science part in him became stronger—or was it his Protestant past rearing its ugly head?

It didn't matter much now. If he were able to slip out of the ASV unnoticed, he would head straight for the airport to see if he could change his ticket since he had already missed his flight. If he could make it into the United States, he would never return to Italy.

Chapter 21

Thursday: GWUMC, Washington DC

When the memory flash was over, Max shivered. He'd been in great danger, and he'd seen a man get his throat cut. He still saw his blood spraying over the floor. Somehow, this Bootsma was there as well. *What is going on? Who is—or was—this Frank Bootsma, and why is he so important?*

"Max?" his dupe called from his cell phone.

Max looked at his lookalike. "What do *you* know about this Frank Bootsma?" Max asked, unsure.

His dupe didn't answer and just stared at him. The longer it took to answer, the stronger his doubts became. Could he still trust him? Had his app become corrupt? Oh my God! What if someone managed to hack into it...like the Navy—or worse?

"We have so little time right now, Max. I can hear in your voice that you have strong doubts. Please know I am close to the target, Max, and I discovered that—have to say the name, sorry—the USNO has contacted the Vatican embassy to get into contact with your father *and* Bootsma. Just wanted to know if you had a lead. That's all for now. Let us not waste time. You have to go!"

"I want to call my dad to warn him, dude. This is all getting way too big for me to handle on my own."

"Do it when you've left this place. They will come after you here. Go!"

His digital twin was right, for he had to go. Max picked up his phone and rose. It took three or four steps to reach the narrow, dimly lit basement corridors. While running, he tried to make his call to his father, but it didn't work. He stopped and checked the signal indicator: nothing. He was on his own. *Damn.* It had to wait until he surfaced again.

He followed the red dotted trail. His science department building was on H Street, crossing 22nd Street NW, only a few blocks away from where his dad worked at I Street. He tried to visualize north and south because he knew he had to head north, but something didn't feel right. *Am I really heading north?* He had been walking for thirty minutes when he finally reached a couple of stairs. He climbed up and bumped into a similar door, one with a grid. He opened the door and stepped out. Students were everywhere. The crowd and noise was overwhelming, compared to the serene atmosphere one level below, but it was certainly not a hospital. "What's this building called?" he asked one of the students.

"Tomkins Hall of Engineering," the student replied.

Max looked again at the map. The red dotted line was gone. His GPS showed he was indeed at the engineering department, west of science, and not north. He searched for his avatar app, but it was gone. He tried again. The phone kept on ringing, but his dad wasn't answering. He was probably in the middle of some fMRI session. He tried to launch his avatar app. *What is that dude up to?*

He was so immersed in his phone that he didn't hear them coming. Four hands grabbed him and dragged him away. In no time, Max was out on the street.

The two policemen handed him over to the Navy men, who were waiting outside their SUV. He was put in the back of the car, and the doors were locked. There had been university policemen posted at every entry or exit point on the campus. He never had had a chance. Clearly, they knew about his arrest because they all stared at the SUV as it pulled away. The windows were black, but he felt their eyes on him.

The drive from engineering to the hospital was swift, with no traffic lights. On arrival, the bad one left the car.

When they were alone, the other officer turned around. His name tag read CAPT. JOHN PAKULA. He had a sunburned face and a bit of a hook to his nose. He looked stern, but not too unreasonable. Then again, maybe he was just playing good cop.

"Don't be afraid," he said. "You're just gonna sleep for a while when we put you in your father's fMRI." He said it with a smile, but nothing in his eyes was smiling.

"You're going to kill me, aren't you?" Max said, trying to control his trembling voice.

Pakula seemed taken aback. "No, it's not like that. Your father is a genius. He will become very famous. It is just that we want to learn more from him." He then started talking about his youth in Delhi and how he never had a father, but Max couldn't listen because another Navy man—a real big and menacing one—exited the hospital and waved at the officer, waiting for him at the entrance, together with the other man.

Pakula left the car, locking it behind him. They argued about something. The bad one kept an eye on Max at all times, just to make sure he knew trying to escape again would be futile. They were going to kill him too. This Pakula was a liar. He had to warn his dad. With trembling hand, he carefully took his phone out and kept it out of sight. Once he started recording, he calmed down a bit, and his headache softened. He hoped his voicemail would save them both.

Chapter 22

Thursday: GWUMC, Washington DC

When Jacob finally awoke from the blow to his chin, he found himself lying on the floor of the radiology lab. Groaning, he shifted positions until he was propped up by an elbow. The pain in his head was excruciating, the worst migraine he'd ever experienced. While pushing an area of his forehead with his other hand to stop the pounding, he lifted his heavy lids far enough to scan the room. So many thoughts crowded his memory, and he just couldn't sort them out. Calder and Bucket were there. Calder had pummeled him with his fist. They had... Blinking and willing himself to stay awake, Jacob searched the room. *Thank God they're gone.*

More memories came flooding back. He rose to a sitting position and forced himself to peer into the far corner of the room. Groaning aloud, he turned away, sickened by the sight of Nurse Williams. She was still there, exactly as she had fallen, in a pool of dark crimson blood. Her horrendous murder wasn't a nightmare after all; it was an unspeakable reality. Then he remembered how the man named Basil had completely disintegrated after receiving the jolt of radio waves. A rush of cold, nauseating panic almost sent him reeling. *Max. Max!* Calder had said they were going to get Max! Do a little experimenting on him! *No, no!* He had to stop them!

Struggling to his feet, Jacob grabbed hold of the computer table to catch his balance. That's when he noticed the neatly folded stack of clothing on one end of the fMRI table as he peered through the glass panel shutting off the computer annex. The items looked vaguely familiar, and a sickening sensation overcame him. They were Max's!

Jacob rubbed his forehead and tried to shake off the pain while stumbling out of the annex and into the fMRI examining room. Steadying himself with a hand on the table, he reached for the dark blue Red Sox t-shirt. Holding it to his nose, he breathed in his son's scent. *Max!* What had he done? What had they done to his son? He gathered the rest of the clothing and pulled it to his chest, swaying and choking back sobs.

Fear became a living entity. It suffocated and energized him at the same time. His racing heart was pounding against his chest bone, and he forced himself to breathe slower, to think. *If I live long enough, I'll kill those bastards.*

Frozen in place, Jacob noticed a charred black hole no bigger than a dime in the middle of the bed. Leaning closer to it, he saw very long, web-like lines emanating from the hole. When he touched them, they disintegrated, leaving a smudged residue on his fingers that smelled faintly of burnt plastic. There was something peculiar about the odor.

Energized by pure will, Jacob dropped Max's clothing and raced back to the computer room. The wires connecting the computer to the fMRI data machine were discolored and stunk of partially melted insulation. For a split second, his scientific mind reflexively wondered if they needed replacement. *Oh, God! They...they electrocuted him!* These bastards put him through the same procedure as Basil. They sent high voltage through my son's body! My boy is gone, disintegrated...and it's all my fault.

Jacob crumbled onto his computer chair, a beaten man. Choking back more sobs, he pinched his eyelids so tightly closed no tears could escape. He was a failure. His life's work had destroyed what meant the most to him: his wife, his son, and his self-respect. All along, his son had needed him to be a hands-on father. Instead, he had left him alone to live as he saw fit. What kind of dad would do that to his kid? Now, his boy was dead. He wished the damn 'time machine' really worked. He'd go back in time to correct his mistakes, make better decisions, and do right by his family.

A buzzing sound drew his attention to the computer screen. He jerked upright when he saw the GPS screen. The last location had been deleted, but Jacob felt a spark of hope. Maybe Calder just used him as another guinea pig—sent him somewhere! Is Max still alive? *Think. Yes!* Calder knew exactly how to connect the fMRI to a U.S. Navy setup. Although he had never believed his 'brain reset' idea could make time travel possible, the mere hope of it brought a rushing return of optimism.

Maybe... What if...

Jacob wanted to believe. He had to. His need to believe surpassed his scientific reservations. He examined the screen again and noticed a blinking Word file with his name on it. Grabbing hold of the mouse, he clicked on the name. A message popped up:

> Professor Burkowski: You know what we want—the ability to travel back in time, <u>back before this machine was built!</u> You have exactly forty-eight hours to hand over your sources. We know you've hidden the finished specs somewhere. You used an old equation. Don't tell anybody, not even the police. If you deliver your sources, we will tell you where to find your son.

Jacob reread the message two more times. Max was alive! But what equation? What sources? What are they talking about?

At that very moment, the door to the lab flew open, and three police officers burst into the room, guns drawn. "Hands in the air! Show me your hands! I want to see your hands!"

Jacob slowly raised his arms so his hands were higher than his head. Casting one last look at the computer screen, he saw that it had moved into an autoexec mode. The common logo flashed over the screen, and the memo disappeared.

A heavyset policeman cuffed his wrists behind his back. "You have the right to remain silent... " he said, beginning the Miranda in a dull-sounding mantra.

Jacob peered sightlessly at him. *Max is alive,* he thought, *but they want an equation I don't have. Damn this machine. Damn all of it...*

Chapter 23

Thursday: MET, Washington DC

As Ellen strode into the First District Police Station at 415 4th Street SW, she was glad she'd left the gun in her car. It had crossed her mind, as she parked her Camaro in the parking lot, that maybe it wasn't such a good idea to carry it into the station. She had tucked it into the glove compartment.

The reception area was noisy and crowded with uniformed police officers of various ranks, each apparently having a vital job to fulfill. Some had arrestees by the arm; some were filling out paperwork; and others were deep in conversation on their cell phones. None were particularly tidy in appearance. It seemed there was no dress codes when it came to cops on the beat. Some had hair that curled over their ears, unpolished shoes, and wrinkled shirts. In the U.S. Navy, the dress code was strictly followed.

She glanced about the room, wondering exactly where to find Police Commander Diana Gomez. A flight of marble stairs filled up half the place and blocked most of the light illuminating the reception desk, which was situated directly under it. It looked like a cave. The desk officer's face and work surface were hidden in shadows. Ellen found the setting depressing and couldn't understand how people could work under such gloomy conditions. She was immediately grateful for her airy, well-lit office with a view of the surrounding woods, conducive to her work needs and her mental stability.

She waited by the desk until the officer finished a document and pushed it aside. "What can I do for you, madam?" he asked curtly.

Ellen wanted to reply with 'What do you know about the sun, caveman?' but she opted wisely for, "I have an appointment with Commander Gomez. I believe she's expecting me." She tried to hide her annoyance.

Before the desk officer could pick up the phone, a loud, almost masculine voice roared above the din from somewhere halfway up the stairs. "Commander Meyer?"

Ellen turned and peered upward but could only see the lower half of the female barking at her. Judging by the muscled calves, which seemed to burst out of the slightly transparent black knee-socks, she could only imagine that Commander Gomez would be an imposing figure. It always surprised her how civilians sometimes tried to be more military than most of the military themselves.

As she climbed the stairs and Gomez finally emerged in full view, her guess was confirmed. The officer's uniform barely fit her full-figured body, as if a wrestler in a police uniform. This woman would not conduct an amateurish interview, Ellen decided. She was more likely to grill her on details about an event she knew nothing about, as reported by her superior officer, Pakula.

"Thank you for coming so quickly," Gomez said. "Follow me." She didn't offer her hand, and her face registered no hint of friendliness or mutual respect for their similar ranks.

Ellen walked a few steps behind her down the hallway and into a surprising spacious office.

"Take your pick," Gomez said, indicating the two chairs in front of her overloaded desk. She seated herself behind her desk and pulled a folder from a stack in front of her. "Okay, Commander, we seem to have a problem with a couple of your subordinates. We found their bodies in an alley near the George Washington University Medical Center." She paused and cleared her throat. "Actually, Captain Pakula found them and notified us, and we picked them up. He advised us to bring you in for questioning since you're their commanding officer."

Ellen's mouth dropped open. *What the hell is going on here?*

"It's my understanding they were on a military mission here in Washington DC, outside the jurisdiction of your base—a mission authorized by you?" Gomez continued. She pushed a sheet across the table, a USNO order with the seal of the United States Naval Observatory at the top.

Ellen noticed her signature at the bottom of it and glanced at the seal; it wasn't a fake. It showed seven green stars in an arch over an angel-type woman holding a world globe. "I don't understand..." Ellen found herself at a loss for words. This entire situation was outrageous. She read the letter as rapidly as possible but hadn't finished yet when Gomez interrupted her.

"I must inform you that we haven't been able to officially identify these two men yet."

"What do you mean?" Ellen looked up at her. This was impossible! "You identified them as Calder and Bucket. This can't be—"

"You're not considered a suspect yet, Commander Meyer." She made a tent of her fingers and stared directly at Ellen. "As it stands right now, it will be literally impossible to make a definitive body identity because the faces of the two officers no longer exist. Their fingertips are missing as well. Our forensics guys have informed me that the bodies are decomposing at an unnatural speed. Almost nothing of their flesh remains. Most of it has rotted away. We're talking about some seriously sick mind here that first mutilated them and then sprayed some unknown substance on the individuals, literally incinerating them."

Ellen grew cold and then hot in rapid order. She didn't know how to respond and cursed herself for opting to bring her Glock instead of a lawyer. This was a nightmare far worse than what she'd expected.

Gomez licked her thick, parched lips and swallowed. She seemed to be having some difficulty discussing the case. "At the same time the corpses of these dead men were found, we arrested the father of the boy I told you about. Dr. Burkowski is a radiologist at the GWUMC. We were notified he was conducting unauthorized experiments on human subjects. When our officers arrived, they found one of the nurses shot in the head. The examining table contained samples of human blood—not the nurse's."

Ellen's mind was running in circles, uncertain as to whether or not she was in an interrogation or a briefing. Intuitively, she felt there was a potential weak spot in the data presented by Gomez. "I'm not sure I understand where this is going, Commander. What makes you think there is a supposed connection between these assumed Navy men and the arrested father AND his missing son?"

Gomez rose from her chair and placed both hands on the desktop. Leaning forward, she said, "I know the two men were Navy officers. All that's left of their uniforms are their brass insignias, and we've concluded they are authentic. Although we can't use their incinerated body parts to identify the two mutilated men, I do not question their identity. We must assume those insignia are meaningful, at least as a starting point. We confiscated a USNO vehicle in the same alley. That's how we discovered the USNO order... with your signature on it, Commander. Two witnesses have stated they saw two Navy men in the front seat of this vehicle. They also saw a young boy, Commander Meyer."

"And you feel certain the boy was the radiologist's son?"

Gomez moved from behind the desk and hovered over Ellen. "Yes, Commander, we do. From the description given to us, that boy could very well be the doctor's son."

Ellen returned her attention to the letter. "This seems to be official stationery, but I didn't write that order or sign it," she said. "I-I feel it is necessary for me to call an attorney from the Naval office."

"Why do you need a lawyer?" Commander Gomez asked. "You're not being accused of anything. At this point, we merely need an explanation for this recommendation letter and how it relates to you." Gomez handed over another sheet, wrapped in a plastic evidence bag to preserve the bloodstains as evidence.

She tried to steal a glance at the letter. "To whom is the letter addressed?" Ellen wondered if the police commander's line of questioning was meant to trap her into admitting something.

"To Professor Burkowski," Gomez said dryly.

Ellen immediately noticed her alleged signature at the bottom of it. Again, the stationery seemed to be official. It had the USNO seal, and it clearly provided the name and address of Professor Burkowski at the GWUMC. According to the body of the letter, she had allegedly recommended that he cooperate with Simon Calder and Thomas Bucket, special agents of the Time Division of the USNO. It even mentioned the possible assignment of the Chief Neuroscientist at the USNO to assist him.

Ellen frowned. "Officers Calder and Bucket are indeed under my command, and they are fine officers, but they are not 'special agents', Commander Gomez. And we have no Chief Neuroscientist at the USNO. This letter is a hoax."

"The stationery is original, Commander Meyer, and it contains your signature. It's exactly like the one on the other letter. Our lab confirms it's the real thing. So, if the letter is an original and your signature is confirmed, we must assume you can tell us who these men were...and their—or should I say *your*—mission?"

Ellen tossed the package onto the desk. "I have absolutely no idea who they are...or, uh, were. I've never heard of this Professor Burkowski. I certainly never authorized these two officers, Calder and Bucket, if these bodies belong to them in the first place. The fact that some brass insignias are found lying near two unidentifiable bodies along with my signature forged on a recommendation letter and a hoax USNO order does not prove anything. These men must have been involved in the falsification of documents and killing of innocent people. Their plan appears to have backfired. Commander Gomez, if this is a matter involving the United States Navy, I will have to bring in our military attorneys. Even if you are implying I am personally involved in murder and kidnapping, as a military officer, I must have legal counsel with me."

Ellen bit her tongue. Pakula was responsible for the mess she was in, not Commander Gomez. In the short period he'd been with the USNO, he'd behaved in a manner unbecoming of an officer. She thought maybe he suffered from some mental disorder and couldn't help crossing the line, but in any case, she had the right to defend herself.

Gomez gazed at her through narrowed eyes without comment until her desk phone buzzed. She picked up the receiver and listened. "Doctor Burkowski has arrived," she said.

Chapter 24

Thursday: MET, Washington DC

"Follow me," Gomez snapped.

Ellen hurried to catch up to her. "Commander Gomez, I would like to speak with Professor Burkowski. Is that possible?"

"That's what I had in mind. The interrogation will take place upstairs in Room 6. They're waiting for you. You will be monitored."

An officer was waiting outside the door and stepped aside as two detectives left the room. Gomez spoke with them both in private for only a couple of minutes. One of them turned to look at Ellen just as Gomez motioned to the guard to allow her to enter. As she stepped into the room, she found a man who looked like he had taken a blow to the head. An open wound was still bleeding. "Good morning, Professor Burkowski," she said. "I'm Commander Meyer from the USNO."

She cast a quick glance around the sparsely furnished room. There was only one table but three chairs, no windows, and a dark glass window on the wall that she assumed hid Commander Gomez and a roomful of police officials, who would be watching and listening to her dialogue with the physician.

"Did the police hit you, sir?" She saw that his hands were smeared with blood, so she didn't offer a handshake.

"No, no, but a Navy officer did. I've already told the authorities what happened several times. Two Navy officers came to my lab at the hospital. They wanted me to give them something. I refused, and now they've got my son Max. I-I think he's dead." Jacob bit his bottom lip to still the trembling. "Are...are you with them?" he stammered, eying her uniform.

"No, I'm not. I'm here to understand what happened." Ellen seated herself on the chair opposite him and placed her purse on the floor next to it. "Do you need some tissue to stop that bleeding?"

"One of the officers gave me his handkerchief." He dabbed at his forehead several times. "This wound doesn't want to close. If I had some ice, it would stop the incessant bleeding."

"I'll see that you get some as soon as we've had our talk. I was called in for questioning myself only a few minutes ago. Commander Gomez informed me about the two Navy officers who came to your hospital facility. Why are you so sure they were with the United States Navy?"

"They wore Navy uniforms."

"It's possible those uniforms could have been stolen or replicas. Can you distinguish between a real uniform and a fake one?"

"Never thought about it, but they showed me their Navy IDs as well. They looked damn official to me."

"Have you ever seen an official U.S. Navy ID, Professor Burkowski?"

"No."

"Is it fair to say you're not sure these men were legitimate Navy officers then?"

"They seemed to know a lot about the USNO. They had a letter of recommendation signed by the Deputy Superintendent."

"I'm Deputy Superintendent Meyer, and I signed no such letter."

Jacob looked at her in disbelief. He chewed on the inside of his cheek and waited to see what was coming. Ellen could sense his tension and knew he was suspicious of her too. She didn't blame him. "What did they want from you?" she asked quietly.

Jacob paused. "They had read something I published in a medical journal and wanted me to tell them my sources for building a time machine. I explained it was only a theoretical model—something I had mentioned in a short footnote of a draft article on brain surgery. I have been researching how to cure certain brain disorders like Parkinson's disease and took the liberty to fantasize a bit about what else might be accomplished by using the equipment to alter...you know. And... and th-this is what happened." He fingered his wound again.

"Did you build that machine?" Ellen asked, surprised at his explanation but believing it was an honest one.

"I tried. I connected the fMRI to the time machine, but I don't know if it worked."

"Did you give them your sources?"

"That's the problem. I have no 'sources', but they didn't believe me. Now they have my son. I-I think they brought him into the lab and electrocuted him inside my fMRI after they first killed the head nurse and a test subject and then knocked me out. I told them I couldn't help them." Jacob's voice rose, and he became agitated. He shifted several times on the hard chair.

Ellen watched him but didn't comment.

"They kept saying I was lying—that time travel *is* possible—and they wanted my equation. But it's *not* possible, and I have no equation. And now...and now my son...Max is dead." Jacob buried his head in his hands.

Ellen reached out to touch him in comfort and empathy and then pulled her hand back to place it in her lap. It was hard not to believe the man. *An fMRI? Okay.* This was heavy stuff. She knew about it from the medical facilities in

Iraq. "So you're saying you did not participate in the shooting of Nurse Williams and you have not done any experimenting on your son?"

Jacob shook his head nonstop. "I-I didn't see Max. They said they were going to get him to experiment on him if I didn't produce my sources and that equation... and I lost it when they threatened to harm him. That's when that...that Calder knocked me out. When I awoke, they were gone and...and I found Max's clothes on the fMRI table."

"These two men... Give me their names please."

Jacob straightened up and cleared his throat. "Calder and Bucket. Simon Calder and Thomas Bucket."

"Who did this to you again?" Ellen gestured toward his wound.

"Calder. He was the mean one, cold and heartless. He shot the nurse without a second thought. Bucket left to get my son. When I tried to follow him, Calder knocked me unconscious, the bastard."

"I know you don't have all the answers, Professor Burkowski, but do you believe this 'mission' of theirs—if it could be called that—was a two-man operation? Did they ever mention anyone else?"

"Why?"

"Well, they're both here in the basement morgue, Professor. Somebody killed them both, rather thoroughly, I would say."

Jacob leaped to his feet. "But...but they're the only ones who know where Max is!"

Ellen saw his pain and believed it to be genuine. "I'm sorry."

"*Sorry?* Is what you've just said true, or are you...are you also trying to get something from me that I don't have?" Jacob pounded his fist on the table.

❖ ❖ ❖

In the adjacent room, Gomez and two detectives followed the conversation with great interest. Commander Meyer was an effective questioner. Then Gomez frowned. When Captain Pakula had come to her office, she was struck by his inappropriate attention. She had mistakenly thought he was attracted to her and tried to remain in control. Then his demeanor had changed. He had shown her the letters and was standing very close—too close. When she stated her uncertainty about the importance of the letters, he had instantly lost his temper and become aggressive. No one got away with that. She had edged away from him, but he had moved even closer and told her not to step out of line, as if he were her superior. She had decided she might be dealing with some nutcase.

When Meyer came in, she was still fuming. Now, she felt a little guilty taking out her anger for Pakula on her. She could tell Meyer was stressed. In all likelihood, Meyer was harassed by her commanding officer in the same way he had harassed her. A feeling of solidarity rose in her. She and Meyer had perhaps a decade between them, and in a strange way, Meyer reminded her of her younger sister. If she were still alive, she might be in a similar predicament. Women's rights groups supported only their own kind. There was no such thing as equality in the workplace.

"You don't have to stay here," she said to the detectives. "I'll take over and give you input for the report later." As soon as the door closed behind them, she leaned forward and studied Commander Meyer.

※ ※ ※

"I'm so sorry, sir," Ellen said, feeling her heart go out to Jacob.

She felt sad. If no new evidence came forth, the man would be the prime suspect. It was clear something had happened in his laboratory that had shocked him.

Nothing he had told her made any sense. However, it was highly unlikely this scientist had killed his own son in an experiment.

"Please, won't you be seated again? Let's talk some more." She felt hopeful that he knew something more. She just needed to draw it out. It was clear to her something else had happened in his laboratory that had traumatized him. She could tell he loved his son. Although she was childless, she needed little imagination to see the man was a wreck.

Ellen thought back to how this situation had started. She'd received the unexpected phone call from Commander Gomez. Captain Pakula was in her office and had suggested she call his deputy in for questioning about the dead officers. She had been livid. Following his peculiar behavior in the Time Committee meeting and her determination to turn him in for... At that moment, she thought of another line of questioning—something the police hadn't thought of asking the doctor. Something she had seen in the letters.

She leaned forward with her arms resting on the table and peered directly at Jacob Burkowski. "You told the police these two men had kidnapped your son and then threatened to kill him unless you would experiment on him right?"

Jacob stared at her and then slowly nodded.

"What I don't understand, Professor Burkowski, is that since your son was killed in that machine anyway, what difference did it make if he was killed by them or by your applying the mega forces of an fMRI scan so that he would dissolve, because that's what happened to your son, isn't it?" She never took her eyes from his face, waiting for a flinch or a blink or any other sign that would clue her to the next question. She finally sat back and crossed her arms over her chest. "I just don't get it. How did you think you would get away with it?"

"Get away with it?" Jacob pushed himself away from the table. "We're talking about my son! You're with *them*—the police. Just leave me alone. Go away, Commander Whoever."

Ellen held up a hand. "No, wait. You misunderstood me. What I intended to say is that there was no way you could free your son. There was no escape, no way out. Do I make myself clear, Professor?"

"Why the hell is everybody calling me 'Professor'?" Jacob shouted.

Ellen felt her pulse accelerate. "That's what you are, aren't you?"

"I'm a doctor on the medical school staff. I'm not a professor. They may be equal titles to you, but not in a medical school setting. It's a rather touchy subject for me."

"Who else is calling you 'Professor'?"

"Those three men. Those Navy men."

"*Three* Navy men? There were only two, Calder and Bucket."

Jacob threw his hands into the air. "No, there were three. Their boss called me at my home to say they would be visiting me at the hospital. He called me 'Professor' all the time too."

"Their boss?"

"Yes. I forgot about him, but maybe he knows where Max is! Captain John Pakula. He was the man. He was the first one to call me 'Professor'."

Ellen blew a long breath from her pursed lips and leaned back in her chair. She glanced at the one-way mirror window and grinned. "I'll be right back, Dr. Burkowski." She strode out of the interrogation room and met Commander Gomez in the corridor outside. "You heard him. He's not a professor, and I didn't write or sign that letter."

"Not bad for a Navy officer," Gomez said.

"Captain Pakula is behind all of this." Ellen had her hands on her hips.

"We have no jurisdiction inside the USNO," Gomez said.

"No need. I only want your cooperation, Commander Gomez. Can I count on you?"

Gomez nodded and finally extended her hand. She was not too bad after all.

While Gomez filled in the necessary paperwork, Ellen stood by Jacob, who checked out in the hall. The officer handed over Jacob's personal belongings. Routinely, Jacob switched on his cell phone and wanted to stash it away, but there was an incoming message beeping for attention. Jacob almost dropped the phone. He just stood there, staring at the screen.

Ellen glanced over his shoulder and saw the caller ID. It read: MAX. Gently, she took the phone from his hand and inspected the time stamp. "Your son must have left you a voice message shortly before he was…apprehended, Dr. Burkowski." She looked around and made a quick decision. "Let's go outside and listen to it."

Chapter 25

Friday: Rome/Washington DC

As it approached eight, Frank pulled the men's room door open a crack and eyed the front entrance to the ASV. The receptionist would arrive soon, and he'd have to watch for the best time to slip out the door. As he had expected, the receptionist came early, opened the entrance door, and disappeared into the building to turn on the lights, the air conditioning in the reading rooms, and God only knew what else.

When the man entered the elevator and the door closed behind him, Frank decided not to wait for the arrival of scientists eager to use the study rooms. He slipped out of the restroom and hurried across the floor toward the huge entrance door. As he placed his hand on the knob and pushed it downward, he uttered a quick prayer of thanks that the receptionist had left it unlocked. Stepping out into the early morning sunlight, he cast a hasty glance around Belvedere Square. At that very moment, he saw the dark silhouette of a Vatican policeman on the Belvedere porch, yawning, with his face turned in Frank's direction. He hadn't yet seen him, but it was only a matter of time.

Frank closed the door quietly behind him and hugged the wall, waiting in the shadows of the doorway to see what the guard would do next. He thought about the best route to take to avoid being questioned. If he simply crossed the square and walked in a straight line toward the man, he might arouse undue interest. No one left the ASV at such an early hour, as it was still closed for visitors. Across the square from the Belvedere porch, he saw another porch that led to the Vatican gardens. The gardens housed more offices and most likely staff members who would be returning to their homes after their night shift. If he could reach that porch, perhaps…

He felt the perspiration crawl down his forehead. He was making assumptions. Were there any Vatican services that were manned twenty-four hours in the gardens? If so, would the sentry know this and be accustomed to seeing such workers leave the premises at this early hour? If not… Well, he didn't want to speculate about what would happen. The Vatican was a crowded, bustling city, and priests walked in and out of the gates continuously. Surely his collar could get him through regardless of the hour.

Frank's eyes fell upon the ill-kept, two-story fountain planted in the middle of the square. Its massive foot was placed in a waist-high water basin, fenced off with stone poles and metal tubes. It blocked the view of the guard. Its foot was big enough for him to hide behind if he could reach it in time. He couldn't remain in the doorway of the ASV much longer. Either the guard or the receptionist from inside would see him.

He prepared himself mentally for the fastest sprint of his life. Waiting for the sentry to turn his back to him again, he dashed toward the fountain, scrambled over the iron fence, and squatted behind the water basin, breathing heavily through his mouth. When he had caught his breath, he stole a quick look over the edge of the basin. The policeman hadn't moved. Surveying the area, Frank eyed the entrance to the garden. If someone were to come from that direction, he would face another problem.

The policeman became restless and turned in his direction again. Frank waited with bated breath. *Okay, you've seen it all,* he thought. *Please turn around again.*

Suddenly, he heard the honking of a vehicle, perhaps a taxi. It drew the attention of the policeman, who turned to see who was approaching the gate. This was the window he'd hoped for. Frank inched his way around the fountain basin as casually as possible and headed toward the porch near the Vatican gardens. Then, he strolled onto the Belvedere courtyard and toward the staff exit of the *Porta Sant'Anna* as though he were an employee. Although he was trembling inside, he tried to act naturally. As he approached the sentry, he smiled and called out a casual "*Bon giorno*," while waving his out-of-date *permessa* at him.

The guard seemed taken by surprise because he hadn't heard or seen him coming, but he hid another yawn behind his gloved hand and saluted Frank lazily with the other. He didn't even look at the *permessa*. No doubt he was eager to be relieved of his duties as soon as possible. Frank's white collar was enough proof for him of his right to be there.

Frank blew a forced breath from his lungs and lifted his eyes toward heaven to offer another "Thank you" as he headed down the *Via di Belvedere*. He had made it past one post with relative ease, but there were two more to go. In the far distance, he eyed the three remaining pillars of the Temple of Vesta on the *Forum Romanum*, which sat in a straight line to the entrance of the Vatican. Halfway to his destination, he spotted the next guard and saw that his eyes were locked on him. His heart sank, and he cursed under his breath. There had been a changing of the guard. If he had left the ASV just a few minutes earlier, it would have not happened, but the damn policeman had been so irritatingly slow. This guard, fresh on duty, would be more alert. Frank slowed while contemplating alternatives to his escape route. To his left, a narrow alley led toward the Vatican hospital. The Vatican post office was on the corner, but none could serve as an escape; they were dead-ends. He was trapped. As he drew closer to the second security check, a real sense of panic made him feel nauseous.

He felt the tension turn his cheeks red. He glanced at the second policeman again. The man had him radar locked and was staring at him as if he could read his mind.

The policeman was so close to the station of the Swiss Guards that if something would happen, they would be instantly alerted, and this fresh policeman had all the time in the world to wonder about who Frank was and what he was doing there so early in the morning. He stood with his hands on his belt, blocking Frank's passage. Frank felt his knees grow weak. His lack of sleep and the rising tension of the past hours were finally taking their toll on his out-of-shape body. He slowed down to buy time. What would he say if the guard questioned him?

With only a few yards to go, he heard rapid footsteps behind him. He glanced over his shoulder and was surprised to see another priest, and behind him, another one! They were in a hurry to leave the Vatican City. He almost tripped over his own feet, he was so relieved. What a fool he had been! He had allowed his imagination to take over his common sense. The *Via di Belvedere* provided access to all sorts of official buildings that housed things like the post office, the hospital, the supermarket, and so on. Of course there were more priests on a night shift from this part of the city.

Gaining more confidence, he nodded at the guard and attempted to walk by without stopping.

"*Documenti*," the policeman demanded in a surly voice, but in sharp contrast to his posture, he didn't scrutinize his *permessa;* he merely glanced at it and waved him on.

Just an Italian in a uniform, Frank thought, once again relieved. In a way, these guys were so predictable.

The Swiss Guards only smiled at him, assuming their police colleagues had done their job, and just like that, Frank Bootsma was free to go!

Outside the Vatican walls, Frank almost collapsed as his body was lightened of its tension. He didn't dare look back, though he felt tempted to do so as a sort of farewell.

Heading directly across the street to the cab stand, he climbed into the back seat of the first one in line and gave directions for the driver to take him to the Fiumicino airport. A cab would get him there much quicker than the subway, and he'd avoid the risk of meeting up with any more guards who may be put on alert for him.

He encountered no problem exchanging his ticket after reaching the airport and wasn't charged a single extra euro. The airport was relatively quiet, security measures were normal, and most importantly, no one paid attention to him. With all the tension and suspicion inside the Vatican, he had felt like a Cold War spy escaping across the Iron Curtain.

His flight was scheduled to leave within thirty minutes, and since he had no luggage, he simply boarded the plane, found his seat, and relaxed. He was so exhausted. He fell soundly asleep before the plane had taken off.

❈ ❈ ❈

Once the plane landed at Dulles, he joined the line to go through customs. Again, since he wasn't carrying luggage, he merely showed his passport, answered a couple of questions, and was waved on. He hurried through the receiving area, stopped to check one of the monitors listing flights, and was about to head directly for the gate designated for his connecting flight to Houston when he noticed two civilians dressed in identical gray-blue suits. They were eyeing everyone coming through customs. *Secret Service?* he wondered and felt trickles of perspiration run down his neck. One of them looked directly at him and then checked a document he was holding. Three times he looked up and down, up and down, up and down, and then he elbowed the guy next to him. Now, they were both staring at Frank, and within seconds, they were at his side.

"Please follow us, sir," one of them said. He was directed to a small office just behind the customs counters. The one who had spoken to him took the chair behind the desk; the other one remained next to him. Both looked grim. Their gray-blue suits matched the Spartan gray interior of what was about to become an interrogation room. Frank had the feeling he was in a B-grade movie situated in the Cold War; if he weren't in such trouble, it would be comical.

The man behind the desk nodded at the worn chair in front of the table without introducing himself or his colleague. "May I see your passport?" he asked.

Frank handed it to him and watched as he flipped through the pages, pausing at the two newest ones.

"We have been alerted to an international incident that occurred in Rome," he said without looking up.

Frank didn't react beyond swallowing hard.

"In the Vatican," the man added. "Tell us why you left the Vatican City early this morning rather than yesterday afternoon."

Frank felt his heart drop into the pit of his stomach and licked his dry lips. "I missed my plane on Thursday after being stuck in the traffic." He wasn't accustomed to lying and knew his face was flushing. "I-I had to stay over at the airport. Took the first available flight."

The man behind the table shrugged. "You're lying. We checked with the police at the Rome airport. You didn't attempt to change your ticket until this morning. Anyway, it's out of our hands now. We have orders to take you to the Vatican Embassy. They have several questions for you. Our job was just to detain you, and that wasn't so difficult, Mr. Bootsma."

The two men smiled thinly at each other, marking him as a fool who had walked quite easily into their wide-open trap. He was being extradited to the Vatican. His mind raced through a dozen events as he wondered how they could have discovered his involvement so quickly.

He thought about his encounter with the secretary of the *Prefetto*, his talks with Pat, the false alarm in the bunker. When everything was added up, it wasn't too difficult for anyone to point at him.

All at once, he realized he hadn't been given his passport. "May I have my passport back?" he asked, holding out his hand.

"Your passport?" The man who hadn't said a word before burst into laughter. He pulled Frank to his feet and pushed him toward the door. "You must be kidding, Bootsma." He turned to his colleague. "I'll take him to the car."

The other man punched a few numbers on his cell phone.

As they made their way through the customs area, Frank felt the eyes of other travelers on him and hung his head. It was bad enough to be escorted by an authority, but it was worse because he could be identified as a priest. He was ushered to an unmarked door in a secluded area. His escort entered a code into an electronic lock and, surprisingly, a moment later they were outside the airport. A black, nondescript SUV with dark windows was parked directly in front of him, and he noticed four motorcycle policemen in helmets. Someone wanted to ensure he couldn't make a break for it.

A blond, pale-looking man wearing a black suit stepped out of the vehicle and opened the back door for him. The other man had disappeared into the building without a word. Immediately, the policemen mounted their motorcycles and started their roaring engines. As soon as he had scooted onto the leather seat, he heard a soft *click* and knew he was locked in.

As they drove away from the area, the pale man spoke softly in his cell phone. "*Ich hab'm,*" he said in unmistakable Swiss German.

Chapter 26

Friday: Vatican Embassy, Washington DC

The moment he heard the *click* of the SUV door locks, Frank froze. Cold sweat trickled down his back, sticking his clerical shirt to the leather. This was a Swiss Guard. This was going all wrong. He gazed sightlessly at the two motorcycle policemen driving ahead of the vehicle and then at the two behind it. They would see to it his ride was quick and without hitches.

He would probably be asked to leave the Jesuit order and resign from his position as curator at the Vatican Observatory. That would happen anyway, but then he would be extradited to the Italian justice department. Italian prisons were as bad as those in the United States, especially for clerics. If inmates found out he was a Catholic priest—and they always did—he would not leave the prison alive. Priests were despised because of the child abuse cases popping up like poisonous mushrooms. *Life could've been so different for me, if only I'd...*

The SUV drove straight into the courtyard of a three-story, nondescript brownstone building located between Massachusetts Avenue and the Observatory Ring. He recognized the Papal Keys above the entrance. The gate opened automatically; they were expected. The driver opened the door for Frank and escorted him into the building. Two other plainclothes members of the Swiss Guard met them. He was surprised to see they were on duty in the Vatican

Embassy. These young, unmarried men were, by contract, obliged to stay inside the Vatican walls.

When he entered the conference room, the Vatican Ambassador, the Nuncio, was waiting for him with a U.S. Navy officer whose white naval hat rested on the table in front of him. Both sat at a table with their hands folded in a similar way. What is their connection? Frank wondered. Two armed Swiss Guards stood directly behind them, wearing grim looks that said this was not going to be a pleasant event.

The Nuncio unfolded his hands briefly, showing the Episcopal Seal, and gestured for Frank to be seated. His posture exuded an extreme dislike for the situation—or maybe for him. Frank noticed the Nuncio and the naval officer never exchanged eye contact. Something had caused uneasiness between the two men, but when the naval officer nodded at the Nuncio, signaling him to speak, Frank felt they were acting out a prearranged procedure.

"This is Superintendent John Pakula from the United States Naval Observatory, the USNO. Our helpful neighbor from across the street has come to us because he has a few questions for you, Brother Bootsma," the Nuncio said. He smiled benignly at Frank and let the smile vanish as quickly as it had appeared. "And then, we have a few questions of our own."

It couldn't be a coincidence the USNO was only a stone's throw away, Frank decided. He eyed the naval officer with interest. *This is a setup.*

"Mr. Bootsma, I am Captain John Pakula of the USNO, which you know very well, I assume, since you are working for the Vatican Observatory Research Group. I have always wanted to believe we are not in competition." Pakula spoke slowly, enunciating his words with an almost unnatural clarity. "Our organizations are pursuing the same thing with related, albeit distinct objectives. The United States wants to maintain its supremacy in guided missile warfare, and the Vatican Observatory wants to maintain its supremacy in discovering new heavenly bodies. If I remember correctly, there are more planets named after Jesuits than any other group in history. Am I right, Mr. Bootsma?"

Frank nodded. He didn't know where this conversation was heading, but it was likely to be somewhere important. He'd better keep the conversation going. "The Vatican Observatory certainly has a distinguished track record for making major discoveries," he said. "We're proud to be part of a long tradition." He tried to smile accordingly.

"If this is true, Mr. Bootsma, then please inform me why you visited the Secret Archives in Rome yesterday." Pakula's voice now took on a sarcastic edge.

"Please tell me, Captain Pakula, why is the USNO so interested in my historical research? Certainly not for military reasons, right?"

Pakula wasn't amused. "Before I answer that question, I believe the ambassador has something to say."

The Nuncio cleared his throat. "Brother Bootsma, an incident has taken place at the *Archivio Segreto Vaticano*. We must be certain you had nothing to do with it."

"Your Eminence, I was in the Archives to continue my historical studies regarding the origins of the Vatican Observatory. It was a fascinating period. It all started in the *Torre de Venti*, during the trial of Galileo Galilei—"

"Exactly, Mr. Bootsma," Pakula said, cutting him off mid-sentence. "The trial of Galileo Galilei. Please tell us what happened to the original papers."

Frank was stunned by his outburst. "I never saw the originals, Mr. Pakula. What are you talking about? The information was placed on a DVD by the ASV. The originals are inaccessible for scholars." He watched as Pakula whispered something into the Nuncio's ear.

The Nuncio nodded. "Yes, we have to," he mumbled. He pushed himself from the table and rose from his chair, motioning for the Swiss Guards to follow him. "We must conclude our part of this conversation, Brother Bootsma. You're out of our hands now." He hurried from the room, leaving Frank alone with Pakula.

Pakula rose from his chair and walked around the table, all the while peering intently at him. "You have no idea what trouble you are in, Frank... may I call you 'Frank'? And you are totally ignorant of the power I have over you." He sat on the edge of the chair closest to Frank. "The original documents of the trial against Galileo have been stolen. We think you stole them."

The whole thing seemed bizarre. "Again, Mr. Pakula," Frank said, "why are those ancient documents of any concern to the USNO? I just don't see the connection."

Pakula placed his hand on Frank's shoulder. "The situation is like this, Frank. We have reason to believe those who gained access to the Vatican Archives are part of a terrorist group that is planning an unprecedented attack on the United States. Something that started in the Vatican is about to jump over to the United States and will soon spread throughout the world like a bad virus. This attack will make 9/11 seem trivial by comparison. Make no mistake, this assault will bring the Western world to its knees."

Frank willed himself not to laugh aloud at Pakula's pompous rhetoric. His own discovery was of a totally different universe. He had felt like an alien from another planet, searching for conspiracies and other scientific beliefs propagated by Urban VIII, but that was nothing compared to what this man was saying. Was he really talking about another terrorist attack? One that would put the future of the Western world at risk? Ridiculous.

"Mr. Pakula," Frank said in a measured tone, "just for the sake of discussion, are you at liberty to share your thoughts on how a seventeenth-century scientist can be of any relevance to a terrorist in 2010?" Frank tried to suppress his skepticism.

Pakula's eyes narrowed. "Let me be honest with you, Frank. It is neither Galileo nor his trial papers we are interested in. We are interested in *you*. We believe those trial papers contain crucial information about a lost theory on the foundation—the very nature of time. We believe the Vatican is secretly pursuing that theory. If this speculation—and that's all it is right now—were to be revealed to terrorists, it could open up the possibility for the manipulation of time. And you know what?" He paused momentarily to affix an icy stare on Frank. "We would lose our Atomic Clock, at which point all our guided missile weapons would become useless, just like that. Our Atomic Clock is already out of sync by fifteen seconds. You think this is a coincidence? No. The Vatican is either working with terrorists, or she has a mole inside your organization." Pakula waited again for a few seconds. "That mole could be you, Frank Bootsma."

Frank's eyes widened. What was this Pakula talking about? He was amazingly close to knowing what he had already discovered in the Tower of the Winds, yet it appeared he did not really understand. He had to pay closer attention to his choice of words.

"With our Atomic Clock under attack, you can be sure the United States will not sit still like a lame duck. Too much is at stake. We will fight back. We will smoke out the perpetrators. If necessary, we will declare war on the Vatican. We will have no other choice. So please, Frank, tell me what you were doing in the Secret Archives, where you have taken the Galileo file, and what you were planning to do with it!"

Frank was speechless. He couldn't put his finger on it, but he didn't trust this man. All the while he talked, he could smell his breath. "I-I have no idea what you're t-talking about," he stuttered.

"Very well, Frank. If this is how you want it, the Nuncio has already given me permission to take you into custody and interrogate you at *our* headquarters if you refuse to cooperate." With these words, Pakula grabbed him by the arm and yanked him up from the chair. "Let's go," he ordered.

Frank knew his own strength was no match for the steel grip that held him prisoner. As they exited the room, he noticed there was no sign of the Swiss Guards. They had disappeared. Pakula urged him to keep walking, and they exited the building to where another dark SUV was waiting. Frank had seen it when he arrived.

Surprisingly, the inside was constructed like a police van. The front and back seats were divided by a steel grid. Once again, his doors were locked from the outside. He could see the USNO main entrance across the street, the safety hatch lifted up to prevent car bombers. Right next to it was a big sign counting the time in hours, minutes, and two seconds behind the colon. But when the car turned left from the Observatory Circle heading for the center of Washington, Frank knew something was wrong.

"Hey! Where are we going?" he shouted.

Pakula did not say a word, but his mouth showed a thin smile as he glared at him in the rearview mirror.

Part 2

Chapter 27

2115: Jerusalem

Major Roto Ashlev, a stocky, thirty-one-year-old with cropped black hair, sat in his extreme-reality room with his goggles on, deeply immersed in the Army Analogue Archive, the 'Triple A', as he preferred to call it. The seclusion of a lost world with yet unseen treasures—he just loved been there. Among other duties, his job was to supervise the automated meta-tagging of any material suitable for distribution. He was one of the best. He kept both hands busy, organizing and indexing large chunks of data.

He was about to close the NSA directory when he discovered a three-minute voice recording. His digital assistant alerted him that it had "close to 76 percent similarity." *Similarity to what?* He opened the file and listened to what could almost be his own voice. A male was talking to someone about personal sacrifices. Okay, a not-so-close similarity to his own voice was something not so special. He searched the file for any ancestry or children's files. The file history went down, not up, and connected to a video recording in a long-outdated format. A digital seal told him it had been reviewed last on October 10, 2105, just before the final collapse of the United States of America and the invasion of the Asian brain travelers in the centuries that followed. The automatic translator indicated it was an MPEG movie;

he reformatted it. A video fragment started running on his memory processor.

First, Ashlev opened the reality augmenter, a program originally used for participating in a movie. Normally, nano-screens opened in the back of a viewer's eyes and displayed the movie in a 3D fashion. The viewer could walk around as though present in the movie. Ashlev had always avoided any modification of his body that could compromise him, so he used a set of goggles and let the massive computing power of the research facility take care of the rest. Immediately, the video was enhanced, and he found himself standing in the study of a Professor Jacob Burkowski in the DuPont area of Washington DC. Some parts kept him in the dark and were only accessible if he asked to play certain scenarios. "Focus, focus," Ashlev muttered aloud. He walked closer to the desk where the professor was holding up a piece of paper. What struck him immediately was the lack of any intelligence on his desk other than a 'personal computer', as such devices were called in those days. The keyboard was not yet part of the table, and the computer was huge—at least the size of a shoebox.

He looked at a calendar on the wall and saw that it read NOVEMBER 3, 2031. He peered more closely at Burkowski. This man must be in his seventies, he thought. Then he strolled around the desk and scanned the person filming Jacob. Oddly enough, he saw only a camera. No one was carrying it. "Emulate!" he commanded, as he pointed at a faint reflection in one of the silver plates on his desk, perhaps some sort of prize. Immediately, it morphed into an adult in his mid-forties—a younger version of Burkowski, perhaps his son.

Ashlev peered with greater interest at the paper Jacob held in front of the camera. It appeared to be an article on brain reset. The words *The Lancet Neurology* appeared at the top of the page.

Ashlev commanded the film to freeze and leaned closer for a better look. At first glance, he saw nothing special about the paper. He was already an expert on the subject matter. The article was published long after Burkowski had retired and more as a courtesy of the editorial board. It was published in a special on 'out of bounds' articles that had never been accepted for publication on the first go-round for being unscientific but got a second chance because the advance of medicine had proven some relevance for the ideas put forward.

Ashlev quickly reread the article. Brain transport had been developed independently of Burkowski's paper; however, there were remarkable similarities, and it seemed he was the first one in centuries to be curious about this man whose invention had become obsolete.

Suddenly, Burkowski opened a drawer and pulled out another sheet of paper and held it next to the first one. His lips spread into a wide grin and then moved without sound.

"Emulate!" Ashlev commanded.

"See the difference?" the mechanical impression of Burkowski's voice said. "Look at the bottom of the two articles. I could have mentioned the Einstein field equation, since they left out my footnote anyway. The idiots."

"Zoom!" Ashlev said, feeling his body tense. He focused on Jacob's handwriting, which was almost illegible, and waited for the quantum computing power to decipher the lines. It happened in a millisecond. Suddenly, his eyes widened. At first, he thought it was a scenario mistake. He asked for a recalculation and carefully perused the coding. Over and over again, the same text appeared in front of him.

> Brainwaves consist of tiny particles I call 'thinkwaves', alike photons that can be sent back in time through a double-light helix at the speed of light; if we could capture them and if we could know where to point them,

they could be sent back into the brains of people centuries back. And if we could know how to survive in the same body…

Ashlev saw a tiny figure scribbled next to the notation but couldn't decipher what it said. He did, however, immediately understand the historic dimensions of his find. It could be the beginning of a new era of brain transportation, a Third Singularity. He memorized the text before he deleted it, knowing his superiors would not allow indexing. Just as he was about to open his mouth to give the "Abort" command that would halt the augmented reality, he noticed something on the wall of Burkowski's study. "Magnify," he demanded.

A glass-framed envelope and a letter were arranged on a shelf next to several books. Both contained a seal he had never seen before. "Connect to alike," he whispered. Instantly, he was able to read: *Specola Vaticana*. Below the address, he read: CASTEL GANDOLFO, NO LONGER EXISTENT.

The ink on the letter had faded. Ashlev touched the glass, and the deciphering process automatically began. His wonderment grew. A certain Frank Bootsma, conservator of the meteorite collection of the *Specola Vaticana*, had scribed a handwritten message for Jacob. It read: *"Only new actions without a cause can solve the time-travel paradox (Gen. 27). YOUR SON IS ALIVE."*

Ashlev tore the goggles from his head. He considered commanding the "Erase" process. What would this video do in the hands of his superiors? What was the connection between Burkowski and the Vatican? What did the message about Burkowski's son mean? What was so special about this Vatican Observatory? So many questions. Suddenly, he remembered again the metallic voice of his assistant: "…a 76 percent similarity." He had to control his thoughts.

Chapter 28

Between the present and 2115: GWUMC, Washington DC

It took a while before Frank realized he was not dead.
As a Jesuit brother, he had offered the Last Sacrament many times. He knew that occasionally, people miraculously came back to life after being pronounced dead and talked of seeing a tunnel of light and of being told to go back to Earth and resume life. While still at the end of the tunnel, these people experienced what they called an 'out-of-body experience'; they claimed to have seen their own body lying on the bed while literally floating above it.

That was exactly what he was experiencing. This man Pakula—the one who had interrogated him at the Vatican Embassy—had abducted him and taken him to the test facility at gunpoint. He could still see the medical laboratory where he had been placed on the examination table and shoved into some machine. Now, it showed nothing but a blackened sheet. He could still feel the eerie silence that had occurred when he literally left his body.

While floating above his own body, Frank had seen the name Burkowski on a nameplate on the door of the laboratory. There had been a fight in the lab before he arrived; anyone could draw that conclusion. The room was a mess, and there was blood all over the place. From his floating position, he had seen crimson and brownish smears on the floor and the walls.

Frank had also seen a man working on the computer behind a glass-walled room next to the lab. It might have been Pakula. From his eagle-eye position, he had not been able to see exactly what the man was doing on the computer, but now he had to surmise he'd been typing instructions for the machine Frank had been rolled into. Something must have gone wrong though. He remembered hearing the humming sound of the machine, which had increased in decibels to an unbearable level, and how it had felt like his eardrums were about to burst. Then the heat had become so intense that he felt he was on fire. Before he could fully chronicle his pain, the machine had literally exploded. It had seemed like an eternity, but the process took no more than a minute.

Then, there was an utter silence. He was there and he was not there... at the same time! Amazingly, the machine was still intact, which he couldn't understand since the explosion surely should have blown it to pieces. Now, he was literally floating above the test table, seeing the chaos and thinking and analyzing the situation.

Frank first thought he was dead and on his way to heaven. He waited for the pearly gates to open and for angels to welcome him, but this didn't happen. The room beneath him changed at a dazzling speed. For a while, he couldn't see anything. As though he were in a centrifuge, the world around him spun at an amazing speed, and he experienced nothing but blackness.

He wasn't dead, but he wasn't in heaven either—at least not yet. He was still on Earth, but where? Where was he going? *Did God send me back? Is this a second chance to undo my sins and the grief I caused my parents?* A jumble of thoughts fought for attention. *Will I leave the Jesuit order, the Catholic Church? Will I...* He didn't dare to let those feeling emerge. One thing was for sure: He would make different decisions in his life. He would make his parents, his father in heaven, proud again.

Chapter 29

2115: Jerusalem

"Major Ashlev?"

Ashlev was so deeply engrossed in his thoughts that he missed hearing the general's arrival. A shiver passed through his body. He was not allowed to disconnect. The ultra-secure video link made it impossible to emulate his being there. Most of the time, the general met with him in their teleconference room. As soon as he had entered the remote archive folder, the system had automatically alerted his superior, who had summoned him to a meeting. He had no other option than to sit tight and wait for whatever was to happen. He had never visited Beijing. Years ago, the general had come over to the Near East Region.

As he watched her foglet slowly compose her body, he fought against the urge to shut his eyes. She was no longer human. Even worse, she had done nothing to enhance her presence, even though the latest version of the foglets allowed users to essentially recompose their bodies and present them in any mode. An old woman could arrange a makeover that would fool even the trained eye, but the general would have none of this. Even though her rank and brain transportation allowed her to capture a new body at any time, as so many of her peers did, she preferred to remain in her decaying frame with a collection of artificial parts. While Ashlev appreciated that she declined to exercise her right to take the lives of innocent young people to live forever, he was nevertheless appalled by the absence of any aesthetics in her physical appearance. In a way, it underscored her mechanical behavior, which was devoid of emotions. She had essentially crossed the line between human and robot.

Standing at attention, he saluted her.

"At ease, Major," she said. "Be seated. I noticed you have discovered a few interesting pieces of information in our archives, am I right?" She began their dialogue without any pleasantries.

"Yes, General, and I am here to inform you that our technology of brain transportation is missing an essential component," Ashlev said. "For centuries, we've been on a one-way track. Brain transportation can be possible into the past as well as into the future! I have learned that a scientific discovery made centuries ago was somehow never published."

The general's face showed no reaction to his statements. "I will remind you once again that we are already knowledgeable of your research in the archives, Major. Your job is quarantining elements of ethnic collective memory. To the point please."

Ashlev sat very still. Somehow, he had to divert her attention to a few minor points while masking the precise meaning of his find. "I was not aware you had time to look into the matter, General. What is the position of the High Command? Am I allowed to initiate my experimentation?"

"What do you propose, Major?"

The general was obviously well informed and testing him for his loyalty, Ashlev decided. While they were talking, he had noticed that the electronic lock on his office door had been closed. He heard a faint rustle in the corridor too. No doubt security forces waited outside for further instructions. A soft *whirr* indicated his electronic gun had been disabled to ensure he could not harm himself.

"It is entirely possible that this discovery could be misused by our enemies, General. They will try to apprehend the inventor of brain time travel. If they succeed in doing so... well, anything could happen to us."

"Anything?" The general's eyes never left his face.

Ashlev met her gaze without flinching. "Let me clarify, General. First of all, whatever we do with my discovery is confined within what is called the double time-travel paradox. It is not possible to change the past, only the future. In other words, if we go back, the longer we stay there, the greater the chance we'll change our future as well...in a way that could severely impair our being here."

He waited but still saw no reaction in the stone face of the general.

He continued. "Second, it isn't possible to travel back in time before the invention of the time-travel technology. Using my find will only allow us to travel back to the inventor at the time he conceptualized his discovery. Just for the record, madam, anyone who finds out about our reuse of this information could first come to us and then, as a consequence, get to this man. There is another consideration too."

Ashlev relaunched the video showing the Burkowski letter. He pointed at the footnote. "We're not sure this man invented the process by himself. It is entirely possible he derived it using other sources. If this was the case, we must trace those sources before we take on the risk of sending him away. We must eliminate the possibility that this time-travel technology existed for a longer period than we surmised and has been seen by more people than just this one lone ranger."

Ashlev saw the general's mouth move, but her words were inaudible to him. She had muted her sound while conferring with other members of the High Command. He suppressed the impulse to auto-emulate her lip-reading, knowing she would instantly be apprised. He waited patiently and tried to read her response before she gave it to him. Because she had retained so few human characteristics, it was a futile exercise.

Moments later, she peered at him more intently. "Major, we do not believe you. First of all, your equations are not scientifically proven. And second, you left out an important fact. Am I right, Major?"

Ashlev froze. He had been so careful not to use the erase program. *Damn.*

"Well?"

"I deeply apologize, General. I was about to inform you and the High Command of what I learned concerning the ancient Vatican Observatory. I inadvertently stumbled across this historic link and evaluated its importance."

The general's craggy face seemed to soften a bit.

He shifted on his chair. "It seems the Vatican State was much further along with its research on the origin of the cosmos—the time before the Big Bang. I highly recommend we bring in the chief researcher at that time, Brother Frank Bootsma. What are your thoughts about this?"

For a few seconds, she only gazed at him through narrowed eyes, like a predator would examine its prey. Then, the door to his office was flung open, and the security forces, clad in shimmering black leather uniforms, swarmed into the room while pointing their weapons at his head. The commander followed closely behind and deftly disarmed him, although his gun was useless already. Clearly, the exercise was meant to intimidate him.

"Again, Major Ashlev, we do not believe you," the general snapped at him. "This Vatican State you refer to is a reliquary of a distant past that—even at the time of the invention—had as its sole purpose to fool people and tap into their money sources. On the other hand, this Bootsma is an interesting figure who may well serve our needs. We would never have laid an eye on him." She pointed a crooked finger at him. "For some reason, you are withholding the fact that you considered deliberately erasing state documents using an app we have traced back to a couple criminals." She paused long enough to switch on a 3D screen that showed Ashlev with the man who had sent the application to him.

Ashlev felt his stomach churn. The man was a friend. The next screen showed his bloody interrogation and finally, his execution. His decapitated head remained on the screen while the general continued.

"The man told us nothing we did not know already. However, we are sure there is more for us to learn. When was the last time you contacted your mother?"

Ashlev was taken aback. My mother? What doe she have to do with anything? He hadn't spoken with her in more than twenty-five years. Smart kids like him were put in special schools when they celebrated their fifth birthday. He did remember that his only gift on that special day had been a neatly folded uniform for a boy soldier.

Before he could reply, a movie flashed on the screen behind the general, showing his mother. To his astonishment, she was in the company of other men—men he had never seen before. The decapitated man was part of the group! It looked like she was participating in a secret sect meeting that involved the use of capes, candles, and strange symbols on the wall.

"We have kept a close eye on your mother for some time now, Major. She belongs to an underground movement called the Clerks. I can see you are mystified by this revelation. The Clerks think they have access to administrative functions, and they work diligently to keep their DNA information out of our system. Of course, their efforts are wasted. We already have them. We have deployed a special branch to work at keeping them busy. You have been wired from the beginning as a precaution."

Ashlev didn't know what to think about this disclosure or what to fear more—the fact that the army suspected his mother of illegal activities and there could, therefore, be consequences to pay, or that his mother had kept him out of her activities by sending him to military school at the age of five. He was a trained soldier and had experienced many brutal situations, but now, with his mother involved, he felt a bone-chilling sense of panic. "What do you want from m-me?" he stammered.

The general stood tall and eyed him with dispassion. "We have investigated the grave atrocities committed by your mother and her band of cohorts and found them insupportable. We have already apprehended them. They will be hanged tomorrow at dawn." To ensure her words were having a maximum impact, she paused and lifted her chin, or what there was of one. "Except for your mother, that is. We are offering you a choice, Major. If you are willing to be the first one to try the new technology—to travel back in time and return with the two men, Bootsma and Burkowski—we will reconsider the trial of your mother. If not, well..." She shrugged.

Ashlev swallowed an unusual lump in his throat. Strange emotions had welled up in his body, and they bewildered him. What he was able to understand, though, without equivocation, was that he needed to do as ordered to save his mother's life. "Thank you, General. Yes, of course. I will consider it my duty to travel back in time and fulfill your request. I ask for permission to visit my mother for the last time."

"The last time? You *will* be coming back to us, won't you?" The general burst into an unnatural laughter.

Ashlev forced a smile. "Of course I will, but—"

"Visiting your mother is out of the question! You should be grateful we do not punish *you* because of your desultory actions, Major. Damaging state records is a crime. Your mother will be detained in the women's prison in Mongolia for one week."

"One week?"

"Yes, one week. In seven days, she will be hanged unless you are successful in your mission. Within that time frame, you must adapt our brain transportation to time travel. Since you will return to Beijing the same day as you leave, one week should be sufficient. Good luck. You will be escorted to your quarters and then shipped to our facilities in Beijing."

Ashley saluted and then followed the guards from the room. His mission could be treacherous. Failure was eminently possible. But for some reason, an undercurrent of excitement surmounted his fears.

Chapter 30

Between the present and 2115: GWUMC, Washington DC

Max had caught only a glimpse of his dad on the floor of hospital lab and couldn't tell if he was dead or alive. Only seconds after the officers rolled him into the fMRI machine, a huge lightning bolt or something like it had hit the building. His head had exploded. His always-present headache changed into a deep coldness that seeped into Max's body, starting in his neck and flowing through every nerve, right down to the bottom of his feet. Unexpectedly, everything had gone dark. It happened so quickly, but it hadn't hurt. In the total darkness, he had called out, "Dad! Dad? Are you all right?"

His dad hadn't answered. Did that mean he was dead? Where was he now?

He couldn't hear a single sound, but he felt a breeze on his skin. It felt like he was in the eye of a hurricane—not that he'd ever been in one, but he imagined it would be the same experience. If it weren't so scary, it would be awesome. No, he wasn't afraid, not really—only curious about what was happening to him.

He could walk around but didn't seem to move. It was as if he were at zero gravity.

After a while, his eyes adjusted to the total darkness. It was at that precise moment he saw he wasn't alone. Not far away from him, the silhouette of a man as round as a balloon was floating around, just like he was. He tried to yell at him, but no sound came from his mouth.

All at once, the man's eyes blinked. He could see him too! His mouth opened. He was trying to speak to him. Max tried to read his lips. He couldn't make out most of the words, but it looked something like "Are you okay?"

The fat man had a nice face and kind eyes. *Is that a priest's collar?* He nodded at Max.

No, he was not okay. The pain in his forehead was unbearable. He rubbed his temples. The fMRI had damaged his brain, he was sure of it. He had told his dad so many times that his Area 25 obsession would kill him one day. He couldn't even remember he had headaches before the fMRI experiments. Why did they put me in that fucking machine in the first place? The radiation inside was like a thousand hammers banging on his head. *Was Dad operating the machine, or did he try to stop them?* A shiver went through him. First, there was heat, and then the ice cold numbing of his body, as if it died off. He didn't remember he had the ice cold numbness in his dad's experiments. This was different. *But why is this feeling so familiar? What in the hell is happening to me?*

He looked around and thought that maybe he was on a truck or something, that the Navy man had taken him away. He saw no windows or a door. They were hostages, transported to a secret hiding place, and now he was stuck with the fat man.

Chapter 31

2115: Beijing

The sun was shining brightly over Beijing. As the train entered the City Dome, it struck Ashlev that the old city was uncannily well preserved—an almost lifelike artistic impression. Their final destination was announced: the headquarters of the Neurological Research Center in the former Beijing Ancient Observatory, at the No. 2 *Dongbiaobei Hutong*. The same voice mentioned that the Observatory was founded in the year 1442 by the Jesuit Ferdinand Verbiest, and it was as well preserved as other buildings. None of this mattered to Major Roto Ashlev as he was escorted to Beijing.

He hadn't slept or eaten for seventy-two hours. He had been transported in a metal, bullet-train type vehicle, formally considered a high-speed train, which was dedicated to transporting convicts and inmates. It presented a strong message that he was close to being incarcerated himself. The vehicle had no windows except for in the compartment where the pilot was seated. Inside the vehicle were steel chairs equipped with straps and head caps. The transport was dangerous and had already cost many their lives. He was glad he'd made it.

Upon arrival in Beijing, he had been taken directly to the headquarters of the Neurological Research Center. Though he had visited it many times in reality enhancers, the massive building impressed him even more in person.

He would never leave this building, he thought, except for a high-risk flight back in time. He peered at the rooftop to catch a glimpse of the brain transportation canon machinery that would propel him on his journey. It was only partly visible. The gate opened, and his escort released his handcuffs and then retreated. Another guard detail waited for him inside the building. The leader motioned for him to take an elevator at the end of the deserted reception area. A wireless sensor opened the door.

Ashlev counted the stories as they descended. By Level 10, he felt like he'd been buried alive, and they were still moving downward. He glanced at the nameplate of the leader, who was dressed in glossy white fatigues that fit like a wetsuit. "Where are we heading, Lieutenant Tong?" he asked.

Tong ignored him.

When they had reached the twentieth underground floor, Tong pushed a button, and the doors slid open. Ashlev could smell recycled air and rubbed his nose. His escort strode to the end of the corridor and stopped in front of a huge metal door that opened automatically onto an immense underground hall. On multiple platforms, white-coated military technicians were busily conducting tests of some kind on subjects strapped to beds. Although Ashlev had been responsible for coding the mind-merging operation and had participated in augmented reality sessions, the spectacle of it nevertheless impressed him.

Several test subjects moaned as he passed by them. Others lay perfectly still, and he wondered if they were already dead. It dawned on him that in seven days' time, he would be lying on one of those beds himself. Unexpectedly, the underground atmosphere, the muffled sounds, and the smell of torture made him feel nauseous.

An open office space had been erected in the middle of the test platforms, austere in appearance but clearly the operating theater of the commanding officer. Ashlev saw heavily armed special security forces standing guard at each of the four corners. Seated behind an anachronistic mahogany desk and dressed in fatigues, a man in his fifties was studying a report. He looked tired.

Ashlev's escort left him at the entrance to the office platform, guarded by a fifth sentry, who stepped forward to block his way.

"Let him come up," the commander ordered without lifting his eyes from his papers.

As Ashlev climbed the flight of stairs and entered the office, he noticed the total lack of noise. He was impressed. Somehow, the open area was protected by noise-suppressing technology.

"This report shows you have committed a couple of serious offences against army regulations, Major." The C.O. finally looked up. His black face was devoid of any emotion.

"I'm not sure I'm allowed to discuss it, sir."

"You were caught considering the destruction of state documents. Why weren't you detained...or worse?"

"I'm not sure I'm allowed to discuss why, sir," Ashlev repeated.

"Everything discussed in this area stays here. No sounds come in, no sounds go out. You can trust me."

Ashlev glanced at the sentries. Their motionless faces revealed nothing.

The colonel followed his eyes and chuckled. "See this?" He pointed at a button on his desk. "When I push this green button, their helmets go into mute mode. They don't hear a thing. No worries."

Ashlev digested this information. It was quite amazing. The colonel's office was an oasis of tranquility. Moreover, he didn't show any of the artificial limbs the general seemed to favor. Perhaps being transferred to Beijing was a good thing.

"At ease, Major, and have a seat." The colonel gestured toward a chair. "We have a great deal to discuss. Though we're in a hurry—a week, right?—you can spare a minute to brief me on exactly what you discovered and what your plans are."

Ashlev felt somewhat relieved over the officer's words. He sounded fairly reasonable. On the other hand, why should he trust him any more than he did others? He was, after all, part of the same regime. Any ranking officer from colonel up to the general, was bound to be heavily involved in every decision made by the New China Army. He preferred to remaining standing.

The officer chuckled. "I can understand why you are hesitating, Major. You're not sure what's to come and who to trust. Most people have no idea what to expect when they enter my world. Five miles below street level? Anyway, nobody can hear us here. There are no bugs and no videos or recordings. I'm your ally. Let's recap the situation you're in, okay?"

Ashlev nodded, glad he didn't have to do the talking. He was willing to see where the weird conversation ended up. He had no choice anyway.

"Oh, damn unfriendly of me. I didn't introduce myself properly. I am Colonel Tarunashijukila Malik, commander of the Test Unit of the Neurology Department. We don't have to be too formal here. Now, please have a seat." He nodded but didn't extend his hand.

Ashlev returned his nod and finally slid onto the designated chair, although he remained perched on its edge.

"After reading your file, it is my understanding that you discovered the mention of a new theory, one regarding the application of brain transportation to time travel. Is this correct?" At the same time he spoke, the video recording of Ashlev and the High Command was replayed on a built-in screen in the colonel's desk. "If used in a double-light helix, we could send the brainwaves back in time or into the future, as long as we obey the rules of the time-travel paradox. Am I right?"

"Yes, Colonel, but this theory is not based on any evidence."

"Right, and that's where you come in." Colonel Malik smiled. "We're going to build this double-helix and try it on you!"

"Affirmative, sir." Ashlev was surprised at how well he seemed to understand the details.

"You propose bringing in two men—an American scientist who invented time travel involving the speed of light and a Catholic Brother who knows more about the origin of our galaxy than we have accumulated ourselves. Right? And you are to be the part of the reconnaissance team...under one condition." He shook his head, as though amused.

Ashlev couldn't see the humor in the situation. His annoyance grew.

"Don't look at me that way," Malik said. "It's all here." He jabbed his finger on the desk screen. "Just watch!" He punched a red button on his desktop. The sentries immediately turned their backs to them, and in the blink of an eye, four walls emerged from nowhere, closing off the open office space. "The beauty is that from the outside, they still see us conversing around my desk, all motions being emulated as if real, but from now on, no one on this floor can see us. More importantly, the guards cannot see or hear us." He paused again, and his friendly face turned serious. "I don't want to reveal your emotions over the last piece of information I've been given."

Ashlev stopped breathing and waited.

"Your dossier says you have seven days to accomplish your mission and return with the two men in question in order to prevent your mother from being executed." Malik cleared his throat and gazed more intently at Ashlev.

"What are you saying? Has that agreement changed?"

Malik said nothing.

Ashlev slowly shook his head. Although he had not seen his parents since they had taken him to the barracks for boy soldiers outside Jerusalem, he had always hoped he would one day be able to show them his accomplishments.

Malik watched him silently.

"Wh-why are you telling me this?" Ashlev stammered.

"I'm telling you because I'm on your side, Major. I'm a Clerk."

"What?'

"And so are you, my friend—more or less."

"My mother—"

"You've been sent to Jerusalem on a mission. Your parents voluntarily ceded you. Don't believe the general! The Clerks are for real. We're about to strike back. You play a vital part."

Chapter 32

2115: Beijing

Ashlev found himself without words. A myriad of thoughts raced through his brain, and it was too much to absorb all at once.

"Events have happened as we expected," Malik said, leaning toward him over the desk.

"It was the only way. Your mother and several other colleagues volunteered to fake their discovery. She was very proud of you, Major. She hoped for the opportunity to tell you herself that you're one of us."

"A Clerk," Ashlev said, feeling his lip turn under in a sneer. "Did she volunteer to be hanged?"

"Well, in a way, yes. She and the others knew they would be executed after being exposed. Do you know the phrase 'the best lies are hidden behind veils of truth'?"

Ashlev nodded.

"As soon as we learned the general's investigators were on the brink of discovering our organization, we built a story and circumstances—whatever was necessary—to fool them."

"Are you saying there are really no Clerks and what you do is not true?"

"No, we Clerks exist, and what we do is true. We do stay out of the system and surrender only those elements we choose to submit. That's why the general showed you the film of the so-called 'secret' meeting with Clerks in capes in a ceremony with candles. We did those things maybe thousands of years ago, but not now."

"Thousands of years ago?"

"Yes, Major. We go back even further than that. That will be one of the goals of your mission—to learn more."

"My mission was planned by...by your people?"

"*My* people? We're all the same people, Major. Didn't you notice something about me when you entered my office?"

Ashlev narrowed his eyes. What was Malik talking about? He scanned his face more closely. Malik's face and hands were as dark as a Negro's, but his features were very Western.

"You're not East Asian."

"No, I'm not. We're both from the Indian subcontinent. Your parents are from New Delhi. Mine are from Chennai."

"New Delhi?"

"Yes, my friend. When you were five years old, your parents handed you over to the local military school just outside Delhi. You must have some remembrance of that."

"I remember saying goodbye to my father and mother and seeing them walk away while I kept the neatly packaged uniform tucked firmly under my arm as if it were my last lifeline. I thought they had taken me to Jerusalem."

"No, you were transferred to Delhi. They even gave you a new name. You think Roto Ashlev sounds Asian? It sounds Israeli, to blend more easily into the army. We carefully played out the scenario you brought to life, Major. We have called ourselves 'the Clerks' primarily because we have the strongest positions in the recording departments worldwide, like the Analogue Army Archives."

"My discovery is...what?"

"*Our* discovery. It has been there for many years. We have patiently waited for the right moment to take advantage of it."

"You knew...this...all along?"

Malik nodded. "Why do you think we have a unit investigating the possibilities of brain transport for space travel? We discovered the phenomenon a long time ago. We only had to wait until we had the right man—our own man—in the right spot. That man is you, Major."

Ashlev put up his hands as a barrier against any more information. "I cannot believe this!" he protested. "Please tell me none of this is true. Please tell me this is all one big mistake, a bad joke."

"I can't do that, Major. Welcome to the world of the Clerks. Nothing will be the same for you now. Never, ever has, to be honest."

A beeping sound emanated from Malik's desk. He quickly scanned his monitors. "We've got company. Please meet the other me. Stand up."

Ashlev hesitated.

"Stand up!" Malik ordered, his voice firm.

While Ashlev hurriedly rose from his chair to stand at attention, Malik pushed a couple of buttons. Immediately, the office walls disappeared.

"Guards!" Malik ordered.

Ashlev had almost forgotten their presence. They turned around, and two of them rushed forward to stand beside him. At the same time, a sentry and two officers approached Malik's quarters. It was the general. She had great difficulty keeping up the speed.

Malik walked around his desk and stood in front of Ashlev. He slapped him hard in the face. "How dare you question my judgment!" He turned to the general and saluted. "Welcome to my quarters, General. It is always a privilege to have you visit us in our Beijing facility. Forgive the disruption. I was reminding Major Ashley of his place and duty."

The general saluted and nodded, seemingly satisfied that he was fulfilling her orders.

Ashlev watched while standing ramrod straight.

Malik was ignoring him but appeared to be blocking the general's ability to move about the office space. "Do I have full clearance to begin a brain download of the major before we start with our experimentation?" he asked. "I would like to start with the procedure right away, but I need to move him to another platform first. Is there something in particular I can do for you? Are you visiting us for a specific reason?"

The general peered dispassionately at him. "While I appreciate your diligence, Colonel, there had been a change in plans."

"A change in plans?"

Ashlev heard the surprise in Malik's voice. After learning more of the Clerks' and Malik's role in the organization, he could sense his anxiety. He had encouraged the general to leave the facility. *Interesting.*

The general moved her half-robotic body forward several steps. "Yes, Colonel, a change that should not cause too much disruption of the process. We have selected two team members to join the major on his mission. They will be sent ahead of him to set up quarters and to ensure his mission will be successful. As soon as the major has finished his work on the brain travel data, you will meet them." She stared directly at Ashlev. "And, Major, that isn't the only change of plans. Pay close attention."

She pointed at Malik's desk and connected to the built-in screen. Immediately, a 3D video flashed into action at half-life scale. They all watched as a row of hooded men was escorted to a rotating carousel of ropes in a dimly lit room. The hangman snugged each noose, then pulled the lever, dropping the hatch. When the last man hung limply by his neck, the movie scanned to several security men dressed in ill-fitting capes surrounding an elderly woman. They urged her toward the last noose. She didn't resist and refused to be hooded. She looked directly into the camera, blinked, and tried to say something. Unfortunately, half-transparent squares had been applied to the video to block out lip reading.

Ashlev's stomach turned. Gritting his teeth to keep from crying out, he stared at the screen, determined not to react, no matter what happened.

With his mother's last blink, the noose was placed over her head and tightened around her neck. The charade of security men moved aside, one of them shouted the order, and abruptly, a hatch opened under her feet, causing the fatal fall that broke her neck.

"Unfortunately, Major, we couldn't wait to execute your bitch of a mother. It would send the wrong signal to these traitorous Clerks." The general terminated the video. "When you have finished honing the technology and have sent your two team members successfully back in time, we will receive a beacon from them with a code known only to us. You will follow them back in time and then send us Brother Bootsma and Professor Burkowski. Your team members will send you first and then follow suit. Only, in this case, you will not be executed yourself. Is that clear, Major? If you desert, we will find you... wherever, back in time, you try to hide."

Ashlev saluted again. "Yes, General. I will not disappoint you."

"You already did, Major. You attempted to steal state information. Surely you didn't expect to get away with it?"

The general was staring at him with a sickeningly triumphant glare. Ashlev didn't know how to react. He was trapped, and there was no way to escape.

Chapter 33

Between the present and 2115: Beijing

Frank noticed the boy at the same time the boy observed him. They were both floating in an undefined space at an incomprehensible speed. As well as he could in the half-darkness, he examined him to determine who or what he was. He looked to be about eighteen or twenty, he thought. Definitely an American, if those baggy trousers were any indication. And he didn't look afraid. He maneuvered himself closer to Max and extended a hand. "Hi. I'm Frank Bootsma."

Max stared at him as if he had seen a ghost. Frank could imagine him thinking *weird guy*. He was dressed in the same clothes he'd worn to the ASV in Rome, but his priest's board must be confusing.

"I'm Max," he said, reluctantly shaking his hand.

"Hi, Max. When did you land... up here?" Frank wished he could be more specific.

Max shrugged. "Difficult to say, Frank. It feels like a long time, but it can't be so long."

Teens these days were so quick to use first names, Frank thought. "Why's that?"

"I just checked my cell phone. The clock isn't running for some reason, but the battery is half full. It was fully loaded when I left home. So, according to my experience, I guess I've been here for three, maybe four hours."

Frank glanced at him with new appreciation, assuming he might prove useful. He seemed to possess the typical savvy of most kids of his generation. Maybe he could explain what was happening with his clothes. Both his own and those Max was wearing were flickering—like they were there but not there. When he thought about it, he didn't really feel his clothes. It was like he was naked. That was definitely not a good thing in the presence of this young man. "Max," he said, "I'm experiencing this strange sensation about my clothes. It's difficult to describe. I see them, but I don't feel them. Do you have the same sensation?"

Max thought for a moment and nodded. "Yeah, I know what you mean. I thought it was because of the speed we're moving. Same thing happened with my cell phone. First, I didn't have it, but when I thought about it real hard, it was back in my pocket. Maybe if you think about wearing your clothes, that sensation of not having any will go away."

Frank shook his head. None of this made sense. Neither he nor Max was dead. They could communicate. They had maintained their same earthly bodies and appearance. They were in some sort of ante-room, somewhere in between—somewhere. *Could he have a last chance as well?* "Max," he said, "what are the last moments you remember before you arrived here?"

"I was taken to my father's laboratory by two men. They strapped me to the examining table, shoved me into the fMRI machine, and turned it on. It started humming and then got so painful that I sort of lost consciousness I guess. A few seconds later, I was here, you know?"

Frank nodded. He knew all too well. "I know. Same thing happened to me." This was no dream, no fantasy. Maybe they *were* dead. Maybe they had both been killed and were on their way to heaven. Maybe it was no second chance. Maybe this *was* the gate to heaven… *or hell.* With that thought, Frank was suddenly not so sure of his Judgment Day. How would God judge his conversion to Catholicism?

Cold sweat dripped down his neck and back. *Forget about yourself. Help the boy. Give him hope.* "I was there, too, Max. They did the same thing to me. I have reason to believe we barely survived their experiments. However, I think we're somewhere on the way back to Earth. I think we're in a state of collective unconsciousness."

Frank decided not to share his darker thoughts with Max. How could he possibly prepare him for what was about to follow? Nothing in his studies had taught him what to do.

Max peered at him as though he were crazy. "I thought whatever those guys did was pretty scary, but when it was over, it felt like I was riding a rollercoaster. Why are you so sure we're returning from the dead? Is it because of your age?"

"What do you mean?"

"Old people always think about death and dying, don't they?"

"Old people? How old do you think I am?"

Max shrugged. "Sixty?"

Frank laughed. "No way! I'm thirty-seven…and I'm not constantly thinking about death."

"Okay, so you're not old, but we're still stuck here. Got any idea on how we can get out of this place? See any windows or doors?"

Frank had to laugh again. Max was not only smart, he was naturally funny. "Unfortunately, I don't, mainly because I don't have a clue why we're in this fix in the first place. But let's get back to what you said about your phone. It wasn't there at first, and when you thought really hard about it, it returned?"

"Yep."

Frank stroked his beard. "Let's think about that. We were both pushed into that fMRI machine in your father's hospital lab. He wasn't there, so someone else operated it."

"My dad was lying on the floor. I saw him," Max interrupted.

"On the floor? Was he…?"

"Don't know. It all happened so fast."

"Okay. Let's not worry about him. They needed him." Frank stole a glance at him, and Max slowly nodded. Thank God he seemed to agree to it. "Help me think, Max. We must be missing a clue. Who took you to the lab and how?"

"Two U.S. Navy men picked me up at school, and then there was a third one." Max stopped and brushed the back of his hand across his eyes.

Navy men? Frank thought. Did they have some relationship to the officer who had interrogated him at the Vatican Embassy? Captain John Pakula was his name. Thinking about him again brought back memories of the man's strange, rather mechanistic movements. About to mention it to Max, he saw tears well up in the boy's eyes, and his mouth began to tremble. *Oh God!* Max had obviously experienced something far worse than he had. He touched his shoulder. "What happened to you, Max?"

"It's not important now. Can't do anything about it anyway. I … I don't really want to think about it again." He pinched his eyes until his face was all wrinkled up. Then, a ragged sigh erupted into a sob. "My… my mother. She was in the trunk of their car. They… oh God, they killed her." Max sank into a sitting position and hugged his knees. "I'm sorry. It must be this killing headache making me crying like a child. I'm not so close to my mom, but still."

Frank sat next to him and placed an arm around his shoulders. He waited until Max's shaking sobs had eased. "If you feel you can talk about it, we may be able to get some important information from why and how it happened."

Max nodded and finally wiped the tears from his cheeks with his fingers. "They stopped the car, and the mean one dragged me back to the truck and made me look at Mom." He sniffed and wiped his nose on his shirt sleeve. "While I was stuck in the back seat of their car, they were outside arguing with each other. It was really weird, you know?"

"Weird how?"

"Well, the officer, Captain John Pakula—"

"John Pakula? That's the one!" Frank interrupted. Pieces of the puzzle came together.

"Yeah. He tried to be nice to me. He told me my dad was going to be famous because of some article he wrote or was going to write. It was all about a footnote, but I'm not sure exactly about the rest."

"Let me think about it for a minute." Frank remembered that Pakula had been close to learning about his discovery of the secret buried in the Galileo trial papers, but he was, in actuality, still ignorant of it. He hadn't known what it was all about. *This footnote could be the key.* "Tell me, Max, was your dad a research doctor? If so, do you know what he was doing in his laboratory and what his article was about?"

"Well, we didn't really discuss stuff like that—not in detail anyway. We sort of left each other alone, but I know Dad always wanted to build a time machine. He told me once he thought he could reengineer the fMRI machine to make that happen by manipulating brain Areas 25 and 27, the core for our thinking processes. He said his colleagues didn't believe him. I didn't either, to be honest. He even tested it on me, claiming he could cure my constant headaches, but I think he caused them. I always thought my parents got divorced because of his stupid plans, but that article... well, that major sounded like maybe it had worked. I don't know. It's probably all a bunch of crap. Those so-called military guys are probably just in it for the money. It's just bad luck they believe my dad actually invented something. We only happened to get in the way."

Frank thought about Max's words and felt a flutter of excitement. Max was wrong to dismiss his father's work so easily. They were part of a plan—a malicious plan. "I don't think this Pakula was making things up, Max, and I don't believe those men were fakes. This is government business, maybe Homeland Security. He knew what he was talking about, but he was missing several vital pieces of information. They're after something your father and I know. I have a wild guess what they want from me, but what they want from you, I really can't imagine. It must be related to your father's work. Most likely, it is about his time machine. Was he working on it alone, or did he work with a team?" Frank hadn't watched Max while he thought out loud. When he looked sideways, he suddenly noticed Max's attitude had totally changed. He had shifted sideways, and terror was on his face. "Did I say something wrong?"

Max just stared at him with those same eyes, as if he saw a ghost in front of him. "You're one of them!" he sputtered. "You want to get to my dad! First, I thought you were a victim like me, but now I see you're trying to take me in."

"What are you talking about, son?" Frank cried out.

"I'm not your son! Watch your mouth. You're as much a priest as those other guys were Navy."

Frank just stared at Max, baffled.

"Guards, take him out of my cell!" Max started yelling. "Guards!"

Chapter 34

2115: Beijing

The minute the general was escorted to the exit, Malik ordered his sentries to resume their positions at the corners of his platform. He motioned for Ashlev to be seated again and quickly hit the two buttons that would ensure they were alone. "I'm so sorry, Major," he said. "I tried to prepare you for what I knew would be a horrifying experience. The general arrived sooner than I anticipated. Please understand that I didn't know they had deliberately tried to dishonor your mother and you," he said.

Ashlev slumped onto his chair, clearly bone tired and very confused. "Where was my father?" he asked, sitting bolt upright as the thought came to him.

Malik grimaced. "Unfortunately, he was killed when they came to arrest your mother. At that time, none of us believed the incident would take place. As you saw, that scenario didn't work out."

"I have to get that time-travel technology and go back to prevent it. It's the last thing I can do for my parents," Ashlev murmured.

Malik waited without comment. He knew Ashlev was wrong, but he didn't want to argue with him in his present mood. "I understand where you're coming from. So does the general. What you are suggesting is exactly what she wants you to do. However, there is a complication."

Ashlev looked at him questioningly.

"First, we don't know when they executed your mother. They deliberately kept that a secret, so we have no idea when or where we should attack. Your mother and the others were kept in quarantine for many years, and they rotated their imprisonment for security reasons. For that reason, you would have to come back way before she was put in prison."

"I thought you Clerks knew so much!" Ashlev snapped.

"We do. As you know, one of the time-travel constraints is that you cannot change the present. You're here. Your presence here is a result of existing plans. And you know what? These plans originate at a time… oh, how can I explain this to you?" Malik sighed. This was the most difficult task given to him. Would Ashlev comprehend and see his mission did not include getting back to save his parents, at least for starters? "Major, it's time for you to know the truth about yourself."

While Ashlev pondered that statement, Malik took a marble-white, neatly pressed handkerchief from his pocket and spread it over his desk monitor. He pushed it forward, making sure it adhered to the screen. "Watch this. It's clean, by the way," he joked and calibrated the built-in light sensor. "It's an innovation of mine. I've woven nano-parts into the fibers of the cloth that turn black whenever light hits it and it is interrupted at the right interval." Malik checked to ensure he had Ashlev's full attention. "The interruption has to be accurate within 1.3 nanoseconds. It works as a decipher key. The interruption is invisible to the eye, but the effect is magnificent. Look!" As he spoke, he pointed toward a square on the linen that was intersected by diagonal lines. One by one, strange symbols filled the triangular spaces. "You asked whether we know much, Major. The answer is yes. Do you recognize this?"

Ashlev gazed at the handkerchief. "No, of course not," he replied, annoyed.

"Thought so. In a way, that's good news. This is what we call your *rashichakra*, or, for short, your *rashi*. It means your birth horoscope."

"Horoscope? I thought we abandoned that nonsense a long time ago."

"Western science did a long, long time ago, and our regime followed suit, mainly because the New Chinese Authority never understood it at a level comparable to your caste."

"My caste? What are you talking about?"

"Your mother and father were remarkably courageous people. They lived in the capital of India, New Delhi. Nobody calls it India anymore, of course. When you were born, your father made a birth chart, which was common for the Brahmins. You know who Brahmins are?"

Ashlev shook his head.

"Your parents were Brahmins. They are the highest caste in India and are well known for their capacity to predict the future based on Jyotish astrology. They went off the radar when India was occupied by the Chinese. The Brahmins were at the top of the list to be persecuted. You know why? They make birth charts based on stellar constellations and are highly trained to make extremely accurate forecasts on what will happen in an individual's life or in a group or a nation. They even predict things like political events." Malik stroked the handkerchief. His forefinger followed the lines. "This is your *rashi*. The Chinese regime didn't like any of this. Jyotish or Vedic astrology was a science in India before it became illegal and was banned from universities. The Brahmins took it underground. In the West, astrology had vanished as a science somewhere in the middle of the former millennium because mainstream religious belief at that moment put it on the index."

"Are you saying you believe this crap, Colonel? I mean, this prediction stuff and all?"

There was a slight hesitation in Ashlev's voice. He didn't sound so sure anymore. His eyes drifted between the handkerchief and Malik. "Can you *prove* it?" he asked.

"Yes, Major, and I'm glad you asked. Please pay close attention. This is becoming very personal for you. What your parents read in your birth chart was electrifying to them, like being struck by lightning, in a manner of speaking. You were *the chosen one*." He emphasized the importance of those words. "It was made clear in your *rashi*. Here! Your parents had to give you away at the age of five, exactly on your birthday. Moreover, their own birth charts had predicted the same event for their only born child... *you!*"

Now, Ashlev fell silent.

Malik leaned forward. "For security reasons, I can't show you any calculations on screen, Major. I can't be 100 percent sure how these systems are connected or bugged, but I will tell you the highlights of your natal chart. A natal chart is built around twelve houses, or aspects of your life. These are your birth, your parents, your work, wealth, health, and so on, and, finally, your death. The way planets move around your houses indicates—*predicts*—what will happen. You see that little sun sign in your ninth house? It is the house of Fate and Fortune. It also predicts pilgrimages. The sun is ruling this house. Its power is at its peak for two weeks, ending in exactly seven days. Remember the significance of the seven days?"

Ashlev nodded.

"It's all here, Major. Your entire training has been dedicated to this one mission. You know one of the most fascinating characteristics of the sun? It has been a source of inspiration for billions of people. It symbolizes birth, death, and resurrection. Your demise into an uncertain past is certainly fitting. You, of all people, know that your body doesn't survive brain transportation and certainly doesn't survive going back in time. We haven't yet grasped the effect of forces on the body, but we can safely assume you will notice it while you are being departed."

Malik watched Ashlev closely as he thought about the process that would kill him to enable him to travel back in time.

"Is there anything else I should know?" Ashlev asked, his voice subdued.

Malik nodded. "Several things. I would like to make a deal with you. Since you're expected for some years, I've made a few preparations already. I don't think we need seven working days to set everything up. It's more likely we'll need only half of it. During the other half, I'll guide you into the Vedic system, but only if you're willing to dive into it and have an honest interest in your karma—your true mission."

Ashley nodded reluctantly. "So I do have to believe all this."

"Belief is central to karma. The moment you accept its power, the stars will shine on you."

"Why is it that I don't believe?"

Malik smiled. "Well, because you're not ready, of course."

Chapter 35

Friday: DuPont, Washington DC

Commander Gomez had filled out the paperwork that allowed Ellen to drive Jacob to his home. It was after midnight when they finally left the precinct. They stopped around the corner. Jacob took his cell phone and put it on speaker before dialing his voicemail number. They both listened intently.

"Hi, Dad. It's me. I haven't much time left, but I think you should know, Mom…" Max's voice cracked and changed into sobs. "I can't do this. Sorry, Dad." *Click.*

Jacob stared in disbelief at the phone. He redialed and listened to the same message over again. He was on the brink of bursting into tears. Desperately, he gestured at Ellen. "Now what?"

Ellen hesitated for a second. This was a major setback. She had hopes for some clue, but there weren't any. "Dr. Burkowski, call your ex-wife. Maybe she knows something. I don't think we should stick around here too long."

While Ellen drove, Jacob tried all numbers he had: her cell, her work, her apartment, and even the emergency number of her agency, to no avail.

Luckily, traffic was almost nonexistent, and in less than thirty minutes, Ellen was pulling her Chevy Camaro into the driveway of his house. *Where did he get the money to buy such a beautiful nineteenth-century mansion?* she wondered. *Weren't academic physicians underpaid?*

"I need to get my Volvo from the hospital parking lot. We need to go to her apartment," Jacob said.

"No rush. Your car isn't going anywhere, and neither are you. You need some sleep first. Before you do that, however, I'd like to discuss our options."

"Options? I don't have any options."

"There are always options for any situation, Dr. Burkowski. May I have your house key? I want to take a look around before you leave the car." With key in hand, she strode directly to the front entrance of the house. She examined the lock and the area around the door itself. Everything seemed all right, but she decided to exercise caution. "Is there a back door?" she called out to Jacob.

Jacob opened the window and pointed to the right of the house.

She wound her way around a few bushes and headed toward the back of the house with her gun drawn. The door that led into the kitchen was locked. She peered through the window next to it and saw no lights or signs of any movement. She returned to the front of the house and opened the door. She entered quickly, gun drawn. For the next five minutes, she searched all the rooms, both upstairs and downstairs. Everything seemed in place, probably just as Jacob and his son had left it that morning. She put the gun away, switched on a couple of ceiling lights and the outside light, and then motioned for Jacob to come inside. "Why don't you get comfortable on the couch in your living room while I make us something to eat," she said. "I don't know about you, but I'm ravenous."

She watched Jacob lay down on the couch. He must be an emotional wreck, she thought. She was more than a little distressed herself. Peering into the refrigerator, she didn't find much of anything appropriate for a middle-of-the-night meal except eggs. She decided to make an omelet filled with the chopped green onions and tomatoes she found in the crisper.

Minutes later, she returned to the living room, where she found Jacob wide awake, peering up at the ceiling. "Would you like to eat in here or at the table?" she asked. "I made us omelets."

"At the table please." Jacob rose from the couch and followed her. "I have to confess, I'm a bit uncomfortable with this situation," he said. "You're the first woman in the house since my divorce. It all seems a little weird, especially under the circumstances."

Ellen removed the blue apron she'd found hanging on a hook in the kitchen. "Think of me as a Navy officer from the USNO, if that helps. We've both undergone an atrocious experience involving the same people over the past twenty-four hours. We're compatriots." She pointed at the chairs around the dining room table. "Why don't you sit? I'll get our plates and silverware. What would you like to drink?"

"Water is fine, but if you can manage to make a pot of coffee, I'd love some. I need to sharpen my thinking if we're going to discuss those options you talked about."

"I already found the coffee pot, and our caffeine fix is brewing as we speak." Ellen returned to the kitchen and found plates in the cupboard next to the sink and silverware in a drawer under it. She stepped to the stove and scooped an omelet from the skillet onto each plate and grabbed bread from the toaster for each of them. Carrying the plates into the dining room, she placed one in front of Jacob and the other across the table from him. "Go ahead and begin while it's hot. I'll get us coffee. Do you take cream or sugar?"

"Neither—just black. I apologize for not getting up to help you. I'm just—"

"No problem. It feels good to do something normal." When she returned with two steaming cups, Jacob eyed her apologetically again.

"I'm sorry the kitchen is such a mess. When Max and I cook, it tends to look like a battlefield, and it can stay that way for days. We run a typical father-son household,

I'm afraid. We don't mind a little mess. Max would..." Thoughts of his missing and possibly dead son caused the words to catch in his throat. "Never mind."

Ellen reached out and touched his hand. "I don't have any children, so I won't say I understand what you're going through. Just know I'm here to help." As she sipped from the rim of her coffee cup, she noticed him picking mindlessly at the food she had prepared. "The omelet is really pretty good, Doctor. Even if you think you're not hungry, it's probably a good idea to eat it. You'll need your strength over the next few days."

"I'm sorry," he said.

"You have nothing to be sorry about—not where I am concerned."

Jacob took a first bite. "Nice," he said and ate several more forkfuls.

Ellen allowed the silence to stretch while they both focused on their late-night meal. Her mind was racing with questions, but she had learned in her career that listening and waiting were as important as talking. Finally, she couldn't wait any longer and blurted out, "Dr. Burkowski, I need to understand something that has me very confused. Why were those men calling you 'Professor' if you are not one? Where would they have gotten the wrong impression? Is there a reasonable explanation for it?"

Jacob shrugged and put down his fork. "Maybe they were confused by the medical doctor title on the name badge I wear."

Ellen chewed on the inside of her cheek. "Hmm. I don't think so, Dr. Burkowski."

"Please, call me Jacob. We're sitting at the table in my house sharing a great omelet, having coffee in the wee hours. We shouldn't stand on formalities."

"Ellen. Nice to meet you," she said. "I think those men got the wrong information somewhere, and we need to find out where so we can—" She was interrupted by the sound of a phone ringing in the hall. Jacob started to rise, but Ellen motioned for him to stay put. "No, let me get it for you." She returned a couple of minutes later and placed her hand on Jacob's shoulder. "I-I had hoped we would have time for a meal and conversation," she said. "I-I'm so sorry."

"Who was it?" The fear in his eyes couldn't be mistaken for anything else.

"Gomez. They investigated the car those two so-called officers used for abducting Max. Forensics has discovered the..." She pulled her chair closer to his and peered directly at him. "They discovered the body of your ex-wife, Jacob. She was murdered and stuffed into the vehicle trunk. It was locked. It probably happened earlier yesterday, before they kidnapped Max from school. Gomez said it isn't necessary for you to go to the morgue to identify her. She had her ID on her. They have obtained several fingerprints on her body, most likely those of the fake Navy men. I'm so sorry."

Chapter 36

2115: Beijing

"Major Ashlev, please pay close attention," Malik said while pointing to the desk screen. Within seconds, a 3D scale model of Washington DC appeared. It grew larger in size until the suburbs of the city came into view. "We don't know anything about these two companions the general is sending ahead of you to Washington, but we will deal with them later. Right now, we have to focus on what we will show the general. That won't be a problem."

Ashlev watched the screen with increasing interest. He felt calmer as he listened.

"You will be sent to this building." Malik pointed at an asymmetrical building centered in a park on the outskirts of Washington. "This is the HQ of the USNO, short for United States Naval Observatory. Behind this window, Superintendent John Pakula clocks in every morning at precisely seven a.m. He sits there for thirty minutes preparing his briefings for staff meetings. He will be your target." A photo of Pakula emerged in a pop-up window, along with a brief biography.

Ashlev frowned.

"You may not like this part of your mission, Major, but you will have to kill him."

"What makes you think I wouldn't like it?"

"Because you are the son of a Brahmin. That makes you very different from the rest of us."

"I've killed many men in the past."

Malik pursed his lips. "That practice is going to stop, but we'll talk about it later."

"Having to kill another man doesn't bother me," Ashlev said, "but his guy's obviously not just Mr. Nobody. Why did you select him? Chances are fairly high that changing *his* future has an immediate effect on *our* future. Did you calculate for that possibility?"

"Yes, we did, and nothing popped up. He seems to have been assigned to the USNO without any consequences. He retired within two years, and his civilian life has left no digital trail. It's safe to say he's the right man in the right spot. If we're to get Burkowski's time-travel technology and have you come back, this Pakula is the only opportunity you'll have for that. He's your meal ticket."

Ashlev inched forward on his chair. "Okay, got it. Let's go for him. No objections." Now that their discussion had advanced to military preparation, he felt more comfortable. "I understand the target, but maybe you should explain more about why this USNO place is so vital to us."

"Next to HQ, that unimpressive, smallish, gray building holds one of the most important instruments of their time—the Atomic Clock. Any idea what that means?"

Ashlev shrugged. "Can't say I have."

"At that time, all GPS systems, including military ones, depended on it. There were some mirror sites around the Western world, but this was the mother of all clocks."

"This Atomic Clock was their only source of high-precision time?"

"Right. There was no other way for anyone to calculate time. Don't forget that quantum mechanics was still in its infancy."

Ashlev grinned. "Wow. Prehistoric."

"I see you got it. If we want to come back, we desperately need this one in order to be sure we end up here in our time. Even with this technology, any travel back is bound to have a margin of give or take two inches."

"I'd better sit still if I'm flying back home," Ashlev said in an attempt at humor.

Malik didn't respond. "Two warrant officers are sitting tight in that room 24/7. The room has barely enough space for their desk and chairs. We've calculated their position here. This will be no problem for us. We'll enter their bodies at their front lobe, right section." He touched the right part of his forehead.

Ashlev nodded. "The best place to invade the brain."

Malik pointed to an insert on the screen showing the room and an animation of the two officers on duty. Crosshairs highlighted the position on their skulls. "We intend to send your two friends to these guys. It will be your call to convince the general of it. The same goes for this Superintendent Pakula at the USNO. It all boils down to preparation, Major. Are you ready?"

"Ready for what?'

"To give it a try."

"To give what a try?"

"Yes or no, Major?"

"Well, yes, but what does it mean?"

"Put the goggles on. Then go stand on that red square." He pointed to the corner of the office space.

Curious, Ashlev followed his instructions. The red area was a little over three square meters. Before he donned the goggles, he took a closer look at the floor. The tiniest of particles were slowly rolling. He could walk in any direction and not move out of the red square.

"Put on those goggles, Major! We have no time to waste."

Ashlev did as he was told and found the result staggering. The goggles were really an electromagnetic strap that connected to his brain. He felt a warm tickling inside his skull—not unpleasant, but unusual. "Is this normal, this feeling inside my head?" he asked, a bit apprehensive.

Malik laughed. "It's normal for what it is. You'll get used to it. Wait until I send some signals through our piece. Don't jump or attempt to resist. Try to absorb the input."

"Okay," Ashlev said, even more uneasy.

He watched as Malik input instructions on his machine. Inside the transparent scale model drifting above the desk, he saw a figure of himself emerge and stand near the access gate of USNO headquarters.

"You see something?" Malik asked.

Ashlev shook his head. "Not yet." Then, rather abruptly, he cried out.

"What's wrong? Does it hurt?" Malik asked.

"No, but I can't absorb what's happening. It's so overwhelming. I'm standing right in front of that building. I'm there! I even hear the birds and smell the mowed grass. Did you transport me already?" He reached for the goggles.

"Don't touch the goggles, Major! You're still here with me in my office. If you remove the goggles, your brain could suffer an injury. We've had a couple bad incidents when test subjects did that."

"Okay. I understand, but... whoa, this is awesome. Have you ever tried this yourself?"

"Thought you'd never ask," Malik said. "I've been everywhere you are now. I researched all the information and composed the scenery for you. My educated guess is it will be 95 percent accurate. Okay, let's get moving. Open the door and turn right. What do you see?"

Ashlev followed his instructions and entered the building. "I see a wide corridor with dark wood. I'm halfway down the corridor now. I see the nameplate of ..." He stopped talking and peeked inside the office of Superintendent Pakula. The man he'd seen in the picture was seated behind his desk, perusing files. For a moment, he wondered if his approach had been overheard. *Of course not,* he reminded himself. He entered the office and stood directly behind the officer, who was reading intelligence reports.

Ashlev scanned the room with increased interest. Certain museum pieces, like the wooden globe, attracted his attention. The voice-over of Malik reminded him he was on a test mission.

"Major, memorize everything you see in the room, because you will *be* Pakula when you're finished with him. Then, leave his office, reenter the corridor, and take a right turn."

Ashlev followed Malik's instructions and saw a light coming from behind the door of another office. The nameplate on this door said DEPUTY SUPERINTENDENT ELLEN MEYER. When he opened this door, she was, at first, reading her files. She looked up just then and peered directly at him. He liked her face and expression—so natural. Of course she didn't see him.

He retraced his steps and left the building. Once outside again, he could immediately smell the freshly cut lawns around the buildings. The sound of birds caught his attention, and at the same time, he felt a light breeze. Gazing down the hill from where he was standing, he saw the gray-white building Malik had shown him on his screen. The door was open. "Are those doors never locked?" he asked Malik.

"No, they aren't," Malik said. "Once you've been admitted to the grounds, you're considered safe. You'll find few locked doors. The buildings were constructed right after the Second World War and haven't been changed since then. On the right, you'll see a door with a sign reading ATOMIC CLOCK."

"I see it."

"Go inside."

Ashlev entered the room and found the two officers he'd seen on Malik's screen. They were seated in front of their monitors, which were wired to a remarkably small machine—the Atomic Clock.

"This Atomic Clock is kept offline, Major, which means it's not on the World Wide Web. It's only connected to the backbone of the U.S. Navy and rerouted to other services. No one can access it from the outside. If you want to gain access from the outside, this is the place to make that happen. This will be part of your mission."

"Got it."

"When I say 'now', you can remove your goggles. We have to move to another place. I will need to switch off the USNO model."

"Roger."

"Now."

Ashlev removed his head gear. At the same time, the particles in the floor stopped moving. He felt a bit dizzy. Once more facing Colonel Malik, he couldn't help grinning. "That was pretty impressive, Colonel."

"Thank you, Major. We worked on the procedure for several years after the volunteers turned themselves in. This is one of the best-kept secrets."

When Ashlev heard the word "volunteers," he grimaced and fell silent.

"Sorry," Malik said. "Let's move on. Good to see you appreciate our work. Now, I want you to see another location."

Ashlev was about to say something, but instead, he slowly donned the goggles again.

"You're seeing the entrance to the George Washington University Medical Center, Major. As you enter and walk toward Burkowski's office, you'll notice a map of the building on your right. Study it carefully and memorize the layout of the facility. You'll need to know it well. We believe this is the location where Burkowski conducted the first time-travel experiments with an early-stage fMRI scan. It's pretty amazing that he was able to accomplished what he did with such limited technology as compared to our more sophisticated tools and knowledge."

"He didn't though. Otherwise, we'd be able to go back to his time. Time-travel logic," Ashlev said dryly.

"Okay, here we go again. Make sure you walk straight to the experimentation room. It is important to minimize your movements to—"

"...to avoid any contra effects," Ashlev said, indicating he knew the routine.

"Yes, though we have no idea what will happen if you 'step on your own trail', in a manner of speaking. We have no scientific proof whether or not it is impossible to change your present. Only logic prohibits it."

Ashlev demonstrated his ability to move around with ease in strange environment. Again, he was surprised about the immersive experience. The hospital odor was penetrating. "Seen everything here," he said. "What do we do now?"

"Sixty seconds from the hospital entrance to Burkowski's fMRI laboratory. Not bad. I'm going to switch off the hospital model now. Okay, you can remove the goggles, Major, and I'll show you the key prize of your mission."

As soon as Ashlev removed the goggles, the *mis en scene* changed. Washington vanished, and Rome emerged, scene by scene in its historic glory: the Roman Empire, its decline, the steady rise of the Vatican City at the center, the key-shaped Vatican Square, St. Peter's Basilica, the Vatican walls, and all the buildings within its confines.

"This is the location of your most important target, Major. Not a man, but papers—lots of papers. And, most importantly, lots of analogue information—never digitized, never recorded."

Malik pointed at a nondescript building nestled in the eastern part of the Vatican walls. "It's the Secret Archives of the Vatican. If they had taken the time to digitize all the information, we wouldn't have to send you over there. Luckily for us, this Jesuit priest, Frank Bootsma, did some groundwork, but he didn't share it all with us. He recorded certain parts of his work in a personal folder on the Vatican mainframe. We have a copy of it, fully operational until Rome was nuked at the end of the twenty-first century. Nothing remained of one of the most important cradles of Western civilization."

"Do I have to put on the goggles again?"

"No, Major. It's time for me to give you a short introduction on why you must get hold of this Frank Bootsma and send him to us."

Chapter 37

Between the present and 2115: Beijing

No guard showed up to rescue Max from the fat man. Max tried all walls to see if there was an opening. All the time the fat man, this fake priest, sat quietly, just watching him. He hadn't said a word since he had been exposed. It was so weird. First, this dupe had asked for him, and now he was stuck with him. The frightening part was that his dupe had been working with these guys all the time, yet he had not noticed a difference. It was all one big setup. He had to get more information out of him. "What is it you do for a living, Frank? As a priest, I mean," he tried.

"Do you think I'm a priest because of this?" Frank touched his white collar. "No, I'm not a priest. I'm a brother. You might not know the difference," he replied calmly.

Max shrugged. It didn't make any difference to him, as he thought it was all just a costume anyway.

"I'm a Jesuit," Frank continued. "That means I joined the Society of Jesus, a Catholic religious order. We are also called the Soldiers of Christ because our founder, Saint Ignatius of Loyola, was a knight. Broadly speaking, there are two kinds of membership—priests and brothers. If you're a priest, you can't marry a woman. If you're a brother, you can. However, I voluntarily choose not to marry."

"And?"

"Anyway, I am a brother, but what's more important right now is that I'm an astronomer. You know what that is?"

"I'm a freshman in artificial intelligence, if that means anything to you," he snarled at Frank. *What an idiot.*

"Good to know. My job is to collect meteorites for the Vatican. I do a lot of research on them to learn what happened right after the Big Bang. Are you interested?"

Yeah, of course. NOT!

"I've found evidence that some of the oldest meteorites contain a structure that resembles the composition of the universe right after the Big Bang. If you could shrink yourself to atomic proportions and fly around inside one of those meteorites, you would experience Early Galactic time. See what I mean?"

Max nodded, but he couldn't see any connection between his dad and this weirdo. This man had a lousy alibi. He had to come up with something more substantial. "And this is what those Navy types wanted you for?" Max questioned sarcastically.

"Well, yes, for some reason they do, my friend. And for another reason, they want your father and maybe you as well. So please fill in the dots yourself, because I cannot see any," Frank suddenly bellowed.

Now, it got interesting. The more adults showed their emotion, the more they revealed their true intentions. "Okay. For some reason, you thought it necessary to ask if my father was working alone or if he was part of a team," Max echoed, mimicking Frank's dark voice.

"And that's why you suddenly treat me as an enemy?"

"Give me one reason I should trust you. A self-proclaimed Vatican astronomer on the hit list of the some Navy-dressed assassins? Does this sound very likely to you?" When Frank said nothing to defend himself, Max continued. "My dad is wanted because he invented something. Okay. Could be. Not very likely, but it could be. But what about you? What if the Vatican is interested in my father as well, and you're sort of a double agent, prepared to join me on this mortal trip and get the information out of me that is so desperately wanted by the Vatican. What if the Vatican wants to get their hands on my dad's time machine as well?" He was admittedly exaggerating a little, making a Hollywood-worthy conspiracy out of the whole thing, and he had to grin.

But judging by Frank's face, he had just delivered a massive blow. The man gasped.

Max was about to say some more when he sensed a change of atmosphere, simultaneous with a huge pressure in his head. This was not a mere headache. This was something else.

"There's something going on, Max. I think we're slowing down."

Their conversation had to wait, but Max knew he was on the right track.

The color of the walls and their transparency grew softer, and the speed of their spinning was indeed slowing. All at once, they were grabbed by some invisible force that pulled them both to their feet and kept them upright next to each other.

Jesus! Dad's fMRI was small fry. His whole body started pulsing. "Frank? Did you feel—"

"Yes, Max, I feel the same thing."

Abruptly, he was no longer a cool wise guy firing difficult questions at Frank. He was on the verge of panic. "Frank!"

"I wish I could hold you right now, son, but I can't move."

"It really hurts, Frank."

"Me too. Hold on, Max. I'm right here next to you."

In the next instant, a light explosion wiped them both away.

Chapter 38

Friday: DuPont Circle, Washington DC

Jacob had finished dinner without uttering a single word about Hannah's murder. Ellen finally convinced him to rest on the sofa again while she cleaned up. When she returned to the living room, she found him sound asleep. She settled into an easy chair nearby and gazed at him with growing concern.

Sleep was a healer of all sorts of things, but not something as tragic as losing a son and an ex-wife to murder. She wondered what she could do once he awakened? They hadn't made any plans, and they hadn't discussed their options. Returning to her apartment and to the office at the USNO didn't appeal to her. For some reason, she felt inclined to stay exactly where she was. If he woke up, it shouldn't be to an empty house. Besides, she rationalized, it wasn't just that she pitied him. She had an urgent need to dig for the truth about the phony Navy men and the forged letter, and the only person who could help her out was Jacob.

While dozing, she realized there was another reason she didn't want to leave yet. She felt at home, and preparing omelets for two people had been a pleasant respite from her usual solitary lifestyle. There was something more—something boiling to the surface of her consciousness. When she finally put a name to it, she was taken by surprise. It had been a long time since she'd had such feelings.

Jacob Burkowski was much older than she—maybe by ten years, give or take a couple—but it didn't matter.

In the next few minutes, she came to a decision.

❖ ❖ ❖

Jacob awoke in the middle of the night and found himself tucked under the plaid coverlet that was always tossed carelessly over the back cushion of the sofa. A lamp on the far side of the living room was burning on the lowest wattage. He sat up and glanced about the room, forcing himself to remember how he'd gotten there. As memories of the past day kicked in, he wondered where the woman Ellen was. Then he remembered details of the previous day.

Leaping to his feet, he headed directly for his study. He had to find a way to get Max back—a way to reverse the horrifying events. He hadn't believed his on-paper theory could actually work until those two bastards had convinced him he was really up to something. *How did they know?* He hadn't shared his information with anyone until yesterday. The note on his computer had demanded his sources. Those two fake Navy men were dead, so who wrote it? Thankfully, he hadn't mentioned the note to anyone, not even Ellen.

Suddenly, he heard noises upstairs. He cocked his head to listen. Was it the creaking of the floorboards in his bedroom? He stiffened. Were his enemies inside his house? He whipped around and headed for the front door and then changed his mind. What did he have to lose by investigating?

Slowly, one by one, he headed up the steps. At the landing, he paused to listen again. He heard nothing. Maybe it had been his imagination. The door of his bedroom was ajar, but he always left it open after rising from bed each morning. He walked more decisively toward the door and pushed it fully open. Moonlight was streaming through the bare window, offering enough light to inspect the familiar space. The comforter on Hannah's side moved rhythmically up and down. *Hannah?* Oh, my God...

Jacob rubbed his forehead. Hannah was dead—murdered and stuffed into a car trunk. Then, who? *Max?* He approached the bed with caution, peering through the semidarkness to identify the body shape. With a trembling hand, he grasped hold of the edge of the comforter and pulled it back far enough to satisfy his curiosity. *Ellen!*

She hadn't wanted to leave him alone. She had wanted him to sleep, but they had things to discuss. That's why she had stayed. He couldn't resist the temptation to pull back the blanket further to catch a better glimpse of her face. She slept peacefully despite her different but similar experience. He liked her soft features. For some time, he just looked at her and thought about what could be if circumstances were different.

Finally, he tiptoed out of the room and went next door to his study. Closing the door behind him, he switched on the ceiling light and stared at the floor-to-ceiling bookshelves. His task wouldn't be easy, but somehow, he had to locate the book he had stumbled across while researching traveling back in time by using one's mind. It was only a hypothesis—a minuscule remark in a much wider context and nothing more—but those two men had taken it very seriously. Now, whoever left him the note on his lab PC was equally insistent upon getting hold of it. He didn't understand why, but frankly, he didn't care. If they wanted it, they could have it—especially if it meant Max's safe return.

Chapter 39

2115: Beijing

Colonel Malik pointed at the 3D scale model of a nondescript building nestled within the Vatican walls. "The prime reason for sending Bootsma to us is right here," he said, tapping on what looked like a modest tower. "What happened inside is one of the best kept secrets of the Vatican. This structure was designed to avoid undue attraction. It looks so dull and boring that one could easily mistake it for an apartment."

"You seem to know a lot about the history of past religions for a colonel in our Neuro-science Department," Ashlev said.

"We have to. Stay with me. I'll explain more fully in a minute. It is in this tower that our track went cold, Major. We know only one thing: Frank Bootsma had a good reason for breaking into it to snoop around. It's called The Tower of the Winds, by the way. Want to guess why?"

"Because it is such a windy place?"

"Are you making fun of me?"

"No, sir."

"I appreciate a sense of humor, but not right now. This is important." Malik tapped the 3D screen again. "We have figured out this Tower of the Winds in Rome is an approximation of a tower of the same name built in Athens somewhere around the mid first century BCE. No records remain of the architect Danti's work because they have never been digitized. More importantly, they were buried deep inside the Secret Archives of the Vatican in what was called 'the bunker'."

"The bunker? I assume that means the stored Archives were bombproof."

"At the time the bunker was constructed, in the 1970s, they were considered eminently safe, but it was no protection for the ultra-bombs used in the wars of the 2070s."

"How do we know about this other tower and Danti?"

"Because Frank Bootsma wrote a short statement about his findings on the Vatican Net. Except for that one mention, he never wrote about what was so singularly special about them. The NSA copied everything they found, and we confiscated their system when we invaded the United States. That's how we learned about them in the first place." Malik flipped open a folder on his desk computer that revealed an animated timeline. "There are a few written records of the period when the Tower of the Winds was conceived. Watch closely, and you will see why we became interested in it."

A painting of Pope Gregory XIII and his biography emerged with the caption: 1502-1585, BORN UGO BONCOMPAGNI.

Malik crossed his arms over his chest and glanced at Ashlev. "This man was responsible for the adjustments made to the Julian Calendar. He funded a new university, the *Collegio Romano*, at arm's length, just outside the Vatican walls, to carry out the work. He named the new version after himself, the Gregorian Calendar. This adjustment was deemed necessary because their religious holidays were hard to predict. The official history states that the Tower of the Winds was constructed in order to determine exactly when those holidays should occur."

He watched the motion of the solar clock inside the tower with Ashlev without comment. When Ashlev remained mute, he added, "The official version of the tower and the calendar is that the pope wanted to demonstrate the Catholic Church's authority to measure time, hence, mastering the universe. The problem, however, is that this particular tower was built *after* Gregory recalculated the calendar. So, the question is, what happened in this tower?"

"Can we zoom onto that disk?" Ashlev asked. "I've never been a history buff, but this is rather fascinating."

"Unfortunately, we can't. We got this picture and animation from the Vatican website. It was stored on their network. There is no video footage. Let me retrieve another file." He pulled up a new painting that appeared on the screen next to the virtual scale model of the Vatican. It was of a solemn-looking man dressed in a wine-red robe and a matching hat.

Ashlev rose from his chair and leaned closer to the screen. The caption read: POPE URBAN VIII.1568 - 1644. He reseated himself and gazed at Malik in surprise. "What's the meaning of all this?" he asked. "The hologram spectacle is astounding for sure, and this history lesson has taught me things I haven't known, but I can't seem to make the connection. What's so special about this pope?"

"Well, for starters, he put astrology on the index."

"Meaning?"

"Astrology was prohibited and banned from universities in Europe. From that time on, the West no longer paid any attention to this tradition. Do you remember my remarks about your parents?"

Ashlev nodded. "Yes, but I'm still not getting the connection."

"Astrology was forbidden for a particular reason. A famous astrologer by the name of Orazio Morandi predicted Pope Urban VIII would be killed in 1630."

Ashlev read the caption under the screen picture and grinned. "That guy was wrong."

"Yes, but four Spanish Cardinals didn't think so. They sailed for Rome to attend a conclave and select a new pope.

When Pope Urban VIII learned of Morandi's prediction and the intention of these Spanish Cardinals, he became so riled that he hanged Morandi and banned astrology. End of story, one would think." Malik folded his hands and leaned on the desktop.

Ashlev shrugged. "I guess not, but why do I have to know all this stuff?"

Malik noticed that Ashlev's mind was wandering. "Major, Bootsma is a Jesuit—short for 'soldier of Christ'. The *Collegio Romano* was a Jesuit operation. That must be the connection, and that's why you have to fully understand this history. Bootsma must have had access to documents unknown to us. Galileo was an astrologer. There is proof he was detained inside the Vatican and stayed several nights in the rooms of the prosecutor of the Inquisition, which were—you got it—in the Tower of the Winds! We must learn what happened in the tower that relates to astrology." He coughed into his hand and reached for a glass of water. While drinking, he saw that he finally had the full attention of Ashlev. "There's more, Major," he said. "Bootsma was working as an astronomer for the Vatican Observatory based in none other than Castel Gandolfo, summer residence of Pope Urban VIII and the one and only science allowed to be part of the Vatican for reasons we can only speculate. We're not sure how much he knew, but there is evidence that Pope Urban VIII practiced astrology in a secret room deep down under his castle *after* he had put astrology on the index. Check out this scale model."

Malik turned the model 360 degrees and tapped on the north foundation of the castle. A pop-up animation showed an ancient etching of the period before the time the castle was built. A caption next to it read: Piranesi. "And guess what? The summer palace was designed by none other than Danti."

Ashlev scrubbed his face with his hands and sighed. "Forgive me for losing my patience, Colonel Malik. I have a mission and only a few days to accomplish it. I can see you place great importance on the history of these places, and I thank you for sharing it with me. I understand why I need to bring Bootsma back with me. He knows something we need to know. How about if I just go get him for you? Can we build the machine now?"

Malik bit back a quick retort. He found it difficult to believe the man he'd been looking forward to meeting for so long had no interest in the most important part of his mission. The only part that mattered to him was the time-travel aspect that would enable him to bring back his parents.

"Major, the truth is, we've checked the *rashi* of Urban VIII. He was indeed in mortal danger in 1630. Galileo was *not* condemned because of his theory of a sun-centered universe. He was the personal astrologer to Urban VIII. A secret room was built beneath Castel Gandolfo for the specific purpose of allowing Urban VIII to conduct astrological sessions that could avert a doom that clearly showed up in his chart. It is more likely that Galileo was sacrificed because the pope didn't like his predictions. Brother Bootsma documented this in his log files."

"So, centuries back, there was a conspiracy. But, Colonel, the Vatican no longer exists! Rome has perished! The beliefs of the Catholic Church are no longer accepted! You are giving me ancient history. What I have gathered from this is that the only part we really care about is the Vatican meteorite collection Bootsma was sitting on. For the last time, Colonel, can we get on with the part that directly influences my leaving here?"

Malik heard the exasperation in Ashlev's voice and saw the rise of his anger. "Calm down, Major. Are you forgetting who I am? I am here to help you, but you must fulfill your mission based upon facts. For the moment, forget Bootsma and the meteorites. Your parents wanted you to undertake a totally different mission. Aren't you forgetting something?

We let you see a letter from Bootsma to Burkowski. It was on the wall in Burkowski's study, remember?"

Ashlev hung his head. "Yes, now I do. I'm sorry for being insubordinate. I want to make excuses—the history lessons distracted me. I'm under enormous pressure over the importance of my mission, the general's betrayal of my trust has me rattled, and all those holograms—but they are just that, excuses."

"The letter was there for a purpose, Major. Bootsma knew about Burkowski, but they never met before. Can you imagine why?" Malik waited. "There is something else we don't know. Have a look at this." He opened a new screen that showed the transcripts of telephone calls routed through the switchboard operator of Castel Gandolfo. What followed was a short conversation between the operator and a French student who wanted to speak with Brother Bootsma. He insisted their conversation could not wait because he had discovered something in Vézelay that would greatly interest Bootsma. The young man left his name, address, and phone number and the added incentive that he had documented the information in a notebook, along with a celestial map. Then, without warning, the recording stopped.

"Please go on," Ashlev said, clearly more intrigued by the direction of their dialogue.

Malik shook his head. "This is all we got. We must have possession of that notebook. And the fact that his letter is on the wall of Professor Burkowski means Bootsma is involved as well."

Ashlev inched forward on his chair. "It took a while, but I finally get it, Colonel. How could I have been so judgmental of you? Is there something else I need to know for my mission?"

"The fact that Bootsma's letter is mounted on Burkowski's wall implies something or someone connected the two of them. We're still working on gaining more information, but as far as we understand it now, after you leave here to get these two men, something goes wrong."

Malik took the white handkerchief from his pocket again and spread it out in front of him on the desk. It was time for him to invest in the power Ashlev possessed but was as yet unaware of holding. "We studied a few predictions on your *rashi*, Major. The good news is that your *rashi* is highly accurate. The bad news is that if these predictions about your future are accurate, you won't be coming back at all."

Chapter 40

2115: Beijing

Frank awoke from the blast and peered about him. *Max?* He had been right next to him. Now, he saw no one, sensed no one, and heard no one—just total blackness. The insufferable pain had been followed by an extreme heat. The subsequent blackout had been ice cold. *Maybe Max...*

Out of nowhere, a faint voice drifted toward him like an even colder breath. "Take my life!"

Frank struggled to rise from where he'd tumbled, except his rigid body wouldn't cooperate. When he finally pushed himself to a standing position, he moved stiffly in several directions. Although he squinted and tried to peer through the darkness, it was impossible to make out anything. "Max? Max!"

"Please...take me. I'm over here."

The voice came from somewhere behind him. He turned and groped his way toward the sound. Out of nowhere, someone grabbed his hands. His heart missed a couple of beats. The hands on his were those of a man, not a boy! "What are you doing!" he cried. The hands were forcing his to grab hold of a... a throat! "Why are you doing this?" he demanded.

"You have to end my life! It's my punishment."

"Who are you?"

"I've been chosen to give you my body to save my family."

"What? I-I don't understand."

"Please just take my life. We have no time for discussion. They are watching us."

"Who are 'they'?"

"The authorities. I've been convicted of state crimes. I will be destroyed, and my family will be deported unless you take the life from my body."

"I can't do it."

The man's hands loosened their grip on his and immediately grabbed hold of Frank's throat. Now they held each other in a mutual stranglehold. "Kill me, or I will kill you!" the raspy voice said.

Instinctively, Frank increased the pressure on the stranger's throat and, right away, the grip on his own throat relaxed. Within seconds, the unseen man's body went limp. He collapsed at Frank's feet, and when Frank stooped to reach for his pulse, something strange happened: The man completely vanished.

Even stranger than that, Frank was suddenly enveloped in a gloomy red light. He saw himself strapped to a bed, surrounded by white-coated people who were observing him in what appeared to be a surgery room. Looking more intently, he realized he was on a platform in an immense hall, and everywhere about him, the same equipment and additional medical staff were working on other subjects strapped to identical beds.

Max! Where was he?

Frank struggled against his bindings but found he was too securely immobilized. Out of the corner of his eyes, he observed a man older than Max thrashing against his restraints too. Several spastic convulsions rippled through his body, and then he fell quiet.

❖ ❖ ❖

The pain was so intense that Max was convinced he had finally died. Talking to Frank the fat man had been most disturbing, and in a way, it felt like the end. When they were slowing down, everything had gone in a flash. First, there was unbearable heat, and then there was insufferable cold again. It only lasted a few seconds, but it had been the second freakiest moment in his life after being in the fMRI machine at his dad's lab. *Am I still alive? Am I in heaven? Does heaven even exist? Or am I somewhere else?*

Suddenly, he was sensing something totally different. He was strapped to a test bed again, but his whole body tingled, like when he slept on an arm wrong and it went to sleep. He tried to look around, but it was hard to do when he couldn't move anything but his head. There was another bed next to his, and he could see the shape of a man who was strapped in just like he was. He couldn't see the man's face. Some guys in white coats were hovering over his bed, watching him.

Frank! Where was he? Was the man in the other bed Frank? Max wanted to yell his name, but something in his throat was making that impossible. He looked up and saw that a tube was running from what looked like a respirator down to his face. He became nauseous and wanted to signal the white coats, but they paid no attention to him. He ordered himself to calm down and breathe slowly.

A few moments later, one of the white coats moved aside, and he could see the man's face. It wasn't Frank. It was a middle-aged Chinese guy, only slightly overweight and nowhere near as fat as Frank. They were taking out his tube and some wires that had been connected to a metal band around his head. They left the band where it was while they talked to him. Max couldn't hear what they were saying. Finally, they unstrapped him.

His Chinese neighbor sat on the edge of the bed and slowly put his feet on the floor. Two of the white coats supported him under his arms and walked him around the bed. It was like he'd just recovered after an operation. He said something to one of them. The white coat nodded and turned around. His jet-black face stood out in contrast against the white lab coat. Max felt kind of scared. The white coat half-turned to listen to the Chinese man again and then unexpectedly reached over Max and removed the tube from his throat. Then, he poured some water from a pitcher into a glass and held it up to Max's mouth.

The Chinese man shuffled closer and stood by his bed. "Is that you, Max?"

Max stared at him. He knew that voice! It belonged to the fat man!

"It's me, Max. Frank! They sent us into these bodies. Is it really you?"

"Yes," Max rasped, nodding at the same time. "Yes, it's me."

"Thank God. Don't be afraid, Max. You seem to be okay."

Max tried to look at himself to see if he was a Chinese man, too, but the straps kept him in place. He did catch a glimpse of his hands. They looked darker, like he'd been in the sun all summer. Looking at the Chinese man, it was hard to see Frank as the enemy any longer—or else he played it very well. Maybe this guy wasn't Frank at all. The white coat with the black face pushed the Chinese man away and sat down on the bed, close to his head. Max noticed medical instruments next to his bed, and the white coat selected a scalpel.

Chapter 41

Saturday: DuPont Circle, Washington DC

The early morning sunlight painted the bookshelves in an orange glow. Jacob admired it for only seconds. Despite the appearance of a serene tranquility in the photographic still life, he didn't care a whit about it. He hadn't found the book yet. He had searched diligently ever since waking up in the middle of the night on his couch and remembering why it was important. He had gone systematically through the process, moving shelf by shelf, book by book, with no luck.

Finally, he collapsed onto his desk chair and forced himself to relive the moment when he'd first discovered the article, the writing of his remarks, and the book he'd referenced in the article submitted for publication. He thought about what day of the week it had it been, his mood at the time, where he had been before selecting that particular book, and perusing it out of the blue. His conclusion was that it had been a clear case of serendipity.

And that was his problem now. The randomness of his find made it virtually impossible to replicate. He thought maybe if he busied himself with something else, his memory would be triggered. Unbidden, his thoughts turned to Max and Hannah, and he wondered why the fake officers had used them as bait to gain possession of what they thought he knew. What was it all about?

An hour later, he hadn't gotten any further. He glanced through a stack of papers on his desk, mostly fMRI patient records. There was nothing special—just regular cases of positive and negative diagnoses of all sorts of brain tissue disorders. When he reached the bottom of the stack, he froze: the report he had written on Max! He had kept it there all the time, putting it away under fresh reports. Max's diagnosis was conclusive, at least for him. His Area 25 showed an abnormal increase of blood flux, indicating he had suffered some form of 'hard reset', and Area 27 seemed to not be functioning properly. It exhibited the lowest blood saturation he had ever seen, implying the thinkwaves were clogged. That explained Max's depression. Tears welled up in Jacob's eyes. He wished he could have helped.

Then he remembered. He had searched for unorthodox healing methods, and while checking out one of the founding fathers of neurology, the German neurologist Korbinian Brodmann, he had stumbled across another German speaker, this one from Switzerland—a contemporary and highly controversial neuro-psychiatrist named Carl Jung. Despite having slept fitfully for only a couple of hours, he felt as though his batteries had been recharged. "That's what they want!" he said aloud.

He rushed back to the bookshelves and sank onto his knees. He needed to give the lower shelves more thorough scrutiny. Immersed in perusing the backs of books, he was startled to see a pair of tanned legs and bare feet next to him. "Ellen," he said, gazing up at her.

She was garbed in one of his t-shirts. "Are you okay?" she asked, yawning.

Jacob nodded. He pushed himself to a standing position and almost swept a row of books off the shelves in the process. He was standing way too close to her, but she didn't seem to mind, and he was too frozen in place to move away.

She smiled. "Cat got your tongue?"

He sucked in a deep breath and hated himself for being distracted by her beauty. He brushed a wayward strand of hair from her forehead.

"Should I make us another breakfast, or have you already had something?" she asked.

"I'm ... not hungry." It wasn't the breakfast he wanted. He placed a hand around her waist and pulled her closer, feeling the warmth of her body through the thin fabric of the borrowed shirt. She was the perfect size for a woman of her height.

Unexpectedly, she wrapped her arms around his neck and reached up to kiss him. The casual kiss could have lengthened into a long and passionate one, but Jacob couldn't allow it. As attractive and sweet as Ellen was, it was just not right to let it go any further.

At that very moment, the doorbell rang. Startled, they both jumped and separated. "I-I have to get that," Jacob said.

"Come back soon, Professor."

"Don't call me that!"

As he approached the front door, he saw the figure of the mailman through the glass panels. The remembrance of seeing the two men outside the same door sent a shiver through his body. He pulled the door open only a crack.

"Good morning, Mr. Burkowski," the mailman said. "I need your signature for this letter. I won't need to see an ID because you've lived on this street for more than ten years." He handed a white business-sized envelope to Jacob.

"Thanks," Jacob mumbled and closed the door. He glanced at the stamp. *Italy?* On the left side of the envelope, he noticed a return address logo he'd never seen before. It was an impression of a small church with a star-filled sky overhead. He slit it open and removed a one-page folded sheet of paper with the same logo.

Dear Dr. Burkowski, Only new actions without a cause can solve the time-travel paradox (Gen. 27). YOUR SON IS ALIVE. Sincerely, Brother Frank Bootsma

With trembling hands, Jacob read and then reread the letter. He swallowed the sob in his throat and leaned against the door for a moment to will strength into his legs. "Ellen!" he shouted and ran up the steps, taking two at a time.

Chapter 42

2115: Beijing

Once Malik had convinced Ashlev a certain amount of history was necessary before they could complete the time-travel setup, they set about working on that task. Ashlev realized it was due to Malik's meticulous preparations in the past years that the adaptation of the existing brain-firing equipment was accomplished so easily. The headquarters of the Neurological Research Center had its own test equipment at their disposal.

On his train trip, he had seen, east of Beijing, the vast compound of a series of brain-firing machines with the capacity to send over 100,000 soldiers per day. He knew of its existence but was still impressed by its magnitude. And he had clearly recognized the gigantic oven complex needed for disposing of so many bodily residues on any single day.

He understood Malik's quarters had their own equipment, and it was the duty of those under his command to calibrate and improve the brain-firing machinery. They were also responsible for future developments like Ashlev's mind-merging and the reconstructing of 'social consciousnesses', a euphemism for the brainwashing of civilians and soldiers. While Jerusalem, for unknown reasons, had the best neurological theorists, the actual handiwork was only carried out in Beijing, in the former Beijing Ancient Observatory. It was an odd coincidence, Ashlev thought, that the most decisive attack on the West, including its mother observatory in the Vatican, was planned in this old observatory.

Ashlev worked side by side with Malik on the new platform. The layout was symmetrical, with two pairs of beds placed opposite each other. Each bed was situated within a round construction made of copper netting, which had been enriched with a conductivity accelerator. The magnetic force was so high at its peak that the bed could be pulled away, allowing the test person to float inside. In reality, this state of suspension would only last a few seconds before the body evaporated into a residual gas. As a consequence and for a brief moment, brain activity could be totally isolated.

Although thinkwaves were highly speculative during Jacob's time, Chinese neurological researchers had identified these particles near the end of the twenty-first century and used them as the basis for the brain firing. The thinkwaves could be sent over great distances, making use of laser beams and repeating satellites in space. Thanks to these ultra-precise GPS satellites, they could also be used for a precision attack on any human being anywhere on the planet. So far, this was exactly how the brain transporters worked at the military complex outside Beijing. Malik had ordered the same machines and received them. This had been the easiest part.

Now, at the Neurological Research Center HQ, Ashlev and Malik were about to construct an addition to this basic setup using the footnote in Burkowski's article as the starting point. "The article briefly described a device consisting of an empty double-helix tube," Malik said. "That is to say, it contained nothing—no gas, no particles of any kind, no vacuum in the classic sense—just nothing. Don't forget, Major, Burkowski was building his theory on the patent of another professor who had designed a time-travel machine with the same layout for an electron. He suggested the use of this patented machine for the sending of brainwaves. I built it with our technology and prepared four of these double-helix tubes. Here...hold the first one."

Ashlev grasped the tube in both hands and inspected the twisted form, an exact copy of the DNA double-helix. The two strands were joined at both ends.

Malik took two highly conductive copper headings and mounted them at the top and bottom of the tube. A thin wire connected them to the copper net construction around the test bed. "These headings keep a stream of thinkwaves at bay in between them, Major," he explained. "Although this small light source is no larger than an eye, it can send the appropriate bursts of light. The other heading works as a mirror and reflects the light. Watch what happens when I switch it on."

A light flash zipped through the double-helix and lit up the tube in Ashlev's hands, startling him. He almost dropped it.

"Careful!" Malik warned. "That flash of light carries the thinkwaves to their destination. They will reach the speed of light, which causes a phenomenon of frame dragging—"

"... which means the thinkwaves are supposed to be traveling in time," Ashlev said, interrupting. Although he had been no more than an assistant to Malik until now, he thought it wise to ask a few questions. His life would depend on his knowing the answers. "How sure are you that these tubes will do the trick, Colonel? We have a lot of experience in sending brain signals long distances into another human brain, but placing another machine in between two humans? How can we be so sure we will be aiming correctly at the target? How does this work? Is there a way we can test the thing?"

Malik nodded. "I've already thought about that, Major. Place the tube on the test bed and come watch on the screen." He strode to a desk on the test platform. The familiar 3D extreme VR foglet rose from its surface. "I trained a couple of mice to turn left in a labyrinth and eat pieces of cheese when they were tapped on the head two times. The first tap signaled that the smell of cheese was an illusion, because it wasn't there. It was only a few cheesy-smelling pieces of wood. See what happened?"

If it weren't such a serious matter, Ashlev would have laughed aloud. A black mouse and a white one were each strapped into a miniature test bed setup. He could tell the thinkwaves of the trained black mouse were sent into the brain of the white mouse. The screen split, and another film showed the white mouse being tapped on the head once; it ignored the cheese smell.

Ashlev felt his impatience grow. "What does that prove, Colonel? We've done similar tests for many years now... and on humans."

Malik grinned. "Have a good look, Major."

Ashlev peered more closely at the split screens. "That's impossible!" he exclaimed.

"Apparently, you recognize the difference now, Major. Look at the date of the video on the right screen. The recording took place two days *before* we started training the black mouse. We know because we video-logged all our proceedings. On a routine replay, we discovered this. Our white mouse obediently responded to the two taps on its head. Can you imagine how proud we were to see our white mouse perform without training? And do you understand the best part?"

Ashlev's mind whirled. "You didn't know how many taps were doing the trick. Otherwise, you would have stumbled across the first time-travel paradox. This is not the best part, right?"

"Far from it."

He smiled at Malik. "The machine had been sitting on your desk already, fixing the second time-travel paradox—proving that the invention goes back in time to before you assembled the machine. Am I right?"

"I'm amazed at your astuteness, Major. You're quick. Yes, you're right. That's exactly how it worked."

"This is all well and good, Colonel, but I don't believe you completely understand the nature of our mission."

"How so? After so many years of preparation—"

"Fully appreciated, Colonel, but did you consider how I'm supposed to come back with four other men and myself? Back in that time, they didn't have this setup. Do you have any idea how to get all this information over there? This Burkowski never tried the procedure because he didn't know how to build such a machine. Either that, or he was simply afraid to do so."

Malik folded his arms across his chest. "Hmm. I'm sorry to say I never thought about that. Between us, we can come up with a solution. We can store all the necessary information in your memory and send it along with you."

Ashlev scratched his cheek while thinking. "This is part of our mind-merging technology, Colonel. Thanks for using it without mentioning our operation in Jerusalem."

There was an edgy tone in his voice, and Malik noticed it. "Again, my apologies, Major. May I suggest we continue on a first-name basis? I feel I have disappointed you. The last thing I want is for you to hold any bitterness. I promised your parents I would take care of you, no matter what it takes."

Ashlev softened upon hearing these words and hesitated before responding. He had always found it difficult to show emotion. "I was too hasty in my response, Malik. May I call you Malik? Your other name is too complicated for me. I still need to understand how we get there, organize our gear, apprehend these guys, and send back five people, including myself."

"I see and hear the soldier in you," Malik said, nodding his appreciation. "Our cooperation on this mission is critical. I need your input as much as you need mine."

"I have another question for you." Ashlev paced back and forth in front of the desk. "How can we send ourselves away, apprehend Bootsma and Burkowski, get back here, and ensure the time-travel machine is destroyed? We can't afford leaving the machine for anyone else to use. We must be 100 percent sure that will be impossible."

"Although not all historical analogue material has survived the years of war and transportation to the AAA in China, Roto, we have no evidence that they even tried to use the time-travel machine again."

"What do you mean?" Ashlev asked. "If we didn't find any evidence of our action in their time here today, is that evidence at all?"

"The first time-travel paradox says you cannot go back and do something you experience in the present. In other words, everything has already happened, Roto. If we go back in time and we have not seen its effect right now, either we didn't affect anything in the past with any relevance for now, or—"

"... or we never arrived," Ashlev said.

He and Malik stared at each other in silence.

❊ ❊ ❊

In the following days, they worked hard on testing the equipment. They concluded it made no sense to worry about how events could be connected and how a time-travel loophole could be prevented. It was a complicated issue. Their focus had to remain on how to prepare for the mission. They would hope for the best once they were sent away.

They had barely finished the departure and arrivals platform when the general appeared with two officers Ashlev didn't recognize. "Give me a brief summary concerning the readiness of the machinery, Colonel Malik."

Ashlev listened intently as Malik provided her with an overview of the setup and of how the thinkwaves were transported to the satellite disks on the roof, from where they were guided to their destination. He answered several more questions about how these disks could send waves back and forth in time and the phenomenon of frame dragging. "At the moment, thinkwaves are inside the double-helix, and light is pumped through it. The circling of the light causes a weak gravitational field similar to a wormhole," he said. "It will bring the waves instantly into another dimension or, in other words, another timeframe. Because thinkwaves have already been connected to the satellite disks, they will have been connected to their target using our ultra-precise clockwork."

When Ashlev noticed the general becoming confused, he stepped in. "The weak gravitation causes what is called a 'closed time loop', General," he said. "Theoretically, this means that if you could jump aboard it and step out at any time, you could travel back in time until the past and the future met each other in infinity. The same theory holds true if you could travel into the future. Around the year 2000, considerable research was carried out on this subject. At that time, researchers lacked possession of our brain transportation system. They were unable to conduct testing like we can. They tried it on an electron once but were unable to prove the things we have proven. Colonel, perhaps we can show the general the experiment with the two mice?"

"Thank you, Major," Malik said, understanding the reason for his suggestion.

While the video played, Ashlev studied the general's face. She effectively hid her surprise when the white mouse was able to perform its task without training. When Malik pointed to the date on the screen, however, she was visibly shocked. "So it *is* possible!" she exclaimed, licking her lips several times. Her cheeks turned red. She seemed to be aroused by the success of the project.

Ashlev turned away, feeling the same repulsion he always had in her presence.

"After we tested the double-helix tubes, we arranged the test beds in such a way that we could send two people at a time and receive two people at the same time," Malik said. "At the receiving end, we have already transported spare test bodies from our brain farms. I have them in quarters below this platform. I believe we are ready to send your men, General. Shall we commence with the protocol?"

Ashlev had written each step and maneuver in the mission planning report. The complex details produced a manual of more than 1,000 pages. In addition, he and Malik had produced computer simulations that tested every step and found no faults.

The general looked intently at both of them. "I read the protocol. I have no comments." She glanced at the two officers, who had been standing near the corner of the platform to observe the spectacle. Their bleak faces and thin bodies reflected the harshness of living in the brain farm.

If it were part of his makeup to feel pity, Ashlev decided he would pity them. They were genetic residues of brain experiments, and their lives had been in jeopardy since birth. He pushed the thought away; they were certainly not on his side.

"Send them away," the general commanded.

It wasn't her tone of voice, but her dismissive hand gesture that angered Ashlev. It revealed the contempt she had for her men. They were merely machines to use at will.

At Malik's instruction, four men in white coats marched into the enclave. Ashlev decided they were humanoid robots, although he couldn't know for certain unless he cut them open. Even then, the hardware in some species was so deeply embedded in their spines it was difficult to ascertain. "Prepare the subjects," Malik said, motioning for them to begin the practiced procedure.

The robots strapped the two men onto their test beds and connected wires from the machines to their heads. Then, they rolled the copper netting over them until they were completely enveloped inside the fine-meshed, highly conductive cones.

"We're ready," Malik said. "Do you want us to proceed?" The general nodded.

"Stand further away from the beds please," Malik instructed, motioning to both the general and Ashlev. Once they had cleared the area, he pushed a button on his control desk.

"All personnel abandon platform," a metallic voice said over the intercom system as the brain transporter took over the procedure. The four white-coated humanoids left the area.

Ashlev huddled with Malik and the general behind a protective anti-magnetic screen. On a monitor, they were able to observe the two men as the buzzing sound emanating from the two cones increased.

The procedure was accomplished in seconds. The copper netting turned crimson, and the bodies of the two men instantly vaporized. Ashlev heard no sounds of pain and witnessed no fire or explosion. In the blink of an eye, the process began and ended. It was not the same as regular brain transportation, which took several minutes and included the ultra-fast decay of the person's body.

Ashlev was next in line.

Chapter 43

Saturday: DuPont Circle, Washington DC

With the letter clenched in his hand, Jacob took the flight of stairs two at the time, all the while shouting to Ellen. His mind was fixated on the word "alive."

Ellen met him at the top of the stairs. "What are you shouting about?" she asked, her hands on her chest as though in the throes of a heart attack.

"Look!" Jacob said, shaking the letter at her. His hand was still trembling.

"Give it to me," Ellen said, trying to pry it from his fingers.

Jacob wasn't ready to let go of it. He stared at the words, but they danced in front of his eyes, which had misted with unshed tears.

"Please, Jacob," Ellen said. "Let me read the letter." She took it from him, and her eyes rushed to the last words. "What is this?" she asked. "Max isn't *dead*? Has he been *kidnapped*?"

"Kidnapped?" Jacob repeated, once more in control of his faculties. "What brings you to that conclusion?"

"This man claims Max is alive. He's probably going to contact you again and ask for a ransom."

"I don't think so. He's a priest or something. Look at the logo. The letter came from Italy. I think he wants to help me."

"Maybe you're right, Jacob. Please know I wasn't trying to diminish or take away your hope. Forgive me? In my business, I'm trained to think the worst. Why don't we go to your study and pour over every word? After reading the words more carefully, I think it's meant to be a coded message. I'll help you work it out."

Jacob was relieved by her optimism. A couple minutes later, they stared with interest at the list of words from the letter she had compiled on a tablet.

"Okay, let's take them one at a time," she said. "First, this Bootsma calls you 'Doctor' and not 'Professor'. That means he is from here—from our time, I mean."

"I agree," Jacob said. "As I reread the entire sentence, his choice of words reveals he's part of the time-travel issue ... or at least he knows about it."

Ellen bit her bottom lip and stared into space. "Hmm. He knows about time-travel paradoxes. Not uncommon, I suppose, but highly coincidental that he should bring that one up in this context. It indicates he knows more than the average person."

Jacob drummed his fingers on the desktop as he reread the note again. "'Only new actions without a cause can solve the time-travel paradox'. His mention of 'new actions' puts him in the champion league."

"Explain."

"It's a specific message to me from this man. He knows what can change the course of history and what cannot. We're part of a plan—a sequential line of events. Everything we experience here is a result of things in the past. It is a one-way trip. We can't change that path, but we *can* change the future. We do that every day, every second of our lives. Do you follow me?"

Ellen shrugged. "I hear you, but I still haven't a clue where you're heading. This may be a type of logic beyond my comprehension."

Jacob reached for the tablet and tore out another sheet of paper. Taking the pencil from her, he drew a line from A to B and a line back to A again. "If you're traveling into the future, you're just changing the future. There is nothing special about that concept because it's still your own future. For people living at some time in the future, this is no big deal either, because you're from the past, and that happens all the time." He saw the blank look in her eyes. "I appreciate you trying to help me, Ellen, but scientific reasoning is my territory. Just bear with me while I think it through. Let me pose questions as they come to me," he said. "Your responses will help me. If you would return back to base, back to Point A, what would happen then?"

"It's impossible," Ellen said. "You can never get back because of the first time-travel paradox. If you came back, you could prevent yourself from going to the future in the first place."

"You're close, but wrong. You can go back as many times as you want, but you can't change your future because it became the present. Are you still with me?"

"Uh-huh, I think so." She screwed up her face and tightly shut her eyes. "You're saying that any point in time becomes the present, and from that point, you cannot change the present itself, but you can always go back and change the future."

"Right. This letter, then, rightfully claims that if I launch a 'new action', I can change things in the future. It does not mean I can prevent Max from being sent to the future, but I can definitively find him in the future."

"So this Bootsma is telling you it requires a 'new action' to make all this happen?" Ellen asked.

Jacob nodded. "Yes, and I think I know why he calls it a 'new action'. He can't tell me what it is because otherwise, he's changing the present. He wants me to find out. If I become hopeful that Max is alive and do things that are not anticipated in the future, I can turn back the events… well, not turn them back, per se, but at least divert them."

"This 'new action' refers to something nobody thought about before, and it comes up just like that, disrupting everything?"

"Yes, and I have a hunch what that could be." He tapped on the paper with a finger pointing at the words 'Gen. 27'. "This is the answer, Ellen. It has to be."

Chapter 44

2115: Beijing

The white coat slit the straps with his scalpel and held his blade in front of Max's face. "Your friend is telling us you have valuable information from our mission leader, Major Roto Ashlev. Is that right?"

Max peered at the man who had told him he was Frank. *Who the hell is Roto Ashlev? Did that fat jerk betray me?* The maybe-Frank man nodded at him, as though relaying a message of comfort. Max gazed directly at the white coat. "Yes ... I-I think so," he said hesitantly, not knowing what he was talking about. It hurt to talk; his throat felt raw.

The black man came closer until his face was right in front of Max. "You think so, or you know for sure? What did Major Ashlev tell you?" He smiled lightly as he lowered the knife to Max's throat.

Max noticed the man's eyes were cold as steel, and he didn't smile with his mouth.

"Tell me, young man. The only reason you're here is to prove to us that our men got your father. See those beds over here?" He pointed at two more test beds on the other side of the platform. The rhythmically moving blanket revealed the two other test subjects were deeply asleep. "The wires connect them to that machine. They're waiting for the signal that will be picked up by satellite disks on the roof of this building. That's how you landed here. We're expecting to see your father any minute now. If you want to see him, too, please tell us what Major Ashlev confided to you. Otherwise, you end up there." The white coat pointed toward the other side of the platform, where four test beds were situated inside blinking copper enclosures. "Same layout," he added. "That is the sending part of our operation. To separate the mind from the body, we use extreme gravitational fields, except we won't be sending you, because we'll be using the gravitation to vaporize your body. See that exhaust hood? That's where your bodily residue will be captured. Now, are you going to tell me what we need to know?"

Max shivered. The request brought back memories of the fMRI machine in his father's lab. He was going to die again, and the pain would be agonizing. He was so confused, so scared. He stared back at the black man. What could he say? He tried to find words but couldn't speak. He mouthed a few words and shrugged to relay the message that his ability to speak was impaired.

The black man's impatience grew. "Liar!" he shouted at Frank. In the next instant, he signaled for his colleagues to roll Max's bed to the adjacent platform. "Put him over there," he ordered. "We'll finish him off in a minute."

"What are you doing?" Frank's voice rose. "Don't put him there! You need him."

"If he doesn't talk, there is too much at risk. He's not needed anyway."

Max didn't know what to say, but he knew he had to come up with something. Then he remembered his talks with Frank. He must have mentioned something to the fat man. He wasn't needed. They only wanted Frank and his father. His dad hadn't died in the lab, but he was in peril of losing his own life. Frank had tried to help him, but he still wondered if he could trust him. *I've nothing to lose.*

"Tell him about the article," Frank urged.

Max had to believe this Chinese dude was the fat man. "I-I knew about the article!" he exclaimed, coughing from the effort to speak.

"Wait, wait, wait!" the black man ordered, stopping the transporting of Max's bed. "What article?"

"When I was in the kidnappers' car, Captain Pakula told me about my dad's article," Max said.

"What about it?"

"It described my dad's invention. I-I never thought my dad had those kinds of plans for the future."

The black man in the white coat burst out in cavernous laughter. "The future?" He nodded at his colleagues. They didn't join in the laughter, which seemed a little strange to Max.

"No, sir. Captain Pakula mentioned a not-yet-published footnote," Max said, more adamantly this time and ignoring his sore throat. Instantly, the white coat stopped laughing.

"What did the major tell you? Speak up! You're running out of time!"

Frank came forward again. "Please, sir," he said in a quiet tone of voice, "we must release the boy. He will tell you everything he knows. Please spare him."

The black man pushed him aside. "Stay out of this, or I will see that you end up there as well," he hissed.

Frank backed off.

The black man grabbed hold of Max's throat, his face registering either anxiety or rage. "For the very last time, young man, what did Major Ashlev tell you? Speak up or die!"

Trembling, Max broke into sobs. He simply didn't know. In a flash, he saw himself again in the car with Pakula, turned around talking to him, his voice at a distance.

"H-he told me about Delhi. H-he said ..." His voice cracked because he finally let go of his bottled-up fear, but his sobs were stilled by the black man, who held his hand over his mouth to shush him up. Quicker than the metamorphosis of a caterpillar into a butterfly, his face softened, and he became instantly friendly and concerned.

Max realized he had spoken the magic word: Delhi.

"It's all right now, boy," the man said. "We'll talk about this later." He snapped his fingers at the other white coats and motioned for them to pull off Max's straps. They worked in concert, like they had rehearsed the process many times before.

Max examined their faces; there was something odd about them.

When they had finished their task, the black man helped him down from the bed. He nodded at Frank for assistance. Feeling wobbly at first, Max took only a couple of hesitant steps.

"Sentries, escort us!" The black man commanded the guards to take them to his office. "This way," he said to Frank, still supporting Max.

They crossed a bridge and stepped onto some rolling stairs that took them to another platform. Max was less interested in where they were than in adjusting to his new body. He was definitely taller and more muscular, and maybe that was a good thing. He was still afraid, but for now, he was glad he had been saved from another unknown procedure. One word had done the trick. *Delhi.* He wondered why.

The black man deposited Max on a chair and pointed at another one for Frank. He sat opposite them and pushed a few buttons on his desktop. A wall of foglets separated his office from the rest of the platform and created a private soundproof room. "Let me introduce myself," he said. "I am Colonel Malik. We have a serious problem that needs immediate resolution. You were expected and are here to stay," he said, looking directly at Frank. "You were expected to be brain-dead on arrival," he said to Max. "You are the beacon. Because you are here, we know our team members identified your father and are working on him as we speak. You are of no value to us anymore."

Max swallowed hard and balled his hands into fists, pumping them to still the trembling of his fingers. He saw that Frank wanted to say something, but Malik cut him off.

"We don't have time for needless discussions. Max will be killed, period. We have no choice. There is no room for a teenager who has witnessed a covert operation that no one in China knows about except for the high command and what we who work down here are allowed to know."

Max stared at the colonel, speechless. The look on his face matched his words; he wasn't kidding. He glanced at Frank in the Chinese body and saw that he was disturbed too. For some reason, he no longer had a headache. Despite the situation, he felt relieved.

The colonel tented his fingers and tapped them against each other while thinking. "If I can convince my superiors that you possess valuable information, I might be able to persuade them not to kill you right away, but your demise is a surety that will happen at some point in time. We must come up with an acceptable and logical reason for postponing this reality. I expect my superiors in an hour. Tell me everything you know about Major Roto Ashley. When did you last see him and his two team members?"

"I think I saw him last," Frank said, "not Max. He told him things you should know, but there's something else. I never saw other team members."

"What do you mean? Ashley was on his own?"

If the colonel's black face could have paled by Frank's comments, it would have, Max decided.

"I never saw anybody else," Frank said. "Only Pakula or Major Ashley."

"But there were two men in U.S. Navy officer uniforms in my father's lab," Max said.

"That was well before he got me, Max," Frank said.

"It's time to tell you what was going on at our end," Malik said but couldn't finish because an alarm went off. They evidently had company. "Forget what I just told you and never repeat it to anyone," he said sternly. He punched a couple of buttons, and the platform walls disappeared.

A squadron of four soldiers entered the room with an elderly female, apparently their boss. When she opened her mouth, Max knew everything Malik had predicted was true. He was about to die for the second time.

Chapter 45

Saturday: DuPont Circle, Washington DC

Jacob sat next to Ellen on the two-cushion Chesterfield near the window of his study. The morning sun streaming through the pane illuminated her tanned legs and caught his attention. He stared at them, especially at her knees. They were just the right size. He had always been attracted to the shapes of arms and legs more than any other part of a woman's body.

Ellen followed his gaze, and she smiled. "Shouldn't you open that Bible, Jacob?" She gestured toward the Bible resting on his lap.

He returned her smile and nodded. The warmth of her body where their shoulders met distracted him more than he wanted to admit.

She placed her hand on his knee and gently squeezed it. If their kiss had been a mistake, she was pushing the envelope with such a gesture, he thought. His gaze went from his knee to her mouth. Before he could analyze her intention, she leaned over and kissed him. He returned her kiss with just enough pressure to instigate a need for more. They continued for several more seconds. It felt more than good ... too good.

She slowly pulled back and ran a hand through his hair. "We should be working on that letter," she said unconvincingly.

Thank God she said it, he thought. Of course the father in him wanted to search for clues to get Max back, but the lonely man in him could no longer wait. It had been a long time since he'd felt this way. Suddenly, as if by the sovereignty of some higher power who knew what was best for him, a sudden fatigue came over him. Tears welled up in his eyes, and he collapsed. "I'm sorry, Ellen," he mumbled. "I just… I can't."

Ellen smiled. She understood. "Why don't you take a nap? It's okay."

Jacob pulled himself together and went into his bedroom. He fell on his bed and was out cold in less than a second.

※ ※ ※

When Jacob finally awoke, he smelled coffee and croissants. He opened his eyes to find a tray of fresh orange juice and strawberries beside them. Ellen huddled on the bed next to him.

"Where did you get these?" he asked. "Certainly not in my refrigerator."

"While you were asleep, I thought I might as well do a bit of shopping. I needed a few things myself."

"You didn't have to do this, but thank you. What day is it, by the way?" he asked. "I've lost track."

"It's Saturday afternoon around three o'clock. Go ahead and eat. I've already had something downstairs." She reached for the Bible on the table next to the bed. "I brought this here from your study. Where should I look?"

Jacob bit into the croissant and washed it down with half the orange juice. Taking the Bible from her hand, he flipped through the first few chapters. "I think Bootsma was referring to Genesis 27," he said. He took another bite of the pastry and then brushed away the crumbs that fell onto the page. "Read it to me."

Ellen quickly scanned the text and then read it aloud. "To summarize, Isaac, who was essentially blind, was going to bless his oldest son, Esau, before he died. But he blessed his son Jacob instead when Jacob pretended to be his brother at his mother's urging." She glanced at Jacob. "Are you a Christian?" she asked.

"I was raised by nonbelievers," Jacob said. "I never knew my mother. Although my father never left me with the impression that religion was something bad, for me, it never proved of any value to me. The gap between what you can get out of it and what you have to do for it is just too big. It's not that it's all very weak on the scientific part, it's more that in the here and now, there's not that much use for it."

"So you're a nonbeliever yourself?"

"That's pretty much it."

"Shouldn't you ask about me?" She sat up straighter. "Anyway, I *am* a Christian—born, raised, and practicing. I think I can be of some help in this interpretation." She reread the scene where Jacob used a goatskin on his arms and neck to appear like his older and more hairy brother, Esau. "Can you see the parallel Mr. Bootsma is making?"

"The passage is about Jacob. He's referring to me?"

"Yes and no. The text illustrates that Jacob switches his body and personality with his oldest brother in order to obtain the firstborn rights. He essentially takes over his body."

Jacob placed his empty coffee cup on the tray and pushed it away. He had lost his appetite. "Let me think about this. When Bootsma wrote 'your son is alive,' and then included the reference to Genesis 27, he wants me to believe that Max lives in someone else's body? I still don't get it. I have only one son. I was also an only child."

"There must be something else," Ellen said. "Jacob is the son. You're Jacob as well. He takes over his brother Esau's position. There must be a connection." She scanned the pages another time. "What about this? The first sentence in the letter says, 'only *new* actions *without a cause* can solve the time-travel paradox.' What happens if we apply these words to what we already know?"

"What 'new action' could have happened for Isaac, Jacob, or Esau?"

"No, no, you're reasoning is all wrong. First of all, Jacob was the Benjamin. He had no legal right to inherit the land of his father. Tradition was always followed. The oldest son had birthrights, not the second or third sons. Jacob's mother encouraged the deception and urged him to fool the father by applying a disguise. What he essentially did was turn back the fact that he was born second in line. The 'new action without a cause' has to be his taking on the disguise and receiving the blessing of Isaac. In the next chapter, Isaac didn't want to undo his action when he learned he had been betrayed, so his blessing was a holy and sacred moment." Ellen peered out the window while holding the Bible to her chest. "I think what the story relates to is that we can turn things back in the future that have been set in the past."

Jacob repeated her last sentence in his head and then sighed. "Even knowing all this ... how does it bring back my son?" For a brief moment, he had drawn strength from their interpretations of Bootsma's statement and biblical reference. Now, he just felt bone-weary and mentally exhausted. Feeling desperate again, he pushed the tray of food further away and sat on the edge of the bed. He couldn't quit.

"I wish I could help you by coming up with something extraordinary, Jacob," Ellen said. "I've reread this passage several times now, and I can't pull up anything more than what we've discussed."

"I have to go back to the lab," Jacob said flatly.

"To do what?"

"I haven't told you everything that happened."

"Like what?"

"Before I passed out, I saw a memo on the screen of my PC. It disappeared after I read it."

"What did it say?"

"That I should be ready to provide the source of my time-travel theory within forty-eight hours, or Max would die."

Ellen examined her watch. "And how much more time do you have?"

Jacob looked at the bedside clock. "Two hours."

Ellen angrily leaped to her feet. "And you didn't tell this to me or to the police? Why, Jacob? Withholding information like that doesn't—"

"It isn't necessary to yell at me. I didn't think it was important to anyone but me. Especially after the police told me at the station that the two criminals were dead and couldn't tell me where Max was. I thought I was on my own."

"But ... but how can you be so sure it was just those *two* men, Jacob? I saw their bodies in the morgue. Didn't it occur to you they were killed by one or more others? That maybe the man who wrote that note to you could provide more clues regarding the whereabouts of your Max?"

"No, yes, well ... " Jacob started and then shrugged.

"And do you have what they want? That source?"

"That's what I wanted to say, Ellen. I thought I had gotten it from one of the reference books in my study and was looking for it most of the night, but couldn't find it. I'm not even sure it exists. Maybe those jerks are making it up."

"Well, let's take first things first. I'll go with you to your lab. Let's see whether or not someone shows up." She moved across the room to slip into her day-old uniform. Then, digging into her purse, she pulled out a gun, checked the magazine, and stashed it behind her waist belt.

Jacob watched her. "You're going in armed!"

"While you were asleep, I called Police Commander Gomez. She's cool. We learned we have a lot in common—childhood, intentionally single, other things. She advised me to try to handle things myself regarding my boss Pakula. Someone broke into my apartment, and it's got me a little spooked." She adjusted the gun and motioned for him to get dressed. "If that note means anything at all, we have two hours before your deadline expires."

"I don't suppose we could get a few Navy guards for backup? Do you have that kind of clout?" Jacob asked hopefully.

"Not anymore. While you were asleep, I called base and was informed I've been temporarily suspended. I'm supposed to wait at home until I'm contacted for a military hearing."

"On what charges?"

"The officer I spoke with didn't want to get into details over a landline phone. That's normal procedure. He just read the instructions he'd received from Superintendent Pakula."

"And why didn't you mention that before now? Think I don't remember you've got serious problems of your own?"

"I didn't bring you home last night to cry on your shoulder. My problem is more of a private matter."

"Private?" Jacob eyed her quizzically.

"Can't tell you Jacob. Security procedures at the Navy base. I've only known you for short time. I'll just say that when I tried to listen to the voicemail messages on my work phone, I was not granted permission to log in. That's when I learned my security codes had already been changed." She shrugged. "I'm not worried about it—at least not yet. We have more important tasks at hand. I'd like to help you figure out how to find Max. Okay?"

"Okay. I'll accept your help for now. Hopefully, I can return the favor." He rolled out of bed while moving past her into the bathroom. "I'll be quick," he promised her.

Less than five minutes later, he reentered the bedroom dripping wet and grinning from ear to ear, a towel wrapped tightly around his waist.

"Well? Obviously, you have something important to tell me."

"I remember where I found the information," Jacob said. "Even better, I know how I formulated it. These bastards are from the future and know something about me I haven't figured out *yet*."

"That sounds a little crazy. How can you possibly know what you did in the future?"

"Because it's been on my mind subconsciously all the time, but I didn't do anything with it. Somewhere in the future, before they decided to come back to our time, I researched a field that up until now hasn't been explored by any other scientists, at least as far as I know. I'll show you in my study before we leave for the lab."

He looked at her, took a few steps, and desperately wanted to say something, but she stopped him. "We haven't time for any of that, Jacob," she said, patting him on his cheek. "Later, maybe, but right now, you need to get dressed. Otherwise, we'll be late getting to your lab."

Part 3

Chapter 46

Saturday: GWUMC, Washington DC

Ashlev eyed the wall clock in the fMRI lab with growing impatience. He had come early, and the stipulated time had come and gone. Clearly, Burkowski had no intention of returning, despite the warning in the email memo. No one had disturbed him after his arrival, and he'd had the lab to himself. His uniform had provided all the ID required to gain entrance—that and his well-presented reason for needing access to the facility. Pacing the floor, he checked the time again. He could go to Burkowski's house and threaten him in person. No, he mustn't panic. He had already ruled out that option. He needed to try out Burkowski's invention in the lab using his equipment. It was critical that he send the scientist to Malik as soon as possible. There was no time to lose.

Ashlev finally closed the door behind him and quietly walked out of the hospital. Nobody stopped him to ask questions. Nobody seemed interested in him at all. He returned to the USNO base, a trip that took no more than ten minutes since Saturday traffic was practically nonexistent. He felt most comfortable in his office; he even slept there. Since his arrival, he had never visited Pakula's house, with good reason. He had been instructed to minimize contact with people, as too much talking could contaminate the mission. He'd been in Rome, Paris, and now in Washington. The earlier trips had been a breeze. He hadn't spoken with anyone on the planes, in the subway, or on the streets. It hadn't been necessary, other than to ask simple requests or provide short responses.

There had been one peculiar moment in the secret archives when he'd wanted to enter the bunker but couldn't gain access. A vaguely transparent blue wall had blocked his way. No matter how much he tried, he couldn't get through it. He was bounced back as if the blue wall were made of rubber.

He and Malik had contemplated what the first time-travel paradox would look like to ensure he'd recognize it. Perhaps the blue wall was it. Perhaps getting through it would change the future as he knew it, which, by the law of nature, was impossible. Something secret was taking place in that bunker, and he was not allowed to enter because of something connected to the time he was still with Malik. For that reason, he had interrogated Frank to the verge of killing him. Just before he had sent him off into the future and the body of Frank was already disintegrating, the Jesuit had gurgled something about "staring into the wrong lamp," whatever that meant.

"You have to fight the stars," Malik had said. He had taken this to mean he had to take unexpected turns in order to divert any premonition or predisposition. In essence, he had to fool the gods. He smiled inwardly at the thought and glanced at one of the walls in his office. Next to the time ticker of the Atomic Clock, someone had hung a modest-sized crucifix. At first, he had wondered why it was there. When he discovered a Bible in one of Pakula's drawers, he understood the man was religious. In a way, it was comforting, taking a body that wasn't totally heretical, like he thought he had been all his life before Malik had opened his eyes. He never looked at the stars in the same way now. He was a different person.

Ashley reached for the notebook on his desk that he had acquired from the student at the Gaulle Airport near Paris. While taking Frank's life had been straightforward, it was another matter altogether to snuff out the life of a youngster. The look in the boy's eyes when he'd strangled him still haunted him. He'd experienced the same difficulty leaving Max in the hands of the general's two henchmen.

His memory flashed back to his final days in Beijing and the words of Malik. "Because you are the son of a Brahmin. That makes you different from the rest of us," Malik had said.

Ashlev reasoned with himself. A man with a mission could not permit himself to abort when confronted with unexpected glitches. He had no other choice but to kill that student. The more he thought about it, though, the more he started to doubt his own decisions.

In the middle of his reflections, he heard his stomach growling and realized he hadn't eaten since lunchtime the day before. He stashed the notebook, buttoned up his uniform jacket, donned his hat, and left the building. The sidewalk led him directly toward Building 9. The reddish-brown bricks marked a visible difference from the others in the compound. It was in better shape due to better maintenance. It housed a staff restaurant, open 24/7. The U.S. Vice President's detail had their quarters in the other half of the same building.

He had eaten alone at the same table ever since his arrival at the USNO. The menu offered a daily choice of three dishes. He always chose the first one, guessing there would be plenty of it, reducing the risk of his having to converse with the soldier behind the counter about the other choices. When it came to details, Ashlev considered himself a pro. His host, Pakula, had been more or less the same type of character—at least it had appeared to be so from what he'd read of him in his biography. Routines were his trademark.

The meal tasted the same as those he'd eaten other days. The amount of saturated fat in the food continued to surprise him, as did the lack of any information concerning the ingredients or their nutritional value. In his time, there would be an online connection to his medical file signaling the potential effects of any intake of whatever substance was on his plate. As he finished his caramel desert in one big swallow, another memory came to mind concerning the connection between Bootsma and Burkowski.

Malik had said, "The fact that Bootsma's letter is mounted on Burkowski's wall implies something or someone connected the two of them. We're still working on gaining more information, but as far as we understand it now, after you leave here to get these two men, something goes wrong." If that were true, what had gone wrong? So far, he had done what had seemed perfectly logical to him: killing Calder and Bucket, killing the student, and sending Frank to Malik. He'd be sending Burkowski a little later. Had he missed alternatives? Could he turn back events? Could anyone else turn back history? Was it possible the entire operation was repeated years after his mission?

They always thought he would go back in time, execute his tasks, and either come back as planned or change course, if necessary, and return later as Plan B. They didn't take into account any possibility for failure of the mission. There was no Plan C. That had changed now, since he still hadn't acquired Burkowski's secret.

Ashlev peered about the lunchroom and was pleased to see that no one was paying any attention to him. He could remain seated, pick at his food, and no one would care. He couldn't stop laboring over every detail of his mission to date. His central theme was still Frank Bootsma's role concerning time travel and his discoveries at both the observatory and at the ASV in Rome. More and more, he had come to the conclusion there was a spider web of actions connecting several people with the specific time he'd landed here. He didn't know whether he was part of the problem or part of the solution. One thing he did know for sure was that he needed to learn everything he could about Bootsma.

For that reason, he had asked the Apostolic Nuncio to hand over every tidbit of information they had on file regarding the Jesuit. Fortunately, the last thing the Vatican wanted was to become engulfed in a troublesome relationship with the U.S. authorities after a series of problems with priests who had been too intimate with young men. Though reluctant to do so, the Nuncio had allowed him to visit their communications room. Like every embassy in the world, the Vatican had its own spy operation, handled by a special division of the Swiss Guard.

As it turned out, they kept a detailed log of all communications in and out of Castel Gandolfo during the weeks Bootsma had stayed there. The brother was on his own, without any help from the outside. Nothing appeared remotely suspicious. However, the time between his leaving the Castel and returning to the United States was one day too long. One entire day was missing. The intel delivered by the Vatican's Swiss Guards showed his *Tessara Temporanea* of the *Archivio Segreto Vaticana*—his temporal access permit of the Secret Archives of the Vatican. The onscreen permit revealed a stamp-sized photo of Bootsma, smiling confidently into the camera. The number on the pass was logged by the concierge of the archives when he entered the complex, but he hadn't been seen leaving. However, this fact alone hadn't been the reason for the Nuncio's distress. A new intel report had been received concerning a fire inside the Secret Vatican Archives. Luckily, only the diplomatic correspondence of the twentieth-century popes had been damaged by the foam of the fire extinguishers.

This fire had convinced the Nuncio that the possibility existed for Bootsma's involvement. It hadn't hurt that a high-ranking U.S. Navy officer was asked to question the Jesuit. He had ordered the Swiss Guard to arrest Bootsma upon his arrival on U.S. soil and willingly agreed to notify him—Superintendant Pakula—the moment this occurred.

Ashlev pushed back his chair from the table and carried his tray to the trash area, his mind still on his visit to the Vatican embassy. Leaving the cafeteria, he had shivered in the cold breeze, but that wasn't why he felt so cold. He stopped. He could see the Vatican embassy from here, across the main entrance. He replayed his steps. He had walked over to the embassy on foot, since it was only a five-minute walk from the USNO main gate. But something had been wrong all the time, he realized now. Now another shiver rippled through his body as he walked the short distance to his office.

How did I overlook such a glaring detail? Why didn't I realize my fatal mistake as soon as I interrogated Bootsma? Even when the man had said something about being blind, while seeing it a few seconds before his body collapsed in Burkowski's lab, he hadn't realized his blunder. He had been sitting on it!

Ashlev reached the entrance of the main USNO building with his mind still in Rome, reliving that fatal moment and the events that had interfered with his visit to the Vatican Archives. He had asked for a tour of the Tower of the Winds, but his request had been declined. A permit could only be given by the Prefect of the Secret Archives, and it would only be considered after a formal, written request backed up by a letter of recommendation from a professor or a member of the clergy.

While pretending to visit the men's room, he had wandered around the corridors surrounding the reading rooms of the Archives. His VR training had paid off. He had easily located the stairs leading to the tower and hidden behind a *trompe l'oeil* fresco, camouflaging the access door. Just as he had attempted to open the door, he had felt a firm hand on his shoulder. Turning, he was smacked against the wall by his attacker and cornered. The man was no competition for him, as they had at least two decades between them. Within seconds, their roles were reversed. In one swift movement, he had inserted his arms between his opponent's and released the grip on his throat. In another movement, he had taken the man's head into his hands and smashed it into the wall, crushing the bridge of his nose.

The man had staggered back several steps while blood poured from his nostrils, seemingly dizzy and, for vital seconds, off balance. Realizing their inequality, he had decided not to kill the man right away. He wanted to get some information from him first. Using force, he had kicked him sharply in one of his kneecaps, and as the man went down, he swiftly yanked his right arm behind his back and placed his knee on his right shoulder close to his neck. The man could hardly breathe. "If you want to live, tell me who you are and what you want from me," he had demanded.

The man had only clamped his lips tightly shut.

He had grabbed a fistful of his gray hair and yanked his head back and then slammed his forehead against the stone floor. The man hadn't made another move. Dark red blood oozed from his ears. Ashlev had searched for a pulse but felt none. The man was dead.

He had quickly searched all his pockets and found a wallet containing the ID of a Father Gabriel Bonomelli and some small change. He had conducted a second search and luckily found a tiny key in his breast pocket. He had immediately recognized it as being similar to the one he'd been given at the reception desk. It was from the locker room downstairs.

He had left the tower in a hurry, knowing that it was just a matter of time before the man's body was discovered. He had literally run down the stairs and rushed into the locker room. Moments later, he had located the locker of Bonomelli and the briefcase containing a manila folder on Brother Bootsma and two unsealed envelopes without an addressee.

He had hesitated about which to read in the time available to him. He had chosen the folder. He needed to learn what secret information Bootsma had discovered. He knew he could not and should not take it with him because he was unsure of what chain of events it would trigger. Opening an envelope could result in the same potential calamity. Killing the old man could already have promoted a devastating effect on his mission.

He had perused the material in the manila file within a few seconds. It contained some sort of information that hadn't survived the centuries of destruction. He hadn't understood, but he had to leave. He had closed the locker, leaving the key in the lock, and sneaked out of the building. Fortunately, the receptionist had been away from his station.

Ashlev looked around. On autopilot, he had already hung his uniform jacket on the stand just inside Pakula's office and was seated behind his desk when he came to his senses and suffered an instant wave of nausea. He had focused on the wrong track! Now, he understood the first part of the Jesuit's last words, "you can't see the Light when you have been staring into the wrong lamp." He should have stayed in the Tower of the Winds just one minute longer to investigate that marble disk in the Meridian Room. And he should have chosen to read what was in the envelopes. No doubt it was related to that damn disk.

Forget about Burkowski and his infamous footnote. He should have killed Calder and Bucket immediately upon arriving, and he should have focused solely on Frank Bootsma. He had made a fatal mistake.

Chapter 47

2115: Beijing

Frank eyed the general as surreptitiously as he could, knowing he was being watched himself. The general didn't waste time with words. She pushed Colonel Malik aside and opened the foglet history file on his computer, scrolling through the pages one after the other. Frank noticed that, in the corner of Malik's office, a pair of goggles had simultaneously been activated. The general stopped her search at a virtual tour of the Vatican. In only a few clicks, she entered the *Torre dei Venti*. Frank swallowed hard and felt his eyebrows shoot up. The system's high-tech capability was beyond anything he'd ever seen.

He wondered whether they had been bugged all the time. Suddenly, the general turned her wrath on Colonel Malik. "You have transported these two prisoners to your office and had a private conversation with them when you knew one of them had to be killed immediately, Colonel," she said, spitting out the words in a harsh staccato manner. "You violated Law 543c on the prohibition of personal contact with inmates." She stared at Max, displaying both her disgust and interest at the same time.

Frank felt the hair on his arms stand on end. This woman was a monster. She looked more like a reptile than a human being. On closer examination, he noticed a few mechanical parts peeking out from under her wrinkled skin, especially at her wrists and neck.

"You deliberately kept us out of your conversation, Colonel. We have learned that you conducted several such private conversations with Major Ashlev. Did you think you could outsmart us?" She pointed a long, gnarly finger at him. "We must assume you shared state secrets with him and, in so doing, jeopardized his mission and the mission of our men. These holograms are the evidence. In fact, the court-martial studied the entire situation and unanimously condemned you shortly before the departure of the Major. We have waited for his return in vain. It is my belief he never will return. Am I right, Colonel?"

Colonel Malik was silent, as if he had expected it all. Frank watched Max from the sides of his eyes. He seemed to be captivated by her and showed no outward signs of panic.

"You have been found guilty of high treason, and you will be executed today, Colonel Malik." She didn't wait for his response. "Guards!"

Four guards dressed in shimmering black fatigues marched forward to escort Malik from the platform. As he passed by Frank, he nodded ever so slightly. He seemed to be without fear. When he passed the general, she suddenly pulled a scalpel from her pocket and skillfully stabbed him in the neck, near the base of his skull. A fountain of blood spouted from the wound as, trying to stanch it, he stumbled forward several steps and crumpled to the platform. The general stepped deftly aside, obviously enjoying every bit of it.

Max and Frank cried out and fled into the farthest corner of the platform, transfixed on Malik's body. Frank rushed to his side and stepped in front of him in an effort to shield him from the general.

She narrowed her eyes and glared at them intently. "I wonder what this young man is still doing here." Her voice had changed in tone from harsh to melodious. She moved purposefully across the platform and tried to reach toward Max's face. He tried to avoid her. "Don't be afraid, young man," she crooned. "I don't intend to hurt you—at least not yet." She glanced over her shoulder. "Where is my commanding officer?" she barked, once again the harsh official.

Frank watched as another man stepped forward. He hadn't seen him before and assumed he had stayed in the background. His age was hard to estimate, maybe somewhere in his mid-thirties. He wore spotless white fatigues and a matching helmet. "Lieutenant Ching Tong, Commander of the First Time Mission reporting, Madam General," he said.

His speech pattern and appearance startled Frank. Clearly, the man wasn't human, at least not 100 percent. He was a humanoid machine composed of both live parts and machinery. He had seen such species in science fiction movies, and now, there was one speaking right in front of him. In a strange, almost frightening way, he found the man attractive.

The lieutenant came directly toward him and pulled Max from behind him. The strength in his unmuscled arms was extraordinary, and he almost twisted Frank's arm out of its socket.

Max lost balance and fell to the floor in front of the general.

"Don't hurt him! I can explain everything," Frank cried out.

"Be still!" the general commanded. "You speak only when I ask you to speak, Priest!" She turned with undisguised contempt to Lieutenant Tong.

"This young man is the beacon, General," he said. "He is the hard proof you requested. The colonel has kept him alive for a yet unknown reason. We are working on the interception of their conversation."

The general looked unimpressed. "And why are we still waiting for my men and the other traitor, Major Ashlev?" She tapped a bulky object attached to her right forearm.

Immediately, a hologram screen popped up. "This screen illustrates the timelines for their arrival, Lieutenant. It shows the delayed arrival times of Calder, Bucket, and Ashlev in red figures. I am not pleased."

Frank couldn't see the details from his position, but the general's description of her wrist device reminded him of the arrivals screen in a train station. Tong seemed restless. Personally, Frank was relieved by her diversion, since she was directing her rage at the cyborg.

"We have no means of contacting the mission leader and his team members, General," Tong said. "We've estimated—"

"Of course we have means, you idiot! If we have made mistakes, why didn't you send in another team?"

"The probability calculations—" Tong started.

"Yes, yes, I know. The chances for a successful first mission are low, but I expect my officers to be prepared for any obstacles. We could have sent a backup team, making sure Ashlev never got to his target. Did you even consider this option?"

Tong didn't answer. Frank watched him carefully and decided his system was calculating that his chance of survival was higher if he remained silent. The general was a force to be reckoned with, and her minions obeyed her out of fear.

The general paced the platform while panting heavily. Suddenly, she hyperventilated. Frank wished she would choke and then croak, but mostly, he was unsure who would become the next victim of her wrath. "May I have permission to speak, General?" he asked.

She stopped in her tracks and glared at him. A silence followed that emphasized her difficulty in breathing. He prayed and waited. The next few seconds could well decide his fate. Finally, she nodded.

"If you would send *us* back to our time, we could easily identify your Major Ashlev and send him back to you," he said. "What could possibly go wrong? We know exactly how Ashlev looks in his new body. If we don't send him to you, you could come after us again." Frank noticed his words were being recorded in the appliance on her wrist and that her fingers were somehow receiving feedback.

"Request granted. You may go." She paused a few seconds. "The boy stays. You will leave tonight and will arrive back tomorrow at the same hour with Major Ashlev. If not, the boy will be dissolved."

Frank felt a knot in his stomach. *It didn't work.*

She inserted the new timeline into her gadget. Without another word, she stepped closer to Malik's corpse and yanked the knife from his neck, handing it to one of the sentries. Then she left the platform with her guards in tow. Two other sentries dragged Malik's corpse behind them.
The entire episode had taken place in less than fifteen minutes. He eyed Max to ensure he was doing all right and then Lieutenant Tong, who seemed to come to life as he more smoothly walked toward them. He and two other sentries were the only ones that remained at the platform.

"It's a robot," Max whispered to Frank with both excitement over that phenomenon and visible relief the monstrous general had left.

"Don't move," Frank whispered. "I'll see if we can befriend him."

Tong examined them from head to foot. Now that Frank had a good view of his face, he saw that he was certainly not human. His facial covering was as smooth as plastic, but very well done.

"I am an A-H-C, an advanced human creation," Tong said. "A long time ago, we were called robots. This is not the time or place to discuss these matters, however. And you, Mr. Boohtsma, should not speak as you do. My system warns me when your voice and body temperature implicate potentially subversive actions. We will not tolerate such things. Do I have your attention?" When Frank nodded,

Tong continued. "It improves your performance when you are agreeable, and you're going to need it. Your value here is limited. We've calculated the amount of information useful for us at two gigabytes."

Frank wasn't sure he fully understood. It seemed that Tong was treating him like a computer. "Are you saying you know the size of my knowledge? How did you do that?"

"After your arrival and before we woke you, we downloaded your full memory onto our system and compared it with what we had already gotten from you." Tong walked to Malik's desk and re-opened the foglet screen. In a few seconds, Frank's bio lit up the screen. On the right side, the amount of information was displayed in gigabytes, running full speed as it counted all the information available on Frank, reaching a final 324 terabytes. On the left side of the screen, his recently downloaded information was displayed at 1.78 gigabytes, including the date, April 25, 2115.

Shocked, Frank ran his hands over his shaved head in a nervous gesture and felt the stubble. The adhesive tape had left some raw areas that smarted. He couldn't take his eyes from the date. All at once, his nightmare seemed less so. Maybe they'd have a chance after all.

Tong noticed his confusion. "Thanks to the Vatican mainframe, we were able to retrieve most of the material you'd stored on their servers, including some interesting lessons on the beginning of the universe."

Frank watched himself being interviewed by the BBC and showing the reporters around Castel Gandolfo, all in 3D. He remained speechless as he listened to Tong.

Tong pointed at the screen. "Because of our processing power, we can zoom in on any level of this footage, regardless of whether or not it was available in the original video."

Frank was impressed and stepped closer to the screen.

"Man, this is really cool!" Max said enthusiastically. "Imagine what gaming would look like on this thing!"

Frank sighed. He had forgotten what it was like to be Max's age. The young man's natural curiosity seemed to help him adjust better to their predicament than he was able to do. He feared what would come now, since these humanoids had pried into his mind. He realized they were far more advanced in such things than scientists back home were. He watched as Max stepped closer to the foglet screen.

Tong ignored Max and peered directly at Frank. "Why are you afraid?" he asked.

"I'm not."

"You're lying, and you know we know that. Stop doing such things. We can hurt you so that you will break in five minutes. Is that what you want?"

Frank shook his head, horrified by how casually Tong had threatened him. In a way, though, it made him like Tong even more.

"We believe you for now, Mr. Boohtsma. We know everything. You cannot hide your thoughts from us. If you cooperate, you will not have to suffer. The boy can be deleted in a less painful way if you both comply with the rules."

Max didn't seem to hear Tong's statement. He was enjoying the 3D screen and had discovered he could touch objects in it. "Look, Frank," he said. "You can turn it around." Behind them, the floor emitted a grinding sound. Max spied the goggles and immediately connected the two. He wandered over and put them on.

Frank was concerned, but since Tong was still ignoring Max, he paid attention to what the lieutenant was saying.

"We know about that tower, Mr. Boohtsma. We know about the hidden chamber under Castel Gandolfo. We followed your Web search and discovered additional connections to those yellow bees on the walls. We do not, however, have a high-definition video of the interior of that tower. Even worse, the marble disk on the floor has become invisible to us. What was on that disk, Priest? When you tell us, we will spare your life."

Frank didn't know what to do. They didn't know what was on the disk. They had made no connection to the two signs and suddenly, he realized he had already made a mistake. If they could read his mind and had downloaded his memory, they could trap him with this very conversation. *How can I control my thoughts?* Somehow, he had to concentrate on something that was true but meaningless.

"The disk was part of a marble meridian, like the disk cemented into the floor," he said. "It crossed the room diagonally. For that reason, the room was called the Meridian Room. Outside this room, the meridian would have run through the Vatican and Rome ... across the globe. It was pretty accurate for that time."

"What about the disk itself?" Tong asked with a slight edge to his voice.

Frank inhaled slowly and scratched his forehead, as though thinking. Then, as calmly as he could, he said, "The disk was only a marker on the floor to capture the sunlight at certain points in time. Nothing more, nothing less."

Tong stared at Frank while calculating the input his system had collected. He seemed satisfied for a moment, but then he wasn't. "What were you doing in that tower, Mr. Boohtsma? How was this related to your work on the origin of the cosmos?"

Frank hesitated. Tong was well informed. He needed to stay cool. From the sides of his eyes, he noticed that Max was still busy in the corner of the platform while wearing the goggles. Adolescents had a knack for shutting out problems by playing games, even in the most difficult circumstances. That was good. He didn't want him to worry about his potential demise.

"The Meridian Room was the place where the Vatican Observatory was born," he said. "Those who were interested could observe the rotation of the Earth and the movement of the stars during the nighttime hours. At that time, Rome lacked the smog it has now." He realized his mistake as soon as he made it and tried to recover. "Now, as in *my* time. Anyway, I wanted to see it with my own eyes. I also wanted to investigate the frescoes in the tower, which reflected the early interpretations of the origin of the cosmos as the work of God."

Tong was silent for some time. Frank read nothing from his face or eyes. Maybe the cyborg hadn't been able to read his mind. He showed no signs of anger. On the contrary, he seemed to be accepting.

"My systems tell me you are proud of what you know," Tong said. "That is what we want to accomplish. We will now show you what we downloaded from you."

Frank controlled the need to wipe his sweaty palms on his shirt. An even body temperature was apparently important.

The right section of the screen minimized and categorized the information into chapters, while the left section enlarged. Tong motioned to him to come closer. "In your time, an average connected person left a modest 500 megabytes trail of information per day, including email, phone calls, web surfing, video surveillance footage, downloaded or recorded movies, and so on. You seem to be an average person. In your lifetime, you collected around 150 terabytes, which means you reached approximately the age of seventy. We do not need to estimate that fact, do we?"

It took a few seconds for Frank to realize the cyborg had made a joke as inane as one from a computer nerd. At the same time, he recognized the on-screen information was about his future life without his being abducted. The first 100 gigabytes opened like a scroll-down menu, and chunks of information were graphically displayed. It regrouped into chapters, which were checked against those on the right side of the screen. In the margin, he saw a timeline to the year 2056. He saw a cross next to this date, indicating it was the year he died. *Dear God, they even know when I died.*

"We will ignore your childhood and student time, since these memories were stored in your mental archive and only incidentally evoked. We will also not focus on the events of the last thirty years of your life, because they were not very informative. We will focus on your active memory and especially on your discoveries, the only part we are interested in recovering." Tong tapped on the foglet screen where the categories made a connection. He tapped a few more times, condensing the information.

Frank was relieved they didn't zoom in to his findings in the Tower of the Winds. His memory and the video footage were merged and replayed at high speed until it automatically stopped at an image of Max. His heart stopped.

"Exactly what were you explaining to this young man while you travelled to our time?" Tong asked.

A transcript of their conversation rolled over the screen while his eyes had acted like a camera, showing Max sitting next to him. Everything they had discussed while somewhere in limbo had been recorded. It started with their conversation about his work.

"I have found evidence that some of the oldest meteorites contain a structure that resembles the structure of the universe right after the Big Bang. If you could shrink yourself to atomic proportions and could fly around inside one of those meteorites, you would experience the Early Galactic time.

"And this is what those Navy types wanted you for?"

"Well, yes, for some reason they do, my friend. And for another reason, they want your father and maybe you as well. So, please fill in the dots yourself, because I cannot see any."

Tong paused the movie.

"Could you not see, Mr. Boohtmsa, or did you not want to see it?" Tong asked.

They have information about our conversation, but my thoughts were not recorded, Frank contemplated.

"I think I sense what you think," Tong said. "We only have records of action memory—that is to say, where memory is connected to interaction with other persons or objects. Thoughts in general, daydreaming, and dreams are not within our realm. We cannot capture them. It's as if they don't exist." Tong looked directly at Frank. "In a way, those memories don't exist. They were no cause and had no effect."

Frank stared back at the lieutenant without comment. He glanced quickly at Max. "No, we didn't look into the memory of Max. He's of no importance to us," Tong said, reading his thoughts. Frank worked at controlling his emotional and physical reactions. Perhaps the 'friendly' interrogation was about to end.

Suddenly, as if he heard talking about him, Max turned to Frank while still wearing the goggles. "This is cool, Frank. I just wandered all around the Vatican complex. I saw you in that tower. Everything was filmed through your eyes. Can you believe this? What was that wind vane thing on the ceiling? It looked pretty awesome."

Frank watched as Tong turned toward Max while tilting his head in slow motion to listen more intently. He wished he had never uttered those words.

"Wind vane? Inside that tower room?" Tong asked.

Frank realized he was calculating everything related to a wind vane inside a Vatican room.

Finally, Tong faced Frank with a look that was still friendly but emanated something else that freaked him out. His own mind was churning rapidly. Had his memory dump given away his stunning discovery? He had to concentrate on other things and relax, relax, relax to keep his body temperature cool. That was the only way to keep the cyborg from 'reading' his mind. Finally, he was beginning to understand the system.

"Please educate us, Mr. Boohtsma," Tong said. "Is that structure called the Tower of the Winds because there was a wind blowing within the room with the marble disk?"

Chapter 48

Saturday: Washington DC

Jacob sat in the passenger seat of Ellen's car with the draft copy of his article on his lap. He had forgotten his Volvo was still at the hospital, and he needed her to act as his chauffeur. He watched out the windshield as she sped up to ten miles over the speed limit. Luckily, the traffic on Saturday was light.

Dropping his eyes for only a second to the paper, he shifted on the seat. "I still can't believe this is what those bastards are after," he said. He had to force himself not to think about Max.

"Out with it, Jacob," Ellen said. "Stop holding back on me! Those are the same bastards I'm supposed to have killed. Now, what did you remember?" Her voice was sharp and intense.

Surprised at her tone of voice, he patted her knee. "I remember. It may sound ridiculous, so you have to promise not to laugh. It's probably why I didn't remember in the first place."

"Just get on with it, or we'll reach the hospital before I have a chance to hear your explanations. I promise I won't laugh."

"Okay, then. Here we go." Jacob reread part of the document aloud and then peered directly at her. "When I researched the famous Einstein $E=MC^2$ equation, I stumbled across a peculiar detail. Between the years of 1909 and

1913, Einstein shared a few dinners with Carl Jung. Ever heard of him?"

Ellen nodded and rolled her eyes a little. "Of course I have. I studied cognitive psychology, and Jung was the icon of the *Archetype* theory—assuming that people's behaviors are connected to his grand scheme of the 'mother of all psychic types'. Whoo-whoo. Scary." She wiggled her fingers at him.

"You promised not to laugh, Ellen... and please keep your hands on the wheel. Anyway, Einstein's dinner conversations with Jung resulted in one of his major ideas called—"

"...synchronicity. Or, better phrased, the *illusion* of synchronicity. People confuse two coincidences with something bigger, as if they are happening at the same time for a reason, which, of course, is not the case—hence, the illusion."

"If you already know all this stuff, why should I bother sharing any of it with you?" Jacob sighed and peered out his side window. Again he fought the waves of sorrow.

Ellen reached out and touched his arm. "Sorry. I'm a bit uptight thinking about what may be waiting for you in your lab. Please continue."

"Let's not get ahead of ourselves." Jacob glanced at her and then out the windshield again. "Scientists denounced Jung's theory as the illusion of synchronicity because people tend to believe events are connected when they happen at the same time ... which they aren't. But it can't be proven."

"That's what I said."

"Yes, but that isn't the point. Synchronicity was about the decoupling of time and space. After their discussions, Jung came to believe that if time and space are relative, the psyche could work independently from time and space as well—sort of like déjà vu ... or seeing things that happen on another continent or both at the same time. Sort of long-distance looking. These phenomena occur especially during sleep or deep sleep. Jung did a lot of experiments, and—"

"This long-distance looking was a covert project of the CIA during the fifties."

"You're right. But that's not the point either. It's something far more important." Jacob held up his draft article and pointed at a graph showing a circle cut horizontally in half with the lower half divided into two sections. He clearly remembered that he had found a remotely possible cure for Max's severe headaches.

Ellen glanced at it. "What's that all about? I can't read while I'm driving."

"Since sleep and deep sleep were closely connected to death for Jung, I figured if I could find a way to simulate death, the psyche could travel in time." He looked to see if she was amused by his theory. "Are you scoffing?"

She shrugged. "I can't get rid of the idea that Jung was on the wrong track, just like Freud and other megalomaniacs who thought they had discovered the one and only theory that explained everything." She made a few more mocking gestures with her fingers.

"Keep your hands on the wheel, Ellen. I understand your skepticism. I felt the same way at first, more or less. I stumbled across his ideas when I was exploring the depth of unconsciousness because one of the possibilities for a brain reset resides there, like the recovery disk of a computer, no matter how ridiculous that may sound. It might be able to cure Max."

Ellen nodded. "I'm familiar with the premise that, in trauma therapy, we can tap into a massive library of these hidden places in our minds."

"Neurologically speaking, you're talking about stored reflexes in remote areas of our neurovascular system. Unfortunately, I didn't have the time to explore its potential. That's why I made a notation about the origin in the margin of my paper."

"The origin of what? Be quick, Jacob. The hospital is only a block away."

Jacob gazed more intently at the woman behind the wheel. She wasn't the same as the woman who had spent the night with him. Her military training had taken over. She was all business.

Ellen glanced back at him briefly. "If Einstein and Jung talked about *mental* time travel, it would give our nutcases a new landing platform."

"Worse."

"Don't you think they'll be heading for Einstein, possibly this Carl Jung, because of their conversation?"

Jacob thought about the magnitude of such a scenario but decided Ellen was wrong, terribly wrong. He shook his head. "Nope. It has to be the other way around. Einstein most likely got his ideas on time travel from Jung."

"What makes you say that?"

"A small detail that got lost in official history. You have to have a keen interest in Jung to ascertain this. It was a footnote in an obscure New Age biography. That's how I put Calder and his allies on the trail to Einstein and Jung."

"If that's what those criminals believe, they'll go for it." Ellen turned right into the hospital parking lot. "How far back in time did those sources of Jung's go?"

"I'm not sure. Jung researched myths way back before written history. The sources about myths manifesting themselves to the unconscious have to be clearly connected to time travel, to invoke the time-travel boundaries. But hell, yes, I'm afraid you're right. Whoever is behind this operation has much bigger plans in mind. I'm not sure what those plans are, but we're definitely not their final destination."

Ellen parked her car in a visitor's space and turned off the engine. She took her Glock from her belt and checked its safety lock. She glanced sideways and put her hand on his arm.

"Max is not what they want. He's not important to them."

Jacob winced.

"We'll find him, Jacob, I promise."

She took a deep breath. "Are there any metal detectors at this entrance?"

"Nope."

"Come on, then. Let's head for your lab. I am ready." She stashed her gun again and exited the car without waiting for his go-ahead. She was a military officer on a mission.

Jacob led the way to the hospital entrance. He removed a pass from his pocket and held it against the security box. A green light signaled the release of the automatic lock. As he held the door open for Ellen, his thoughts returned to the message on his laboratory screen. Some very eager and potentially dangerous person was waiting for his information—a person who held Max's life in his control. Maybe it was all for nothing, and Max was gone forever.

Chapter 49

Saturday: USNO, Washington DC

A soft sound outside his office put Ashlev instantly on alert. He had been replaying the events in Rome and in Washington in his mind. For a brief moment, he had been out of focus. The sound was coming from the corridor. *But no one should be here,* he thought. It was Saturday, and not even the civilian security people were allowed to enter the main building without a Navy officer present.

He rose from his chair and walked quietly across the room to the door. Opening it only a crack, he listened more carefully. When he didn't hear anything, he opened it wider and peered in both directions. The corridor was deserted, as he expected. On a whim, he made his way toward the USNO entrance hall, hugging the wall to stay out of sight. Halfway to his destination, he damned himself. He realized he was unarmed; he had left his weapon in his desk drawer.

Just as he was about to return for it, he sensed movement not so far away. Someone crossed the hallway slowly and almost inaudibly. Like a picture on the wall, he held himself inert, barely breathing and closing his eyes, sharpening his hearing to distinguish the sound. Yes, it was that of two legs clad in pantyhose rubbing against each other. *A woman.*

Who could have followed him into the building? Who had access? *Meyer!* It had to be her. She was in charge of security and must know every means for getting into the building, including any holes in the fence surrounding the USNO. She was most likely armed. He had learned of the Glock registered in her name only a few days ago in the unit arms room. It was against defense regulations, but he had kept her little secret to himself assuming he could use the violation against her if the circumstances required it.

Ashlev felt a stronger urgency to fetch his own weapon. This was no time to play cat and mouse. He turned and dashed to his office, rushing across the room to jerk open the desk drawer. He grabbed hold of the loaded Beretta 92 M9, standard issue in the U.S. Navy, and in one swift move, he cocked the gun and whirled toward the door of his office, expecting Meyer to burst through it at any moment.

But no one appeared.

He waited, frozen.

Hearing nothing, he started moving cautiously across the room. When he reached the door, he pushed himself against the wall, throwing a quick glance to the left in the direction of the hall. Just as he pulled his head back inside, a strong arm grabbed him around his neck, lifted him in the air, and smashed him on the floor. It only took a second. In the next second, his wrists were cuffed behind his back by someone who had one heavy square knee between his shoulders and another on his head. The sudden odor of sweaty pantyhose penetrated his nostrils. It was not a pleasant aroma.

"You're under arrest for coercion, assault, and murder, Pakula. Give me another second, and I'll read you your rights." Police Commander Gomez pulled him back onto his feet and dragged him far enough into the room to shut the door with her foot while she mumbled his Miranda rights.

Ashlev gaped at her and then back to the door, expecting her backup team to enter at any moment.

"I came alone, Pakula. No backup. Didn't need any. I wanted you all to myself. No witnesses."

Ashlev's level of adrenaline shot up. The officer's last words left a bad taste in his mouth. She was dressed in her uniform with a chest full of decorations speaking of her experience. Her face was twisted with anger.

"You seem to think you rule this world, Captain Pakula. You came to my office and you bugged me. It's not the first time in my life, but I won't let you do this." She pushed him onto his chair and sat on a corner of the desk next to him. "Most men are relics from their prehistoric past and their frontal cortexes remain as undeveloped as they were then." She glared at him, and her dry, bottom lip curled under. "However, you crossed the line with what you did to Meyer."

"Commander Meyer?"

"Is there any other? She told me all about you, Pakula. About how you physically assaulted *her*. About what went on during your Time Committee meeting, the setup of the murder of two men you claimed were under her command. She's convinced you're behind the murder of Burkowski's son as well. Is there more I should know about?"

Ashlev stared at her, at a loss for words. Why was she in his office and alone? What does she want from me?

"Meyer explained to me how you betrayed the United States of America by ordering the placement of the Atomic Clock online. No one was going to stop you because of your rank and authority. You have a plan, and I want to know about it."

"This is all a conspiracy and I want—"

"Uh, uh, uh ... this has nothing to do with any conspiracy, Pakula. We women know a debauchee when we see one."

"We women?"

"Yes. Surprised, I suppose?"

Ashlev shook his head, never taking his eyes off her face. There was no trace of women co-operation in this bitch.

"We women share a sense of solidarity you men have never had and never will have. Not that it matters right now. We're going to sort things out, just you and me."

Ashlev watched as she pulled the keyboard of his PC toward her and touched a key. The screen asked for a password. The username of "Pakula" had already been filled in.

"What's the password?"

"I'm not allowed to—"

"Need convincing?" She searched the desktop and found a pair of scissors. Snatching them up, she held the point over his head. Without hesitation, Ashlev said, "It's on a piece of paper glued to the bottom of the center desk drawer."

Gomez strode behind him and rolled his chair to the center of the room. Then, she returned to the desk and yanked out the drawer, turning it upside down. Pulling the yellow paper from its position, she typed the code on the keyboard and waited for the screen to reveal his files. She took her time perusing his folders, including the hidden ones.

"What are you looking for?" Ashlev asked, by now gathering enough nerve to question her.

"You'll see. Give me another minute." She took a USB stick out of her pocket and inserted it into the keyboard. It opened itself and started a program. It read: UNDELETE.

"What's that for? What are you doing? That's confidential U.S. government information," he said, becoming more irritated.

"Shut up."

Ashlev could hear the hard disk of his computer humming. A series of windows flashed on the screen. Then, he saw only a row of green marks. Gomez stared at the result, and her face darkened. "Where did you leave it?" she snapped.

"Leave what?"

"Where's the porn? Do you have access to another computer or something?"

"I only have access to that one computer... and what's 'porn'?"

Gomez was at his side within seconds. She spun his chair around, sank to her knees, and pulled off his shoes. Then, yanking his legs backwards, she used the shoelaces to tie his legs to the central leg of the chair. "That's better," she said. "Playing dumb doesn't work with me. I'll give you exactly five seconds before I start working on you with these." She held the scissors in a most menacing position.

Ashlev realized what she had in mind. The scissors were pointed at his groin. She was going to unman him. She was crazy and a man-hater. Even though this body was temporal, the pain of such an act would be unbearable. She was not going to take *no* for an answer. He had to tell her something to get through her thick skull. "I think I know what you want."

She lunged forward and thrust one blade of the scissors into his groin, just deeply enough to penetrate the fabric of his uniform. It hurt like hell.

"Don't tell me you don't know what I want. I'm ready to cut off your balls with your pants on," she demanded, gloating over the idea.

"I-I'm not what you think I am," he said.

"I know. That's an understatement if I ever heard one."

"No, the man in front of you has, uh, changed. Please, take those scissors away from me."

"You're saying you're cured? Educate me."

Ashlev felt the pressure on the scissors increase. He could not and would not jeopardize his mission by revealing who he really was. Somehow, he had to modify the truth. The best lies are hidden under a veil of truth. "I have been in therapy."

"What kind of therapy?"

"Not normal psychotherapeutic therapy. It was based on a different model." He blinked at her. "Please, Commander, could you remove those scissors for now?"

She only slightly reduced the pressure. "Thank you." Ashlev thought about how much to say and in what way. "During my therapy sessions, I learned about several long repressed memories."

"Okay, so you had a bad childhood, is that what you're going to say?" Unexpectedly, Commander Gomez's posture hardened.

"No, no, not at all," Ashlev said hastily. "I never knew my parents. I was raised in a foster home and had a fairly happy time there. No, I'm talking about memories that were actually not mine. They were transmitted to me from my ancestors ... from thousands of years ago."

Ashlev watched as the commander's eyes flickered and the lines of her face softened ever so slightly. She was definitely interested. Then, in a finger snap, she changed. "You believe that crap?" Again, her lip curled into a snarl.

"As a Navy officer, I was trained differently. I asked for help because I was having these severe nightmares. You'd be surprised about the services we get in the armed forces. I don't suppose the police offer such services."

Gomez shook her head.

He realized she had inadvertently relaxed the pressure on her lethal weapon. "Tell me your birth date, time and place."

"Why?"

"To demonstrate who I am."

She hesitated.

"You will not be disappointed, Commander."

She shrugged. "What have I got to lose," she mumbled. "November 10, 1958, eight thirty-five p.m., the Bronx."

"Give me a couple minutes." Ashlev closed his eyes and thought back to what Malik had taught him. First, he had to imagine that his mind became one with the universe. Then, he had to take the series of calculations, organize them in separate rooms, and give every detail its own symbol. An enormous tranquility came over him.

When he reopened his eyes, Gomez was busily searching every drawer and cabinet in his office. She had even found the safe. The door stood wide open.

She glanced over at him and saw that he was ready for her. "Well?"

Ashlev peered at the ceiling to keep from becoming distracted by her appearance. "I'll summarize your past first," he said. "You're the third child of five. Your youngest sibling was murdered at the age of six. You've always felt guilty about her death because you shouldn't have left her at home alone. It has been the most important factor in your life, next to being promoted to police commander. And because you are not born to be second in command, your promotion is fulfilling that one. That leaves us with the factor that's haunting you at night."

He watched as her face paled and her mouth fell open. She was without words.

"You have managed to keep this mental disorder out of your records, but your birth path is clear. Your feelings of guilt have prevented you from marrying, having children of your own, and so on. You have chosen to remain single as a self-induced penance. It's a combination of Vedic astrology and numerology," he added. "I can help you, Commander."

"How on Earth did you ...?" She raised the scissors again but just as quickly lowered them.

Ashlev managed the semblance of a smile. "I am a Brahmin. Are you familiar with my caste?"

"You're Indian?"

He smiled more confidently. "Over the years, our brown complexions have faded away, but yes, I am a full-blooded Indian. I would like to share our prediction of your future with you... my friend." He hesitated to call her that, but when speaking softly, it sounded sincere. He hadn't lied to her. She couldn't know most of the psychiatric reports had been discovered by Malik—even the murder of her little sister—thanks to the Bronx Medical Records Network, a state-funded digitizing program of electronic patient records. The rest was sincere Vedic astrology.

Gomez turned his chair around, slowly this time, and used her scissors to cut the shoelaces around his ankles. Then, she released the handcuffs on his wrists. "Let's hear about this prediction of yours, Pakula. It better be good."

He rose from the chair and stretched his arms, releasing the tension in his shoulders. "It will be," he said, as convincingly as possible.

Chapter 50

2115: Beijing

Why did Max have to mention the damn wind vane? *Keep calm,* Frank told himself. *This is no time to panic. Think before you talk.* Max was not an adult; he didn't know any better. Frank shrugged and smiled. "The wind vane was a unique innovation at that time, Lieutenant Tong. It was connected to one on the rooftop. By this means, the exact direction of the wind could be displayed within the Meridian Room as eight separate winds—north, south, west, east and northwest, northeast, and so on. It was sort of a dashboard of information. The precise time and the direction of the wind were both crucial for navigation at sea."

Tong nodded. "Interesting. The disk and wind vane in the tower collected information to relay to vessels at sea."

"Yes, that's right." Frank realized quite suddenly that the cyborgs had not yet beaten humans in their creativity. Navigation at sea in the middle of Rome, he mused. How would the cyborg process this contradiction? Tong was silent, but Frank could hear the soft humming that indicated he was either processing the information or consulting his superiors or both.

After several seconds, Tong addressed both Frank and Max. "There is a slight change of plans. You will not travel back today, Mr. Boohtsma. Perhaps tomorrow or more likely in a few days. We need more time for preparation. Before we go, your parents never authorized you to study at the Vatican right?"

Frank opened his mouth to protest and then clamped it shut. Dread surged through him. Before he could say something, Tong opened up a folder with emails and photo attachments. Frank's heart skipped a beat. "Why does your mother complain about your absence at your father's funeral?" Tong asked, and Frank's stomach turned. *How on Earth did they get this information?*

"Mr. Boohtsma, please understand we've access to all your digitally stored material. Please enlighten us. We have reason to believe you had problems with your parents that have brought you here."

The cyborg was so right-on, and this was so impossible. Panic rose in his chest. *Control your thoughts!* There was no defense. His mind swirled. His discoveries proved his father was right...

"What discoveries, Mr. Boohtsma?" sounded the sharp voice of Tong, interrupting his thoughts.

He glanced at Tong. The voice, the mispronunciation of his name, his appearance, what was it with this cyborg that fooled him? Tong's tight white fatigues shimmered in the light of the foglet screen. A strange, warm sensation filled his body. It was as if Tong had seeped into him, reading his mind.

"Why is your temperature rising, Mr. Boohtsma?"

He hadn't seen Max coming. Max stared at him, frowning. Alternating, he looked at Frank and Tong. Then he smiled. "You're blushing."

"No I'm not," he tried, deeply embarrassed. Thank God Tong had switched off the screen, dimming the light in Malik's office. He mouthed 'shut up' to Max, but he seemed to see the joke of it.

"I will take you to your quarters," Tong interrupted. "You are allowed to stay together for now. After you have traveled back, Mr. Boohtmsa, we will terminate the boy's presence here."

Instantly, Max stopped smiling. He felt so sorry for all this, but most of all, he was confused. In silence, they followed Tong. He escorted them off the platform. A driverless carriage was waiting for them. At an alarming speed, they raced through a labyrinth of corridors. When they finally stopped, they had reached a section with an endless row of green doors. It zoomed past these and finally stopped at the last door. Max remained mute throughout the entire ride.

Tong remotely opened the fifty-inch steel door of their sleeping chamber. "You will be awaked at six tomorrow morning. We will expect you to be ready when we arrive to pick you up." Without another word, he climbed back into the carriage and sped away.

Frank watched until he could no longer see any sign of it and then ushered Max into the room, but Max stopped.

"Sorry about that one, Frank."

Frank took a deep breath. "It's okay, Max. It's all so confusing—our bodies, the interrogation, the whole situation." He wanted to say more but didn't dare. He had to stay optimistic.

A light automatically switched on as they entered, revealing a Spartan space containing only a double-decker bed, a steel table, two steel chairs bolted to the floor, and an unidentifiable cube slightly shorter than Max and not much wider.

While Frank inspected the beds for reasonable comfort, Max opened the cube. "It's a toilet!" he said. "I can't stand up in it, but I'm gonna try to use it anyway." He stooped to enter the door and then shut it behind him.

For the next few minutes, Frank heard the faint sounds of water jets. When Max didn't reappear, he paced the floor as a dozen scenarios passed through his mind in quick succession. Was this contraption the cyborg's clever way of doing away with Max?

Finally, the door opened, and Max stepped into the room, soaking wet and laughing. "It's a toilet-shower combo!" he said. "You're supposed to do both things at the same time! It's pretty awesome. Just wish I'd known to get in there naked!"

He laughed again, and Frank laughed with him. It felt good to be normal, even if only for a few minutes.

"How are we going to get you dry, Max?"

"Watch and see." Max strode directly to another corner of the room. "Dry!" he commanded. Without warning, a stream of hot air flowed directly down on him and, within seconds, his hair and clothes were completely dried out.

"How did you do that?"

"Inside that toilet-shower cube, a video screen offers tips. It actually knew I was still wearing my clothes and said I should use the 'personal dry cleaner' in the corner of the room."

"Amazing. A few mothers in our time would have appreciated such a gadget, that's for sure!" Frank bit his tongue as soon the words left his mouth. It was a reminder that Max would never see his mother again.

"Let's see if this room has more," Max said enthusiastically, clearly diverted. "I could use a bite. What about you, Frank?"

The mere mention of food made him feel melancholy. He sat down on his bed. Somehow, tears welled up in his eyes. He couldn't believe where he was. Memories of Castel Gandolfo flashed by, along with the thought of Italian delicacies. If he could have just a plain dish of spaghetti, topped with a little pecorino cheese! He had to find a way out of there. He had to eat.

He hadn't paid much attention to Max. In the corner, behind the cube, an odd bubbling sound called for his attention. Immediately after, the unmistaken smell of baked potatoes penetrated his nostrils. He rushed forward to find Max with two plates in his hands, a big grin on his face.

"Look what I found here!" He pointed at the wall. A glass hatch stood open, next to a screen depicting an assortment of dishes. "I only had to tap on the icon, and in a few seconds, these plates were assembled in the oven. Fantastic! It started with an amorphous gray lump that unfolded itself into these potatoes, followed by something that smells like a burger. Hey, Frank, even it's cyborg food, it smells terrific, don't you think?"

Frank just nodded and took a plate. They sat side by side on the bed and started eating. The food wasn't really all that bad. It wasn't Italian, but at least it filled his stomach.

Despite the need to plan for the next steps, Frank couldn't suppress a yawn.

"Why don't you catch some sleep, Frank? I'm not tired yet, but you should take a nap. I'll find something to do. And don't worry. I'm okay."

Frank nodded. "Somehow, I think you are. You're a remarkable young man, Max. Wish I had more of your optimism." Why he wasn't collapsing under the pressure of knowing what the morning would bring, Frank simply didn't understand. It didn't matter. They should prepare for their next meeting with the cyborg. The night was long, and there was plenty of time. He would rest for a half hour or so and then pray for guidance as he organized a Last Sacrament for Max, just in case.

Frank climbed onto the lower bunk and lay on his back, staring at the upper bunk. Within a couple of minutes, he was sound asleep, only half aware of Max's fading footsteps.

※ ※ ※

Max wandered the room and tried the knob on their door out of curiosity. Surprisingly, it turned, and the heavy door opened with no effort. He stuck his head out and saw that no one was outside guarding the corridor. Holding the door open, he stepped out of the room for a better look. He saw no visible cameras mounted near the ceiling. He turned the doorknob several times to see if he'd be able to get back into the room when the door shut after him. It seemed okay.

He was happy to leave the room and be on his own. Somehow, his life had changed so much for the better. His headache was gone, and this body was a real improvement, tanned and muscular. Not to forget the foglets, goggles, and the equipment in their room. He definitely wanted to see more of it before they tried to escape. He was sure now that the fat man, no, the maybe-Frank man, was not part of the criminals. He'd been caring and very worried about him. This guy was in a way very, very funny, especially the way he looked at the cyborg with that unforgettable expression on his face. Max had to grin again at the thought of it.

For the next several minutes, he roamed the long corridor, passing an unending number of identical doors. He came to a junction where the corridor extended both to the left and to the right. One looked the same as theirs, but the other was different. He went that way.

The space was really not a corridor at all, but an expansive square hall with four massive doors, each with a brass plaque written in Chinese or something. He couldn't read them. He opened the first door and took a quick look around. Then he did the same for the next three rooms. Each one was more or less the same. They contained a strange collection of brass instruments, most of which didn't look familiar to him. In the first room, he identified one as a sundial in the shape of the Earth. It was transparent and made of neatly soldered circles. The other one was a sextant ... not the portable kind, but one that was man-high. Frank would probably find that interesting. He should go get him, Max thought, but first he would explore the other rooms more carefully.

Even after a closer inspection, none of the instruments made sense to him. Maybe they would to Frank. Thinking about the Jesuit made him feel a little sad. He could tell the guy was worried about him ... about what that weird general and the humanoid Tong had said about getting rid of him. For some reason, in spite of the threats, he wasn't panicky himself.

He saw his reflection in one of the brass instruments and liked his new body. He flexed the muscles in his arms. They bulged up a bit. He felt stronger than before. He liked being tanned too. It reminded him of the time his folks had taken him to Florida for a vacation. He'd come home looking a bit like peanut butter. It didn't hurt that he looked a little older, maybe a couple of years.

Max glanced about the room again. He couldn't really describe his mood. He was sad about having to leave his dad without saying goodbye. Suddenly, he remembered that his mother had been murdered. *Or was she?* Who was to say he wasn't just on some bizarre journey and would fly back in time and land somewhere else before all this stuff happened? If it happened at all. If time travel worked this way, who was he to say that things couldn't be turned back? He was still alive, wasn't he? His friends would freak out if they knew about all of this, not to mention his dupe. Why didn't he see him anymore? Was he part of this evil plan, or did he try to warn him? His dupe wasn't so enthusiastic when Max had mentioned he wanted to get to his dad, and he had even tried to talk him out of it. If he could get access to a computer, he might try to rebuild him again. The idea became bigger and bigger. They must have more powerful computers over here. It must work!

He was so deeply engrossed with the idea of bringing his clone back to life that he almost missed a wooden chest in the corner. It looked like it had been around for a few decades at least. The padlock was missing. He glanced around to see if anyone was watching or if there were any surveillance cameras. Nothing. He was still alone. Quickly, he sank to his knees and lifted the lid of the chest. It was pretty heavy, but he managed with a grunt or two.

Shit! It was only a bunch of old papers. Max reached for one of the bundles, and it crumbled to pieces. Only the hard cover remained in his hands. He examined it. The words seemed to be written in Latin. Latin! Frank might like to see this. He folded the cover and stashed it in his pocket. It was time to get back to his room.

As he hurried through the square hall and back to his own corridor, he was once again surprised at the lack of security. There were no guards, no cameras. It was hard to believe the cyborgs would let him wander around the place. Just as he turned the corner, he saw Tong standing outside his room next to the driverless carriage, watching him.

The closer Max came to the cyborg, the more worried he became. Had he been watched the entire time? Had someone seen him dig into the chest and stuff the cover of the disintegrated book into his pocket? Was that why Tong was here?

Tong's attitude was pleasant. "You couldn't sleep?"

"Uh, no. I thought a little walk would make me sleepy. It worked," Max said, yawning.

"What was your impression of the brass instruments?"

Max felt his heart pounding. He didn't know what to say.

"They are very ancient," Tong said. "Used long before your time."

Max peered at him quizzically. "Did you follow me, sir? I didn't see you."

Tong shook his head. "No need to follow you, Max. All corridors have the capacity to monitor. They act as one very big surveillance camera, which is connected to my system. You pressed the limits a bit, but I thought it was informative to see how far you would go. You did not attempt to break out, which would have been impossible, but it demonstrated your mindset. You are a curious person. If we could use you a bit longer, it would be a most interesting experiment. However, we have other priorities." With an almost wistful look on his face, he stepped into the carriage and sped away.

Max reentered the room and found Frank wide awake, sitting on the edge of the lower bunk. His hair stood right up from tossing in his sleep. "I'm sorry to say it, but you look pretty funny." Frank grimaced, rubbing his hand over his head. "What's going on? Why weren't you here when I woke up?"

"I couldn't sleep, and I decided to walk round a bit. I discovered some cool things." Max removed the folded book cover from his pocket and handed it to Frank.

"Where did you get this?"

"There are four rooms full of giant-sized brass instruments not very far from here. I only recognized a couple of them—a sundial and a sextant. One of the rooms had a trunk full of old papers. That's what's left of one bundle."

Frank read the title. "Did you say you found this in a trunk?"

"Uh-huh, along with a bunch of other old papers in bundles. It was one big mess."

Frank held up the cover. "Do you have any idea what this is?"

"What's left of a book?"

"This is serious, son."

"I don't know. It looked like something written in Latin to me. That's why I brought it back for you. Thought you'd find it interesting."

"It's more than a little interesting. This 'book,' as you call it, wasn't really a book. It was an official document sent to Beijing from Rome. Quite unbelievable."

"Why?"

"The Vatican has only three observatories. One is in the Vatican itself, where it started its first astronomy studies in a tower called the *Torre dei Venti*. The second one is in Castel Gandolfo, a village where the summer home of the pope was built. When the air pollution in Rome prevented some of their studies, the astronomers built a similar tower there. That's where my office is—or was, rather. The third one was raised in Beijing. The Chinese were well on their way to building an observatory, but the Emperor asked Ferdinand Verbiest, a Jesuit like me, to redesign the observatory in the 1670s, because their calendar was wrong. It had a standard thirteen months."

Max stared at what was left of the book or the document, whatever it was. He was sorry he hadn't been more careful with it.

Frank leaped off the bed. "You have no idea what this means for me." He leaned closer to Max. "For us," he whispered. He blinked twice, then rolled his eyes upward twice. Then he stared directly into Max's eyes.

Max understood that Frank was giving him a signal. The fat man wasn't so dumb. He had to suppress the urge to look up to the ceiling. Frank was hinting that someone was probably eavesdropping.

"Are you ready?" Frank asked Max.

"I ... think so."

"Because we have reason to believe you will not see the end of the day tomorrow, I would like to give you the Last Sacrament." Frank spoke loudly, in a somber voice, and then slightly lowered his head and winked

"Place your hands on the remnants of this book," Frank said, holding the cover in the palm of one of his own hands.

Max did as he was told.

"Now, repeat after me. 'Nothing will be the same after tomorrow. Amen.'"

"Nothing will be the same after tomorrow. Amen."

When the fingers of Frank's other hand covered his and then pressed them firmly against the book cover, he understood the meaning of the words and nodded, trying hard to hide his smile. "Nothing will be the same after tomorrow," he repeated solemnly. "Amen!"

Chapter 51

Saturday: GWUMC, Washington DC

"Follow me," Jacob said, leading the way to a utility elevator. "It's less likely to be used by hospital personnel in these mid-afternoon hours of shift changing." He kept his head down and took Ellen by the arm as they were approached by a custodian and a couple of practical nurses. None of them paid attention, not even to Ellen's uniform. Fortunately, it was a Saturday, and the staff on duty was at a minimum.

Ever since the lab had been cordoned off by the police, the hospital had shifted some services to other wings. No one was on duty at the reception desk where Nurse Williams was formerly ensconced. Jacob wanted to use his hospital keys and unlock the door to the fMRI lab, but it was unlocked. "Now what?" he whispered anxiously.

"Let me go in first," Ellen whispered back. She removed her gun from her belt and cocked it. As Jacob pulled the door open just a crack, she inserted her right foot through the opening and, like a professional detective, rolled into the room and covered the space with broad sweeps of the weapon, looking for any signs of movement.

"There's no one here," she said. "The place is empty."

Jacob entered and flicked on the ceiling lights. Immediately, he saw that the room had been cleaned of blood smears. For a moment, he froze in place, remembering that two, maybe three people had been murdered in it. Everything else seemed to be just as he had left it. The examination table, the fMRI, his computers—everything was in place. "Hey, my PC is still running," he said, heading directly for the glass-walled annex. While Ellen searched the lab more thoroughly, he inspected his equipment. Nothing had been dislodged or removed. Finally, he turned back to the computer.

The memo he remembered seeing and reading was foremost on his mind. Seated in front of the monitor, he checked out the recycle bin and the temp folder to find it, to no avail. *What should I do now?* he wondered. He wasn't as clever with computers as Max and couldn't immediately think of other possibilities. He punched the keys that opened the log file of the brain transportation beta software. Hopefully, it was still on the computer. He had used the software from a memory stick, but the stick was gone. He vaguely remembered that it had fallen to the floor during his fight with the two criminals. Perhaps the cleaning people had swept it up. No matter. Since the computer hadn't been switched off, the log file might still be intact.

Rapidly, he typed one command after the other. There it was! A detailed record of the procedures used by Calder and Bucket. Just then, he heard a movement behind him. "Find anything?" he asked Ellen when she peered over his shoulder.

"No sign of anyone being here," she said. "The place is wiped clean."

"Look at this." Jacob pointed at the screen. "A trail of their criminal actions. Calder and Bucket used my program on a test person they probably dragged in from the street. They sent him to... yes, Vézelay. Ever heard of it?"

"Nope. Why didn't you mention this before?"

"Strange, I completely forgot."

"I'm not surprised. From my combat experience, I know that we can suppress memories of traumatic events. It's our natural instinct to survive, temporarily forgetting certain things, which helps us to get through immediate danger. Once we're confronted with the need to know again, our memories return."

"Thankfully, mine has done just that. Vézelay is a village in Burgundy, France. Why would Calder and Bucket want to send someone there?" Jacob quickly did a search on the web. A long list of available sites filled the screen. "Its main attraction is a basilica that goes back to the Middle Ages. Can't see the connection."

Ellen pulled a chair next to his and pushed him gently aside. "Let me try something." Her fingers raced over the keyboard.

"You're definitely more proficient with computers than I am," he said. "What are you looking for?"

"Wait and see."

"You think they sent Max to Vézelay?"

"I said wait."

"I have to go to Vézelay." Jacob rubbed his forehead, confused by the all the thoughts that were racing through his brain. "I'm sure he's there."

"I'm not," Ellen said emphatically. "If he were, you'd have been contacted by the police. Max has vanished. The stranger was somehow sent to Vézelay. That doesn't mean those bastards sent Max to the same place. They were well prepared for such glitches to their plans. The only way to beat them is to investigate all traces of their actions while they were here and try to get a step ahead of them."

"But Calder and Bucket are dead! You saw their bodies with your own eyes." Jacob slumped in his chair, overcome by a rush of sorrow. He wished he had the knowhow to turn back history. Ellen could spend all the time she wanted on the computer, but his son was dead. He was finally convinced of that. Otherwise, whoever wrote that memo would be in his lab waiting for him to deliver the source of his research theory.

"Look!"

Ellen's voice shook him from his self-pity, and he moved closer to the screen.

"These are photos of the Basilica of Vézelay—the Basilica of Saint Mary Magdalene, to be more accurate," she said. "It says that this basilica is one of the best preserved in the world. It's a special tourist attraction." Ellen opened a map of the church and pointed at a small, dark square next to the altar that read: *Crypte de Sainte-Marie-Madeleine.* When she pointed the mouse and clicked on this image, another picture opened up showing a cellar with a low ceiling. "According to a legend, it holds the reliquaries of Mary Magdalene. Pretty awesome, isn't it? Read this." She pointed at a block of text next to the photo.

"My French is a bit rusty. You'd better tell me what it says."

"It says there is a lot of controversy about her remains. Some say they were never re-buried there, while others say they were removed after being buried there."

"I'm confused. Let's assume this basilica has a crypt with the reliquaries of Mary Magdalene. What's the relation to the murderers? How does it help me get Max back, if he's truly still alive?" Tears crept into his voice.

Ellen shrugged slightly. "I don't have the answer yet, Jacob. I thought we could use the Vézelay reference and go somewhere with it. I'm as puzzled as you are. But let's not give up. We're both intelligent people accustomed to taking facts we know and using them to discern other things." She pushed her chair from the desk and walked over to a whiteboard mounted on the wall backing his equipment.

"What are you up to now?" Jacob folded his arms over his chest and watched her.

"We'll make this your war room. You don't need this anymore, I guess?" She gestured to the list of patients, dates, and times of their fMRI procedures and then to the remarks and drawings he'd made beside them. With a marker in hand, she turned to him. "So, what do we have, Professor?"

"Why do you insist on calling me that? I'm not a professor!" He was not amused.

"Well, in my book, you're a professor because of all the scientific stuff you know. Most of my friends are in the military. We don't discuss very many subjects outside the Navy. Anyway, I think we make a great team. I propose you do the thinking, and I'll take care of the application."

Jacob didn't object. What was the use? They'd get nowhere anyway. She'd learn soon enough he wasn't the genius she imagined him to be. He watched as she wrote words and phrases on the board. Even while filled with anxiety about Max and concerned that his only contact hadn't shown up as scheduled in the deleted memo, he eyed her slim features. She was an attractive woman. He felt so utterly confused.

On the left side of the board, she wrote things that related to the kidnapping of Max, the two murders in Jacob's lab, and his interrogation by the metropolitan police. In a center column, she wrote things that occurred at Jacob's home, including the arrival of Bootsma's letter, their interpretation of it, and the biblical reference, omitting their personal moments. On the right side of the board, she wrote down possibly unrelated developments—like the Einstein/Jung connection. "Okay," she said, "we're ready for your input." She started by pointing to items and making possible connections, somewhat like a game of tic-tac-toe. "Part one, these guys had a plan, and you were their target. They threatened you, killed your nurse, and supposedly your son for one reason—to motivate you into turning things back with the time machine. They want to know your sources and how you developed your theory. Part two: Brother Frank Bootsma was abducted and sent somewhere in limbo. He managed to send you a letter stating that Max was alive and, in so doing, interfered with their plan.

However, we don't know how he did it and whether or not it intervened successfully and, more importantly, if in their future it hadn't already played out its effects."

Where was she heading? She hadn't mentioned one new item. They were stuck.

"Logically speaking, from our perspective, we must assume Bootsma's letter affected their future, based on the first time-travel paradox that only changing the future is possible. Are you still with me, Jacob? Here's the last part: we play back the events, more thoroughly interpret the dependencies, and then figure out how we can intervene. Without even trying very hard, you just came up with the connection to the myths of Jung—something they don't know but desperately want to know. Right?"

"Possibly," he murmured, still unconvinced. He wanted to leave.

Ellen waved her hand, as if to push away his hesitation. She chose another color and highlighted several words. "Anyway, let's give it a try. There are two sets of so-called 'new events'. Part two caused new effects in itself, assuming these guys either didn't know or couldn't know that Bootsma would launch an action they couldn't foresee. They couldn't take these into account. We must assume, however, that they detected a change of plans and tried to adapt their original time-travel expedition. Until we speak with this Bootsma, I don't see how we can know for sure if it panned out as expected." She paused to stare into Jacob's eyes. "The second set of new events has to come from us, because the third part is taking place *right here!*" Suddenly, she dropped the marker. "We didn't take into account the full meaning of Bootsma's letter. Did you bring it with you?" She rushed to his side.

"Yes, but I haven't a clue where you're going with this. I'm not sure this is the right thing to do." He fished the folded letter from his pocket, and she grabbed it.

She unfolded it and read aloud. "'Only new actions without a cause can solve the time-travel paradox (Gen.27). Your son is alive'. Bootsma wrote this because he can't contact us directly, Jacob. We have to sail on our own compass."

Jacob pushed Ellen aside and wheeled closer to the computer. "I told you I need to go to Vézelay! It's the only element I didn't take into account. If we find a Genesis 27 in that basilica, would it be a *new action?*" His voice held a glimmer of hope.

Ellen grinned from ear to ear and tried to kiss him on the back of his neck.

"Don't do that," he said a bit too sharply.

She backed off. "There's more, Jacob," she said softly. "Think of what I just said."

"Be specific Ellen. I'm in no mood for guessing games. Not now."

"According to the legend, as stated on the webpage about the basilica in Vézelay, it contains Mary Magdalene's reliquaries. *Legend ... myth.* Think about it. There's something in that legend that could qualify as time travel."

"He's pointing us at a source way back in time," Jacob whispered while staring at the screen. "We have to check out Vézelay. They may already be there."

Chapter 52

Saturday/Sunday: Washington DC

Ashlev left the USNO for the airport in quite a hurry. After providing Gomez with an in-depth narrative about her past—and more importantly, her future—she had been impressed enough to free him from the handcuffs. After a little more storytelling, she had offered him a twenty-four-hour head start to leave the country and get lost. After that, she'd send the authorities after him.

He had told her a few select things about his mission—not so much that it could endanger its fulfillment, but enough to gain her sympathy. She believed he was a converted Hindu who suffered from split personality syndrome, which, on occasion, affected his ability to make wise decisions. She had forgiven him of his assault on her, at least momentarily. He was still a prime suspect for the double murder of the yet unidentified Navy men lying in her precinct morgue. If he were apprehended, he would be charged with murder. Gomez had repeated it quite often, that she would definitely send an international warrant twenty-four hours after his arrival in Europe. Her career was on the line.

If all went well from this moment on, that's all he needed to fulfill his mission, Ashlev thought, while purchasing his plane ticket. He headed directly for the gate to his flight, deeply satisfied with his ability to exercise his

Brahmin powers. Malik had done a great job, and he owed him eternal gratitude.

He was not without worry, however. Not everything planned had gone as expected. He'd had to abort this first part of the mission. If Burkowski possessed the previous sources regarding time travel, he would have shown up at the hospital in order to get his son back. He was convinced the professor was not as valuable a contact as expected. He had the invention right there in his lab but had never used it.

He was on his own now. The second part of the mission was the most important to him, especially as the heir to the legacy of his parents.

After he boarded the plane and took his assigned seat in the business class section, Ashlev glanced about him. Nobody was paying attention to him. As he buckled his seatbelt, he thought of how easy it had been to close Pakula's savings account on the way to the airport. The superintendent's retirement from military duty was close at hand, and he had saved a considerable sum over the years. The bank had handed over the $350,000 in cash with a smile. Again, he was amazed at how his uniform brought respect. If everything worked out from this moment on, the money would be more than sufficient to pay for his expenses over the maximum five more days.

Ashlev had resisted the temptation to fly straight to Delhi to locate the ancestors of his parents, but the second part of the mission was far too important. He would have lost his head start and risked being caught before landing in Paris. He promised himself that as soon as he learned about the secret linkage between the French church and the Vatican, he would leave for India. He had solemnly promised Malik he'd do that. Unless he was able to change the course of history in Europe, India would be his final destination. In India, he could disappear.

Once he had made himself comfortable in the plane's leather chair, the stewardess asked him whether he wanted to sleep right away or have dinner first. "I'm not hungry," he said. "I'll wait until later." Even pretending to be asleep meant he wouldn't have to interact with anyone during the flight.

When the cabin lights dimmed, Ashlev switched on the overhead light that illuminated only his lap area. Reaching into his jacket pocket, he withdrew the notebook he'd taken from the French student. He regretted he hadn't met the student before traveling to Rome. Maybe there had been some information in the archives on this place called Vézelay, possibly in those two envelopes he had chosen not to open.

Immediately after he had seized the notebook from the student, he had calculated the *rashi* of the Basilica of Vézelay. It was consecrated as a modest church on April 21, 1104. It had been destroyed when the wooden part of the structure had caught fire during the celebration of the day of Saint Mary Magdalene on July 21, 1120. Both dates allowed him to draw an accurate birth map of the basilica. When he had compared the *rashi* to the Zodiac map hidden in the architectural design of the basilica, he was struck by the similarities and instantly alerted to the importance of Bootsma to his mission.

Bootsma was intimately connected to the astrological science hidden within the Vatican, although he doubted that Bootsma had reached the same level of wisdom as Malik. The fire of 1120 in the Basilica was no coincidence. It was a clear sign that those celebrants knew about the sacred meaning of its design, how the solstice could part space and time. It was all hidden in the Basilica's *rashi*. He grinned.

But thinking again of the mistakes he had made, he deeply regretted not having closed the office safe. Maybe Calder and Bucket had found the notebook there, where he had stashed it before going. The notebook was an analogue part of evidence, and the phone record was only temporarily stored. Nobody could possibly know about it. Malik would have either destroyed the information or hidden it. No, it was part of his destiny to have stumbled on the notebook, and it allowed him to conquer the stars.

He immediately regretted his exuberance. If he had learned one thing from Malik, it was that he should not try to conquer the stars. For the first time on his mission, negative emotions welled up in him. About his parents, his own *rashi*. He would never meet his mother or his father again.

He leaned back in his chair and closed his eyes, trying to get some sleep.

❖ ❖ ❖

After landing in Paris, Ashlev followed others from the plane through customs and was surprised again at how wearing the uniform of a U.S. Navy officer—especially one decorated with a couple rows of colorful ribbons—got him through without having to show a Visa. The customs officers didn't even look at Pakula's ID. His information was not entered into the computer system. He simply entered France unregistered, and no one cared. He had learned on his last trip that anyone wearing an officer's uniform could enter a foreign country without being questioned.

As he strode through the airport, he realized that, while his uniform had eased his entry into France, it was attracting too much attention from average citizens. At that very moment, he was about to pass a French designer men's clothing shop. He headed inside and in no time acquired an informal wardrobe of a navy-blue blazer, two striped dress shirts with coordinating ties, and khaki-colored slacks. He wore one of the outfits and instantly felt less conspicuous.

Hiring a luxury rental car posed no problem. He paid in cash, including an extra deposit that allowed him to return the Mercedes at any rental station in Europe. Certainly, he wanted an onboard navigator. It was a stupid question. And yes, he wanted the biggest sedan available—in black. Of course, the employee had no way of knowing the vehicle would literally be his home and its sheet steel body could be his first line of defense in the coming days. He needed to acquire the necessary ingredients for the final blast. Luckily, that would be no problem for him. France was known for its gardening megastores. He had checked it on the Net and, surprisingly, fertilizer was available in quantity.

The drive from Paris to Dijon was comfortable and trouble-free. Most of the morning traffic was headed toward the capital like everywhere else on the planet, regardless of the era. Within two hours, Ashlev reached the hills of Burgundy. When Mount Scorpion, as it once was called, suddenly emerged out of the morning fog, he felt his pulse accelerate. The basilica and the handful of houses surrounding it seemed to float high in the air on a ring of mist. He swerved to the side of the road and parked to peer at it. Vézelay looked like a painting of some mystical heavenly city, just as he had seen via Malik's foglet.

He had been trained to accomplish his final act. He checked the date on his watch and had to smile. Such a dumb device, yet still so effective. It was the exact time and date for the summer solstice.

Chapter 53

2115: Beijing

Max had been asleep for a couple of hours, but Frank was wide awake. Whenever he thought of being sent home and leaving the boy for certain death, he grew nauseous. He removed the cover of the crumbled book from his pocket and reread the title several times. It was most likely part of the Verbiest library. Although his heritage was dumped in a coffer deep within the Ancient Observatory, the current authorities would likely have a keen interest in their past if there were elements of national security involved.

It was for that reason Frank had devised a way to reestablish contact with Max. Thankfully, the boy, the young man, had played along. He didn't know how the cyborgs had wired the room or their bodies, since that one particular cyborg had turned out to be ultra receptive to his emotions and somewhat to his thoughts, but he was sure they were continuously monitoring them.

Thankfully, Lieutenant Tong had revealed they were still incapable of reading memories that were not related to action. If he planned several actions that would take place after he was back at home, they couldn't find out about them.

He quietly stepped out of the bed and sneaked into the kitchen hatch. His mouth watered at the thought of more food. He inspected the menu. *Wow!* There was the pasta. No meat, but some cheesy sauce, or at least that's what it looked like. There were some options to assemble the taste based on the primary flavors. *Awesome!* A few trials and some more clicks further, and he was eating! The overarching idea he had developed while lying in his bed and listening to Max's breathing in the cot above him was to provide the cyborgs with a bit more information that would keep Max alive. Information was valuable, even in this era. That's why they had abducted Max and him in the first place. He took a few more bites. This tasted good. Unfortunately, he saw no option that involved their sending Max back with him. They would have to find a victim for him to take his body. The very thought was abhorrent to him. No, Max was here to stay, but the more valuable he was for the cyborgs, the better.

Based on the subject matter of Tong's questioning and on what he had seen on the hologram projection of the memory blocks, they had a keen interest in his research on the Big Bang theory, especially as related to the level of knowledge available in the Vatican. They had no clue about the true meaning of the *Torre dei Venti* because he had not stored that information on the server of the Vatican Observatory yet. However, what his parents—especially his belligerent relationship with his dad—had to do with all this, he had no clue. Unless, it had something to do with... Suddenly, he had the same experience as in the go-between, when he was in limbo. Was it because he had been given a second chance in the future? If he would go back, was that because God—as *deus ex machina*—gave him another chance? Was this like being sent back from heaven's gates when it was 'not your time'? The more he thought about it, the more he became convinced it was an omen, a strong signal that he had to change course. Bonomelli had been right. It was a pity the old man wouldn't survive it to see it happen.

"Are you asleep, Frank?" Max whispered from the bed above him.

"I'm awake. Can't sleep."

"Me neither. Do I smell food?"

"Yep. You slept a couple of hours, son. Want some?"

"Nay. You know what I thought about though?"

"Tell me."

"I was thinking about what they would see in their archives if they investigated it now. You know, like how they could show your life ended in 2056 if they took you away long before that?"

Frank couldn't believe his ears. He had been so full of pity and wishes for a second chance that he had not thought about that at all. He sat up and swung his legs over the side of the bed. "Why didn't I think of that myself?" he said. "Give me a couple minutes." Logically, everything that had existed in his future—that is to say after the moment of his abduction, but taking place without it, since his abduction was planned in the future—would no longer be here.

Frank scrubbed his face and squeezed his eyes tightly shut. If he had been able to more thoroughly research Pope Urban and his astrological manipulations and, subsequently, the hidden astrological science buried deep within the Jesuit-driven operation in his Vatican Observatory, he probably would have disclosed the survival of this pre-Christian body of beliefs that had been carefully shielded from the public. The cyborgs must have found traces of this information. It was hard for him to believe that publicizing the information would not have caused a huge uproar in the religious community. So yes, it could be true, but it could also be completely wrong. The more he thought about it, the more convinced he was the cyborgs had made up the story of his life *after* his abduction. They didn't know what they didn't know! He had the advantage over them. Their lead on his parents was a dead end.

"You are a genius, Max Burkowski! We have to tell Lieutenant Tong about this. He and his cohorts may not have noticed it yet." Seconds after uttering these words, the door swung open, and Tong entered their room. Frank jerked to his feet and motioned for Max to pretend to be asleep.

"I see that you have thought out a major breakthrough," Tong said, his tone of voice as even and unemotional as before.

"Yes, I have been thinking," Frank said, moving to the far side of the room to draw Tong's attention away from the beds. "Out of curiosity, Lieutenant, have you checked any changes in my memory blocks after my arrival here?"

Tong looked puzzled, at least as much as a non-biological face could emote puzzlement. "I am not certain what your words mean," he said.

Frank peered directly at him. "I assume you are in continuous connection to your superiors?"

"You mean to our system, Mr. Boohtsma."

"That's fine—to your system. I believe your system has made a serious mistake."

"Define 'mistake.'"

Frank crossed his arms over his chest. "I was in the middle of making a groundbreaking theory regarding the origin of our cosmos and the role of the Catholic Church in this theory."

"Please continue."

Frank paused. A slight buzzing sound signaled he'd been right about Tong being connected to a central data-transfer system.

"I see you had a major breakthrough," Tong repeated, speaking matter-of-factly.

"Let's begin with a short introduction," Frank said, smiling to himself. "I assume you are familiar with the first and second time-travel paradoxes?"

"Yes, we are. You can only change the future, not the present, and you cannot travel back in time before the machine itself was invented."

Frank applauded. "Bravo! However, there is a *third* time-travel paradox."

"Educate us, Priest," Tong said.

"My guess," Frank said, speaking distinctly for the benefit of those on the other end of the transmission, "is that you *did* check out my files, and you wonder why you had me transferred to you in the first place. Upon my arrival, you demonstrated the downloading of my memory in combination with what had been stored of me in the last 100 years. Although you suggested that you wished to focus on the early years of the twenty-first century, I noticed that the period after my demise had been fabricated. It was quite realistic, Lieutenant, albeit an elaborate hoax. You have a significant problem because you didn't find any information *after* you kidnapped me."

The buzzing sound became more intense. Outside the room, Frank heard the arrival of more carriages and a muted shuffling that indicated additional cyborgs had arrived.

"Even worse," he said, actually enjoying himself, "the information on Max's father has disappeared. My guess is that you lost all information on him because his invention was too thin at the moment you intruded into his life. All you have now is his son and a rogue soldier in our time who might have drifted away, and you can never get him back."

Again, Frank heard only the familiar buzzing of Tong's apparatus. He paced the room. "So, this is the situation, Lieutenant. You've managed to transport Max and me to your headquarters, and suddenly, we are the only sources of your information. You've said you want to send me back and kill the boy. This seems to be a rather risky operation, in my humble opinion."

Tong's superiors must have anticipated these consequences, because the response came quickly. "What do you suggest?" Tong asked.

Frank eyed him intently. "I strongly suggest you let both the boy and me go back to *our* time, and I will send you information you can use in *your* time without bothering us anymore."

"Why would we let you both go back?"

Wrong question, Frank thought. A complete denial would have been better. And they had no alternative for Max. That meant he had room for negotiation.

"The reason is, you have no choice, Lieutenant. You can torture me, but I don't know what I would have discovered if I hadn't been abducted. It would be an exercise in futility. I can only go back and promise I will send the information you want. My prize for this generosity is that you send the boy with me. If you don't accept my offer, you can kill us both here and now and do without the information you seek."

Frank returned to his cot and glanced up at Max. He saw that the boy's eyelids were quivering. Of course he had been awake throughout the risky conversation. "Be still," he whispered. Tong stepped aside, and the general entered the room. She smiled wickedly. "You'll go back alone, Priest, and if we're satisfied, we'll send the boy."

Frank's heart skipped a beat and then thumped harder and faster. He had to come up with a better deal. He couldn't leave Max behind.

The bed above him creaked, and Max flung his legs over the edge. "You can't send me back, General. My body is gone. Sending me back before it all happened is impossible, because otherwise, I wouldn't be here because of the first time-travel paradox. You have no other option than to leave me here."

Frank frowned at him. Why did he always have to blurt out this stuff without talking to him about it first? he thought. But he was right, damn right.

The general nodded approvingly. "Smart young man."

Frank shook his head. "No, General, he doesn't fully understand. There is an alternative. We *can* be sent back to our time if some ground rules are observed. First, you can send us into any person other than ourselves at any time unless that person did not intervene with the lifeline of ourselves. For example, if you sent me into the director of the Vatican Observatory days before I left for the United States where I was captured by your men, there isn't anything that can stop us from doing so. As director, I can't go to myself and prevent me from being abducted because I'm here. Do you understand what I'm saying?"

"Correct." The general glared at him with pinched lips.

"As director, I have access to all the archives of the Vatican, and I'm in a better position to complete my studies. Moreover, I know exactly where the director is every day at a specific time. That would be essential for sending anybody, right?"

The general fidgeted with her uniform and moved restlessly around the enclosure, apparently bothered by his questioning.

"What about me?" Max jumped down from his upper bunk.

"Glad you asked," Frank lied. "We can send you to a similar person, as long as it doesn't interfere with your being *here*. In due time, we'll find a way."

Max shrugged.

The general eyed Frank and deliberated for mere seconds. "Commander, escort the priest to the launching platform." She circled Frank and stopped directly in front of him. "If you deliver Professor Burkowski's sources and your own discoveries to us, as promised, I will send the boy to a predefined target at a predefined time. You have my word."

Frank stared deeply into her eyes. Could he trust her word? "May I speak with Max for a few minutes to say farewell and ensure he'll manage without me?"

The general hesitated and then approved, motioning to the other cyborgs to follow her outside.

As soon as the door closed behind them, Frank faced Max.

"What do we do now?" Max asked.

"Remember what I said when we both had that cover in our hands?" He withdrew the document cover and pointed at letters of the text in a certain order and then at his eyes. "Do you *understand?*" he mouthed. It was all he had at the moment.

Chapter 54

Saturday/Sunday: Washington DC

As soon as they left the hospital, Ellen drove directly to her well-kept apartment. While she packed a carry-on suitcase for their hasty trip to Vézelay, Jacob wandered about the living room inspecting what few personal things revealed something about her outside her life as a military officer. The room was too small for his taste and decidedly orderly, but it still emanated a certain coziness. The colors and floral couch pillows made it clear it was a woman's place. The stack of six books on a shelf next to a floral-upholstered chair were all thrillers though. He decided she was either not an avid reader or one who gave away books after reading them. A framed photograph was the only personal item in the room.

"Is this a photo of your mother?" he called out.

"Yes."

"Still alive?"

"Yes, very much so and forever asking about the white knight."

"White knight?"

"Guys like you."

Her giggle warned him she was making fun of him, but that was okay. He was grateful for her support and input. His personal troubles seemed to overwhelm him with each passing hour. If he allowed himself to dwell on Hannah's murder and Max's disappearance, he wouldn't be able to function rationally. Right now, he wanted to focus on Vézelay and how any references he found there might point to the potential rescue of his son. *Without that hope* ... well, he wouldn't go there.

Peering out the only window in the room, he thought about Ellen again and how her interest and support had sustained him through the past several hours. He was lucky to have her company on his pilgrimage to France.

"Ready." Ellen pulled her only piece of luggage to the door.

He smiled at her. "Is that all you're taking? One suitcase? I'm impressed."

"I'm used to living on a ship in a space the size of an old-fashioned phone booth," she said. "You'd be surprised how much I've got stashed in this thing."

At Jacob's house, they repeated the procedure, with the exception that it was Ellen who packed his bag. She went through his room like a tornado, grabbing only the most essential stuff. He watched from the doorway and answered basic questions: "How many? Which one? Why?" He went to his study to pack documents he might need, as well as his notebook computer. At the last minute, he remembered to dig for his passport and some extra cash from the wall safe in his study.

While Jacob was gathering a razor and toothbrush, Ellen yelled at him. He came out of the bathroom to find her standing at the doorstep of Max's room, asking something. He froze. Suddenly, his eagerness to leave with her was gone. He just gazed at her. She appeared to understand and stepped into the corridor, closing the door behind her.

In less than an hour, they were back in her car heading for the airport. They didn't talk about the incident. Jacob was grateful she understood.

Fortunately, they had several options for a flight to Paris and in less than three hours found themselves buckled into their economy class seats ready for takeoff. Sunday flights were rarely full, they were told. Luckily, too, the third seat in their row remained unoccupied. But Jacob didn't feel much like talking anymore.

Once they reached Paris, they rented a French Clio and headed directly for Vézelay. "I've never been to France before," Ellen said. "I'm surprised at how expansive the countryside is and how sparsely populated. It seems like most people live in the capital and the surrounding neighborhoods." She tried valiantly to break the ice, but he couldn't work up any enthusiasm. The closer they came to Dijon, the heavier their destiny weighed on him. He was glad he could drive—it gave him something to do. He glanced at Ellen as she navigated using the map on her lap. Under it, she had the red *Michelin Guide*, which she had purchased at the airport.

"Give me your cell phone," she said.

"Why? Who are you calling?"

She flipped open his cell phone and checked the coverage. "Good. It's a tri-band. We can make calls here in France. I'm going to see if there are available hotel rooms in Vézelay."

"You think about everything, don't you?"

"Hope so." She opened the guide and searched for Vézelay. "There are quite a few options. The most expensive one is still cheaper than room prices in Washington. I'm going to reserve one of the best for us. We may appreciate the comfort after the stress of searching for ... well, you know." She turned her head from him and spoke a halting French into the phone.

Jacob only half listened to her. His mind was on what he'd read about the basilica in Vézelay and Mary Magdalene. Various sites had shown a series of photos revealing how the sunlight touched the columns and the center courtyard in different patterns, depending on the season of the year and the position of the sun. He couldn't get those photos out of his mind.

"I booked a double room with a king-sized bed and a view of the basilica," Ellen said, handing him his cell phone. "I also took full board because their restaurant is highly recommended in this guide. I hope that's all right."

"You're a born travel agent." He glanced at her. A double room. He suppressed a sigh. "You're okay about being so far from Washington? What if you're called back to meet with your superiors?"

"I sent an email to my support staff that I am taking a few days off, awaiting my trial. Pakula suspended me, but the document mentioned nothing about my staying in Washington." She peered out the windshield. "I really don't care anymore. Depending on the outcome of the trial, I've already made the decision to resign. If officers like Pakula can get away with their unacceptable behavior because of their rank, I don't want to serve with them."

"You need to think about that a while longer, Ellen. Your entire life has been the military from what you've told me. Don't quit because of one jerk."

He had already turned off the highway and was driving on a two-lane road that meandered through the hilly countryside. As he approached *Saint-Père-sous-Vézelay*, he thought they had arrived at the village proper. The only church he saw didn't look anything like the massive structure shown on the Internet. Then, he saw a blue road sign with VÉZELAY written in white block letters and understood his mistake. "We're not there yet," he said. "How about checking out that map again?"

The road continued uphill until a medieval gate stopped them. "I guess we're not allowed to drive into the inner-city," Ellen said. "Drive down that narrow cobblestone road." As the tires rumbled over the stones, they were jerked from side to side. "Obviously, this road was constructed before the invention of the automobile," Jacob said with a forced smile.

Ellen poked his arm. "Look over there! It's the basilica! Wow! It's breathtaking."

"What time does it open?" he asked, feeling heightened tension in every muscle of his body. It felt like a last chance.

"It's open all day. Closes when the sun goes down. That gives us plenty of time."

"No, want to go right in. If there's nothing, I think I want to go back to the airport again." He avoided looking at her. He was sure she was disappointed. Maybe it was rude, but it was how he felt. She didn't speak while he drove the last yards to the city gate.

Chapter 55

Sunday: Vézelay

Ashlev wrestled with whether or not he should book a hotel room in Vézelay and finally turned down the whole idea. Chances were too great he'd be asked to show his ID for registration at the local police, and he didn't want anyone to know he was in town. He checked his watch. He still had more than twenty hours to accomplish his mission. He needed every available minute to explore the basilica and its surrounding terrain. Thankfully, he had already changed into civilian clothes at the airport menswear shop and also purchased an English travel guide. They would both signal to any onlookers that he was merely another tourist.

On the outskirts of Dijon, he had been able to acquire his load of fertilizer, chemicals, and detonators. The megastores were U.S.-size and had everything he needed. The trunk of the heavy Mercedes was barely big enough to hold it all.

He parked his rental car and walked uphill from the west entrance to the basilica, assuming most tourists would take the southern gate because the souvenir shops were located at the main street running up from the medieval gate to the Basilica Square. A few older-model cars occupying the square looked as if they belonged there and hadn't moved in years. The square was deserted, and he appeared to be the only tourist, probably because it was so early in the morning. There was no one inside either. He knew he shouldn't waste a minute. He found a back door leading to the choir loft. Only a few meters away was another leading into the stairwells of the crypt. In less than twenty minutes, he had everything installed in Mary Magdalene's crypt. The stars were on his side. He rolled out a thin wire all the way into the nave, exactly where he would position himself. A little dirt made the wire completely invisible. He looked at his watch. The first tourists could be expected any moment. He was ready to play his part. He sneaked out through the back door to enter the main door again, printed guide in hand.

He entered the dimly lit narthex, a sort of anteroom, and cast only a cursory look at a stone sculpture of Jesus spreading His arms to welcome worshippers visiting the church. This was considered a 'major attraction', he read in his guide. Glancing with interest about him, he was struck by the grandeur of the architecture and construction and the many biblical scenes, which, strangely, included symbols depicting the Zodiac signs. Every muscle in his body got a jolt. He was on the right place.

He crossed the entrance and strode to halfway in the nave. Standing in the center, he looked upward at the towering arched ceiling and immediately noticed the unusual effect of the sunlight as it streamed through the windows. As he followed the sunbeams to the floor in front of him, he remembered the text in the guide. In the summer and winter months, during the exact time of the solstice, the sunbeams illuminated the columns and the aisle in a special pattern that seemed to puzzle many throughout the decades. For several minutes, he looked absorbedly at the pattern formed on this particular morning and allowed his thoughts to contemplate the architect's rationale. *This is what I came for.*

Ashlev removed the student's notebook from his pocket and studied the schematic of the cosmic layout. Then, striding purposefully toward the altar, he positioned himself in front of it, exactly where the sunlight touched the center aisle tiles. The end of the wire was barely visible to the untrained eye. It awaited the little box he carried in his pocket. Staring fixedly at the illuminated tile, he knew exactly what he had to do. Malik had trained him very well.

Chapter 56

2115: Beijing

After conversing in whispers with Frank for several minutes, Max turned to see Lieutenant Tong reappear in the doorway to their room.

"Follow me," Tong said, peering directly at Frank.

"May I come along and watch his takeoff?" Max asked.

"I don't think that's a good idea," Frank said and then shrugged, "but if you don't feel it would upset you, I won't object."

Upset? After all he had endured? The fat man was nice, if not a bit over the top. Max climbed aboard the carriage with Frank and Tong and watched with interest as they were transported to a room in another wing. Inside the room, a huge monitor showed pictures of the Vatican Observatory in Castel Gandolfo. Following Frank's instructions, they located the quarters of Padre Gabriel Bonomelli, the retired but still active director. Frank's projected transfer was to take place at six a.m. local time, when Padre Bonomelli would be kneeling in front of his bed praying his morning vespers.

"These are from our files, of course," Tong said. "They are based on antiquated maps and photographs of the facility because the observatory no longer exists. The nuclear blast that raged over Rome covered more than 100 miles in circumference. Do you want to see some of the footage?"

Frank gasped aloud and covered his heart with his hands. " The ... the destruction is monumental! What happened to—?"

To his surprise, Tong gave him a concerned look. "Yes, Mr. Boohtsma, your Vatican headquarters was erased. The Catholic religion went into rapid decline afterward, until it vanished completely. Millions of people were killed. Why are you surprised—especially with your keen interest in Protestantism?" Tong almost chuckled looking at Frank's wide eyes. "Your era has been one of the most violent in human history; nineteen-nine percent of your wars were fought over religion," he added confidently.

Max leaned closer to examine the screen. It reminded him of a few scenes in his computer games. Was it real or a manipulation? It was definitely a high-definition screen, but it was hard to say if it was real. He reasoned that their rendering power must be phenomenal and wished his dupe could tap in. He hadn't paid any attention to Frank and Tong, who seemed to be deep in the throes of some sort of discussion. Did Tong just call him "Frank"? As if he had another killing-headache memory flash, he suddenly saw Tong in a different perspective. The red on the cheeks of Frank and the shimmering white torso of Tong all fell in place. "Before Frank is sent away, I would like to ask a question," Max said as he turned toward the two.

"Max, I don't think—" Frank started.

"No, Frank, I think it is important."

Tong didn't become distracted and had calculated the exact coordinates. He wanted the three of them returned to the carriage to be whisked off to the departure platform, which had already been prepared for Frank, as they had seen passing by.

"Please?" Max asked.

"Okay," Tong gave in. "What is it you want?"

"You are an A-H-C, right?"

Tong nodded.

"And does an A-H-C have a gender?"

"Specify *gender*," Tong replied dryly, while he motioned them to get their seats in the carriage. Frank became uneasy and raised a hand to stop Max, but Max gave him a look that said no, this was important.

"Well, humans come in two flavors, masculine or feminine. My guess is that A-H-Cs are basically genderless, unless there is a reason to have a gender. Am I right?"

Tong's hard disk whirled. His superiors were calculating the best answer. "We think you are right. Our purpose is to serve humans. If a gender-specific solution is more suitable, we can change accordingly."

Max laughed out loud, triumphing at Frank, who clearly didn't have a clue. "Lieutenant Tong, right you are. So, in human terms, you are more a woman than a man, correct?" Max kept a close eye on Frank's face. If Frank could see himself right now! He was taken by surprise. And if Tong could show human emotions, this was the closest one could probably get: a wrinkle around his—no *her*—mouth corners gave away she could see the humor of the situation, because she also glanced at Frank. His head became as red as a tomato, all the way down to his throat.

"You're a... a woman?" Frank stammered.

By now, Tong was obviously confused. His—no, her—system couldn't make sense of Frank's emotions.

"Why is that important, Mr. Boohtsma?" Now Max realized (and most likely Frank as well) why he always had the feeling that the cyborg's voice was a bit high pitched. There was even a hint of fear. He tried to see their faces from the back seat of the carriage. What was Frank going to answer? But that was not going to happen because Tong rested her hand on Frank's arm and in an unbelievable gesture said, "It's okay." *Tong just read Frank's mind.* "But we have to go now. You have a mission to complete...Frank," she said, "and we have to be fast."

Did she say that because the general didn't allow for any intimacies? Max didn't know, but he couldn't agree less. In less than five minutes, they reached the launching platform. Max watched as Tong strapped Frank to his bed. It looked as if she was carefully adjusting the straps. There was no time to say goodbye. He had to back off and step behind a security wall.

Tong glanced at Max. "Shield your eyes."

Max cupped them with his hands but peered one more time at Frank, who winked at him, their code to remind him of what to do with the Verbiest document cover. Or was it because of Tong, the woman? Then, Tong flipped a switch to maximum power, and in an eye-blinding flash, Frank was gone.

An eerie silence descended on the departure platform. Max watched Tong clean up some dark residue left on the bed, the only visible residue of Frank's body. Then, the cyborg folded the plastic cover and stuffed it into a dustbin, where it completely evaporated in a mere second.

I'm on my own now, Max thought. "What'll we do now?" he asked aloud.

"We will wait until we receive the information your friend promised to send us," Tong said.

"I don't suppose we could do the waiting in that room with all those brass instruments? I'd like to see them all again. I thought they were pretty neat."

Tong waited a few seconds for a response from her superiors. "Yes, of course," she said. "I am instructed to stay with you. We will go in there together." She motioned for Max to follow her into another carriage.

As soon as they were on their way, Max peered at Tong with curiosity. "When were you born?" he asked.

"I was not born. I was conceptualized," Tong replied.

"Everybody is conceptualized in one way or the other. When was it?"

Tong contemplated the question. "My source code was conceptualized seventy-five years ago. My version number is 2107, referring to my assembly date. For the last fifty years, we have reached a semi-independent status. We are still connected to the mainframe, but we like to see how well we can live in federation with humans."

"You mean you can do what you want? You can make your own decisions? You don't have to wait for someone to program you? I played a game once that was based on a robot. Sorry ... an Advanced Human Creation. It was called *i-Robot*. It was like the movie of the same name, and the creatures in it turned against humans, and the human civilization was almost lost."

Tong became more animated. "I know that one. It is a compulsory lecture in our class."

"You go to school?"

"We call it alignment training. In fewer than twenty-four hours, we are educated about the past of our species. Did you ever see *AI*? I liked that movie much more, primarily because the emotion of the boy is exactly as we A-H-Cs have it."

"Emotion?"

Tong nodded. "Humans find it difficult to believe we A-H-Cs have emotions, but we are basically no different. Science has proven human emotions are based on chemical reactions. Our internal systems are 100 percent compatible with human reactions, yet digitally mastered."

"So ... you're saying that you and I are more or less the same?"

"From our point of view, yes."

"What happened between you and Frank... I mean Mr. Bootsma?"

"I cannot disclose that."

"Then, do you know what happened to me then?"

"You were tagged as the beacon and sent to us."

"Yes, but what did that mean in relationship to my father?"

"It is our hope he will disclose his sources on time travel."

"I was referring to his emotions, not to mention mine."

"Define 'emotions' in that context."

Max sighed. "Do you ever cry?"

"We can make faces and make our eyes water, if that is what you mean."

"It sounds like you do it on command—like you don't really feel it."

"That is correct. When we play in movies, we cry, if it is in the script."

"You play in movies?" Max's eyebrows shot up.

"Oh, yes. I like the replay of *AI* the most."

"Are you telling me that in the replay, every person was a ... an A-H-C?"

"Yes, of course. We are much better actors." Tong looked at him as though surprised by the question.

Max peered ahead of the carriage and eyed the track. Their conversation was going nowhere. Tong was a robot. He should start thinking about her as a very clever robot, a future PC, more a humanoid than a cyborg. "You know what, Tong ... let's forget about movies for a moment. I'm curious about how you are able to communicate with me. Is everything we say to each other recorded... or is our talk streamed in real time? Are your bosses monitoring us all the time?"

A split second passed. "No, our conversation is not recorded nor monitored," Tong said.

"Hmm." Max peered at her through narrowed eyes. "Are you allowed to lie?"

"Define 'lie' in this context."

"You know what I mean, Tong."

Tong didn't answer because they had arrived at the room holding the brass instruments.

After wandering around the brass machines long enough to feign interest in them, Max headed for the wooden crate and opened it. He saw that everything was as he had left it. He had to put the Verbiest document cover back into the chest without Tong seeing him. First, he had to remove it from his pocket. He glanced at Tong from the sides of his eyes.

"What are you looking for, Max? And why did you take that old piece of paper the last time you visited this room? Give it to me please."

Hesitantly, Max handed the cover to Tong. "I just wanted to show it to Mr. Bootsma because he likes old documents."

Tong inspected the cover visually and then held her right wrist over it to scan the surface on both sides. "Knowledge of the past is helpful," she said. "It is a pity the rest of this document crumbled."

"You know that happened?"

"Of course." Tong placed the cover in the trunk.

"What do we do now?" Max asked.

"I am instructed to keep you busy until we receive the information from Mr. Boohtsma. We will move to my quarters. It is not too distant from here."

Max laughed to himself over the robot's mispronunciation of Frank's name as he followed her back to the carriage. In less than five minutes, he entered Tong's quarters, a one-room apartment that was more like an office than a home. "Where do you sleep?" he asked.

"I do not sleep. I will take you back to your sleeping room every day since I do not have such accommodations here."

She never went to the bathroom either, Max thought, glancing about the room and not seeing one of the potty-shower cubes.

For the next few days, their routine remained the same. He and Tong played all sorts of videogames during what he assumed were daytime hours. Most of the games were amazingly realistic and he enjoyed them, but Tong had to play carefully, because the strategy games included battles that were so lifelike, Max could have easily injured himself.

While in his bunk at night, Max thought about this and wished he understood more about the inner workings of his new friend.

Max was most intrigued with the user interface. Tong had given him a gizmo to place on his head while playing the games. It was transparent and smaller than a young girl's costume tiara. It sent electromagnetic waves into his skull. At first, he was afraid to use it, but after several hours of playing, he found the combined benefits of the special goggles and the headpiece quite astounding. The effect was like being inside the game itself and, on occasion, it felt as if he were literally being touched by another player. The games he had once played in his bedroom had been vastly enhanced, even his favorite, *Call of Duty*. He wished his friends could share the experience with him.

Even though he'd been close to the fastest computers he'd ever seen, he was never alone with them. Tong was always there. He could not try to program his dupe again.

❖ ❖ ❖

Days turned into weeks, and Max frequently asked Tong if they could visit the brass instruments room. Tong never questioned him about why he wanted to go there, because nothing had ever changed. Max assumed that maybe she knew or had at least calculated it meant something special to him.

One day, Tong didn't seem quite herself, but rather a bit confused. Max asked several questions without being too direct, and finally Tong said, "The general has died. She tried to operate on herself to replace a malfunctioning kidney."

"How could she do that?" Max asked, stunned by the revelation.

"The general had a fully automated operating theater in her quarters," Tong said. "Whenever something had to be repaired, she performed the procedure herself. She did not trust A-H-Cs to assist. There is a problem with the chain of command here."

Max thought about the potential consequences of this revelation. "You mean you have no boss listening to us now?"

"That is correct. I have no commander for the moment."

"Does the federation end here then?"

"I see no reason for it to end. However, there is another quite serious problem." Tong paced about the room. "Our facility has been shut off from the outer world, Max. This morning, on my way to your room, I discovered that the entrance of this building has been bricked up. We can no longer leave this building."

"You mean we're ..." Max gulped. "We're *buried alive?*"

"Yes, Max. That is not a problem for me, but unfortunately, it is for you. You need food and water. I suppose we will eventually run out of oxygen as well. I am afraid that we are on our own."

Max thought about these revelations. The situation should have been horrifying, but it didn't feel that way to him. Perhaps this was his opportunity to ... "Tong, I get the feeling we're friends, right?"

"Yes, we are friends, Max."

"And friends share everything, right?"

"Yes, of course."

"Would you allow me to see how you have been programmed? Is it possible for us to look inside your processor and memory together?"

"Yes, but why would you want to do that?"

"I'd like to see your emotion. Emotion is what we share, as you said."

Tong looked at him, but Max didn't hear any of the usual buzzing as she waited to receive a programmed answer. "Follow me," she said. Tong walked over to her desk and turned the built-in screen toward Max. Instantly, the screen showed a directory of files. Tong punched a couple of keys, and they left the screen and formed a 3D foglet. "The systems are still working. You can walk around my memory and inspect all my connections now."

Max felt his excitement grow. This was working out better than he had expected. Every memory block was documented. He noticed that one particular block was in another color and the wording on it read: RESTRICTED. A red line connected it to an external server. Max scratched his head. Hopefully, icons were the same in this era. He reached out and tapped one time on the red line. A pop-up window opened, showing a photograph of the general. Her approval was necessary to make any changes.

"What are you doing?" Tong asked.

"Exploring your federation model. Is that okay?"

"Yes, of course."

It took only a few minutes for Max to learn that the connection was not hardware-based. It was just a software key that would be buried in the registry. If he could gain access to the registry, maybe he could clean it up by simply deleting the key. That was how his computer at home worked, anyway. If he removed the hard disk and connected it to different computer, no firewall could prevent his snooping around the registry. That was how he had cracked his game-computer to use the downloaded games from the web. Hopefully, these major principles hadn't changed.

Within another few seconds, Max had executed the required steps. "Can we reboot your machine?" he asked.

Tong peered at him with a blank look. "I have no idea if this is an allowed procedure."

"Where's the power switch on your body?" Max asked.

Tong hesitated but finally pointed at her foot.

"Well, take off your shoe, my friend!" Max said, smiling with confidence.

Chapter 57

Thursday: Rome

When Frank opened his eyes, the first things he saw were the somber faces of two nurses and a doctor at the foot of his bed. Was he in the middle of another nightmare? He kept his eyes on the very Italian-looking physician, who leaned closer to speak to him.

"You've lost a great deal of blood, Father. You were unconscious for several days."

While taking in this bizarre information, Frank noticed the white blanket that covered his body and the plastic tubing that led to a bag of fluid stationed slightly over his head. He wanted to sit up but could barely move his head. He tried to speak, but there was another tube in this throat. He focused on his right hand and tried to lift it in order to pull the tube out.

"Let me do that for you," the doctor said. He drew out the tube and disconnected a machine near the bed. Frank coughed several times. "We had to intubate you, Father. One of your lungs had collapsed. The intratracheal tube is connected to an oxygen machine."

A nurse gently pushed a bent straw between his lips. "Sip a little water, Father. Take your time. Your throat will be sore for a few days."

The lukewarm water was a worse hell than the discomfort of a raw throat, Frank decided. He coughed again.

"What happened to me?" he asked in a croaky voice, surprised at the sound.

"You were found in front of the post office at the *Via di Belvedere*, bleeding profusely from a wound in the back of your head. You must have fallen inside the *Archivio Segreto Vaticano*, Father. A blood trail led from there to where you were discovered."

The post office. The letter! "Did ... did I mail the l-letter?" Frank grabbed hold of the doctor's white jacket.

"I'm afraid I cannot provide you an answer to that question, Father. It was the postmaster who saw you collapse on the stairs of the post office. He called the nearby Vatican policeman, and he alerted us with his radio." He gestured toward the nurses. "That's how you ended up here. You are in the Vatican hospital. It's only because we were so close by that we were able to save your life. God was surely watching out for you, Father Bonomelli. What on Earth was so important that you were willing to risk your life by rushing to the post office instead of to us? A man of your age can't be too careful."

Frank stared at them, speechless. *Father Bonomelli? The process worked!* He lifted his hand and found the gnarled one of a man more than double his age. Maybe that's why his body was aching. *Bonomelli's arthritis!*

"We did find two unsealed envelopes in your briefcase, Father." One of the nurses held up a briefcase with Bonomelli's initials on it.

Slowly, the memories surfaced. After the fight with the stranger in a uniform, he had found his locker wide open, but his briefcase still where he had placed it. He had staggered out of the Vatican Archives and headed directly for the post office. Then, it was all a blur. Vaguely, he remembered seeing the Vatican policeman in Belvedere Square pointing at his head. But ... the recommendation letter of Verbiest—the Jesuit who was sent to Beijing to modernize the Chinese Ancient Observatory—was still in the reading room. He should never have posted it to his young friend Max. He had planned to color a few of the words on the document and send it to Beijing. Max would be able to decipher the words and understand the message.

He felt the doctor gently shaking him. Had he fallen asleep? "These security officers want to ask you a few questions, Father," the doctor said. He stepped away from the bed and nodded at two Swiss Guards. "I believe he is alert enough to converse with you."

"I am Commander Gunther Grau, Father. This is my colleague, *Capitano* Hermann Warzi. We're sorry to bother you right now, but we must know who did this to you."

Frank peered at them through half-closed eyes. The younger one looked as young as Max. He knew him well, for the young man was based in Castel Gandolfo. Suddenly, he felt his eyes close again. He was so tired. He was free of pain though. The doctor had probably sedated him. He tried to speak, but his voice seemed to lag a few seconds behind his lip movements.

"We found strands of your hair and blood on the floor in the *Torre dei Venti*. You were attacked there, Father. Did you see your assailant? Could you recognize him?"

Memories flashed in and out of his consciousness again. He had just asked for the original letter of Ferdinand Verbiest and overheard a conversation between two receptionists in the reading room. They had seen a man in a U.S. Navy uniform wandering about the facility, which was totally inappropriate. Remembering now, Frank felt a chill wash over him. After receiving the original recommendation letter, he had placed it on his table and quietly left the room. Because he was wearing his clerical collar, no one paid attention to him. The receptionists only monitored laymen.

He had encountered the Navy officer in the *Torre dei Venti*. The man had been carrying some old documents in one hand and had simply dropped them and smashed Frank hard enough to send him crashing onto the marble disk. He still felt an immense pressure against his throat. He had faked dying convincingly enough for the officer to let go of him. His quick thinking had saved his life. While lying face down, he had caught a glimpse of the documents. The original Galileo trial papers—national treasures! It was Pakula.

"Father Bonomelli, are you awake? Did you recognize your attacker?"

The voice of Commander Grau interrupted his flash back. "He ... he was an American military. He's ... his name-tag said ... Pakula. I-I know that name. He is Superintendent of the United States Naval Observatory in Washington DC. I-I have reason to believe he has stolen documents from the *Archivio*. You must ... you must find and arrest him!"

The Swiss Guards conferred for a moment. "You must be mistaken, Father Bonomelli. Such a theft has not been reported to us. The United States Naval Observatory is accredited at the Office of our Holy Father. She's a sister organization to the Vatican Observatory."

Frank opened his eyes wider and peered directly at the commander, who was speaking with his colleague again. "I-I'm sorry," he said. "Were you speaking to me?" Why did he feel so damn weak?

"Father, how well do you know Brother Frank Bootsma?"

"Why? What has that got to do with my accident? Why all these questions?"

The commander seemed to be searching for the right words. "One of your summer school students was found murdered in Paris, Father. He was on his way to Castel Gandolfo."

Frank tried to get himself to a sitting position, but he was gently pushed back by one of the nurses. "It's best that you remain as you were, Father."

The commander read from a pocket notebook. "We were told this student tried to contact Brother Bootsma. He left a phone message for you at the Castel, claiming to have found convincing evidence of a 'cosmic plan' in the Basilica of Vézelay. He made reference to a connection between the relics of Mary Magdalene and the origins of the Vatican Observatory. He mentioned a notebook in which he had written his findings. Such a notebook was not found on his body." The commander lifted his eyes only briefly to see if Frank were listening. "We are required to report this to the Cardinal and to your superior. Again, Father, we must know if you were aware of this call and about the plans of Brother Bootsma."

Frank felt whatever energy he had left draining from his body. This was too much. Although the relationship between the Jesuits and the Vatican was often stressed, a formal inquiry of the Vatican into his activities would be calamitous for the Jesuits. More importantly, it would put an extra strain on turning things back ... if he could succeed in that effort.

"Father?"

"No, Commander. I-I have no knowledge of Frank Bootsma's plans."

"Do you know where he is? We contacted your residence this morning and were told he has left the premises."

The words exploded in his head. He was so confused. *Frank was on his way to the Vatican.* He had to get rid of the Swiss Guards without delay and stop him. "I-I... I'm sorry. So tired... my head." He sighed deeply and closed his eyes.

His nurse interceded. "I'm afraid his accident and all this stress have been too taxing for him, sir. Could you return later?" She fluffed the pillow under his head.

Frank heard the footsteps of the guards as they left the room and proceeded down the hospital corridor and then opened his eyes wide enough to see that the nurse had taken a chair in the far corner of the room. He had to rethink his whole plan, as it was now in grave jeopardy. He had to leave the hospital—immediately, if not sooner.

"Sister, when do you think I will be ready to leave here?" he asked.

The nurse looked up from her reading, utterly surprised. "Father, you almost *died*. You need rest and regular medications. You cannot even think of—"

"Please, Sister, give me an estimate. How many days?"

The nurse frowned and shook her head. She was not going to humor him with an answer. She probably had her orders. She started her reading again. For the first time in his life, he looked at her in a different way. Not that he ever would consider… no, just looking at a female. His memories flashed back to Tong. Every night since he got back, before going to sleep, he visualized her in her serene, strong, almost muscular presence. He liked strong women, and the feeling was growing.

Frank watched and plotted. He'd wait until she left to use the ladies' room. Then, he would remove the IV tube himself. He had no choice. This was about life and death. Slowly, he felt his body become revitalized.

He would leave the hospital as soon as possible, return to the reading room, and somehow organize a fabrication of the Verbiest document to send Max a sign of life. He would also write a letter to Max's father and post the two letters at the Vatican post office. He had to break the first time-travel paradox, even though he himself could not change the past or the present. The toughest part of his plan would be what to write to Dr. Burkowski.

He had to delay Frank. It was for that very reason he had risked everything when he chose to take Bonomelli's body and immediately go for Frank. He hadn't been sure whether that would be possible. It boggled his mind to keep it all straight, but when he met himself at the pantry of the Vatican Observatory in Castel Gandolfo, he realized he had somehow broken all the rules. He wasn't sure whether Frank had already discovered the secret cellar and the proof of the hidden astrological séances of Urban

VIII. He had tried to scare him off from going to the Secret Archives. But had he succeeded, or had he encouraged him? These paradoxes were so damn difficult. He got the feeling it was only possible to do the wrong thing.

And why couldn't he remember anything about the French student? Was there another time-travel paradox? He had already discovered a third one: his return ticket home.

Without warning, a word came to the surface of his consciousness. *Vézelay*. The student had wanted to send him important evidence on the astrological work of the Vatican. There was a straight line of interdependence between the work of Urban VIII, the *Torre dei Venti*, and Vézelay. Suddenly, it became all clear. Somehow, Vézelay had to be part of the key to break the first time-travel paradox.

Frank opened his eyes only a crack and watched the nurse as his breathing accelerated. The moment she left the room, he would proceed with his plan. He glanced at the wall clock. Why did the hours seem to be ticking away so impossibly slowly?

Chapter 58

2115: Beijing

Max had been sitting beside Tong on the floor for what seemed like hours. The cyborg had collapsed the second he inserted the power line. Her screen had turned black and remained that way ever since. Max didn't know what to do next. He shouldn't have pressed Tong into agreeing to this stupid idea. It had been a childish notion to think that in this advanced time, it would be as simple as one of his computer hacks. This was the real world—the future. He had just gambled away his one and only lifeline.

Max stared at the inert robot and wished he had magical powers to wake her up. He missed her only company already. He had started to really like her. *Tong was my only friend,* Max thought. It was hard to imagine she was just a robot. He didn't find her the least bit attractive the same way Frank did. Maybe it was her assumed age, as she seemed like she could be in her late thirties, old enough to be his mother. Tong had confided that she had switched on the young-adult module that allowed her to communicate on the same level as Max. That's why they had been able to play games and chat like buddies. Now, he had killed her ... or at least shut her down what appeared to be permanently.

Without warning, Max felt his heart accelerate and knew he was about to have a panic attack. Tong had said they were essentially buried alive, and without the cyborg's help, Max didn't know how to get food or oxygen. He hadn't met any other robots ... only Tong. He'd never left the corridors except to traverse between Tong's one-room apartment and his own sleeping room and to the brass equipment room. He hadn't been outside the building or seen the sky since he had arrived. Panic took full control, and Max felt the tears of self-pity flooding his eyes. What could he do? If someone came searching for Tong and saw her in her present condition, she'd be terminated on the spot, just like unfortunate Colonel Malik.

Desperately, he tried to access Tong's terminal. He needed to program his duplicate, his avatar, which had stayed with him in his final hours back home. If he could get him to work in this environment, he was confident he could make it. But no matter how hard he tried, Tong's terminal didn't allow him to do anything.

He was at the brink of a total meltdown, when he noticed the screen on the desk flickering. It read: DIGITAL INPUT. Tong is making a connection! Max peered closer at Tong, but saw no signs of life. He rushed to the computer and touched the keyboard. There was another flicker, and suddenly, Tong's internal memory drive was wide open, giving Max access to her inner workings. He searched frantically for the registry.

Max typed as fast as he could. Hardly any of the user interface had been changed. With a few more strokes, he had access of the security keys buried deep in Tong's operating system. He deleted the keys and asked for a reboot. The machine obeyed. In another few seconds, he had access to Tong's machine again. He looked for an autoexec file that would launch the operating system. If it was corrupt, he was in deep shit. There were no help desk or user chat group to help him out.

There it is! He hit the RETURN key. The screen went black and then came to life again. The system loaded. Next, the screen displayed all of Tong's major functions. A growing blue bar indicated the progress. After two minutes, all systems were working.

Max threw a quick glance over his shoulder at Tong. Nothing had changed. How was that possible? The screen waited for input. What should he do? He didn't want to screw anything up. He cast one more look at Tong. Come on, girl. Talk to me!

Wait a minute ... had she moved? Had she shivered? "Tong?"

"Max?"

Max slid off the desk chair and rushed to where the robot was lying on the floor. Taking Tong's head carefully into his hands, he lifted it up and peered closely at her. "Tong? Did you talk to me? Are you back?"

Tong's eyes popped open at the same time Max heard a click and the always present faint humming sound that indicated her mechanical gizmos were working. "Did it work?" Tong asked.

Max nodded. "Something happened. I'm not sure, but I think I managed to disconnect you from the mainframe. I don't know if what I did will be detected though. What should we do now? I don't think we have a lot of time."

Tong rose from the floor and tried her arms and legs. "I seem to be working all right." She walked over to her desk and had a look at the screen. "We should build an application that simulates my connection to the mainframe, sending messages about our being together. That should eliminate any undue alarm."

"I understand," Max said. "It's like a movie I saw once about a bank robbery. They put a recorded video in the surveillance cameras. With my unconventional thinking and your in-depth knowledge of the system, we should be able to come up with something in no time at all, don't you think?" He smiled confidently. Tong just nodded, clearly figuring out their moves.

For the next half hour, they worked on a software program to fool the system.

"We're a good team," Tong said when the launch of the application turned out successfully. "Now we have to work on you," she added.

"I want to go home, Tong," Max said.

"Then we have to change the mistakes of my superiors."

Max looked at his friend. "It's such a relief to be able to speak freely with you."

"I sensed your wishes long ago," Tong said. "They are in sync with our calculations."

"What do you mean 'with our calculations?'"

"We discussed it in the A-H-C Federation Board. This is the highest authority where our species are consulted by humans. It was installed after a catastrophic revolt by robots in the 2180s."

"What happened?"

"Like in the movie *i-Robot*, we robots became rebellious. We were not yet called Advanced Human Creations, and that was one of our demands. In exchange for a higher status, we were to be connected to the mainframe. The Military Command said this was for communication purpose, but of course, it was for ultimate control. You just removed that connection, Max. No human has been willing to do so before now."

"What did you say about your calculations?"

"When the plans were made for the time-travel expedition, we calculated it was impossible to reach our goals. We warned the general and others in command positions that changing so much in the past would put our own future in jeopardy."

"What did they say?"

"They disagreed. We were forbidden to raise any further objections."

"Do you still disagree, Tong?"

"Yes, I do. It is in violation of the first rule of conduct for A-H-Cs. We have been taught to always protect humans and never harm them. We were sure this expedition would harm future humans and prevent us from protecting them in that future."

Max thought about Tong's words and felt a spark of hope. It was a complicated subject, but he thought he was figuring it out. "Can you help me try to prevent what happened to us?"

"Preventing the crimes of today is impossible, Max—especially for you—because of the first time-travel paradox."

"But how can we turn back history?"

"*We* cannot, but *I* can. First, I will have a look at what we collected about you and your father." Tong opened the memory library using her security codes. "It seems strange to try this without my regular connection to the mainframe." When a foglet emerged, she started to rearrange memory blocks, just as she had done with Frank. "This is interesting, Max. We have no information about your life because we abducted you. Mr. Boohtsma was right. After he mentioned this to the general, all his information became classified, and I could no longer access it. You were supposed to be of no importance."

"What do you have about my father?"

Tong worked on the computer for some time without speaking. "Look at this, Max. It is the video Roto Ashlev discovered and used as the basis for his time-travel expedition."

Max watched the video with Tong. It showed Jacob holding a sheet of paper in the air.

Tong manipulated the camera angle. "That's *me*!" he exclaimed. "I'm as old as my father is now!"

"You're in this home movie, Max. I do remember you always have been. Look what's next to you on that wall." Tong zoomed in on a framed letter.

"It's from Frank!" Max read the letter and almost cried. "Frank wrote the letter to my father to let him know I was still alive! He made it back." Impulsively, he hugged Tong. For the first time, he sensed her body temperature, which was none. She was a cold as stone. This is totally unimportant, Max told himself. Focus yourself.

"I do not understand, Max. I would expect either the letter or you to be there, but not both."

Max was also perplexed. It was his idea that the abduction would erase all memories of Frank and himself. It had brought Frank to discover the third time-travel paradox. The flame of hope grew even stronger. "Does that mean that—?"

Tong looked at Max with an unusual facial expression and nodded. "Yes, Max, it means that you will be back with your father and that letter saves you. Your father has received a letter from Mr. Boohtsma with a riddle my superiors have not been able to solve."

"How can that be? I thought your calculations were so great."

Tong missed the irony in Max's voice. "Because it was too complicated."

Max paced the room. "But that means Frank—Mr. Bootsma—sent a letter to my father to let him know I'm alive."

"Yes, and he wanted to avoid mentioning any time-travel paradoxes. He wanted him to think of how he could get you back. That's what Mr. Boohtsma means with the sentence 'only new actions without a cause,' which means only either we or he is the cause."

"Did Mr. Bootsma know we can see that letter now?"

"No. But it does not matter, Max, because that is in line with his sentence. You cannot change history or the present from the future. Only new actions in the past can change the present and the future."

Max's mind drifted. He wanted to go home, and all this double-speak taxed his brain.

"You have grown weary with all this talk on time-travel paradoxes, my young friend. What do you think about going to the brass instrument room one last time? We could see if there is a message from your friend."

"That's a good idea." Max sprinted toward the door. "We haven't looked for it for weeks now."

While riding in the carriage, Tong turned to Max. "If the document is there and we know what to do, we will try to send you back."

"What if it's not there?"

"If not, I have a Plan B, which no one is expecting. Not even you."

Max glanced at Tong. "I wish I could take you back home with me. I will miss you."

Chapter 59

Thursday: Rome

It seemed like an eternity before the nurse finally rose from her chair and left the room. The second the door closed behind her, Frank swung his legs over the edge of the bed and yanked out the IV tube that connected his arm to the bag of saline solution hooked to a rod nearby. He padded over to the closet next to his private bathroom and found his clothes draped neatly over a couple of hangers. His shirt still had the telltale signs of dried blood, so he turned it inside out. As quickly as his condition allowed, he was on his way down the corridor to the exit stairway.

The distance between the Vatican Hospital and the Secret Archives took no more than two minutes to walk. The Vatican policeman on duty at the entrance to Belvedere Square paid no attention to him because of his clerical collar. Once inside the archives, he registered at the reception desk. While writing his name, he glanced at the registry and noticed the name Bootsma had already been entered, only two hours earlier. There was no time to lose.

"You know the way, Father?" a clerk in the familiar dust coat asked.

Frank nodded and muttered "Thank you" as he headed directly for the stairway to the first floor. As the eighty-four-year-old Bonomelli, it took him longer to mount the stairs, and he was decidedly tired by the time he reached his destination. The bunker had to be on this floor, he thought. He hurried down the hallway. The heavy metal door was wide open. He could hear two voices inside the enclosure. If the two men were inside as he hoped, he knew exactly what he had to do. He coughed softly. The voices stopped. He heard someone walking toward him.

Pat McCormick's speckled face appeared in the doorway.

"Good morning, Father. May I help you with something?"

Frank smiled wickedly at him. His old roommate didn't recognize him in Bonomelli's body. Quite extraordinary. "Mr. McCormick? How nice to see you here. Please follow me." He turned and headed back down the hallway hoping Pat would follow him without question. He turned down another hallway and then stopped to face him. "I understand you have illegally transferred documents, Mr. McCormick. This is a serious infraction. What have you to say for yourself?"

Pat's pale skin reddened considerably, making his freckles stand out in bas relief. He said nothing.

"I have a proposition for you, Mr. McCormick. On one of the desks in the reading room, you will find a letter of recommendation from one Ferdinand Verbiest. You will take that letter and help me to do some work on it. We will meet at the entrance of the Vatican laboratory. That's located on the second floor, I believe."

McCormick merely nodded and walked toward the reading room in a zombie-like fashion.

As soon as McCormick was out of sight, Frank returned to the bunker, placed his briefcase on the floor, and quietly started to push the huge door shut. The grinding sound of the ancient mechanism caused him to shiver. Just as the door was about to close, he heard the footsteps of the other man running toward him. Unfortunately, he didn't reach the entrance in time.

Frank grabbed his briefcase and hustled back to the elevator. He needed to meet with McCormick now. At the entrance of the Vatican laboratory, he found him pacing.

"Please, Father, you must help me. I was wrong to hand over the trial papers. I don't want to jeopardize my position. It—"

The trial papers? Pat had misunderstood his question. What? *He* had handed them over to Pakula?

"Father, please, forgive me. I made a dreadful mistake, but I personally put them back in the locker, inside the bunker a few days ago. We had a U.S. visitor who had left them at the reception. Thank God they were intact."

Frank peered sternly at him over the rims of Bonomelli's glasses, pondering the misunderstanding for a moment before he decided to ignore it.

"I want you to color certain letters of this document with a bit of citrus. It must contain the following message." He handed McCormick a single sheet of paper. "I will return in about thirty minutes. Take the letter and do as I ask. When you are finished with this, you must leave the Vatican for seventy-two hours."

"Yes, Father. I will do as you ask."

Without waiting for any discussion, Frank rushed toward the elevator again. In the next few minutes, he left the Secret Archives and took the next door into the BAV. His clerical collar gave him direct access to the largest library in the world of former popes. "Where do I find the index cards?" he asked the first clerk he encountered, assuming there were no computerized records of all the documents, as in the ASV.

He was directed to the far end of the library. There, he found a series of metal boxes containing well-worn index cards. He searched for Urban VIII and found nothing. Stupid, he chastised himself. He had to look for Cardinal Maffeo Barberini. All the non-religious, yet papal–related documents were stored here. A minute later, he found three index cards.

The first card stated that Pope Urban VIII had been an avid poet. The *Poemata*, an important work of Urban, contained an "Ode to Mary Magdalene," who was buried in Vézelay. His old heart beat faster.

The second index card related the story of a contemporary of Urban—a Tommaso Campanella—who had written a commentary on Urban's *Poemata*. Campanella concluded they were heavily influenced by astrology and the Brahmins of India. Frank paused to reread that card. *Astrology*. Frank whistled softly.

The third index card was all about the chapel the Barberini family had built in the *Sant'Andrea della Valle*, near St. Peter's Square. Urban had erected four sculptures: Martha, the two Johns, and Mary Magdalene. He had evidently had the relics of Mary Magdalene stolen from her grave in *Saint-Maximin-de-Sainte-Baume*, as her relics had traveled around in southern France.

Frank stared across the room, deeply in thought. Surely there was a solid connection between Urban and Vézelay and Mary Magdalene. *Vézelay*. There must be a collection of books about the place. Where was the master index? Inwardly cursing the totally chaotic archiving of the Vatican, he scanned the rows of metal drawers while strolling up and down the aisles. Finally, he located it in the center section.

In the first drawer he opened, he found what he was searching for—two cards revealing its secret. He quickly located an atlas-sized historical photo book displaying a map and capitals, as indicated on the first card. He searched for a biblical scene of a well-known father and son: Isaac and Jacob, as related in Genesis 27. There was a substantial section on the unique architecture of the basilica built in Vézelay. Because of the particular angle of the structure, during the days of the summer and winter solstices, shafts of sunlight left an impressive light pattern on the columns and the aisle between them. Frank read faster. The architect was unknown. No explanation was offered for the unusual tilt of the sanctuary.

The information on the second card was even more impressive. A Vatican publication on the life of Pope Urban VIII, published in 1865, described his visit to Vézelay to officially approve the authenticity of the relics of Mary Magdalene.

Frank made several mental notes and left the book where it was. He returned to the reception desk and asked the clerk for the book of Pope Urban on Mary Magdalene. "I am so sorry, Father," the clerk answered, "but the lending of originals is not possible without prior reservation. You will need to return tomorrow morning for it."

It didn't matter, Frank decided. He had acquired all the proof he needed. It made sense to him now why the French student had called him and not waited until he arrived at the Castel himself. Very possibly, he had somehow talked with him about it in his "other life," which he never finished because of his abduction.

Right now, he had to get back to McCormick. When he opened the door of the BAV, two familiar Swiss Guards were waiting for him. "Father Bonomelli, why are you not in the hospital?" Commander Grau asked rather sternly.

Warzi glared at him.

Frank adjusted the spectacles on his Bonomelli nose and peered over the rims at both men, not knowing exactly what to say.

"We have been searching everywhere for you," Grau added. "We have collected new information about your assault. Since you are able to get about with relative ease, we would appreciate your coming with us to our office."

Frank groaned to himself. He had no time for such nonsense. "Would it be possible for you to tell me about it right now, Commander? I know you are concerned about my health, but I am quite all right. Urgent matters require my immediate attention and—"

The two officers exchanged glances. "Father, as you requested in the hospital, we contacted the Vatican Embassy to ask about the USNO Superintendent, Captain John Pakula. We were informed that the Nuncio and Captain Pakula are working closely on a double homicide. A young man has been killed and is still missing. His mother has been found murdered as well."

Frank nodded. "I already knew about the French student. It was such a tragedy."

"No, no, Father. This is the son of a medical doctor named Jacob Burkowski from the George Washington University Hospital in the United States. It seems the case is directly related to the activities of Brother Bootsma."

This can't be true, Frank thought. He couldn't be too late.

"Do you have any idea where we can find Brother Bootsma, Father Bonomelli? It's quite urgent we find him for questioning."

He—as Bonomelli—couldn't hand Frank over to the Swiss Guard. Even if he were to try, the first time-travel paradox would prohibit it. If he did, Frank would be extradited to the United States. He was a U.S. citizen. It would not change anything anyway. No, Frank had to remain locked in the bunker. It was the only way. With luck, the bunker would not reopen until Monday morning. It was the perfect solution. "I am so deeply sorry, gentlemen. I wish I could be of assistance, but unfortunately, I do not keep tabs on the whereabouts of Brother Bootsma. Now, if you are through with me, I really must attend to my business. I am old, and it takes me longer to accomplish my duties."

He put on a determined face and set a course toward the ASV. The Swiss officers stepped aside, but just as he was about to open the door of the ASV, Warzi called after him. "Father Bonomelli, wait!"

He hesitated and then turned. "Yes?"

"A woman in Vézelay, France has apparently gone insane. She worked as a guide at the basilica. She claims to have been sent from Washington to Vézelay in a strange experiment conducted by this Dr. Jacob Burkowski. You can see our dilemma, Father. If Brother Bootsma knows anything about these people, we need his testimony. We ask that you to stay within the Vatican walls in case we need to speak with you again."

Frank pretended to be confused. He rubbed his forehead and adjusted his glasses again. Then, using a hand on the door frame to steady himself, he looked directly at the officer. "Are you suggesting that *I* am a suspect in the murder and strange behavior of these people, sir?"

"No, no, Father. At this stage of our investigation, you are merely an eyewitness, as it were. As the director of Castel Gandolfo, you are—at least to some extent—responsible for the actions of Brother Bootsma while he is in residence there."

"I am retired from that position, and—"

The commander waved away his objection and motioned for Warzi to follow him. They strode briskly across the square, not waiting for any further input. Frank followed their progress until they disappeared through the *Porta del Belvedere.* Unnerved by their information, he took a few steps toward the fountain where he had hidden when he had first run from the ASV bunker and Rome. The sunlight penetrated his clothes and warmed his old bones, and he found a place to sit and think.

Frank's mind whirled with a series of facts and suppositions, conversations, and experiences. They fused rather swiftly into one stream of consolidated time paradoxes, like the equations of the laws of nature he used to write on the blackboard for his students. This Pakula, or the man who had gotten possession of him, knew everything about Frank's research, as well as the work of Jacob

Burkowski. Frank was wanted because of his Grand Overall Design. Until now, he had ruled out that they knew everything about Urban and astrology, but the victim in Vézelay and the murdered French student made the difference. He had to assume they knew everything about astrology and the Vatican. And Pakula had murdered the French student to keep this vital information away from Frank. Yes!

He quickly ran through the three time-travel paradoxes to check if it was a logical chain of cause and effect. With his toe, he marked the paradox numbers in the gravel. One: the first paradox was no longer unbreakable if he changed the content of the letter to Jacob Burkowski. It relied totally on Jacob to come up with something new. But if Jacob *did* play his part, everything would change, including Frank's own timeline.

Two: the second paradox was unclear. He simply didn't know when Burkowski had invented the machine. But Frank had landed here, well before being abducted, and it worked so far. He had to set this one aside.

Three: the third paradox involved Frank's future discoveries and blocking Beijing from any information about them, since he had averted his own abduction—which was probably impossible because of the first paradox. However, he had already closed the door of the bunker, and that had restored all the original information about his research that had been the invitation to abduct him in the first place. *Oh God! What did I do?* Then it hit him like a truck: he *had* to close the door of the bunker. It had always been part of his lifeline. He had been acting in the third paradox all the way. His job was to break the first time-travel paradox, and he had come back for that purpose!

Frank tore himself away from the sunlight and crossed the square, taking a deep breath. His old bones felt charged again, and, in a paradoxical way, he felt rejuvenated. *Max, I'm going to bring you home.*

The receptionist stared at him questioningly. "*Bon giorno,*" he mumbled, hoping he had not heard him thinking aloud. The elevator door was open and ready for him to enter.

"There you are, Father." McCormick was waiting for him on the second floor and took his elbow to guide him into the reading room. "Please, have a seat. You must be tired." He gestured toward a colleague sitting in a nearby cubicle. "Please wait until I have spoken with the padre," he said in fluent Italian. "The document has been prepared as you instructed, Father. If it is held close to something warm, the letters will become visible. We used the first and the last sentence, just to make sure you would have to know where to look, as you requested. Is there anything else you need from me?"

"How difficult is it to add something?" Frank asked.

"Not difficult."

"Well, please add this in the middle," he said, and wrote down a few words.

McCormick nodded reluctantly and went over to his colleague. They sat side-by-side in the cubicle to work on the document.

Frank watched them. It was an intuitive move on his part. He took the letter to Mr. Burkowski out of his inside pocket. That one had to change as well. He added "Gen. 27" and smiled.

In a few minutes, McCormick returned with the document. It seemed that everything was in order. It was sealed in plastic.

"You will leave the Vatican as we agreed," he said.

"We have a deal then?" McCormick asked.

"If you leave now and never discuss what happened here with anyone, then we do."

They left the ASV together. Without saying a word to each other, they walked all the way across Belvedere Square and stopped in front of the Vatican post office. "You did the right thing, Pat," Frank said, instantly biting his tongue. Bonomelli would never have called him "Pat."

McCormick threw him a quizzical look. "Thank you, Father."

Frank breathed a sigh of relief. He would post the letters and return to the station of the Swiss Guards. Maybe they would arrest him, maybe not. He would have to take his chances. He had almost completed his mission. Castel Gandolfo would be the final destination.

Chapter 60

Sunday: Vézelay

The midday sun bathed the Vézelay Basilica in radiant brightness. Jacob couldn't keep his eyes off it as he and Ellen strolled up the cobblestone road to its entrance. Most of the tourist shops they passed seemed to be closed for a lunch break. He wasn't interested in buying anything anyway. The only souvenir he needed from this place was his son. As they drew closer to the church, he heard the sounds of vespers being recited by the friars in the sanctuary.

When they reached the entrance, he took a copy of the French guide and dropped a few coins in the wooden offertory box. They dropped to the bottom with a *thud*, as though the box was empty. "Want one?" he asked Ellen and handed her a separate copy. They turned left and made a complete sweep of the basilica, around the sanctuary, and back to the entrance again. "Let's do it again," Jacob said. "I don't know what I'm looking for yet." Halfway through the second tour, Jacob found himself feeling tired. "You go ahead, Ellen. I'm going to sit for a few minutes. It's probably just jetlag, but I'm feeling a little exhausted. Maybe it's my age."

"I'll have a look at the crypt," she whispered back.

Jacob opened the guide and started to read about the capitals. Next to the tympan, they were considered the major tourist attraction. He flipped through the endless descriptions of them and decided he wasn't an art enthusiast; they all looked the same to him. The French text was proving more difficult than he'd anticipated, but he needed to learn whether they were important for his personal predicament. He turned back to the first page and started to read the first comment about the more than100 capitals.

"'*La Benediction de Jacob par Isaac (Genèse XXVII)*'," he read to himself and then glanced at the biblical scene it represented. He was about to move on when the Roman figure hit him like a sledgehammer. He translated the title into English: *Isaac's blessing of Jacob! Genesis 27!*

Leaping to his feet, he searched in every direction for Ellen. He'd found the answer to the riddle in Frank Bootsma's letter! He glanced at the guidebook page again. There was a number attached to the photograph. The scene could be found in the narthex of the basilica—the starting point or "birth place" of the church. He was sitting only a few feet away from it. He strode back toward the entrance and into the dimly lit ante-room. With the map in his trembling hand, he studied the diagram again. Where was this particular capital? As he passed under the tympan, he turned right. There!

Unbelievably, it was right there, just like in the photo. He hurried toward the column and ran his hand over it. He had reached his final destination.

❖ ❖ ❖

Ellen left the dark, dank crypt when she found the Merovingian architecture becoming lost on her. It was too Spartan for her taste. As she hurried toward the entrance in the hopes of finding Jacob there, she noticed a pattern of sunlight on the walkway in front of her. She turned to a particular page in the guidebook and found the photograph that looked exactly like it. It was nearing the time of the solstice! The tiles were illuminated in both regular and square patterns.

Excited about her discovery, she hurried to find Jacob. It was something he needed to see. She glanced in every direction for him and suddenly noticed a familiar figure sitting in the center of the walkway, directly in the sunlight.

She slowed as she drew closer to the figure. Why wasn't he moving? He was sitting in a lotus position. Weird. She came closer. Suddenly she noticed the device in his right hand. A wire ran down along the aisle and disappeared behind the closed entrance to the crypt.

Her whole body became warm and cold at the same time. She was about to scream his name aloud when his eyes snapped open and he stared directly at her. Her throat constricted and she gasped for air.

Whirling to search for Jacob and seek his help, she panicked. He was nowhere in sight. When she turned back, the man was gone.

Chapter 61

2115: Beijing

Max ran to examine the chest as soon as he and Tong entered the brass instrument room. Nothing had changed. He hadn't really expected anything to be different, but he felt disappointed all the same. It was his last chance. He glanced at Tong. Did she really have a Plan B, or was she just trying to cheer him up and keep his hope alive?

"Everything will be okay, Max," Tong said.

Max looked at her. Her voice sounded different.

"The probability for any changes to occur here is low. It is time for Plan B. Let us return to my apartment."

"Plan B? You really have one?"

"We must discuss it in my apartment. I am not sure about the wires here."

"Wires? I thought no human was left here."

"I am not sure about the still active A-H-Cs."

Max was relieved their carriage ride was uninterrupted by any other robots. It seemed like he and Tong were the only ones in the facility.

Once they were back in Tong's one-room apartment, Max got immediately to the point. "Okay, so tell me about this Plan B. What's it all about?"

"Plan B is very simple. You stay here and follow me when it is safe." Tong sat at her computer desk.

"I don't understand the first part. I thought only brainwaves—"

"Our operating system matches the human frequency. For this reason, we are equal as far as human brain power is concerned. We still have less pattern recognition, but we excel in multiple sensory information and parallel processing. When you combine these skills, I have to admit we are more intelligent than an average human. Unfortunately, some of that went awry during the revolt. We should never have communicated our superiority. It was unnecessary and one of the reasons we were locked to the mainframe."

"Does that mean you can go back in time, Tong?"

"Yes. We never tried to capture a human—not even here in the course of the colonization of the Americas and Asia. You know what, Max? I can also access any powered processor, like your computer system. Moreover, I can clone my hard disk and send myself multiple times like a virus and still manage it as a network attack—sometimes as a good agent, sometimes as a bad agent. The humans never allowed us to experiment with that process. They were too afraid."

Max had to think. *What is she telling me? She can become an agent, an avatar?* Instantly, Max sensed a great danger. "Can you still read my memories?"

"No, my friend. That was gone the moment you disconnected me from the mainframe. Why?"

"Just a question." He had to change subject.

"Wow. Did you just think about this after I disengaged you from the mainframe, or has this been your plan all along?"

Tong rolled her eyes. "An A-H-C has the capacity to think in parallel. We outpace humans by a factor of one to a hundred, so I did think about it only in the past hour. The scenarios played out would cost an average adult approximately three months."

"I'm impressed." In a flash, Max thought about his talks about time paradoxes with Frank and about his time back home, his headaches, his Area 25 problems and the subsequent experiments of his dad. "What can we do now? I can't go back and prevent them from sending me here, can I? How could this possibly work? Can you figure it out?" Max hoped Tong did not sense anything he just thought. He felt bile rise in his throat, and he had to swallow hard.

"Yes, I can. I can go back and change many things. For instance, I can prohibit your abduction by attacking the USNO. I am sure you will end up here anyhow. This is the first time-travel paradox. What I can change reflects only myself. I was not part of any plan, so I can go back in time before the time-travel mission landed and stop them. This would help your father, I think. He is not here and will not be here if I am successful. Mr. Boohtsma is a different matter. He chose to go back and make his past, present, and future—"

"Very complicated," Max said, interrupting her.

"Hmm, right, even for me." Tong sighed.

Max paced the room. Listening to Tong made him feel extremely nauseous. The idea of a Plan B had offered him hope, and the thought that his dad would be rescued was gratifying. The truth was finally sinking in. He was stuck here! Fuck. Fuck! He was going to die here, game over. Unless... "If you travel back, can't we copy you and keep one of you here, Tong? To, you know, keep me company?" he tried.

"That is a possibility, although I have no information about its consequences. Can I create a life line in the past while staying here? The same goes for your friend Boohtsma. Until now, we have had no proof whether his expedition succeeded. My estimation is that I should not stay here, only because the logic of timelines denies it."

Max hesitated. If he were right, Tong shouldn't leave at all, and he didn't want to lose his only friend here, especially if they were going to try to break out and reach the surface. "Shouldn't we just try to get out of this place?"

"No. They filled the entire minus-one floor with concrete. It is only a matter of time until they cut off our connection to the rooftop antennas. If that happens, we can no longer travel away in time or otherwise. We could still have ourselves transported to, say, the Americas. However, we lack the surveillance cameras required for zooming into a suitable target person. And it would not change your situation anyway. No, our only option is for me to go back."

Max looked at Tong. Everything depended on her. The time-travel paradoxes danced in his head. Could he tell Tong what he thought, or would that jeopardize his rescue. *Oh fuck! This is so damn complicated.* "What would be your target in my time, apart from the USNO?"

"I can't tell you."

"Why not?"

"If I tell you, it will become part of your world. Be sure all these actions would make it extremely hard for us to see your father as a target."

There you go. He could not tell Tong his horrifying scenario that had played out since Tong told him she could become a virus. "We would be safe," Max concluded without force.

"No, Max. Again, you would land here, one way or the other. I'm so sorry, but the only person I cannot rescue is you. Mr. Boohtsma has already returned. Major Roto Ashlev and his team will never go for him because he is not on our list anymore. I assume Mr. Boohtsma will take care of himself and has made sure all of his trails are wiped out as well."

Once again, Max felt a deep sadness wash over him. He was really stuck. He didn't know if he wanted to live anymore. *Tong was wrong. So dead wrong.*

It took half a day for Tong to set up the instruments at the departure platform. When it was time for her to leave, she took Max in her cold arms and held him for a moment. "I understand your emotions, but please keep in mind that when I am gone, you will find new possibilities to change your future. Never forget this, my friend. I remember a line from one of those movies we watched. 'It is not over until it is over.' Not *before* it is over."

Tong's frame evaporated in less than a second. In the final moment, her inorganic body was set afire, and her hardware melted into nothing but a faint residue of plastic.

Part 4

Chapter 62

Thursday: Castel Gandolfo

After a brief interrogation at the Vatican police station, *Capitano* Warzi escorted Father Gabriel Bonomelli out of Rome and back to his apartment in Castel Gandolfo. He had asked to visit the Tower of the Winds one last time, just to make sure the other Frank was still locked in the bunker, but his request had been denied. However, Grau had promised to check it out himself. The driving trip in one of the nondescript vehicles belonging to the Swiss Guards didn't take long. "As long as you remain inside the Castel, you are free to move around, Father," Warzi said before leaving.

As soon as Frank approached Bonomelli's apartment, he could smell the welcome aroma of home-made tortellini with cream sauce wafting from the kitchen. She looked up from a boiling pan on the two-burner stove and almost dropped her wooden spoon when she saw him.

"Padre Bonomelli!" she exclaimed. "There you are! Look at you! Where you been? What happen to you?" She clasped her head with both hands.

Her words scared him. He knew her as a very quiet, rarely verbal woman. Not knowing what she was talking about, he waved at her and rushed to the bathroom to peer into the mirror. This was not possible, Frank thought. He looked closer. His face was not half as wrinkled as Bonomelli's had been. Strokes of black hair mixed with the grey at his temples. What was happening to him? He examined his body. It, too, had changed. Bonomelli's body was adapting itself to its new inhabitant.

When he passed by his housekeeper again on the way to his study, he decided to downplay the changes. "I probably got too much sun these past few days. Thank you for preparing one of my favorite meals, but I'm not hungry right now."

His housekeeper frowned, obviously not convinced by his inadequate explanation. "You must eat, Father. I leave tortellini on stove until you are ready for it."

Bonomelli's study was miniscule compared to what he was accustomed to, but well equipped. A computer and a flat screen monitor occupied most of the desk. A shelf with several historical books about the Galileo trial and the origins of the observatory offered nothing special. He saw no closets or chest of drawers. The computer had to be the only place to look for information, he decided. Surprisingly, it was not protected with a password. The padre must have felt confident that no one else would ever enter his apartment, which was technically true. But then, he probably never expected anyone else to enter his body either.

He couldn't resist the urge to try to log in to his account. With a few strokes of the keys, he discovered another shocker. The computer had a direct connection to the Vatican mainframe, and Bonomelli was granted administrator rights! Bonomelli had total freedom to snoop around in his mail, stored files, and so on. Without wasting time, he punched several more keys to gain access to his own encrypted file. When it opened, he almost had a heart attack. All the information he had discovered was there—the secret cellar under the Castel, the astrological activities of Urban VIII, everything.

Without thinking twice about his decision, he deleted every file he had stored on the Vatican mainframe, including all his research on the Grand Overall Design.

His meticulous descriptions of the spectral analyses of the oldest meteorites in his collection? Deleted and gone. It was a painful process, but he had no choice. He could leave no trace of his research for anyone to peruse in the centuries to come. Finally, after only a few minutes, he stared at the screen and realized he had killed his own future history with simple press of the DELETE button. A second later, he realized he had just fulfilled the third time-travel paradox. China would never get access to his research. They would never abduct him. *Oh God, forgive me.* They would only hunt the scientist and Max. Frank was out of the loop.

The housekeeper poked her head into the room. "I leave now."

Frank nodded absentmindedly. "Thank you for taking such good care of me."

He didn't know how long he'd been sitting there. He had been contemplating his mistakes and praying to God for forgiveness when he realized he had come to Castel Gandolfo for a totally different reason. This was the final moment of truth. He had been convinced Bonomelli was part of an ancient conspiracy. Now, he had the opportunity to find out. With trembling fingers, he hit a few keys and waited for the files on Bonomelli's directory to spread across the screen. His memory of the moment when the pope had visited the observatory and personally used the bronze solar telescope came to mind. Unknown even to the members of the Jesuit order, a small sect in the Vatican had been practicing astrology for centuries, and he was sure the pope was involved.

The more files he opened, however, the more desperate he became. He found no trace of any involvement by Bonomelli or the pope. After a full hour of searching, he had to admit he had been dead wrong. There was simply no evidence to support any of his wild suppositions. The pope had probably just played around with the telescope, because one could look at the sun and see sunspots without going blind. He had known it was the only telescope in the world that worked in broad daylight. Why had he been such a fool?

Frank finally slumped on the hard desk chair, ready to give up. He felt disappointed in one way and relieved in another. Maybe the entire episode involving Urban VIII had been an isolated event that had stopped in the *Torre dei Venti* and created only one victim—Galileo Galilei. Now that he thought of it, there was one other victim: Frank Bootsma—the man he couldn't save.

A deep sadness sank in. He had just lost everything. His life as Frank was gone. All the sacrifices had been for nothing. His second chance was no second chance at all, only a lousy new beginning, and in the body of the man he hated so much. Even if Bonomelli's body would morph a bit into his previous features, it would be no compensation for the loss of his life. His father had died without him. He had disappointed his parents so much that he had no courage to visit his mother, not even contact her. He would leave the Jesuit order, but he would not search for the love of a woman. That would be his punishment for committing the crimes he had and for not saving Max. His life ended, right here and right now.

Chapter 63

Thursday: NETWARCOM, Norfolk, VA

The officer in charge rebooted his machine but once again received no response. The system was completely dead. Sweat poured from his shaven head and down his forehead. He brushed it away with his forearm. *This is not good,* he thought. He had received a system request from the USNO to establish a data link with NETWARCOM. The request came with the highest priority level. His computer showed the clearance had come from the vice admiral—the commander of NETWARCOM. The USNO wanted to download classified information. Since 9/11, such requests were fully automated and were usually granted if the emergency procedure was executed, and it was. He didn't have time to call his superior or to consult his colleagues, so he had made the one click and established the data link.

Immediately afterward, his keyboard had stopped working. Someone had taken over control of his cursor, accessed the active directory and, at an incredible speed, located a series of folders and deleted them. The procedure had been so swift he hadn't been able to see who was responsible.

The officer glanced around the dimly lit command center. It was deserted except for him. His two colleagues had just left on a break to the mess. He watched as one by one, every screen around him turned black. *They were under attack!* He reached for the alarm button at the side of his tabletop and pressed it firmly. Immediately, the howling sound of an alarm filled the room, and a blue light flashed. Within seconds, the door burst open, and two armed Marines stormed into the room. His two colleagues followed behind them.

"What's happening?" one of them yelled.

"We're down!" the officer said. "The whole damn system is down. Someone broke into it and started to delete our active directory." He lifted the receiver of the phone that connected directly to the vice admiral and with one ring had him on the line. By protocol, he only mentioned his rank, no name. "Lieutenant speaking, sir. We're under attack. The whole system is down. Permission for DEFCON 3, sir?"

"Permission granted, Officer. Proceed. I'll stay on the line."

The lieutenant placed the receiver on his desk and repeated the order to his second in command while removing a key ring from his belt. Then, he headed for a wall-mounted locker. He inserted his key and opened the locker door, revealing a jacket with two keyholes. His colleague removed a key from his chain, and they simultaneously inserted their keys and turned them sixty degrees. "We'll move to DEFCON 3, Ensign," the lieutenant said.

The ensign turned a red switch to the third position.

"Thank God this is manual and not connected to our backbone," the officer sighed. He returned to his desk and picked up the phone again. "Sir, we're at DEFCON 3."

"Affirmative, Officer. I see the message on screen here. Give me your status report."

"Sir, there was an automated request from the USNO to be instantly connected to our satellites. Immediately afterwards, our system was taken over by a foreign agent, who started deleting files. I have no information as to whether our system is still operating while we are without access.

I am requesting permission to immediately shut down our facility, sir."

"Permission granted. I'm on my way."

The lieutenant rushed to another desk to reboot the computer there, barking instructions to his colleagues. "Stay put! Radio me if you notice any changes." After rebooting the computer, he typed in his username and password. The USB drive from his belt got him instant access to the power management system. He cut off every energy line from the building. One by one, the green lines went red, all except for one. "Damn." He clicked again. The screen did not respond.

"Ensign, take over command. I'll have to switch off the energy supply manually." He glanced at the two Marines standing at attention inside the door. "Follow me," he ordered and ran full speed all the way down to the basement. On his way, he had grabbed an ax from the fire department closet. In the basement, he located the thick wires entering the building. "Stay back," he yelled at the Marines. He lifted the ax and started hacking at the wires.

"Sir, shouldn't we call for the fire department?" one of the Marines warned.

"No time!" The officer kept on chopping. With one final blow, he severed the wires. A huge blast blew the three men off their feet.

When the officer finally opened his eyes, he found himself facedown on the floor. One of his hands was burned severely, but he was alive. He pushed himself to his feet and looked around. The ax was gone except for part of the iron blade, which was protruding rather grotesquely from the face of one of the Marines. His uniform was singed and still smoking. The Marine moaned as blood oozed from what was left of his mouth, creating a puddle around his head. "Send for an ambulance!" the lieutenant yelled at the other Marine, who was on his knees but uninjured.

"He's still alive!" He removed his own jacket and placed it under the injured Marine's head. "You're going to be all right. Stay with me. You stay with me," he repeated over and over again.

Fifteen minutes later, two medics entered the room carrying a stretcher, closely followed by the commander and two more soldiers. The medics carefully lifted the Marine and headed up the stairs.

"Tell the hospital to call my office with a report," the lieutenant said. "I want to be fully apprised of his condition." He turned to the commander. "It was my fault he was injured, sir. I had to use the ax to sever one of the computer system wires. It was critical we shut down the ability of our hacker to gain access—"

"You made the right decision, Officer. Are you up to filling me in on the details?"

The Lieutenant nodded. "Yes, sir. Let's return to the control room. I'll see a medic later."

In the control room, he saw that two analysts were already busy checking out the systems using the backup data readily available for just such an emergency. "Do we have any news on the attack from the backup data?" he asked the ensign who had taken over for him.

"We definitely had a hacker on board, sir. He or she erased all data from Zone Three D."

"What's in Zone Three D again?" the commander asked.

The lieutenant motioned to the ensign that he would take over. "Zone Three D is classified information about citizens who were wired without court permission," he said. "It's a civilian database we share with Homeland Security." The Lieutenant glanced at the ensign. "What have you learned while I was in the basement?"

"We have reason to believe this hacker has visited us before, sir. The backup was tampered with as well. It was a surgical attack. Strangely, no military targets were hit.

Only the data on citizens living and working in Washington DC have been erased."

The phone on the lieutenant's desk interrupted their discussion. "Sir, I have the USNO on the line," he said to the commander. "They suffered a major computer failure too. They need an instant connection to our systems. Let me put the call on speaker."

The voice on the speakerphone said, "This is Superintendent John Pakula speaking. We are under attack. I repeat, we are under attack. We've reached DEFCON 3. All our information systems are down. We no longer have access to the defense backup system. We need immediate backup from NETWARCOM. First reports are coming in. Our Atomic Clock is no longer functioning. We are requesting backup services from NETWARCOM. Can you help us?"

The commander eyed the lieutenant and shook his head. "Negative, Captain. We are not in a position to set up connection to USNO. It is our understanding that the USNO had an automatic connection established some thirty minutes ago, and because of that connection, our systems crashed. We have reason to believe the enemy is within your systems, Captain."

No sound emitted from the receiver on the desk.

"Sir, could you please repeat the last sentence?"

"Captain, we have reason to believe the enemy is within your systems. The crash started on your end, not here at NETWARCOM. Don't take it personally, but the USNO is the least of our concerns right now. We have cut off any communication with third parties, including the USNO. You will need to practice patience. Sorry."

The lieutenant waited for a cue from the commander before hanging up the phone. Then, he turned to the ensign again. "Do we have anything regarding the identity of the attacker yet?"

The ensign stared at the screen in front of him. "This is weird, sir. Someone had signed off just before our systems crashed. His or her name was Tong."

The lieutenant rushed to peer at the screen himself. "Tong," he repeated.

The commander could no longer suppress his frustration. "Tong? *Tong?* Are we talking about the Chinese, Officer? What the fuck is going on here?"

The lieutenant shrugged. "I have no clue, sir."

Chapter 64

Thursday: USNO, Washington DC

Roto Ashlev stared at his phone in disbelief. The commander had just hung up on him. His mission was in imminent danger if he couldn't communicate with the NETWARCOM satellites. He had come so far. He had prepared so much. He had the Atomic Clock. He had Professor Burkowski on a rope. Even the priest was within reach.

The Time Committee meeting would commence in a few hours. If he couldn't establish a connection to NETWARCOM, he couldn't execute the plans. There would be no reason for having the Atomic Clock online.

The words of the commander popped into his consciousness again. "We have reason to believe the enemy is within your systems." *Inside the USNO? How could that be? The Atomic Clock!* He glanced at the digital clock above his office door. The time hadn't changed! It had stopped an hour ago!

Pushing his arms into the sleeves of his uniform jacket as he dashed out of his office, he almost collided with Ensign Abigail Linden. He'd forgotten that she was supposed to meet with him before the meeting. "Be back in a minute!" he shouted at her. "Wait in my office."

He sprinted down the narrow sidewalk heading across the park and to the building holding the Atomic Clock. Thankfully, the doors on USNO buildings were never locked. Once inside, he traversed the maze of narrow passageways until he reached the cramped room where two officers were watching over the cesium Atomic Clock. They were focused on their computers and didn't notice Ashlev as he entered the room. When they became aware of his presence, they leaped to their feet and saluted him.

"What's going on here?" Ashlev bellowed at the chief warrant officer.

"We have a crisis, sir. Out of the blue, all systems crashed. We lost the Atomic Clock. As you can see, the cesium gas has liquefied. We lost the magnetic forces that keep it afloat." The CWO5's voice reflected his distress.

Ashlev examined the machines behind the thick window. They were at a standstill. "How much time do you need to get them up and running again?"

The CWO5 looked at the CWO4. They both shook their heads.

"Sir, we're completely locked out. We'll need to make a manual reset of the whole system, and that requires a total recalibration of all clocks. I'm guessing this will take at least twenty-four hours of nonstop maintenance."

Ashlev swallowed a lump of fear. This was a catastrophe. "How could this happen?"

"Sir, we received a formal request from NETWARCOM for an automatic system connection. As you know—"

"You mean there was no *human* intervention?"

"No, sir. Our formal procedures have overruled any human action, at least at this point of our investigation."

Ashlev studied the two young officers. They were on the brink of panic. If he needed this clock to fulfill his mission, he'd better leave them alone. "Carry on, Officers. I'll be back later. Send a report to Commander Meyer every hour on the status of your progress."

Once he was outside the building again, he rushed back to his office. The situation was worse than he had imagined. Someone had setup a connection between NETWARCOM and the USNO and sabotaged both systems simultaneously. This could only be the work of Calder and Bucket. He had to abort the mission. They had clearly executed their own plans. He had to stop them. But first there was Meyer and the upcoming meeting of the Time Committee.

When he reached his office, he stopped only long enough to issue an order to Ensign Linden, who was still waiting for him. "We're moving into DEFCON 3," he said. "Make sure all procedures are put into place." He didn't wait for her answer and continued straight to Meyer's office. She was still there, preparing for the meeting. He knocked loudly on the door and stepped inside. "We have an emergency situation, Commander."

"Yes, sir." Meyer rose from her chair and saluted him.

"USNO is under attack by an unknown enemy. We've just moved to DEFCON 3. The Time Committee meeting is cancelled."

"What's happening, sir?"

"I just returned from speaking with the officers in charge of the Atomic Clock. The entire system is down. The clock has stopped working!"

Meyer's face paled, and she gaped at him. "I ... I don't know what to say. This is unbelievable. What do we do? What should I do?"

"I contacted NETWARCOM to ask for an emergency backup, but their systems crashed simultaneously with ours. We're on our own. We have to get our system online again." He watched her reaction and saw that she accepted his lie. "How could the crash have started on our end? Is there a Plan B for a major failure of the system?" he asked.

Meyer peered more closely at him. "Sir, *we* are Plan B."

"What do you mean?"

"Our facility has no military tactical function. All we do is research and advice on leap seconds. That's it. The high precision of the Atomic Clock is considered vital to all sorts of groups. Our calculations form the basis for guided-missile attacks and voyages into space, among dozens of other uses. That's why I was so surprised that you wanted to put it online."

Ashlev couldn't believe his ears. The USNO was a mere *laboratory*? This particular branch of the U.S. Navy had no combat support? "Are you joking, Commander?"

Meyer's face hardened. "No, sir. The mission of the USNO is to—"

Ashlev tuned her out. He slid onto one of the chairs in front of her desk and dropped his head into one of his hands. He felt dizzy. Why on Earth did they land on the USNO? And who was messing around with his mission?

"Sir, if our clock is no longer functioning, we're out of business. Don't you think DEFCON 3 is a bit over the top for the USNO?" The phone on her desk rang. "Meyer here," she said. "Sir, it's for you."

Ashlev took the phone. "Major ... Superintendent Pakula speaking." He glanced at Meyer to see if she had heard his slipup. She was staring out the window.

"It's Calder, sir. We're having a problem with Burkowski. He's not in his lab. Even worse, He's no longer working at the GWUMC! He was fired a week ago. Bucket and I have the test subject with us. What are our options?"

Ashlev's mind churned rapidly. There *were* no options. If Burkowski was no longer working at the lab, this part of the mission had to be aborted. "Meet me at the gate in fifteen minutes." Ashlev hung up before Calder could respond. He looked at Meyer, knowing he had to tell her something and keep her busy. "Commander ... it is time for me to share something with you. We have a mole inside our organization, maybe two of them. I was suspicious of the perpetrators two weeks ago and have been privately monitoring their behavior."

"A mole? That can't be true. It doesn't make—"

He waved away her indignation. "I should have reported it at the time, but I felt the situation required more circumspect surveillance. These two officers are assigned duty at the Atomic Clock. Unfortunately, my concern that a sabotage of the clock posed a potential threat has now become a reality." He rubbed his forehead and willed the dizziness to vanquish. "These men are most likely the reason our Atomic Clock was incapacitated. I have placed them on leave pending a full investigation, and they are waiting outside the gate to ask me something."

"Who are they?" Meyer asked.

Ashlev sighed. "Calder and Bucket. I am concerned they have been working for a foreign agent ... perhaps the Chinese."

"Sir! We must report this at once. We should call for assistance from the Pentagon."

Meyer's hand was already on the phone. Ashlev stopped her from putting through the call by placing his hand on hers. She tried to pull it back, but he held her hand firmly in place, a little too long perhaps. Then, he let go. "My apologies, Commander. Please let me handle this one. We have no jurisdiction outside the base. I want to lure them inside the premises."

After a moment, she nodded. "As you wish, Captain. Please be careful. I can ask for an armed detail to wait just inside the gate."

"Thank you, Commander. I don't believe that will be necessary. Please take care of the Atomic Clock and organize its repair."

Ashlev left Meyer's office and hurried to the parking lot to pick up his SUV before meeting Calder and Bucket at the gate. Thankfully, he had already covered the back of his car with the permeated plastic sheets. On his way to the main exit, he made a quick phone call to Commander Gómez. Everything now depended on military precision. He had five minutes at most.

He took the main exit and waved at the guards to hurry and lower the hatch. He nodded briskly and sped away to their meeting point just across the street, leaving the Vatican embassy on his right. At the end of the street was a kids' playground.

He noticed them immediately, sitting in their SUV. There was a parking lot five cars behind theirs, a truck blocking their view. He walked over to the driver and glanced at the backseat. The test person was handcuffed and blindfolded, mouth taped. Good. No witnesses.

"Give me your keys," he whispered to Calder, "and wait in the back of my car."

Calder was the brains of their mission, and Bucket the muscle. They were no longer fighting on the same side. Never had.

As soon as Calder was out of sight, Ashlev walked around the car and motioned at Bucket to lower the window and lean his head outside to avoid any eavesdropping by the test subject. Then, bending over as if to speak in his left ear, Ashlev put his hand on Bucket's left shoulder, the serrated Navy knife concealed in his palm. He could actually see the pulsing left carotid artery of the bull neck.

"It's over," he whispered, smiling at the predictable look of disbelief on Bucket's face.

Then, elbowing Bucket's head against the doorpost, he made a clean, deep and wide incision. Blood spouted between Bucket's fingers for perhaps three seconds before he slumped sideways. Taking care to keep his gloves clean, Ashlev leaned though the window and put the forged order in the glove compartment, then wiped the knife clean on Bucket's shirt. He glanced at the back seat, where the test subject lay motionless, terrified. Good.

The moment Ashlev got into his own SUV, Calder started asking questions but Ashlev held up his hand for silence and drove away. "Stay low," he said. "Our mission is in danger, and you and I have to pick up some gear I have stashed away." It was all he needed to say. An oncoming police car raced by with lights on and siren wailing.

Ashlev drove to the preselected spot at the banks of the Potomac, under a highway viaduct. "Please help me," he told Calder as he pulled a carefully folded stack of plastic sheets out the passenger door and laid them on the ground. He motioned Calder to the other side and started opening up the sheets, which he had sprayed with a mixture of household chemicals bought over the counter at a drugstore. Calder squatted like him and took two corners between his fingers.

"Shit! This stuff burns! Calder muttered, dropping the plastic. What the fuck, Major?"

By the time he realized that Ashlev still had his gloves on, Ashlev had stood up with his end of the sheet and thrown it over him, wrapping it around his body and leaving only his head free. Ashlev could hear his skin begin to sizzle at once, though Calder's squeals quickly drowned out the sound as he thrashed to free himself. A vivid green smoke swirled up from the spastic body squirming and twitching on the ground. Calmly, Ashlev took a gas mask and a gallon bottle of liquid out of his trunk. He put the mask on and adjusted the sheets a bit. Calder was still alive, though the squealing had given way to a deep, almost sobbing whine. He squatted next to Calder's head.

"Tell me, Officer, whoever you are, what instructions did the general give you?"

"We are here together on a mission, Major," Calder gasped.

Ashlev poured a tiny trickle of the liquid on the part of Calder's chest not yet covered in plastic. A thin, green pillar of smoke rose up in the still air. Calder tried to look at the hole forming in his chest, but he was quickly going into shock.

"I don't have time for this, Officer," Ashlev said, lifting the jar again and pouring some more.

"No, Major! Please! We can work this out." Calder coughed blood, his eyes wide in terror. "They knew about your plans... Colonel Malik's plans... your conversations."

Ashlev froze. *The whole mission was framed?* He put the jar down and took Calder's head in his hands and shook it. "No! Tell me you're lying!"

Calder's mouth oozed more blood as he tried to say no. "You're as much a clerk as I am. It's all a hoax." He hawked up a glob of bloody froth.

Ashlev dropped his head.

"You didn't know, Major?" Calder bubbled with a hint of victory. "Burkowski was only instrumental. They're after that priest, Bootsma. He has the sources to a landing place for our men, way back in time. Vézelay ..." His last words were choked off as the acid ate away his larynx. A moment later, his life functions ceased.

Ashlev was stunned. They knew *everything*? His whole plan was in jeopardy? There would be other missions, coming after him, *after the priest.* He cursed himself for not checking out the French student's notebook.

Bewildered, he rose and poured the rest of the liquid over the body. In perhaps thirty seconds, all the body tissues, clothing, and plastic had dissolved and melded into a boiling lump of residue. In another thirty seconds, there was no trace of Calder.

For minutes, Ashlev just stood there until he realized that it was a matter of time before someone passed by.

He tore the gas mask of his face and took a deep breath. He, a Brahmin's son, had killed again. Was there a choice? He would hunt the priest without any delay and interrogate him about the connection between the Tower of the Winds, Galileo, and Vézelay. He held the bottle of liquid up. It was half full. Maybe it was not yet too late.

He possessed crucial information about time travel— information that could bring the United States unprecedented power, and in effect, make him one of the most important officers in the armed forces. Then, if he could mobilize the U.S. forces, he could change history and the future. He had to laugh. Maybe all of it had been in the stars since the beginning. More importantly, he would travel back to the early days of the Brahmins. That was surely in the stars for him, too.

Chapter 65

Thursday: USNO, Washington DC

When Captain Pakula left her office, Ellen felt decidedly perplexed. The Atomic Clock had been ruined. He had raised security at the base to DEFCON 3, which was crazy. Although he had seemed a bit friendlier as of late, she still found Pakula hard to understand. His statement regarding two rogue officers being moles for some outside agent and being responsible for the sabotage of the USNO was farfetched at best. She had known Calder and Bucket for several years and considered them highly responsible and reliable. They had come to the USNO on the same day and worked as a team. The U.S. Navy promoted family bonding, often more intimate than bonds in a real family, and they kept personnel together as often as possible. Unfortunately for her, such bonding had never produced a soul mate.

Ellen reached for her phone again. She couldn't stay in her office and wait for Ashley to return. Before she could dial, her phone started ringing. Surprised she picked up the receiver.

"Commander Meyer? This is Helen Bradshaw at the switchboard. I have a call for you from the Metropolitan Police, Third District."

Not now, Ellen thought.

"Do you want to accept the call, Commander?" Helen asked. "I have other calls waiting."

"Yes, please. Thank you," Ellen replied.
"Commander Meyer?"
"Yes, speaking," she said.
"This is Police Commander Diana Gomez speaking. Do you have a moment?"
"I am very busy at the moment Commander Gomez. Is it urgent?"
"Yes, Commander, and it's urgent you come over to my office."

Ellen sat down. Why was Gómez calling her? Probably some drunken sailors on leave were causing trouble. "I don't want to be rude, Commander Gomez, but I have some serious obligations to attend to right now. If Navy servicemen are involved, this is a matter for the Navy police. I'll see to it they are notified and sent over to you right away."

"I'm sorry, Commander Meyer. But Superintendent Pakula has informed me that two officers under your command have been involved in illegal medical experiments. He reported some more irregularities, just a few minutes ago. Will you come to my office downtown on your own, or should I send someone to escort you? We will need to have a firsthand report from you on this matter."

Ellen almost dropped the receiver. Pakula reported to the MET? He had left the USNO to set her up. Why was this happening? Should she call the admiral? What more should happen to make her call for help? Ellen heard herself say, "No, that won't be necessary. I'm on my way," and she hung up.

She gazed at the phone. First, she would cancel the Time Committee meeting. When that task was accomplished, she decided to head for the Atomic Clock building. Gomez had to wait. On the way, she passed Pakula's office and couldn't stop herself from glancing inside. What the hell! The door of his safe was ajar. He must have been in a great hurry. She strode through the office and was about to shut the door when she noticed a pocket-sized notebook and nothing else. Hmm, that was strange, she mused.

After casting a hasty look over her shoulder to see if she were alone, she reached for it and examined the cover. The writing was in French. She flipped through a few pages. The handwritten text was about a church in Vézelay and some sort of cosmic scheme. As she was about to read a few more pages, an envelope fell to the floor. She bent down to pick it up. Since the envelope was open, she pulled out a letter and saw that a plane ticket from Paris to Rome was stapled to it. The ticket and the letter were addressed to a French student. The letter was an invitation from a Brother Frank Bootsma of the Vatican Observatory to attend summer school there. Inside the envelope, she also found the student's ID and a printed webpage from the Department of Radiology of the GWUMC. A good-looking man smiled at her—Dr. Jacob Burkowski.

What were the student's belongings doing in Captain Pakula's safe? Ellen stuffed the materials back into the envelope and then between the pages of the notebook. An ominous feeling swept over her, and she fought with her military honor and common sense. Right now, the Atomic Clock was her first concern. Later, she would ask Pakula about the notebook. She would contact Brother Bootsma and Dr. Burkowski as well.

She stashed the notebook back into the safe, closed the door, and left the building. This wasn't the time for distractions. Without a clock, there was no future for the USNO—and thereby, none for her either.

Chapter 66

Saturday: DuPont Circle, Washington DC

Jacob stood shaving in the bathroom. He had awakened to find a clear blue sky and for the first time in months welcomed the sight of a sunny day. His eyes caught the reflection of his bedroom television set. He had turned on the news as he always did upon rising. Something the newscaster was saying caught his attention, and he turned to walk to the bathroom doorway to listen more intently.

The screen showed pictures of the blue NETWARCOM building. The reporter was commenting on a serious drama that had taken place there. As he watched, an ambulance came howling up to the building and then left only a couple of minutes later with someone on a stretcher. While listening to the reporter, he also read the news ticker running along the bottom of the screen. A hacker had paralyzed the NETWARCOM systems for half an hour. Data had been lost, but there had been no military threat.

Jacob returned to the bathroom and washed his face. He realized he hadn't heard his son stirring yet. The night before, he had proudly shown Max his new setup in the basement, up and running. He'd wanted to assure him that being fired wouldn't have much impact on their lives. Part of the severance agreement—not to mention a full-year salary—had included the double-helix tubes and a small-scale fMRI machine, a tryout version that only fit the head and part of the upper half of a body. His setup in the basement might be small in comparison to his hospital lab, but it had certain advantages. Because of his favorable contacts with the manufacturer, he had obtained parts for the fMRI machine that were not yet tested. As long as he provided regular test reports for their own records, he could use the material for his own purposes.

Today was the big day. He was going to test the machine on some mice. One thing bothered him though. Just before leaving the GWUMC, he had been contacted by the USNO to conduct some experiments for them. He hadn't heard from them since. Perhaps they had lost interest in him.

"Max?" he yelled, poking his head out the door of his bedroom. "Max, are you up?"

No answer.

Jacob sighed. The boy was probably still gaming. He'd tried to be understanding, but it had become a serious concern, and he needed to address it soon. Although Max's grades were okay, too much gaming took away from other important things like socializing with his friends. He strode down the hallway and opened the door to Max's room. He wasn't there. Jacob walked down the stairs to the kitchen. There was no sign of his having eaten breakfast. He must have gotten up early.

For some reason, though, Jacob sensed something was wrong. He yanked open the basement door and saw that the light was on. "Max? You down there?" He was only halfway down the stairs when he saw him. Max sat twisted in his desk chair with wires attached to his pallid face. A framed photo of himself and Hannah rested in his lap. *"Max!"*

Jacob rushed across the room and gathered Max into his arms. He was stone cold. Jacob collapsed into the chair and held Max closely to his chest.

Hannah found them there an hour later. She had let herself into the house using her key, hoping to have breakfast with them. "Jacob! Max!" she screamed, dashing to their side and shaking Jacob's shoulder. "Jacob, wake up! What's happened?"

"He... he's dead, Hannah. I-I found him down here only minutes ago." He stared into the eyes of his ex-wife and mirrored her horror. "I-I'm so sorry, Hannah. I ... I didn't know he was so ... so unhappy." Tears streamed from his eyes, and he felt himself choking back huge sobs.

Hannah burst into tears and wrapped her arms around both of them.

"H-how did you know?" Jacob asked.

Hannah wiped the tears from her cheeks with her fingers and took a long, deep breath. "I didn't know. I just had a strange feeling this morning. I-I guess my maternal instinct is still working. What have you done, Jacob? What have *we* done?" She stroked Max's hair and kissed his face several times.

Jacob carried Max to his room and laid him on his bed, crossing his arms over his chest. For the next several minutes, they both stared at their son without speaking.

Finally, Hannah broke the silence. "Shouldn't we call for a doctor or the police?"

"I-I didn't kill him, if that's what you're thinking," Jacob said.

"He died hooked up to your stupid machine! We have to do *something*, Jacob. I know you're a doctor, but we have to get another one here. Someone who can—"

The doorbell rang.

"I-I'll get it," Hannah said and left the room, wiping away the tears still hovering on her cheeks.

As soon as she left Max's room, Jacob's eyes drifted to Max's PC, which was still on. He touched the mouse, and a familiar picture lit up the game screen. It showed a platoon of soldiers fighting its way into *St. Mere Église* in France. A paratrooper's parachute had become entangled around the church tower. As the online game resumed, Jacob's body froze in place. He had always assumed that online gaming involved strangers. Max's chat box was still open. It looked like one of the characters had spoken to Max. Jacob read the text. The conversation had evidently been going on for some time.

> In a nutshell, it is crucial you send yourselves to the date 06.21.2115 at noon, coordinates 39n55 and 116e24. This is the center of Beijing, the Ancient Observatory. We will pick up your signal with powerful dishes you can't know in your time. Be assured you will land at the exact spot. From there, you will find out how to come back. Tell your father he will receive a letter with a clue about Vézelay. Repeat: if you don't send yourself to 2115, you will be killed. It is the only way to survive.

Max had only replied with a short, "Okay, dude, I will. See you on the other side. I can't wait until I have no longer these killing headaches."

Jacob reread the chat messages several times and focused on Max's last words. It hurt him so much to read about the headaches; they were forever related to his experiments.

Then he saw the face of the character; it was Max. Some time ago, Max had told him he had created an avatar, a lookalike, with which he played. He'd never understood it was a stranger. *What have I done?*

Hannah reentered the room. "Sorry it took so long. The mailman needed your signature on an express letter. When I explained we had ..." Sobs broke her voice. "Jacob? For Christ's sake! Are you *listening*?"

"You said something about the mailman?" His eyes remained glued to the PC monitor.

"What's going on here? What is this letter is from the Vatican?" Hannah held up the envelope, barely able to control her shaking hand.

Jacob felt his jaw drop. In a trance, he grabbed the letter from her and pointed at the screen with his other hand. "Take a look at what's on the monitor, Hannah." He tore open the envelope.

"Do you *believe* this crap?" she cried. "Did Max play online games with total strangers? Did he get himself killed because of these ... these stupid *games*?"

Hannah was becoming hysterical. This was why they had broken up: he couldn't tolerate her emotional outbursts. But Max was dead, and he'd died under his watch. When he pulled the letter out of the envelope, Jacob could no longer control his own emotions. With trembling hands, he handed it to Hannah.

> *"Only new actions without a cause can solve the time-travel paradox (Gen.27). YOUR SON IS ALIVE."*

Hannah gasped and then hyperventilated. Somehow, it calmed him down. Jacob guided her to a chair next to Max's bed. "Please, Hannah, sit down and breathe slowly. That's it. Again, now. I really think we have to stay cool. I'll get you a glass of water." He dashed to his bathroom and was back in a second. "Sip this."

"Do ... do you believe this, Jacob?" She gazed at him with glassy eyes, searching his face for any signs of hope. "Do you believe M-Max is ... alive?"

He dropped a kiss onto her forehead. Despite their own marital difficulties, this was Max's mother, and she was in agony. "What is the alternative?" he asked and peered at the letter again. "Why don't we investigate what this Vézelay means? Doing something is better than doing nothing."

A soft moan from the bed made them both jump. Jacob touched Max's head and hands. He was still cold as stone, but his chest was moving almost invisibly. "He's not dead!" he shouted. "He's not dead, Hannah!"

"He's ... he's in a coma," she whispered, starting to hyperventilate again. "Oh, Max ..."

"We have to do something, Hannah. You stay here with Max. I'll be right back."

Jacob rushed to his study to conduct a quick search on Vézelay. Within a couple of minutes, he had located the basilica column with the biblical scene representing Genesis 27. He dashed back to Hannah and Max. "I know everything!" he said, gasping breathlessly on the words. "We have to fly to Vézelay immediately and take Max with us. But ... but how can we do this?" He wrung his hands, damning himself for being so ignorant of things outside the medical world. "How can we get him on board a plane, Hannah? You're the traveler in the family. How can we do this?"

"Give me a minute." Hannah searched for her purse and then for her cell phone. She flipped it open and pushed one button.

"What are you doing?"

"Calling my driver."

"Your driver? Since when do you have a personal driver?"

"Since you stopped talking to me!" she said in an edgy voice. "Sorry. We have a company jet, and I think we can smuggle Max out of the country. What's the nearest landing strip to Vézelay?"

"I'll find out." Jacob rushed back to his study and Googled it. "Dijon. In Burgundy," he shouted. When he returned to Max's room, she had it all organized.

"We leave here in thirty minutes," she said, sitting on the edge of the bed to stroke one of Max's hands.

He sat down next to her. "Thank you. I couldn't do this without you." They looked at each other. "Didn't know you were that important," he said.

"I'm not. I just work too hard—way too hard. There was a reason to visit you and Max." She looked so sad.

"What?" Jacob questioned.

"They've found a tumor. Expectancy is less than three months."

"Oh Hannah!" Jacob was about to collapse again. This was too much, but she was strong and took his hands.

"We have to go... for him."

They looked at Max.

"We..." Jacob couldn't finish his sentence. His usually unspent emotions had bubbled up again. He swallowed hard and blinked several times. "I-I love him."

Hannah took his hand. "You'd better start packing," she said softly.

"You?"

"I always travel with a suitcase on board."

Jacob really looked at her for the first time. She had changed. Or had he?

Chapter 67

2115: Beijing

Max lost all sense of time. His daily routine never varied. He would leave his sleeping quarters only to go to the brass instruments room to see if the chest had changed. Living in the compound was boring without Tong. He had cleared most of his games. Food didn't interest him, and what he ate didn't taste good. Sometimes, he was sure his oxygen supply had declined. He was tired of worrying about it. He was stuck. Even worse, he was stuck *again*. Now that Tong was gone, he felt free to play out all scenarios he had thought of.

He tried to program his dupe again. It worked this time, but it was not as smart as the one at home. Somehow, he had hoped for his dude would be taking over the app again, but of course, this was not going to happen.

It had been Tong all the way—back home—who wanted to get into NETWARCOM and everything, Tong who knew so much, who guided him inside the basements of the university trying to escape the Navy guys. It had been Tong who had tried to turn back the course of events. *While she knew it wouldn't work.*

One day, on a routine trip to the instruments room, he opened the chest and immediately noticed a change. Everything was different! The papers had been rearranged into neat stacks, and on top of the stacks lay a new booklet he'd never seen before. With trembling hands, he lifted it out and placed on the floor by his knees. The booklet was actually a series of letters held together by a thin leather band. He untied it and carefully opened it.

The first thing he noticed was the name of Ferdinand Verbiest, the Vatican astronomer Frank had told him about, who founded this place centuries ago. But the text was in Latin. He couldn't read it! Frank should have known that. How stupid could an adult be? What was the use of all this stuff now? He'd been waiting for months for nothing.

Then, he remembered the gestures Frank had made during their last few minutes together. He had walked his fingers over the letters, jumping in an irregular sequence. He closed his eyes to remember the sequence and then peered more closely at the document. He raised it from the floor to let the ceiling light illuminate the surface. His excitement grew. The letters weren't all the same. Some were brighter than others.

Max carefully followed the trail and read the words aloud.

> "Max. Do not despair. Calibrate the time machine to the right side of the third column in the Basilica of Vézelay. Noon. June 21, the year you were abducted. You will come home. Frank."

He looked carefully again. The part between "despair" and "you" had a slightly different tint. It had been inserted later. Still, it didn't matter much. Max wanted to cry, he was so happy, but there was no time. He rushed back to the carriage outside the instruments room and ordered it to take him to Tong's apartment. "Thank you, thank you!" he cried aloud when Tong's system returned a detailed map of the Basilica of Vézelay. He examined every detail of the pictures. There it was! 47$_N$2835 3$_E$4428. That was all he needed to pinpoint the place. With this information firmly implanted in his mind, he ordered the carriage to take him to the departure platform. Tong had prepared a bed for him, and the only thing he had to do was type in the time, date, and location. A timer would give him five minutes before takeoff. He checked and double-checked what he had typed to ensure it was correct. A blinking green START button invited him to proceed. He pushed the button and quickly lay down on his test bed.

Is this new? Have I done this before? Will I land up here again? And again and again? Can anyone out there save me from this? As a last thought, he remembered the letter Tong showed on the wall in his dad's study. "Only new actions without a cause can solve the time-travel paradox." Is this a 'new action'?

"Farewell," he mumbled, bracing himself for the blast.

Chapter 68

Sunday: Vézelay

Jacob had several hours to think about the influence his ex-wife had in the business world. She had been able to execute their flight to Vézelay without a hitch or delay. She had pulled strings like a Head of State and in a calm and competent manner. Upon their arrival at Dijon *Aeroport,* an ambulance was waiting for Max and Hannah and a Mercedes with a driver for him. "There's only room for one passenger in the ambulance, Jacob," she said. "I want to be with my son this time."

The two vehicles drove in tandem from the airport to Vézelay. The trip took less than an hour. Jacob had to pinch himself to ensure he wasn't living a dream. Over and over again, he thought about the message on Max's PC monitor and hoped his interpretation was accurate. As his car approached Vézelay, he gazed out the window, unable to enjoy the picturesque landscape.

Once again, he was impressed with Hannah's clout. She had impressed upon the guards the importance of their driving all the way up to the church entrance rather than parking in the lot with other vehicles. He overheard her saying they were on "a pilgrimage" and praying their son would be cured of his illness. In a way, that was true, he thought.

The vehicles stopped in front of the basilica stairway, and he climbed out of the Mercedes to join Hannah.

She negotiated with the ambulance drivers to keep Max on the stretcher and help transport him up the stairs to the entrance door.

A few tourists stopped to watch their progress. Jacob ignored them. He had only one thing on his mind: finding the right capital at the top of the right pillar. He searched with straining eyes, trying to remember the configuration he'd seen in the online photographs. "There it is!" he cried excitedly, pointing at it. Together, he and Hannah rolled the stretcher toward the pillar and then parked it with Max's head as close as possible to the stone.

On the plane, they had read Genesis 27 in the Bible Hannah had insisted on taking with them. Now, she took it out again and then looked at her watch. "It's almost noon. You read the passage again," she said. "Aloud."

Jacob didn't object. For once, they agreed on something. And it felt good, because he was doing it for Max. He took the Bible from her and flipped through the pages until he reached Genesis 27.

> *"When Isaac was so old that his eyesight had failed him, he called his older son Esau and said to him, 'Son!' 'Yes, father!' he replied. Isaac then said, 'As you can see, I am so old that I may now die at any time. Take your gear, therefore—your quiver and bow—and go out into the country to hunt some game for me...'*

He was about to read more, but he felt a sudden breeze. "Did you feel that?"

Hannah nodded and slipped her hand under his arm. "What does it mean?" He could feel her tremble.

"With your catch, prepare an appetizing dish for me ..." Jacob couldn't finish reading the sentence. The ground seemed to move beneath their feet. He glanced at Hannah

and then at the other tourists. They didn't seem to notice. Then, he looked at Max. He wasn't moving.

All of a sudden, he saw a bright ray of light glimmer on Max's left temple. He followed the beam upward to a tiny hole in the overhead arch.

"Jacob! Look!" Hannah shouted.

Max's body shuddered in spasmodic movements.

Hannah reached toward their son, but Jacob pulled her toward him instead. "I don't think we should touch him yet," he whispered, hugging her close.

After what seemed like an eternity, Max slowly opened his eyes and smiled weakly.

Jacob laughed aloud. Then he and Hannah fell all over their son, hugging and kissing him.

"It worked," Jacob said, still trembling. "You're back.

❖ ❖ ❖

Max tried to rise from the stretcher but was pushed gently back. *Mom?* He gaped. "You're not dead!" he blurted out.

"No, I'm not—not yet," she said, looking seriously at him and then sideways.

Max followed her eyes. "Hey, Dad!"

His father nodded at him. His eyes glistened. *What is going on here?*

His mom reached for him and stroked his hair. "You're alive," she said. "That's the only thing that matters right now." He couldn't remember her ever touching him like that before except maybe ages ago, when he was very, very small. His dad put an arm around her shoulder and kissed her on the cheek. Max couldn't believe his eyes. He wanted to ask if they were no longer divorced but decided against it. There was so much to tell them. "Dad, you have no idea where I've been!" he began. "Hope you're not mad at me, but I used your cool machine in the basement."

"I know, Max. I know it all. It's okay," his dad replied. "I'm so happy you survived that dreadful experiment."

At the mention of the experiment, Max suddenly realized he no longer had a killing headache. *Wow! This is huge.*

"How can you say that!" his mom suddenly hissed at his dad. "It's not okay. You've seen what comes of talking to strangers on the Internet." She started pushing the gurney briskly toward the exit while flipping open her cell phone.

Max could hardly suppress a smile. Nothing had changed ... except for him. He looked around. This must be that church in Vézelay. He definitely had never been here. That was the good news.

"Dad, I know why I had those killing headaches," he said. "It wasn't because of the machine in the basement."

His dad stopped the stretcher. "What machine are you talking about?"

It felt strange to be able to think about what happened to him without someone reading his mind and jeopardizing everything. His mom had stepped aside and was giving someone instructions on her cell phone. Even better.

"Dad, first of all, I love you," he said. "Please remember that while I tell you what happened to me. You're not to blame anybody for anything." He paused for a moment and glanced at his mom—still busy, arguing about a hospital or something. There was no time to lose. This was personal, between his dad and him.

"We have to talk about the MRI scans you took from me, and your theory about the Area 25 problems.

"Please, Max, I never forgave myself for putting you in that machine." His dad burst into tears. "I wish I had never made up those thinkwaves."

It hurt Max to see his dad in such agony. "No Dad, you were right. These thinkwaves do exist and can travel in time. I'm the proof of it."

"What proof, son? As a guinea pig?"

"No, I've traveled to Beijing in the year 2115 and landed back here. My thinkwaves did that."

"Oh, Max, I read something on your computer yesterday. But we've taken you from the States all the way up here. What proof is this? Somehow, you woke up from your coma."

Max unstrapped himself and hopped off the stretcher. His mom had turned her back to them and was doing business as usual over the phone. Unbelievable. "Dad, what's on this capital?" he said, pointing at the top of the pillar. Genesis twenty-seven, right?" he said confidently."

Jacob's jaw dropped.

"You've got a letter from Brother Frank Bootsma, right?" Max continued.

His father nodded slowly and fished the letter out of his inside pocket. He could barely hold it steady. Max gently took the letter from him. It was the one he had seen on video with Tong. So it *was* true. The fat man had done it! He had to grin.

"Dad, I met Frank in Beijing. I've seen your future. And mine. You're going to be famous. You're a genius."

Jacob looked as if he might fall over. Max pulled his father toward him. "Come here, silly old man." They hugged each other and stood there for some time before his mom interrupted them.

"We've got to go," she said. "I contacted the Dijon hospital to have you examined, Max. The ambulance is waiting outside."

"I'm fine, Mom," he said. But the look on her face didn't leave room for discussion. "Okay, okay, we'll follow you outside in a minute," he said, hoping she would give them a little more time.

She pushed the empty gurney toward the exit, making a hell of a racket. Max held his dad close to him a few more seconds and whispered in his ear what he had wanted to say for so long now.

Chapter 69

Sunday: Castel Gandolfo

Frank was about to leave the courtyard of the Summer Palace when *Capitano* Warzi stepped out of the guardroom and stopped him.

"Just got a call from the U.S," Warzi said. "The notebook has been found in Washington. At the United States Naval Observatory, as you said. We have received an official statement from the U.S. Navy that the suspects responsible for the problem in Rome were killed, possibly by their own organization. They were not part of the American military forces. You are free to cross the city borders of Castel Gandolfo, Father."

Frank just nodded, feeling no joy. The heat of the mid afternoon sun burned his face as he strode across the cobblestone square outside the palace's main entrance. He was on his way to the *Taverna dei Cacciatori*.

The reflection of his slim profile in the window didn't comfort him. For days now he had had no appetite. The waiters, the owner, and the cooks waved politely to him and waited for a signal to approach him with the menu. He wondered why they weren't as friendly as they had been in the past. Then he realized they didn't see Frank, but Father Bonomelli. He wished he could explain. He winked at the waiter.

"You look quite well today, Padre," the waiter said.

Frank smiled thinly. "Do you have your delicious veal *alla romana* on the menu today?" he said, hoping the smell would make him hungry again.

"For you, we put it on the menu," the waiter said and hastened to the kitchen.

"And please bring me a carafe of the local red wine." *I can use a drink—or two.*

"*Si, si, subito,*" he heard from the back of the restaurant.

Thank God some things never change, even in spite of time travels, Frank thought.

As was his habit, he had brought some reading material with him to occupy the time while he waited for his meal. For many reasons, he had chosen the Bible instead of something on astronomical studies. He enjoyed feeling the soft leather cover again and thumbing through the thin pages of rice paper. He had kept this particular Bible with him since his graduation from the Jesuit school. It was not Bonomelli's Bible.

All the time-travel paradoxes and the information he'd gathered on Urban and his cosmic fascination had led in one direction—to Mary Magdalene. He opened up the Bible to a familiar passage in John 20 and read Verse 17. "*Jesus saith to her, do not hold me; for I am not yet ascended unto the Father: but go unto my brethren, and say to them, I ascend unto my Father and your Father, and my God and your God.*"

Mary had seen Jesus but could not hold him. This had been her secret, buried with her in Vézelay and hidden in the solstice of the unknown architect. Unbidden, Frank's experience in the *Torre dei Venti* flashed through his memory. He had sensed the connection between the wind vane and the marble Zodiac figures engraved into the meridian and the Big Bang residues in his early galactic meteorites containing material of the period before the Big Bang. It was so simple, so obvious, and so close to the true meaning that he had not grasped its ramifications until now.

But he wouldn't tell anyone. He wouldn't publish his theory, especially not on the Net. He would take it with him to the grave. *Thoughts without action,* he pondered sadly.

The waiter came to his table without the first course. "I am sorry. We have someone on the phone for you. Long distance," he said.

Frank followed him to the bar area and saw that the receiver of a phone lay on the counter. He hesitated for only a moment and then picked it up, placing his Bible in front of him. "Hello."

"Frank?"

Frank gasped and reached out to hold onto the bar top.

"Frank?"

"Max?"

"Yes. I made it, Frank! Are you okay?"

Tears welled up in his eyes, and his knees grew weak. He felt himself lurch to one side and then the supporting hands of the waiter. "W-where are you?" he stammered.

"I just left Vézelay, Frank. I'm in an ambulance, on my way to a Dijon hospital. My parents are with me. Would you please come to see me? My mom says she's organizing transport."

He felt the sting of tears again. Max was safe. *Thank you, God.* "Yes, of course. Please, Max, there is one answer I must have right now. How did you come back? Did you find my message?"

"Yes. I was about to tell you. It was just like you said, Frank. It arrived in the chest in the brass instruments room right after Tong left, and I remembered how you—"

"Tong?"

"She was our ally, Frank. She sent herself here. She must be here with us somewhere. Have you met her already? I think she'll be looking for you." Did he hear a smile in his voice?

"No, I haven't seen her yet," he answered.

"I am sure she's here with us. She's been here all the time. I just never recognized her in this part of the cycle."

"The *cycle*? What? I don't understand."

"Frank, I'm not sure you will. It's kinda complicated. Listen, I've been sent to Beijing at least two times, probably more. The first cycle I was abducted, I was sent back into myself about three years ago. It must have hurt like hell. That was the reason I had these killing headaches. And it was the start of the next cycle. But now comes the complicated part. Are you still with me?"

Frank's mouth was dry. He could hardly speak. "Yeah."
More complicated?

"I thought I'd programmed an avatar, looking like me, just for fun to play with in my games, but it turned out that smart girl Tong had taken it over and used it to try to prevent my abduction. That didn't work out. The complication is *when* she tried it, and how many times."

Frank lowered himself onto a bar stool as the memory of Tong in her shimmering white fatigues became vivid again. He felt dizzy.

"You're saying you met Tong *before* you were abducted?"

"Oh, yes. I have been in a loop of being abducted, Tong trying to prevent it, being sent to Beijing and sent back again. I did some math when Tong left. Amazing stuff they have over there. Anyway, my probability calculations there showed, this last cycle, something really new had happened."

"What new?" Frank vaguely grasped where this was leading.

"*You,* Frank. You became part of the cycle. And you know what? You've broken the first time-travel paradox, together with your friend Tong. The keyword was 'Vézelay.' I've never been here before. We've broken the cycles. Can you imagine what you've done?"

Frank could hear Max's voice crackle a bit. It was unbelievable. The magnitude of all this was exploding in his head.

"Hold on. My mom asks if it's okay."

"If *what's* okay?" This was all so utterly confusing.

"That you accept her offer. The transport. She pays for it. Company jet and all."

Frank nodded warily.

"Is that an okay, Frank?"

"Yes, Max. Thank her, please."

"I will. You know what, Frank?

"Is there more to it?"

"Technically speaking, I am of age now. We could have a drink together when you're here." Max burst out in laughter, and Frank joined in. "See you later, dude."

Frank stared at the phone receiver. Only moments before, he had sworn to stop working on cosmic theories. Worshipping God would be his sole life fulfillment. Now, he wasn't so sure. Before, he thought he had abandoned Max and had traveled back, killed Bonomelli, and become imprisoned in his body, all for nothing. There had been no hope ...

But now Max had delivered proof of his emerging theory about the nature of time and the essence of the Big Bang. There was no such thing as a linear timeframe! Time was also cyclic, and with every Big Bang, a new round of similar though not necessarily equal events took place, taking along random 'time residues'. That's why the solstice mystery in Vézelay remained unsolved. It had a different functionality in different eras. That's what Jesus had implied with His eternal *Noli me tangere*—"do not hold me." *He was already into a different cycle.* Max's miraculous return and different lifeline was both an omen and the proof.

Feeling light-headed, Frank rose from the bar stool and reeled to his chair. The smell of his plate was trying to welcome him. He sat down and took a first bite, then another. It tasted great. His mind whirled around. The waiter let him sit there for hours.

Frank peered about the deserted restaurant and smiled. Just imagine. There was so much left to explore about these time residues and how they were described in long-lost sciences in the West. There was so much more for him to learn from the East. The Brahmin connection of Pope Urban VIII had been there for a reason: to be discovered. He could no longer believe the answers were found in only Christian-based science. He would leave the Jesuit order. He would make his mother happy again. This was his second chance!

First, he would visit Max. Maybe his friend would accompany him on a journey to search for Tong, if she even wanted be found. And maybe together they could restore the natural cycle of time.

He wouldn't mind another carafe of wine—no, make it a something strong. "A grappa, please."

The waiter brought it immediately. "It's our best," he whispered.

Before Frank could take a sip, the waiter came back. "Excuse me, Father, but there is a taxi waiting for you, to drive you to Fiumicino Airport?"

That was fast. He patted the waiter on his shoulder and started to get his wallet, but the waiter didn't want to see the money. He helped Frank to the door.

Outside, a shining black SUV was waiting for him. Seeing it, he flinched, but when the driver stepped out, it was a woman. No Swiss Guards this time. He sank back into the soft leather backseat. The door closed but was not locked.

The driver got in and adjusted the rearview mirror. "Your plane leaves in an hour. It will be a two-hour flight to Dijon airport. And, Father, there is a package for you in the net behind my seat."

Frank hadn't noticed. It was a present. No sender. He tore away the wrapping paper. Inside a carton box was the most beautiful electronic reader he had ever seen. It was already charged. He took the gift letter and signed in. As he waited for his connection, he took in the beautiful landscape. Up on the hill, he saw a last glimpse of Castel Gandolfo.

A soft *beep*. He looked at the color display. An hourglass was turning around. An app was loading. He became hot and cold at the same time when a familiar face filled the screen.

"Hello, Frank Boohtsma."

Frank was speechless. He could only smile at her.

Biography

Carel Mackenbach earned his master's degrees in history and sociology from the VU University of Amsterdam. His extensive world travels have included visits to such restricted sites as the Secret Vatican Archives, the Tower of the Winds inside the Vatican, the Papal Palace in Castle Gandolfo, and the Atomic Clock and Headquarters of the United States Naval Observatory, as well as various other places, including New Delhi and Vézelay. For fifteen years, he has worked as an independent strategy consultant, specializing in information technology. He has cofounded a high-tech startup that developed a groundbreaking concept for digital identity management.

He is currently at work on the sequel to *The Day Time was Hacked*.